XZARDAK

SCOTT CATO

Should words and phrases in this manuscript appear jumbled or out of sequence, please consult the instruction manual issued with your translator chip.

CHAPTER 1

It had been a long day. Xzardak was slouching uncomfortably in his armchair, awaiting the evening news report. A contact within the coalition had informed him that it would be in his interest to watch the broadcast. Xzardak had been anticipating trouble, and here it was.

Wearing a blue satin dress and diamond earrings, a silver-skinned, female space alien was sitting behind the news desk in a garishly designed TV studio. As she introduced herself, images of Xzardak's busy day were playing out over the news feed. "The first human survivors from the dying Earth planet arrived at the coalition's Science Division today," she began. "The mobilisation has been dubbed 'Operation Xzardak' after the man in charge, Robert Xzardak."

Xzardak raised an eyebrow.

The voice went on, "The program's administrators have salvaged a specimen of every remaining life form from the Earth planet, due to be declared a dead star later in this sun cycle."

Images of a coalition freighter docking and unloading several silver-grey metal caskets appeared on screen. "Our reporter was there to speak to the man in charge, Robert Xzardak."

Xzardak let out a groan as the broadcast cut to a reporter who had breached the safety perimeter and was thrusting a microphone into Xzardak's weary face.

"Can you give us any information, Sir?" called the reporter, wrestling with a coalition assistant. "Are you proud of the work you've been doing?"

Xzardak looked uncomfortable, the cameraman and reporters all rudely jostling around him. Any other coalition official would have fled or told the reporter in no uncertain terms to scram, but Xzardak would not do that. He dutifully turned, intent on being his usual polite self.

Having been asked a question he felt obliged to answer, his mild manner and good nature at least assured the TV crew of a decent soundbite for that evening's broadcast. "Yes, it's true; the program is going ahead. It's hard work and yes, the project is very controversial."

"Lots of people think the program is just too dangerous!" cried the reporter, clearly thrilled to have been granted an audience with the man of the moment.

"Well, I've had death threats so you could say that, yes!" said Xzardak solemnly. "The Earth people have a bad reputation. They've destroyed their own planet, let's not forget that! But it's my job to make sure that the coalition's plan is put into action and the Earth creatures are safely delivered to their new home."

With that, Xzardak departed and pushed his way through the gaggle of TV news personnel.

"When will we get a chance to see one?" called another reporter, being tackled and pushed back by coalition officials who'd come scurrying out from the government building.

Xzardak did not respond this time.

The studio announcer's voice continued, "Not everyone is a supporter of Xzardak and his operation, as we found out." Aerial pictures played out of creatures breaching the security cordon and surrounding the silver cackpto. "Today saw mass demonstrations across the lawn at Commission HQ," she continued, the images changing to scenes of alien protesters gathering at the front of the ministry building. One by one, different species and specimens of alien life came shoving their way to the front of the crowd to speak to the

CHAPTER 1

TV cameraman, each one eager to give their opinion. A small, rotund purple creature was jabbering enthusiastically into the reporter's microphone. "These fellas are dangerous; we've all heard the stories!" he proclaimed.

"I don't know why we're helping them," complained a tall grey creature with bulbous black eyes. "They've destroyed their own world, and now we've brought them onto our own patch!"

"They're gonna cause trouble for sure!" shrieked an outsized green creature in a red gown. "It's those damned do-gooder liberals getting us involved! These guys ain't soft and cuddly! They're little monsters!"

Back in the studio, the news anchor rounded up her report. "This controversial operation, which has been condemned by many in the coalition, will see the Earth people relocated to a high-security compound. Supporters of the program are calling it *Earth 2.*"

As the bulletin ended, Xzardak closed his eyes, rubbing his scaly silver forehead. "Earth people." He sighed, wondering what he had done to deserve an assignment like this one.

CHAPTER 2

"**W**hy do you want information on that dirty place?" the librarian asked.

"I'm researching the Earth for a paper," Xzardak answered.

"Not worth bothering with if you want my opinion," the librarian declared.

"We don't," Xzardak's mechanical assistant, Mono, chipped in and smiled.

"It's a dead planet, you know," she whispered. "But they reckon they saved some of them... What did they call them? *Humans!*"

"I wouldn't know," replied Xzardak, reluctant to inflame speculation. "I'm working with the coalition." He smiled. "I can assure you it's just a rumour, and nothing else."

The librarian shuffled away and soon returned with a ledger marked 'CONFIDENTIAL.' "I'll need to see your government pass and a deliberation order if you're to see these."

"Of course." Xzardak presented his badge and the necessary paperwork.

"This pass only goes up to Category B," the librarian said.

"Yes," said Xzardak impatiently. "I know what it says."

"Well, many of these files are Category C."

Xzardak thought for a moment. "Why would they be classified as Category C?" he asked "There must be some mistake. Please, can you check again?"

"No mistake." The librarian smiled. "I expect there are some quite colourful stories in here!"

Xzardak pulled a face.

"Sorry," she went on. "But I can only show you the relevant documents for your badge grade. I'm sure you understand that."

He understood, but it didn't make the news any more palatable and he scrunched up his face.

She rummaged through the stack, handing Xzardak just half of the files. "You'll have to get authorisation before I can let you see the good stuff!" With that, she snatched up the ledger and slammed closed the library hatch.

Xzardak considered his handful of intel files, retiring to a pod to begin his research.

Quickly reading through, it soon became evident he had limited information about his new assignment. As a child, he had often heard stories about the Earth planet and of the hideous creatures dwelling there. Earth was a dreadful, dark place, in a tiny remote solar system far out on the fringes of nowhere. Terrible crimes were committed in this horrible world, and it was a place to which little children were told they would be sent if they didn't do as they were told.

"Behave yourself, or the humans will get you!" parents would warn. As an infant with an overactive imagination, Xzardak had frequently wondered what terrible monsters must be inhabiting this strange place, but it was better not to think of it for fear of bad dreams.

"A kingdom of nightmares!" an older schoolboy had called it. "Even more terrible than the Planet of Night!" he'd cried excitedly, eager to scare the younger kids. He'd succeeded.

As the years passed, Xzardak never heard another mention of the mythical world, until one day, he got a call at his office. A small planet was about to die, a commissioner had been overseeing a rescue mission, and a task force had been assembled to salvage the remaining life forms. The saved creatures would be arriving that week, and Xzardak soon received instructions to take care of the matter. To say he was thrilled would be an understatement; after years as a senior clerk, he had grown to despise all the long hours and boring paperwork that his role entailed.

"At last, a case of some merit!" he'd cried, convinced it sounded like a project with purpose.

"We'll need you down at Bay Y to oversee the integration," the voice instructed.

"Great!" replied Xzardak excitedly. "I'll draw up the relevant deliberation order now! By the way, for the paperwork…" he asked. "What's the planet called?"

"Earth," replied the voice. "Not a big deal, apparently."

Now in quarantine and out of bounds in terms of space travel, the planet Earth had officially been declared a dead star. Earth had been on the government's danger list for some time and in the preceding years, coalition agents had been sent to the small blue-green world to harvest and preserve as many life samples as they could. A variety of flora and fauna specimens had been collected, every species duly conserved except for one, the human being.

The coalition had turned a blind eye to the humans' dwindling numbers, reluctant to get involved with such a volatile entity.

Since the dawn of time, the 'Galactic Government of the Infinite Everything' had represented every civilised species in the cosmos. The universe had since been split up into twelve sectors, and a representative for each sat on the government panel. For many millennia, the government had been debating whether planet Earth's inhabitants should be invited to join with the other kingdoms in the planetary coalition. It seemed obvious that a creature as intelligent and technologically advanced should be inducted, but in the end, it was agreed that these primitive life forms were too dangerous and unpredictable to be given a place at the table.

Quite simply put, it wasn't worth the risk.

The planet Earth's demise had happened quite suddenly. After many billions of orbits around its galaxy's sun, observers on nearby worlds began to report that things on Earth were changing.

Generally accepted as a stable planet, certain Earth creatures had begun to rapidly evolve.

The usual mundane routines of life such as eating, drinking, sleeping, and everyday survival in the universe were becoming replaced by more destructive pursuits.

Indeed, it appeared that the human beings had discovered how to make clothes and tools and as time passed, had also developed the ability to produce machines, motorised vehicles and eventually, a whole exhaustive array of terrifying weapons.

Most civilizations had, by this point in their development, abandoned weapons.

For most fledgling societies, armaments had only ever been a fad, and the more advanced life forms had worked out that violence never solved anything. So usually, brutality came and went quite quickly in the evolution of an average species.

Not so with the Earth people. They were *not* an average species.

No, planet Earth had been a different matter. The period of time between the first incidence of a human life form striking another human life form, up until the last dying breath of the planet had been so short that most 'non-humans' refused to believe it was true.

Unfortunately, however, it *was* true. The impact on the humans' home planet was such that within a few thousand years, their world was dead, the soil poisoned, the seas polluted, and the majority of life destroyed. A radioactive wind now howled across the once beautiful planet's barren wastelands.

Occasionally, agents of the coalition who had been sent on reconnaissance to Earth would appeal to the high tower, pleading for someone to intervene. "It's getting worse and worse," they would implore but the government never did nothing but talk and the Earth quickly died.

Then, in the last dying hours of the planet, a group of well-meaning souls had gotten together to highlight the plight of the poor misguided Earth people. There had been much media coverage of the protest and finally, the embarrassed government, in their infinite wisdom, had capitulated to the pressure group's impassioned appeal. After much discussion, they reached a decision.

And this was that a party should be sent to Earth to save its last remaining souls.

The academic community expressed a view that they should preserve the human being for scientific observation; after all, a specimen of every other living organism had been collected from the planet. "Human beings must be collected too, for future analysis!" insisted the Chief Scientific Officer. Thus, after many sessions in the chamber, the government managed to reach a decision. They would save the Earth people but classify the salvaged beings as a toxic virus, considering them a 'harmful substance.'

The rescue mission had been a success.

Soon, the coalition cargo ships had collected every remaining life form from the planet Earth and assembled them at the science division HQ. Sedated and laid out on a slab, the assembled Earth people were in a most sorry state. Xzardak counted them.

132 he made it, men, women, and children of all ages, all in an equally deplorable condition, hours from death, riddled with disease, their bodies poisoned and rotting.

It was clear their notorious human spirit had been broken.

Xzardak was aware the rescue mission might come as a surprise to the surviving members of the human race, unaware as they were that alien life even existed—or at least, no one had ever confirmed it in an official capacity. The government was convinced that nothing good would come of interaction with the savage Earth inhabitants, so they had made great efforts to ensure that the Earth people did not discover extra-terrestrial life.

Many remarked that humans were so fond of war, any interplay with them would end in catastrophe. Thus, not one of the neighbouring settlements wanted anything to do with Earth.

"Poor wretches." Xzardak said and sighed, shaking his head. This was his first contact with human life. "They're nothing like I was expecting." He spoke solemnly.

"Don't get too close!" exclaimed a technician. "We have been instructed to maintain a perimeter. If one of this lot wakes up, they'll have your hand off!"

"Such feeble specimens," he whispered, scrutinising the Earthlings. "How could these creatures have gotten it so wrong?" Xzardak approached one of the smaller humans, a child, he surmised, laid out in her summer clothes. She had the most angelic innocent face he had ever seen. "How were you able to destroy an entire world?" he asked.

Xzardak requested a council with the coalition the following day.

Once in the regional chamber, he put forward a motion.

"Gentlemen, there has been a mistake," he suggested. "I fear we may have failed in securing specimens of human life." The committee grumbled as Xzardak continued, "I have never been to Earth, nor ever wanted to visit—"

"Me neither!" interjected a coalition member. "Awful place!" he scoffed, and the assembled council whooped and laughed.

Xzardak looked unimpressed. "These creatures we have supposedly rescued cannot be human," he insisted. "They do not match the specification. The crimes of Earth could not have been committed by these insignificant life forms! They appear fragile, puny, underwhelming."

A tall man in a green suit stepped forward. "Look, Xzardak, your lot sent us to Earth to rescue the humans and that's what we've done. You asked for humans, we got you humans! We cannot help the fact that the specimens we retrieved are poor quality. We took what was left. We couldn't exactly pick and choose, you know. There wasn't a menu!"

"But they're not human," Xzardak asserted. "We have all heard the legends and read the reports about planet Earth, and these beings don't match the order description! These creatures are not capable of the fabled atrocities. They have no tusks or claws, and they are weak!"

The commissioners mumbled and fussed.

"I would like the Earth lab to cross-reference all existing life profiles and tell me what these creatures are!" Xzardak concluded, getting to his feet. "I fear we may have missed our chance to save a rare species of creature! And we have ended up with goodness only knows what!"

Sometime later, the results were back and Xzardak addressed the local council via a video link. "You're wrong," he insisted, looking at the sleeping child through a vision portal. "You may well have discovered a whole new species, but I refuse to believe that this sleeping child could be responsible for..." Xzardak stopped himself. The coalition members were becoming agitated.

"Xzardak, listen," said the commissioner. "This case is of such little importance; quite frankly, you are overreacting. The laboratory has presented you with the scientific evidence you demanded, and the Peace Corps has confirmed that these are indeed human beings.

"If you have further reservations, please present them now and we'll be only happy to pass the case on to another agent."

This was a major opportunity for Xzardak. A relatively high-profile job like this would give a boost to his career plan. "No." Xzardak stood. "I do want the case," he said, realising he may be talking himself out of a job. "I just want to make sure we are doing this right. I'm sure you can understand my position."

"Of course," the commissioner agreed. "I admire your diligence, Xzardak, but it's all there to see in the data log. You must understand these human beings are a menace!" Xzardak lowered his head. "Now if I were you, I'd get to it!" demanded the commissioner. "They'll be waking up soon, then you'll see everything they're capable of! *Then* you won't be coming to the council saying they're weak. Believe me."

Xzardak nodded—the commissioner had firmly put him in his place. Switching off the video feed, he set about preparing for the next stage of the operation.

Time was passing slowly, and the humans were sleeping, unaware of their strange alien environment and the second chance they had been granted. Robotic assistants had initiated the regeneration process and they would isolate, examine and neutralise all ailments and diseases.

They would soon wake up, all in good health, free from poison and decay. Xzardak was excited for that moment, imagining how grateful and high spirited they would be. He was certain it wouldn't be anything like as horrifying as the commissioner tried to make him believe; he was convinced that these desperate specimens could not as bad as the humans in the data log.

"When can we wake them?" Xzardak asked excitedly.

"Two rotations," the medic replied stiffly.

"Not long now," he said, smiling. "I'll show them!"

CHAPTER 3

Sitting back, Xzardak considered the strange new alien world he had created. "We tried our best. We couldn't do any more." He sighed, staring up at the milky blue horizon.

"Yes," agreed Dr Jay, a purple-grey, velvet-skinned, humanoid creature in a white lab coat. "Just a pity we couldn't save them all."

The transition from the old Earth to the new had been too much for some of the weaker humans and despite their best efforts, of the 132 brought in on the cargo, only seventy-seven had survived. Dr Jay had witnessed the demise of the Earth planet first hand, being part of the task force that had evacuated the humans and been granted extensive access to the doomed world. Once the mission was complete, he had volunteered to stay on and help Xzardak recreate the humans' old world in its new-world location, many light years away from home.

Dr Jay and Xzardak had worked together to oversee the research process, design, and construction of the compound facility. Once complete, the habitat would safely house and maintain the Earth people whilst at the same time, securely containing them from the wider universe. "Incarceration!" exclaimed a disgruntled looking commissioner during a heated consultation meeting. "I'm all for saving them but for the sake of us all, don't let them escape!"

"And keep the costs down!" interjected another official. "We've already wasted a fortune on this vexatious operation! And for what?"

"All they require is a patch of fertile soil and a breathable atmosphere!" called out Xzardak, getting to his feet.

"All anyone requires is a patch of fertile soil and a breathable atmosphere!" rebuked the commissioner. "But those things don't come cheap! And I don't see why we should provide these worms with resources paid for by an already fractious public!"

The commissioner was less than sympathetic to the plight of Xzardak and his earthworms.

It was Dr Jay who had managed to charm the coalition into granting the funding for their grand design. "You must consider the scientific value of the program," he said with a superior air. "If we are to evolve to our full potential, it is important that we study every species of life inside of the everything." Eventually, after much huff and bluster, the coalition became bored with the conversation and granted the pair the requested resources so they could flee the tedium.

With the blueprints finalised, it didn't take long to construct an environment similar to that of their origin Earth before the ravages of industry and war. Over many centuries, visitors had managed to harvest so many different examples of life that Xzardak and Jay were spoilt for choice when it came to the design process—eventually electing a simplistic European design, with many trees, shrubs and a small water feature.

"We are giving the Earth people a second chance!" Xzardak had explained to another overzealous TV reporter, who'd managed to infiltrate security and obtain a few moments with the project facilitator whilst out on reconnaissance. "I'm working closely with the science division, and we hope to have the facility up and running very soon."

The science division had been hard at work and the compound was now complete. Using the most advanced fertilisation process, they had accelerated the development of the lush green plant life and flora. "Essential in the creation of breathable oxygen!" explained Jay in a high-pitched trill, "Now that the trees are fully matured, we are ready!" he announced excitedly.

"What happens next?" asked Xzardak.

"We wait for them to wake up," cooed Dr Jay as if the next part would be a breeze. "Then the trouble begins." He laughed. Xzardak rolled his eyes and looked unimpressed.

Despite their collaboration, the two beings were worlds apart when it came to their opinion of the project assets. Xzardak was there to make sure that the Earth people were safe and would be given a fair chance in their new environment.

"I'm only here to observe," announced Dr Jay coldly. "I'm going to be writing a paper on the Earth people and I'll make a fortune!" he pompously bragged.

"Isn't that just a little cynical?" Xzardak enquired, his personal intentions purely altruistic.

"That's one way of putting it," admitted Jay. "But be realistic, facts are facts and science is science!"

"And money is money!" proclaimed Xzardak, bringing the doctor down a peg.

During the construction process, the coalition had little to say about the project. "I'm surprised they weren't all over us, interfering and bossing us around!" Xzardak confided.

"Truth is, Xzardak," Dr Jay explained. "They don't care about the project. Simply put, this is purely a public relations exercise. My sources within the coalition reckon they will pull the plug the moment anything untoward happens. I just hope I can get my blasted paper finished before it all goes belly up! I'll have to get a move on."

"And you're sure it *will* all go belly up?" said Xzardak stiffly.

Dr Jay nodded his head. "Of course, it will! Don't get drawn in…" He scowled. "Look, you've done a marvellous job; you've created a wonderful Earth substitute but you must understand, they won't be grateful and once you turn your back, they'll only wreck it! I saw the origin planet; they poisoned it and everyone on it. They're no good! Believe me!"

Xzardak had heard it all many times and couldn't think of anything to say.

"Those trees you see would take a lifetime to grow on Earth. Yet they were given little respect by the Earth people, cut down on a whim to supply pulp for their trivial so-called novels and newspapers." He shook his head. "Don't get me wrong"—he sighed, slightly backtracking so as not to sound as ruthless and twisted as the degenerate Earth wretches, all laid up in the infirmary—"I'd truly love to see the program succeed, but I've seen these creatures in their natural environment and the odds aren't stacked in your favour."

Xzardak shuddered as he thought about his own home planet and how resources had been in such short supply, but with mutual cooperation, they had somehow managed to make it work.

Then he considered Jay's words for a moment. "I appreciate your advice, sincerely I do, but we must try. What if, like some life forms, they have a bad side and a good side? They can't be *all* bad. No one's that bad. Everyone deserves at least one chance."

Dr Jay gently chuckled. "All credit to you if you want to look for the humans' good side! Good luck to you! But you're in for a surprise—a nasty one—if you think they have a shred of decency between the lot of them. Don't be fooled, these creatures are very dangerous. They have an innate darkness in their hearts and are hellbent on destruction."

Xzardak shook his head disparagingly. "Sorry, but I think you're wrong."

"So be it. Well, either way, my paper will be a runaway success!" announced the doctor. "I just hope you will still be alive to read it!"

Soon, Dr Jay would be gone. His video surveillance system would capture all the research footage he needed and his trusty robot 'Zork'—with its legion of special worker robots—would compile progress reports for the doctor. "I hate to leave you at a time like this," he confessed. "But the coalition have me scheduled on another evacuation mission. Nowhere near as interesting as this one. Brain dead, the next lot! Not even worth writing a paper about!

"It's a shame as I wanted to be around when these Earthlings hatched. I'm curious to see what kind of mood they'll be in." Dr Jay giggled, slapping his thigh as if this was the funniest thing.

Xzardak smiled. "I'd make sure they don't all escape then, before your return."

"You do that."

Dr Jay gathered his cargo containers and readied himself to leave.

Standing on the command centre deck and surveying all the flowers and trees, Jay turned to Xzardak and looked him straight in the eye. "I shouldn't really do this, but I fear I must," he said, talking in a hushed tone. "I need you to wake up to the task you have been given. I would like you to go back to the library vault and ask to see Rhodar. She's an ex-pupil of mine and is doing very well in their research and analysis division. Mention my name and she will be able to grant you access to the entire planet Earth file. There, you will find the truth in all its glory.

"And there, Xzardak, you will see the horrors of their world, all recorded information at your disposal. I suggest you study it… all of it!" he whispered. "Should the coalition find out that you have been granted authorisation above your grade, Rhodar and I will be in serious trouble. But for your own good and for the good of the Universe, I consider it's worth the risk."

Xzardak looked unsure.

Jay had not finished all he had to say on the topic. "Xzardak, you're too good for this lot; most would have let them perish. So, for your compassion at least, I commend you."

Dr Jay held out his hand. "On to pastures new, as they used to say on Earth," he proclaimed.

Xzardak shook his hand and smiled though he wasn't sure where the pastures came into it. "Thank you. I'll make sure that the humans know all about you when they are settled."

Dr Jay laughed. "Know all about me? I'll demand a statue if we pull this off."

CHAPTER 4

Xzardak had received some exciting news from the infirmary. The moment had arrived. The first of the Earth people had awoken! It was late afternoon, and the purple sun was beginning to set. A light breeze blowing across the compound was causing the Earth trees to gently sway against the strange, pinkish-blue alien backdrop. Xzardak's assistant Mono had overseen the entire conversion process. Together, they sat side by side in the control unit, watching the live feed of the ward. Xzardak looked on with nervous excitement as a pink-faced Earth man silently stirred.

When the Earth people had been brought to the medical facility, they'd been so sick that Mono and his team had predicted they would all be lost. Yet together under Xzardak's supervision, the facility had managed to save a high percentage of them. Now, each one would be slowly resuscitated, having been in a deep sleep stasis for many Earth rotations.

"It's a miracle that so many are all still with us!" exclaimed Xzardak. "I never expected anything like this survival rate. And it's all down to you fellas!" he added, beaming as the medical team worked to rehabilitate the visitors and restore them back to full biological health.

Joined by his deputy, Bungo, they observed in stunned silence. They could see the Earth man on the video feed being beamed via Zork's surveillance pod. The Earth man's eyes were open. He lifted his head from the stuffed pillow and opened his mouth to speak.

"Hey, man!" he called out. "What's going on? Where's my leather jacket?"

Xzardak looked to Bungo, unable to determine whether this was a positive or negative statement. Bungo shrugged, struggling to make sense of the Earth man's first communication.

They looked back to the live feed, eager to hear what the visitor would say next.

"Who are you guys? Where am I?" The Earth man was sitting upright in his bed. Xzardak thought it prudent to give the man a few moments to gather himself before he ventured in to make first contact. During the consultancy process, there had been many discussions about the mental state of the humans. Traditionally, the coalition insisted that a full brain cleanse be administered to any individual from an undesirable species. However, in the case of the peculiar Earth humans, the board, led by Dr Jay, wanted to observe their behaviour in their natural mind-state. In short, they wanted to see if the Earth people really were as deranged as the rumours implied.

The first human got up out of his bed. "Hey there! What is this place, a military jail or something?" Xzardak placed the protective helmet on to his head.

Although the human would have been fully cured and purified, Xzardak still thought it sensible to wear his barrier contamination suit. The outfit would also conceal the alien's appearance from the Earth man. Xzardak wanted to get inside the pod and speak with the human up close, assessing whether he was mentally equipped to handle the news of his planet's demise.

Each human was being cared for in a small, plainly decorated room similar to that of an intensive care unit back on Earth. The walls were plain white, dressed with medical charts, and a lightweight opaque curtain surrounded the small single bed sited in the centre of the room.

"The Earth people call it a *hospital,*" explained Xzardak, having discovered pictures of such places in the research vault.

Concerned that feelings of disorientation may upset the frail Earthlings, Xzardak wanted the humans to wake up in familiar surroundings, hopefully shielding them from any unnecessary stress or trauma. The Earth people would awaken and convalesce in homely surroundings until it was deemed a suitable time for the big reveal.

Xzardak couldn't resist it anymore. For many rotations, he had patiently been waiting to converse with an actual Earth person and with an overwhelming feeling of excitement, he made his way towards the pod. Standing outside the door, he could hear the Earth man knocking at the viewport window. With slight trepidation, Xzardak's uncontrollable curiosity got the better of him; he opened the door and made his way inside.

"Hey, man! Where is this place? Who are you?" The Earth man lunged toward Xzardak. "What's going on?" he asked, anxiously.

Pinned up against the unit door, Xzardak was unable to speak, the Earth man having placed his hands around his neck. This did not seem to be any kind of friendly Earth greeting. "I'm going to ask you one more time, man, where am I?" Xzardak had never felt fear like this before and this new sensation was not a pleasurable one. He would have much preferred a simple handshake.

"Please, let me go," he croaked, flailing his arms around.

"Stand still!" urged the Earth man, his face pressed up into the reflective helmet visor. The Earthling tightened his grip and Xzardak let out a shrill plea. "Please!" he beseeched. "Release me!" The human's hot breath made Xzardak's shield fog up. His eyes bulging in their sockets and his nostrils flaring, the human intensified his hold. "You better start talking, soldier!" the Earth man insisted, giving one final shove before finally letting poor Xzardak go.

Xzardak pulled away quickly and stumbled across the room, straightening his sealed collar, and fixing his protective visor. "You are quite safe!" he proclaimed reassuringly with an apologetic cough. "You are in a health facility very far from your home!"

The Earth man said nothing, just stood and stared, studying Xzardak.

"You were saved from a life-threatening situation, and we have brought you here to convalesce," explained Xzardak, but the Earth man still did not respond.

Gathering his composure, Xzardak continued, "There are several of you here at the unit. We are taking good care of all of you! Please try to relax!"

At last, the Earth man smiled. "And who... are you?"

"I am the administrator of the facility. I am responsible for the welfare of you all," Xzardak attempted to explain.

"Administrator?" quizzed the Earth man. "What's that? A doctor?"

"Not quite," came the reply, but the Earth man looked dissatisfied with Xzardak's answer. "Well, yes, sort of," he backtracked, out of fear of some form of negative reprisal. Gesturing to the chair, the Earth man's beady eyes followed Xzardak as he sat opposite in an empty seat.

Xzardak rubbed his neck. The Earth man was certainly in good health; his strong grip around the administrator's throat had revealed that.

"I want out, Doctor," he said. "This isn't the can, is it?"

"The can?" enquired Xzardak. "What's the can?"

"The can! Prison, jail!" hollered the agitated Earth man. "C'mon man, tell me the truth!"

"No, of course not!" replied Xzardak. "This is a hospital! We are making you well!"

The Earth man looked unconvinced. "Well, you'd better let me out! For the good of your own health!" he growled. "You'll be needing intensive care after I'm finished with you."

Hoping to avoid another physical altercation as the communications between himself and the Earthling continued to decline, he wondered what to do for the best.

The human was certainly robust enough to endure the shock of more news. Thus, Xzardak, anxious that another misunderstanding might result in him lying strangled and dying on the infirmary floor, decided it would be prudent to just tell the truth as the Earth man had demanded. So, as unsympathetic as the human had been to him so far, Xzardak would try to break the horrible news as gently as he possibly could.

"This isn't going to be easy for you to hear," he said softly.

The Earth man pulled up a chair and sat opposite him, resting his feet on the foot of the bed.

Xzardak cleared his throat. "My name is Robert. Please, what is yours?"

"Grotesque." The man smiled, exposing his broken teeth. "They call me Grotesque but please, Doctor, my friends call me Tesk."

Xzardak hesitated; did this mean they were now friends?

The Earthling studied Xzardak's darkened visor, trying to see inside the reflective helmet.

"Okay, thank you, Tesk," ventured Xzardak taking another deep breath. "Tesk, I'm afraid to tell you this, but the Earth planet is dead. You are on a small moon many light years away from your home, and it is my job to see that you are safe. Now, if at any point you have any questions, please stop me. And if there's anything you don't understand, please ask. I understand this is a lot to take in, so I will take my time."

"So, you're not the cops?" said the Earthling, sitting forward.

"No," answered Xzardak, appearing puzzled.

"Sheriff's Department?" enquired Tesk.

Unsure of what a Sheriff's Department even was, Xzardak shook his head.

"Phew, praise be!" said the Earth man, looking relieved. "I thought I was back inside the big house again. Already jumped bail a bunch of times!" He snickered, reclining back into his chair.

Xzardak signalled to Mono, concerned that the Earth man might be experiencing a psychotic episode. In Xzardak's earpiece, Mono relayed the man's health statistics.

"Heart rate good. Blood pressure good. Blood oxygen normal. Lung function normal, and for a human, brain activity… normal," he reported.

The Earth man suddenly appeared quite relaxed. He got to his feet and returned to his bed. "Well," said Xzardak, unsure of how to proceed. "Is there anything you would like to ask me? Or anything I can get for you?"

Tesk smiled. "Doc, is there anywhere I can get a drink? I haven't felt this good in years!"

"Yes, of course," said Xzardak. "I'll call my assistant who will provide you with refreshment!"

"Can you make it a double?" cackled the strange Earth creature, stretching his back and placing his hands behind his head.

Confused and unsettled, Xzardak made a quick exit out of the room. On the other side of the door, he ripped off his visor, his heart beating out of his chest.

"Well, that was strange," said Bungo. "At one point, I thought we were going to have to come in there and get you!"

"Very strange!" exclaimed Xzardak, trying to catch his breath. "Very strange indeed."

"They're savages! I thought he was going to kill you!" remarked Bungo.

"Yes, me too!" admitted Xzardak. "But put yourself in his place. It must be an awful lot to take in." Xzardak's encounter with the Earth being had left him unnerved and shaken, but he felt he must give Tesk the benefit of the doubt since he surely must be feeling the same.

"He took the news very well I thought," Xzardak suggested. "He seemed quite calm once I explained I wasn't law enforcement!"

"Well, I don't like him, Xzardak. Don't turn your back on him for a second," warned Bungo. "These Earth people are going to be trouble," he added, sighing. "I can feel it."

Xzardak was trying to take something positive from the experience, desperate to convince himself that the Earth man was probably acting in self-defence.

"His behaviour was quite understandable under the circumstances," he cheerily enthused. "We must not give up on him just yet!"

He was determined to give these humans the benefit of doubt. Well, so far.

Back at the compound command centre, Xzardak noticed it was getting late. He decided it was time to call it a day and sitting at his desk, poured himself a drink. Replacing his helmet back into his locker, he let out a sigh. "Well, that's enough excitement for one day." He yawned and no sooner had the words left his lips than the video-port intel flashed a light. It was Mono again.

"Come in, Xzardak, do you read me?" he called.

Xzardak reached over and flicked a switch, patching Mono through.

"Yes, I read you, Mono. What's going on?" he asked. Mono buzzed and twitched excitedly.

"Great news!" he chirped. "You might want to get over to the infirmary; another one has woken up! A female this time, and I understand she's conscious and lucid. I thought you might like to come over and speak with her. I hear you're quite good with them."

Even Xzardak wouldn't have said quite that.

Xzardak jumped to his feet and reached for his protective headgear.

"I'm coming over now, Mono!" he called. "We need to take things slowly this time, so don't startle her by sending in the service robots before I get there."

Xzardak put on his gloves and quickly gulped down his drink.

The earlier weary feeling had dissipated, replaced now by a familiar nervous excitement. His dealings with the first Earth man had been unsettling but he was sure that not all of the Earth people would be quite so hostile.

Entering the infirmary, Mono greeted him. "Good evening, sir!" said the service robot cheerfully. "The Earth female is still awake. She appears to be doing very well!"

Xzardak smiled. "Where is she?"

"Room thirty-seven. Come, I'll take you up." Mono led the way.

"Do we know anything about her?" enquired Xzardak.

"Not much," answered Mono. "All that I can say is the conversion treatment appears to have worked very well! Her vital signs seem promising. We estimate that she is roughly twenty-eight origin sun rotations old. She was unconscious when we picked her up. I believe she arrived on the same transport as the Earth man you were talking with earlier."

Xzardak felt a sudden pang of apprehension.

"Perhaps you should inform Bungo," he quietly intimated.

Arriving at room thirty-seven, Xzardak gently suggested that Mono stay outside and keep an eye on the Earth being's health readings. He put on his helmet and giving the visor a wipe, took a breath, quietly opening the door so as not to startle the Earth being. Unsure of what to expect, Xzardak braced himself. Hearing someone enter the room, the Earth female slowly flickered her eyes open.

"Do not be afraid," said Xzardak softly. "You are in a health facility; we are making you well. Please do not panic. All is good."

The Earth woman looked confused but not scared. She also spoke softly and had none of Tesk's aggression. "Where are we?"

"Please relax. We will come to that soon enough," said Xzardak quietly. "But first, we must assess that you are well enough to talk."

She smiled, looking up at Xzardak. "Oh, I'm fine," she whispered. "Just wondering how I ended up in this fancy place?"

Xzardak sat down on a chair adjacent to the bed, a safe distance away from the young woman. "You were rescued," he said sympathetically. "Your situation had made you very unwell…"

"I have no memory of it… None of it."

She sat up a little, trying to remember her final moments before the darkness, before waking up in the health facility. "The dirt cloud, that's all I remember," she said solemnly.

She studied Xzardak's overall and protective face shield. "Hey, what's with the garb? Am I radioactive or something?" she enquired, sounding concerned.

"Please relax!" he said reassuringly. "The outfit is to protect you from me as much as it is to shield me from you." He tried to explain, becoming flustered as he spoke.

"Well, then… you better tell me how I ended up here," she said calmly with a friendly smile, nothing like the Earth man's from earlier in the day.

Xzardak looked over to the readout panel. "I just need to check your test results," he said. "It won't take long." Suddenly, she appeared frightened. The words *test results* had unnerved her.

"Am I sick?" she called. Her tone had changed. "You guys know I ain't got health insurance, don't you?" she blurted. "There ain't gonna be a big medical bill at the end of all this, is there?"

Xzardak didn't quite understand. "Oh, no, no! The medical facility was set up to help you and your fellow Earth…" He paused, correcting himself. "Er, to help you and your companions to convalesce! Our only concern is to make you and your friends well."

"When you say *friends,*" she ventured, looking perturbed. "Which friends, exactly?"

"I have estimated that there are seventy-six, er, *friends* of yours present," Xzardak was trying his best to keep the woman calm, sensing she was becoming anxious and irritable.

"I ain't got seventy-six friends!" she said, raising her voice. "What's going on? Who are you talking about? Gimme the names!" she demanded.

Fearing another confrontation like the one earlier in the day, Xzardak began to panic.

"I do not know their names," he explained. "So far, only one of your friends has regained consciousness! The others are still in stasis. Sleeping if you like?"

"Is that friend of mine Alice?" she asked.

"No."

"Is it Ruby? Small girl, tough as hell, very sharp tongue…"

"No, not Ruby."

"Is it…" It seemed she was going through her few friends to determine which ones had ended up in this unfathomable predicament with her. "Is it Marvin, big guy, not the smartest, but heart of gold?"

"Sharp tongue? Heart made of gold?" repeated Xzardak. Who were these people? "No!" he insisted. He lowered his voice in an attempt to placate the girl. "So far, the only other 'friend' of yours I have spoken to is a man named Tesk."

"Tesk!" cried the girl. "Tesk ain't no friend of mine, I can tell you that!" She was becoming angry. "Now tell me what's going on!" she insisted.

Xzardak was beginning to wonder if he was cut out for this kind of work. For now, he'd have to end this conversation.

"We can go into the finer detail as time progresses." He stood, discreetly eyeing the exit.

"Hey, hold on, mister! You need to tell me more or I'll call the cops. You better tell me right now! Or I'll scream this place down! I'll scream until I'm sick!"

Sensing he was losing control of the situation, he darted across the room and peered into the two-way viewport. Xzardak motioned for Mono to enter the room.

"Hey, where's my stuff, you scumbag!" the woman bristled at Xzardak. "Who put me in this robe!" She was only becoming angrier.

"Please, try to calm down," he pleaded. "This really isn't helping!"

The woman had turned scarlet in the face. "Helping who, buster?" she screamed. "Me or you?" Xzardak headed toward the door, anticipating another physical altercation as suddenly, Mono entered the room.

"What the..!" she said.

"Please!" cried Xzardak, aware that he had uncharacteristically raised his voice.

"You must sit back. You are still under observation!" insisted Mono.

"What's this?" cried the woman. "A robot? This place is weird, and you, sir, are a CREEP!" She shut off as if a switch had been flicked.

With a feeling of exhaustion, she fell back, unaware that she had already been under sedation for many months and that the slightest rise in her activity level would put her right out of action again. The sudden burst of excitement had taken it out of her.

"I'm going to give you one last chance," she whispered. "What the hell is going on?"

Xzardak looked to Mono. "Please, can you show me the technical readout for this woman?" Mono set off chirping and bleeping, the sensor lights on his head beginning to pulsate.

A square of pale blue plastic appeared to squeeze out of his body like some form of a small token, in fact bearing a minuscule printout of the female's medical results.

"Here it is, Xzardak!" chirped Mono. "She's actually doing very well, all things considered!"

"All things considered?" said the woman. "All what things?"

Xzardak quickly read the report printout, eyes darting left to right, and back. "Ah."

Concerned the woman might again lose her temper, he made a snap decision. "In lieu of anything else to say," he began, "I believe it best to proceed with the truth."

The Earth girl folded her arms. "You better start talking, man…" she warned.

Xzardak cleared his throat, "Would you mind telling me your name?" he asked.

"Sure, it's Cheryl! What is to you?"

"Cheryl, I am confident that you are strong enough to hear this and I think under the circumstances, I should be clear with you," he asserted. "I am working with the government, and our only interest is to make you well, keep you safe and preserve your life."

The girl listened intently.

"When we found you, you were gravely ill—unconscious, in fact. Your environment was unsafe, and the air around you putrid and horribly poisonous."

"Yes, sir," she interrupted. "That's Detroit!"

Xzardak looked bewildered and stopped for a second. "As I said, you are in a medical facility. A long way from Detroit. Very far away from Detroit in fact." He paused. "Cheryl, I want you to brace yourself now because what I am about to tell you may be difficult for you to believe. However, I assure you it is the truth." The girl's eyes narrowed and Xzardak took a breath.

"You are on a small moon many light years away from your home planet. The world you inhabited, 'planet Earth' has been declared unsafe and condemned. You were airlifted from the planet and you and the remaining seventy-six people are all that are left of the Earth race!"

Xzardak stood and took a few steps away from the puzzled looking girl, fearing a physical reprisal, but she did not move, eyeing him with a slightly open mouth.

"I realise this must be very difficult for you to understand," he repeated.

The girl smiled and looked around. "Okay, where's the camera?" She smiled. "This is a put-on, right! I knew this was a set up! Come on, guys, you can come out now! Oh man, am I going to be on TV?"

Xzardak looked perplexed, unsure if this was a good reaction or not.

The girl was smiling, so surely this was a positive.

Mono was able to read the situation better, sidling up to Xzardak. "I believe she thinks you are joking," he said. "Humour was very big on the Earth planet!"

Xzardak looked even more puzzled. "Humour?" he repeated. "Not a concept that I fully understand," he confessed. "What did I say that was humour?"

"All of it!" exclaimed Mono.

The girl tried to get up but realised again that she hadn't the strength.

"I'm afraid there is no camera; this is not a joke, unfortunately," offered Mono, hoping to help out the confused administrator.

"Not a joke, huh? Well, you better wise up, mister, and tell me what's really going on!"

Xzardak tried again, explaining in detail the dying moments of the Earth planet, the rescue mission, the evacuation, and the conversion therapy but the girl would not believe what he was saying.

"You must believe me!" he insisted. The tired girl began to sob, exhausted and exasperated, all of Xzardak's words seeming to cause some kind of misfire in her brain. "Please, will you tell me the truth?" she pleaded. "Am I in hospital or is this the nut house or what?" she cried. "Stop playing games with me!"

"I want you to take a breath," he said. "Please sit back." Mono checked the girl's vital signs once more: blood pressure good; heart rate okay; lung function all fine.

"I think it's time," suggested Mono. "Quite safe to proceed from a medical viewpoint!"

Xzardak released the clasp on his helmet. "I'm not like you," he said to the Earth female, about to make a grand reveal. "But I feel you must know the truth. For your own wellbeing."

He felt the visor clamp release and slowly, he lifted the helmet to reveal his true appearance. The girl looked suspicious, staring at Xzardak's dark silver-blue skin and unusual red eyes.

The woman's jaw dropped. "That's a mask, right?" she whispered.

Xzardak shook his head. He had been chosen for the assignment as his build and height were not dissimilar to those of the Earth people. However, with his face uncovered, it was clear that he was not human, and it took the girl a few minutes to come to terms with what she was seeing.

Stretching out her arm, she placed her hand on Xzardak's exposed cheek.

"I don't believe it," she said softly.

Xzardak took a step back. "I want you to know that you are not in any danger. We have only your best interests at heart. I realise what a troubling revelation this must be for you," he said.

The girl was silent, but Xzardak sensed an inner strength. "Maybe I'm crazy?" she said eventually, wiping away a tear. "But actually, I do believe you. My father always used to talk of the visitors, he was convinced—"

"You are quite safe," repeated Xzardak, reapplying his helmet. "But I must put this back on. We are still concerned about cross-contamination." But the girl didn't reply, just staring blankly and silently into space. "Perhaps Mono could administer something for your nerves; a sedative pill, a drink, maybe?" he suggested.

"No need," she said, wiping her face. "The Earth?" she asked. "Are we, the seventy-seven survivors, really all that are left?"

Xzardak lowered his head. "Yes, seventy-seven. I'm afraid so." The woman wiped her nose, gathering up as much strength as she could. She looked at Xzardak.

"And what do they call you here, sir?" she asked politely.

Xzardak paused. "It's a hard name. Just call me Robert," he replied.

"Robert?" she repeated. "Oh, come on. That ain't no space alien name. What's your real name?"

"Well, my true name is unpronounceable to an Earth person, so the language implant in your brain will translate it to a more familiar moniker."

She laughed. "Well, I ain't calling a space alien Bobby! Please try to tell me."

Xzardak thought for a moment. "To translate my family name into human, the nearest I could manage would be 'Xzardak.', X-Z-A-R—"

He stood back to see if the Earth woman would settle for the translation.

She considered it. "Hmm, Czar-Dack," she enunciated. "Well, that's a little more spacey than Robbie or Bob," she said contentedly. "Xzardak it is then. Must be my lucky day!" She smiled. "Waking up in this fancy hospital and meeting my very first space man!"

"Yes," agreed Xzardak, unsure of how to proceed. "And I also met my first human today, the Earth man… Tesk."

"Mother Mary!" exclaimed the woman. "Tesk was the first human you met? Lord help us. Never mind me!" The robot better give you that sedative!

CHAPTER 5

Mono and his worker robots had resuscitated all seventy-seven of the surviving Earth beings. Xzardak had spoken to each one individually and had tried his best to explain the situation as sensitively and delicately as possible. Each one of the humans had received the news differently. Many had broken down, horrified that the end of the world—or at least their world—had finally arrived. To some, Xzardak's revelation had come as little surprise. Their existence on the planet had become so uncomfortable, that they were thrilled to be far away from the terrible place.

A handful of people had hardly responded at all on hearing the news.

Xzardak suspected that these stubborn and sceptical sorts were the ones who did not believe him.

"Don't believe you?" exclaimed Bungo. "Where do they think they are then?"

"They believe they are still back on Earth and that this is some kind of trick," Xzardak said.

"Sounds a little far-fetched to me," offered Bungo.

"Yes quite," agreed Xzardak. "But then I imagine it's not as far-fetched as their actual predicament."

Regardless of the Earth people's feelings, the reality of the situation was that they were now under Xzardak's supervision, and it was up to him to ensure that they were fed, watered, entertained and most importantly, incarcerated for the duration of the project.

Now that they were fully fit and healthy, Xzardak suggested that Mono should gather all the Earth people into the town square. Xzardak wanted to make a speech and it would be a good opportunity for the whole group to meet and interact.

The Earth 2 compound had been divided up into sectors. Xzardak, Bungo, Mono and the service robots were inhabiting the command sector, where they oversaw, monitored and controlled the entire compound. Dr Jay's assistant robot, Zork, was also based there, where he compiled data, making sure that he kept the good doctor up to date with every eventuality.

The Earth people inhabited the housing sector. From the research materials, Xzardak and Doctor Jay had designed a housing complex similar to that found all across the western continents of the origin Earth. "They like to call it the suburbs," declared Dr Jay. "Rows and rows of uniform dwelling units, as devised by the most intelligent of the Earthlings."

Each Earth human had been provided with a modest house with a front and back yard. Families were housed together there, while single citizens were given the option of living independently or cohabiting. Each house boasting soft furnishings and a plethora of mod cons.

Xzardak and his designers had paid special attention to the interior design, decorating each home in muted tones in an attempt to keep the inhabitants calm and sedate.

The quiet streets were ringed with tall birch trees and at the centre of the complex was a town square. A general store, a non-denominational chapel and a community hall were situated to the north of the town square and to the south stood a large video monitor. The giant screen had been erected to entertain the humans, playing looped footage of the old world from the research vault.

Authentic in every way imaginable, the team had realised and constructed a genuine non-Earth 'Earth environment' for its residents. The only factor shattering this illusion was the zone's lack of litter and debris, making the square resemble and feel more like an old-time movie set.

Beyond the housing complex, a thousand tall trees had been planted and were carefully nurtured, sweet-smelling air circulating the entire compound. The temperature had been regulated to an extremely comfortable seventy-two degrees and the only sound to disturb the Earth people was the bird-song emanating from the dense forest. The cumulative effect, everyone hoped, was that the Earth people would feel safe and secure and settle quickly into their brand-new home from home.

"Such a wonderful environment," remarked Xzardak on the morning of his planned get together, overjoyed that their grand design had finally reached fruition. "I could happily live here myself."

"And such a beautiful day for a communion," replied Zork cheerily. "I'll be sure to inform Dr Jay about your little gathering. He will be very interested to hear what you have to say!"

Mono had been around the entire housing complex, informing each of the Earth people of Xzardak's planned get-together and with a little muscle from Bungo, had managed to assemble almost everyone in the town square. It hadn't been a simple task to rouse the Earth people from their slumber and convince them to convene in the square, but after much bitching and moaning, with the promise of coffee and doughnuts, the strike force had eventually succeeded.

"Who is missing?" asked Xzardak, noting that a few of the seventy-seven chairs were empty.

"Tesk and a few of the Detroit humans," said Bungo. "They aren't interested in socialising." "As the humans like to say," chirped Zork "They 'keep themselves to themselves.'"

"Well, that's disappointing," Xzardak said. "I had hoped to get them all in one place at the same time. I thought it might do them good," he said, scratching his head. "You want to try rounding them up and convincing them to get out of bed before midday," grumbled Bungo. "It's a miracle we managed to assemble this many!"

"The humans have a saying for that too," Xzardak said. *"Better you than me."*

"Precisely."

In due course, the majority of the Earth people were collected together and Xzardak stood on a small makeshift stage that had been constructed in front of the large video screen. He cleared his throat and addressed the company over the compound's loudspeaker system.

"So very nice to see you, friends!" he started. "Almost everyone is assembled, and I must say, it is good to see you all up and about and looking so lively!" The assembled humans yawned and scratched themselves, present in person but perhaps not in spirit.

Xzardak had previously conversed with Mono about the Earth humans' sleeping patterns. "They will sleep twelve hours a day, if you let them" said Mono. "As long as you feed them and let them watch the video screen, they are quite happy to lie around all day!" he confirmed. "They appear to have very little in the way of personal motivation."

"Yes," Xzardak agreed. "I was expecting them to be a little more animated. They are certainly more docile than I had been anticipating."

"Docile? They're lazy," insisted Bungo. "I've never known such a lacklustre bunch, bone idle!" he spat dismissively. "They could do with an exercise class!"

Ever the optimist, Xzardak had leapt to their defence. "It's probably the gravity," he suggested. "It's slightly harsher than that of the origin planet. That and the length of the days. They'll be fine once they become adjusted."

Bungo shook his head, keeping his mouth shut so as not to cause trouble.

"They just need time," asserted Xzardak. "They'll liven up, you'll see."

Bungo raised an eyebrow, fearing Xzardak might be tempting fate.

"Unfortunately, our friends from Detroit could not join us," continued Xzardak as a burst of feedback emanated from the broadcast system. He looked around to see where the strange wailing sound was coming from.

"Here they are now!" exclaimed Mono as Tesk and his friends appeared through the tall trees and made their way towards the proceedings. Wandering over at a leisurely pace, they did not seem to be in any hurry, but the caffeine and sugar bribe had been enough to entice them to Xzardak's special event.

"Ah, Tesk, Stevie, Ruby, all of you!" called Xzardak like an overenthusiastic schoolteacher, "Welcome, friends, and thank you for joining us!" Tesk grimaced as he and his cohorts took their seats at the back of the improvised amphitheatre.

With all of the Earth people in their places and all eyes fixed upon him, Xzardak consulted his speech notes. "I want you all to understand that the program has required a lot of hard work on my behalf," he announced nervously. "I do understand that your new surroundings are a little disconcerting, but we are all in this together. We are your fellow countrymen now, your allies, your friends and family. Together, we can do anything and everything we set our minds to!"

Xzardak had been watching library footage of all the great Earth orators and despite some initial trepidation, he quite fancied himself as a public speaker. It looked straightforward enough; the essence of it was that in all great speeches, no matter the topic, the core message had to be one of coming together, uniting as one and being one great family. He had attempted to weave all these core elements into his speech. "And so, the time has come for us to come together!" he called. "We must work as one if we are to make this project work!" There was a faint ripple of applause from the audience but Xzardak's rallying cry was failing to rouse the assembled crowd. "For where there is effort and will, no man shall ever fail! Where there's a will, there's a way!"

A grumbling murmur was followed by a paltry scattering of claps.

"Who is this guy?" snickered Little Stevie.

"I would now like some of you to come up and tell me how you are feeling," Xzardak declared. Mono circled the crowd, ready to help any willing participant up onto the stage.

He extended his hand, then his elbow, unsure which was the appropriate etiquette. He did not wish to offend by offering or grabbing the wrong body part. So, he waited for them to reach out to him.

"Is anyone brave enough to come up and speak to me?" he called out desperately.

From the front row, a large older woman stood up. Feeling sorry for Xzardak, his efforts not amounting to much of a response, she grudgingly accepted his invitation to say something. Mono helped her up the steps and Xzardak gracefully took her hand as if about to propose to her. "Thank you. What is your name?" he asked.

"Hi, my name is Pam. I'm from North Carolina," she said nervously. Some more muted clapping emanated from the underwhelmed audience.

"And how are you finding your new life?" asked Xzardak. "Is everything to your satisfaction?"

"Oh, you know. Ups and downs," she answered, blushing. "I can't say it's how I envisaged spending my retirement, but still, it's better than that care home." Xzardak nodded his head as Pam continued, "Not that anyone ever came to visit me there, but that's families. The sun is out at least and as long as the rain stays off, I'll be okay." Xzardak appeared confused; unable to tell if Pam's response had been favourable, he looked to Bungo who rolled his eyes and shrugged.

Next up was a tall gentleman. "Hi, my name's Clive," he announced.

"Hi Clive!" called the unrehearsed crowd.

"And how are you finding your new life on Earth 2?" enquired Xzardak, ever hopeful.

Clive took the microphone. "Well," he said. "Everything was going great 'til I realised you'd saved my ex-wife too!" The crowd erupted into laughter. "I thought I might get some peace out here, then I bumped into her in the general store!" Another laugh rang out. "I kinda wish you'd left me to die!" he cried enthusiastically. The crowd let out a cheer. "The only good thing," shouted Clive, enjoying his moment in the spotlight, "I just heard, there's no alimony in outer space! And no Child Support payments!" The crowd was in uproar by now.

Xzardak thought he was beginning to get the hang of Earth humour and although he didn't understand the jokes, he smiled and clapped along with everyone else.

As the afternoon progressed, more and more people got up on stage and Xzardak could sense a thawing in the Earth people's icy mood. He was almost certain they were beginning to relax. Humans from all over the globe had been saved and evacuated; it seemed the entire planet was represented and Xzardak beamed as they cheerfully interacted with one another. The translation chips installed into the Earth people's brains had by now served to break down any language barriers. Together, the Earth 2 humans were acting unified and unlike during their unhappy times on Earth, were getting along more or less fine—better than expected.

With the exception of course, of Tesk and his cronies.

"Tesk, perhaps you would like to come up here and say something?" suggested Xzardak encouragingly.

Tesk got to his feet and cried, "I'm Tesk, and I'm an alcoholic!" The entire crowd let out a cheer. "Well, I'm not one for public speaking much," he called. "But I'm pleased to see so many people out here enjoying themselves."

"Excellent," Xzardak said, encouraged that Tesk had stepped forward.

"Thing is, I'm still having a problem with accepting my current predicament."

Xzardak furrowed his brow, concerned that Tesk was about to spoil the party.

"Something ain't quite right and I'm not buying it, Xzardak! Let's just say I smell a rat."

Xzardak appeared well and truly befuddled. He looked to Mono for a definition, but Mono shook his head dismissively.

Whatever Tesk had meant, it seemed to resonate with his fellow humans, unsettling them.

The Earth people let out a gasp as he gathered his jacket and kicked over his chair, making his way from the assembled symposium. It was already clear that Tesk's unpleasant little contribution had served to suck the life from the afternoon's proceedings and as he stormed off, the Earth people sat back down in their seats, most doing the only thing they excelled at.

Grumbling and whingeing.

Fearing that he was losing the Earth people's attention, Xzardak continued to badger the crowd. "How about you, little girl? Would you like to come up and say a few words?" He gestured to the small blonde child in the front row. Her mother looked delighted that her child had been noticed, beaming as she led her up onto the stage and timidly encouraged her to speak.

The crowd *oohed* and *aahed* as the shy little girl, embarrassed to be up in front of everyone, hid behind her mother's voluminous but still fairly short, cotton skirt.

Occasionally, the child peeked out with a grumpy face.

Xzardak knelt down. "How are you enjoying yourself?" he asked but the little girl refused to speak. "Isn't she wonderful?" Xzardak smiled, patting the girl on the head. "She's such a little angel!"

He pinched her chubby pink cheek.

Suddenly, he let out a scream. The small girl had taken much offence at being pinched and pointed at and had snapped; his finger was spurting blood, her small teeth clamped tight, with no intention of releasing him. "Yowch!" he cried as the mother tried to prise open the girl's jaws.

The digit was throbbing and gushing bright blood. Green, not red.

The mother's voice was clear as she said to the girl, "Let him loose, you damned brat! Let the nice man go!" The girl releasing her snack, her mother pulled her over by her arm. "How many times have I told you, you cannot bite people. Look at you, you could have caught something off him!"

A little something about that statement seemed slightly… warped. But Xzardak could not work out what it was in the moment. Somewhat perturbed and embarrassed, he felt it was time to call an end to the day's festivities. Eventually wrapping his bulbous and bleeding finger in a lump of gauze produced by Bungo. He thanked the crowd for attending and beat a hasty retreat back to the command centre.

"Maybe we should call in at the infirmary?" suggested Mono. "You heard what the woman said. Not only could you have infected the girl, but she could also have given you a nasty Earth disease! Who knows what they're infected with?"

"Nonsense!" exclaimed Xzardak. "It was just a nip, and I'm sure the children are mostly clean."

Indeed, it was the *mostly* that perturbed his robot cohort.

His almost luminous green blood persisted in dripping onto the orange robe in a terrible clash of colours. "Anyway, I thought that went pretty well," he said cheerily. "All things considered."

"Let's just say it was very entertaining!" agreed Bungo.

"Don't you want to get out of this pantomime?" cried Tesk, holding Nelson, one of his oldest buddies, up against the wall by his throat. Back at the housing complex, a few of the Earth people had gathered, a handful less than satisfied with the new arrangement.

As time progressed, their agitation was beginning to show.

Naturally, Tesk had become the leader of the disgruntled bunch and as the unelected spokesperson, he was holding his own rally. "Have any of you people stopped to ask yourselves, *where is this place?*" He paused for dramatic effect, the crew of Detroit humans listening intently. "Have you been thinking, *How did I get here? What am I doing here?* Earth 2? Does all of this not seem a little far-fetched to you?" He held up his hands. "After the mess we were in, neck deep, we should wake up in some kooky 1950's B-Movie!"

The crowd grumbled and murmured in agreement as Tesk paced the floor.

"This guy, Xzardak, and his creepy robots… are you really telling me he put on this whole parade out of the goodness of his heart? Do you really believe this Earth 2 crap?"

The small crowd jeered and clapped in agreement.

He carried on, "You're telling me that this all-powerful, superior 'alien' race"—the crowd gently giggled as Tesk put his fingers up to his head and wiggled them to symbolise antenna—"Yes, that's right, alien race… You're telling me that they have been monitoring planet Earth for all these years, watching all of the hoopla that's been going down and allowing it to happen?" He paused. "Then right at the end, when the sky disappeared and the breathing stopped being breathable, they decided to step in and beam us out of there!"

Some members of the crowd had got to their feet.

"Bullshit!" cried one of the Detroit crew. "It's bullshit, Tesk!"

"They're demons, Tesk, sent by the devil himself!" cried an elderly onlooker.

Tesk nodded, lowering his voice. "Now you'll admit it's a little far-fetched at least? The whole damned thing!" The crowd purred in agreement. "Truth is, I don't know where we are or how we got here. Or who this Xzardak creep even is! We could be anywhere. I mean this place, it could be Mars, Jupiter, Venus, Heaven or Hell, Paris, France or Miami, Florida!"

A man in a plaid shirt gave a whistle then a whoop!

"I just don't know…" Tesk cackled. "But I'll tell you what I do know. I know I don't like it! I don't like this place, I don't like him, his people or this whole damned situation!" Tesk was a convincing orator and the small, unified crowd was becoming animated.

"Damn right!" called Pam.

"Now you guys are welcome to sit back, relax, enjoy the surroundings; take it easy all you want, but I warn you, it's not what it seems. Let me ask you, when was the last time anyone ever gave you something for nothing? In this cursed existence of ours, when was the last time anyone ever reached out a hand without expecting something in return?"

"Not for a long time!" called Little Stevie.

"Not for a long time?" growled Tesk. "Not ever, I'm guessing!"

In truth, most of the Earth people were quite content with their new lives but Tesk's ranting and raving was beginning to draw a crowd. An ensemble was starting to grow as curious onlookers gathered to see what all the commotion was about. Tesk climbed up onto a chair. "My thought is"—he was becoming angry—"the birds, the trees, the food, it's just too good to be true!"

"Amen, brother," cried Clive.

"Maybe it's a hunting lodge or science lab… maybe we're the lab rats? It's just a little too easy and a whole lot of crazy!"

Swept up in the fervour, many of the crowd were cheering and whistling.

"Not like crazy at home. I can handle crazy at home, but this place is crazy weird! For one thing, it's too good to be true!" Tesk yelled.

"What we gonna do then, Tesk?" cried Little Stevie.

Climbing down from the chair, Tesk lowered his voice to a whisper and gestured to his followers to come closer. "I'll tell you what we're going to do, good buddy. We're going to do nothing. If we're part of a science experiment, they'll be monitoring us to see what we do next. So, for now we wait, we get organised, and WE study THEM!" Tesk spoke calmly and quietly. "I need to know who's with me."

Looking over their shoulders as if being monitored, silently and uneasily, members of the assembled crowd raised their hands. "Looks like we all are," croaked Little Stevie.

"Okay!" Tesk grinned with an evil look in his eye. "Here's the plan…"

CHAPTER 6

Mono entered Xzardak's bed chamber with a canister containing a moderate breakfast, a light-blue nutrition capsule and a progress report of the previous night's activity. The rotations on the new Earth world were shorter than those of Xzardak's home planet and he was finding it difficult to adjust to the time structure. "Another busy day, Xzardak?" enquired Mono—even though he himself had planned out the itinerary.

"Yes, lots to do, Mono." Xzardak sighed. "I should really be getting up, but the nights here are just so short as you well know!" With a stretch, Xzardak reluctantly got out of bed, and rubbed his pinkish-purple eyes.

"Now you must eat," insisted Mono. He left the chamber and set off to prepare the transport craft. The small robot had a feeling that an unusual day lay ahead of them.

"Unlike Xzardak to be late?" mused Mono. An hour had passed since they had spoken and Xzardak was yet to appear from his chambers. "Very strange," he mumbled to himself, before noticing his master tardily approaching the cruiser with a slow and shuffling gait.

"I do apologise, Mono. I was looking at some of the surveillance footage from the housing complex. It appears that some of the Earth people had a bit of a get together last night after our meeting. I knew it would do them good to mingle." Mono remained silent, secretly wondering to himself what misdeeds the Earth people were planning. He didn't trust any of them.

"Now where are we off to?" said Xzardak brightly.

Mono was doing a good job of masking his frustration. "Data Archive," he announced. "We're behind the clock," he said stiffly.

At the archive reception, Xzardak presented his commission pass, then strolling slowly into the library, a data servant approached. "May I assist you?" enquired the robot.

"Yes, I think so. I'm looking for Rhodar. I've an appointment to see her."

"Certainly," replied the probe. "Let me just find her for you." The robot scurried off and a few moments later, returned with the tall, slender, grey-blue library assistant.

"Xzardak, isn't it?"

Xzardak smiled, assuming this must be Rhodar. "Nice to meet you!" he said.

"Yes! You too. I recognise you from the television." She blushed as she said it. "I've been following the Earth Project with great interest," she said enthusiastically. "Such a sad predicament the Earth people find themselves in."

"I quite agree." Xzardak smiled.

"The coalition should have stepped in a lot earlier." Rhodar sighed, shaking her head.

Xzardak nodded reassuringly. "The damage is done now, but I intend to put it right."

Rhodar agreed and led Xzardak and Mono into the brightly lit octagon.

Following her lead, Xzardak said, "Dr Jay suggested that you may be able to help us; we are looking for any additional information you might have on the Earth people. I'm trying to piece together some alternative ideas I have." He was pleased to at last be conversing with someone who shared his compassionate viewpoint.

"Well, I'll try," said Rhodar. "I can take you into the vault. Your commission pass wouldn't usually get you that far but as Jay has vouched for you, I'd be quite happy to let you have a rummage around. What exactly are you hoping to discover?"

"I'm trying to find anything whatsoever that would support a claim that I am making. So far, everything I have read about the Earth people has been negative. I'm sure if you have been following the project, you will be aware of their reputation?"

"Indeed," said Rhodar. "But the archivers do have a habit of collating and preserving the more, how should I put it, salacious and scandalous pieces of information." She laughed. "You must understand that working in the archive is not the most exciting of jobs and the researchers do tend to live vicariously through these more colourful news reports."

Xzardak gently laughed, surprised to be sharing a joke. "Well, that's what I'm finding. I've spent time with these people and in my opinion, not all of them are bad. Some can be unpleasant and unruly but on the whole, they are nowhere near as bad as their reputation would suggest."

Looking into the data monitor, Rhodar located the area housing the Earth findings and with the press of a button, she requested that the archive be brought up to the vault.

"How is Dr Jay these days?" enquired Rhodar. "He told me you were coming. It was good to hear from him as I haven't seen him for an age."

"He's doing very well; he's off on his adventures. He thinks I'm insane for taking on this project." Xzardak winced.

"Well, he's forever the pragmatist and like you say, we've heard such terrible things about them," said Rhodar. "Someone told me they even bite! It's not true, is it?"

"Not all of them." Xzardak blushed, concealing his bandaged finger. "On the contrary, they are quite docile on the whole, and they do love their beds."

Suddenly, the monitor flashed a yellow light. "Ah, it's quite a big archive, so you'll have to go up to portal fifty-four to view it. I'll make sure a curator will be up there to grant you access."

Shaking Xzardak's hand, she smiled. "It's a big vault, so hopefully, you'll find something of use up there!" Rhodar escorted Xzardak and Mono on their way along the corridor, guiding them into the elevator which would whisk them up to the 38th floor.

Portal 54 was a small bright room with a reading station and a video monitor. Once the Earth file was loaded, Xzardak began to examine each document. Together, they made up a list of every significant event in the Earth's history. World War 1,2,3 & 4, the great plagues, the great famines, the economic collapse of the west, enslavement of the west, economic collapse of the east, enslavement of the east, World War 5, and so the list went on. Studiously, he searched through the data archive, trying to discover something positive, but to his disappointment found nothing to give him hope in this unabridged history of the planet Earth.

If anything, it served only to enforce the notion that the human race was beyond redemption and indeed a danger to the civilised universe should they ever make it out of the Earth 2 penitentiary. "I know there must be more to the story," Xzardak said under his breath. "There has to be something."

He instructed Mono to summon Rhodar again and within a few minutes, she was back.

"How's the search, Xzardak? Anyone got anything nice to say about them?"

Xzardak looked perturbed.

"Nothing. All I've discovered are more and more reports of their terrible deeds."

Rhodar looked disappointed.

"Maybe," interjected Mono, "they really are just terrible?" Not usually one to voice any kind of an opinion, it seemed clear to him that if the data bank stated they were terrible and there were no studies to oppose or refute that view, maybe it was because they were, well, terrible.

"Yes, I hear you Mono," Xzardak said. "But I just have a feeling about them. It's awfully dismissive—if not to say defeatist—to write off a whole population. An entire species!"

"Surely, no one in the universe is without redemption," offered Rhodar.

Xzardak shook his head. "I've never read such biased expert analysis. According to this, they are beyond hope!" Mono remained silent. "There's something not right about this project, I can feel it," Xzardak said disparagingly.

"Listen, Xzardak," whispered Rhodar. "I know a way to get access to the restricted coalition archive. I shouldn't really do this, but Dr Jay said you were a good soul so I'll give it a go."

Sitting at the control terminal, Rhodar entered the information granting her access to the private archive. The monitor flashed and whirred as clearance was granted. She typed in the letters E-A-R-T-H, and crossed her fingers.

"This is the highest level so there's got to be something good in there for you! Beyond this, Xzardak, you've had it!" Within a couple of minutes, the result came back. Indeed, there *was* more to the archive. Rhodar sniffed. "Well, there's good news and there's bad news."

Xzardak sat up straight with nervous anticipation.

"The good news is there *is* more in the archive... a lot more," she said, her eyes widening.

Xzardak smiled. "I knew it!" he said gleefully.

"And the bad news?" said Mono flatly.

"The bad news is… it's all Category D."

"Category D?" questioned Xzardak.

"Yes, Category D," confirmed Rhodar. "You'll need a commissioner to clear it if you want to see what's inside. I really can't help you any further, I'm sorry."

"Category D," repeated Xzardak. "So, there is more to the vault?"

The fact that the additional archive material had come up as Category D made the result all the more mysterious. Intrigued, Xzardak was not willing to concede defeat quite yet, pressing Rhodar to go further. "Is there anything else you can tell me about it? I really must know."

Rhodar had already exceeded her clearance status and was beginning to feel uneasy, poking around in classified case files. "There's nothing more, Xzardak, as I said. It's top level, Category D. All of it." Rhodar paused. "All I can tell you is it looks like it's a massive file, data and artefacts, and it's currently being housed at the coalition HQ."

Xzardak raised an eyebrow. Rhodar hurriedly logged out of the portal.

"You're in with those government people, Xzardak. Surely you know a friendly commissioner?" she said softly, ushering them out of portal fifty-four. But Xzardak did not respond. Relieved to have made it from the private coalition archive undiscovered, Rhodar politely nudged Xzardak and his friend out into the teleport lift.

"I must say it's a little strange"—said Rhodar, pondering the afternoon's events in the lift down from the 38th floor—"that the lead facilitator would have information withheld from him. Especially on such a high-profile project as this."

Xzardak was deep in thought and did not respond.

Still ill at ease, having not provided Xzardak with anything positive to go on, she offered, "Maybe it's just a duplication? Maybe the coalition backed up all of the data and they're keeping a copy safe, just in case there are any problems? You said yourself that it was a complicated and controversial project."

Xzardak scratched his head. "And would that be in keeping with coalition protocol?"

"Not really," she answered. "Category D would usually indicate something—"

"Unusual!" interjected Mono abruptly. "Anomalous!"

Back in the transport craft, Mono could sense that Xzardak was unhappy. "Would you like me to contact the coalition?"

he suggested. "We could request to see the hidden archive if we enact Protocol 4536H."

"No, my friend." Xzardak sighed. "I fear we will only incriminate Jay and Rhodar if we do any more digging." Mono had run out of suggestions and the pair sat in silence as the craft entered a wormhole portal which would deliver them back to the Earth 2 sector.

Xzardak had made duplicate copies of all of the documents within the data archive library vault. Every piece of research literature, every news story and every eyewitness account now lay at his disposal for consideration and perusal at his own leisure. The craft cruising gently through space, Xzardak began the gargantuan task of reading the file.

Once collated, the information presented Xzardak with quite a horrifying picture of his Earth pets. The Earth, once a beautiful planet, had been ravaged, polluted and destroyed by what seemed to be the alpha predator inhabiting it: the human being. These turned out to be a barbarous savage race of individuals capable of horrific cruelty and wanton destruction on a massive scale.

It appeared from this research folder that these creatures had an inherent capability for evil and had gleefully indulged in every act of violence and destruction imaginable. Instances of murder, torture, assault and battery, deranged acts of selfishness, dishonesty and depravity all considered trivial occurrences on their troubled, broken world. Greed, gluttony, envy, pride and every other undesirable and dislikeable trait possessed by a life form commonly and openly displayed by these underdeveloped Earth devils.

Furthermore, it seemed within a couple of thousand rotations in their sun orbit, they had managed to completely poison and ultimately destroy the delicate ecosystem into which they had been born. The descriptions of humankind had not been accurate, he concluded at last. The humans were far *worse* than any of the documents and warnings had ever intimated!

Xzardak shuddered. So now, he could only think, what if he was wrong, after all?

What if he was fighting a losing battle? What if he'd been telling the powers that be that the humans were bound to come with redeeming qualities, and there were none? He would be ruined.

After all, the evidence sat right here in front of him. If these files contained the truth, would Xzardak be enabling the Earth monsters to commit further crimes? He felt like a fool and wondered if these terrible deceitful creatures might be conspiring against him.

"Mono, I'd like you to tell me the truth," he said, the craft slowing to exit the wormhole.

"The truth?" enquired Mono. "Of course, I will tell you the truth."

Xzardak took a deep breath in as if preparing himself to ask the unimaginable. "Do you think I am being foolish for giving the Earth people the benefit of the doubt?"

Mono considered Xzardak's question carefully. "Yes," he said flatly. Xzardak looked hurt. "And no," added Mono. Well, that was helpful.

Xzardak felt more confused than ever.

Mono continued, "All of the collated evidence would suggest that the Earth people are beyond help, beyond salvation. The intelligence states that very clearly, so yes, it would be foolish to ignore these findings. However, in your predicament, you have been assigned the task to look after and nurture the Earth people, so in doing this you are not being foolish; you are merely following the correct protocol."

It had been a long day but Xzardak kind of understood what Mono was intimating.

"That is why you are and are not being foolish," he concluded. "Plus, I believe a great deal of your reckoning concerning the Earth people comes from a gut instinct that you possess. Personally, I do not recognise or believe in gut instinct, but I must add it is rather strange that an entire artifact archive is being withheld from you. So for now, I will reserve judgement."

Xzardak rubbed his head. Still very confused, he at least felt somewhat vindicated.

CHAPTER 7

Commissioner Turner had called in unannounced to see how Xzardak's new Earth Project was progressing. "It's incredible!" he enthused. "Awfully impressive! The attention to detail is quite exquisite!" Xzardak blushed coyly, clearly very proud of his achievements. "I visited the real Earth myself many times, you know!" declared the commissioner. "Such a wonderful environment! Blessed with such a glorious landscape, it's hard to understand how the Earth people turned out so rotten."

Both shook their bulbous heads despairingly.

"I really didn't think you'd be able to recreate the Earth conditions this far out," whispered Turner encouragingly. "The ground must be incredibly fertile, far nicer than the dirt bowl where I am stationed! You really have done very well for yourself with this environment."

Xzardak nodded excitedly. "Yes, it's the moisture in the air," he said. "Dr Jay devised the propagation system and together, we designed the hill, the valley, and the main compounds. We harvested many of the plant and animal specimens from the life vault. My plan is to reintroduce as many species as we can."

"Are the humans settling in, would you say?" enquired Turner.

"Yes, they seem to be, far better than I'd expected," said Xzardak, appearing relieved.

"Hard to believe with every report we received about them! You must have the magic touch. And what about you? Are you enjoying yourself?"

Xzardak looked at him. "Yes, very much so," he said, nodding his head.

"Good, I'm glad." Turner smiled reassuringly.

"I did wonder why you'd given such a big project to me," Xzardak announced nervously. "I'd have thought you'd be more likely to entrust such a case to someone with more... experience?" He hesitated. "I'm hardly qualified for the position."

The commissioner put his hand on Xzardak's shoulder. "Ah, well. That's where you may be wrong. The coalition members have been watching you, Xzardak. We noticed something in you very early on." Xzardak looked reassured. "You are young, enthusiastic, and most importantly, compassionate. That is what this project needs. There are far more experienced agents than yourself, but our concern was they hadn't the patience or the good nature to see the job through.

"This is a sensitive project," he insisted. "The human race is a violent and destructive species yet strangely, their natural habitat is that of a delicate ecosystem! They need guidance and education if they are to survive a second time around. They must be handled in a most sensitive and thoughtful manner." He looked Xzardak in the eye and smiled. "It was your kindness that got you the job and it'll be your patience and sensitivity that sees you get through it. You should be very proud, Xzardak. You've created something very special."

"I could take you on a tour!" suggested Xzardak excitedly, choosing to ignore the commissioner's compliments as they did make him cringe a little. "I'd love to show you around the place! Show you what we have achieved so far. If you would like me to."

The commissioner smiled mischievously. "I shouldn't really. I'm not meant to be here in the first place but go on, a tiny sliver of time won't hurt!" he said, chuckling. "You see, Xzardak, you've managed to twist my arm. These powers of persuasion will go a long way."

Xzardak simply smiled, then said, "Follow me, sir."

He guided the commissioner down into the hangar bay where a small silver craft was gently idling. Boarding the transport charger, Xzardak instructed Bungo to drive them over to the housing complex. "The commissioner doesn't have much time, but I thought we'd show him some of the wildlife!" he said enthusiastically. "Give him something nice to remember."

"Oh, there's plenty of wildlife!" grumbled Bungo with a disdainful smile.

Strapping Xzardak and Commissioner Turner into their seats, Bungo hit the electric battery pedal, launching them through the gates and out across the main Earth 2 compound.

"It really is wonderful!" said the commissioner, marvelling at the multicoloured birds in the tall trees surrounding them. "It's like Earth in the good old days! Before they messed it up!"

"This time will be different," vowed Xzardak. "I've a feeling the Earth people are going to be just fine this time! They will take pleasure in what we have created and preserve it!"

Within a few minutes, the transport craft entered the housing complex and Xzardak was in full flow, explaining to the commissioner the exact engineering processes they had employed to recreate the origin Earth environment. Suddenly, the vehicle screeched and swerved as Bungo hit the emergency brake, forcing Xzardak and the commissioner to bolt forward in their seats.

"Please, Bungo!" cried Xzardak. "What have I told you about speeding!"

"Sorry, Xzardak," moaned Bungo, rubbing his head which had ricocheted off the windscreen. "But we nearly hit him!"

Xzardak peered up to see the obstacle in the road.

"That's all we need," he whispered. Tesk was standing right there, out in front of the craft.

"Ah, sorry about that!" called Tesk, laughing and noticeably unshaken. "I wasn't looking where I was going. We don't get much traffic around these parts! And that craft is so quiet."

The commissioner straightened his collar, the jolt leaving him disorientated.

Xzardak rubbed his neck. "Please watch where you are going, Tesk," he said with a nervous laugh, trying to remain calm in front of Commissioner Turner. "We could easily have killed you."

"Heaven forbid," uttered Bungo sarcastically. "That would be such a loss."

"Thank you," voiced Tesk, taking the comment as a show of affection. "Guess it's my own fault, out jaywalking on the street. Just enjoying the beautiful weather."

The commissioner nervously eyed the Earth man as they disembarked from the vehicle. Standing for a moment, Xzardak attempted to regain his composure.

"Ain't you gonna introduce us?" Tesk asked, smirking.

"Yes, of course," said Xzardak hesitantly. "Commissioner Turner, this is Tesk, one of our most favourite Earth 2 inhabitants." As Tesk stepped forward, Turner looked to Xzardak for reassurance. Xzardak gently nodded and the commissioner reached out to shake Tesk's hand. "Tesk, this is Commissioner Turner from the coalition."

"Pleased to meet you," said Tesk and the commissioner respectfully bowed.

Xzardak cursed his bad luck. "Of all of the people for the commissioner to meet," he said under his breath as he shot Bungo an irritated look. "We have to bump into that idiot."

"So, you're a commissioner, are you?" Tesk said. "Gee, we've heard a lot about your kind." Tesk looked at Xzardak and smirked.

"Oh!" said Turner. "That's interesting. And yes, I've heard a lot about you too!"

"All good 1 hope." Tesk grinned. "I do hope Xzardak ain't been telling tales out of school!" The commissioner looked confused and Xzardak signalled to Bungo to move Tesk along. Noticing they had mounted a paved area near to one of the dwelling units, Xzardak had an idea.

"Let's just get inside this house here," said Xzardak, pointing to the closest small property. "Let's see who lives in here."

The plan had been to take the commissioner for a circuit of the complex and then pack him off on his craft before the Earth people could say or do anything to upset him. Despite the commissioner's friendly demeanour, Xzardak knew that his actions were being observed, and any slip up at this stage could hinder the program. The last thing anyone wanted was more coalition interference. This was an unplanned stop off but as they were standing outside the small house, Xzardak felt it would be a good enough diversion to shake off Tesk.

Nervously, Xzardak ushered the commissioner away before the boneheaded pedestrian could say anything else. Bungo apologised to Tesk, and they went their separate ways. "Great to meet you, Commissioner Turner!" hollered Tesk with a mischievous laugh. Turner smiled awkwardly.

"I must admit I'm a little nervous!" confessed the commissioner as they walked up the pathway and approached the compact dwelling. "I visited the Earth many times but usually under the cover of darkness and I never actually got that close to a human being."

"Don't worry," said Xzardak, ringing on the doorbell. "They don't bite! Not often, anyway."

The front door opened and Xzardak, Bungo and the commissioner were nervously welcomed in by Sherry, the mother of the little girl who did bite. Xzardak could not believe that yet again, fate had delivered another twist. Of all the houses on the complex, it had brought them here.

Xzardak put his gloves back on as they walked through the house and out into the neatly tended garden space where he immediately spotted the little girl, sitting glumly on her own.

Xzardak approached and apprehensively spoke to the child, the commissioner standing well back in fear of his life.

"How are you today?" asked Xzardak, hoping this time the little girl might be a little more responsive. Unfortunately, she wasn't.

She sat on the ground, barely lifting her head in recognition of the visitors.

"Say something!" insisted the girl's mother. "Come on now, don't be rude!"

Her admonishment had no effect on the child who seemed to be in a permanent state of grumpiness.

Xzardak stood and awkwardly addressed the mother. "This is Commissioner Turner from the Coalition of the Kingdoms. He's just called in to see how we are doing."

The mother curtseyed and smiled shyly. "Oh, gee, thank you, Commissioner. Very nice to meet you. We're good thanks, considering the circumstances. We're just still getting over the shock, you know! It's been a lot to take in," she muttered, gazing off into the middle distance as if lost inside a dream.

Xzardak agreed. "Yes, my dear, we quite understand. If there's anything else you need, please don't be afraid to ask Bungo or myself." Bungo gave a cautious smile.

"I'm bored!" interrupted the little girl. "It's boring here! There's nothing to do!" The mother looked horrified.

"Boring?" asked Xzardak, his eyes widening, an ominous feeling growing in his stomach.

"Yes!" replied the little girl impudently. "Booorrrrring!" Dismayed by the girl's negative appraisal of the facility, Xzardak reluctantly knelt beside her.

"How can you be bored? Surely, you have everything you need here, and more," he insisted. "Ask your mother. She will tell you, there's so much for you children to do."

The little girl folded her arms and slunk away, hiding behind a nearby chair. "Please, excuse her," begged the girl's mother, looking to the bemused commissioner. "She's going through a rough patch!" Concerned that the little girl's outburst might have caused the family some trouble, the mother quickly grabbed the girl and pulled her up off the floor. "Say you're sorry! You little beast!"

But the little girl would not apologise.

Acknowledging the mother's discomfort, Xzardak let out a reassuring laugh. "Boring, is it?" He chuckled, hoping to defuse the situation. "If you only knew all the trouble and hard work that we put into this place—"

"And money," interjected the commissioner. "Let's not forget that." The mother smiled awkwardly, putting her arm around the girl protectively as Xzardak went on.

"And you tell me you don't like it!"

The girl wriggled free from her mother's clutches.

"I do like it! But it's still boring!" the girl shouted. Perplexed by the child's behaviour, Xzardak looked to the embarrassed mother for guidance.

"I am sorry, sir." She blushed. "It's really not boring. Compared to where we were living, it's nice to have a little peace and quiet. I think she's just tired. We've been through a lot, what with the travel and everything."

Xzardak eyed the bewildered commissioner.

"Well, we'd better be off!" Xzardak said cheerfully. "I'll get Mono to try and devise some activities to keep you entertained! I don't want anyone feeling bored! Least of all you."

He gave the problematic little child a huge smile, putting the mother at ease.

"Don't worry about it," he said to the mother. "She's a delight and I can tell we're going to get along just fine."

With a fabricated cackle, he, Bungo and Turner left the little girl and her mortified mother. Hoping that the incident hadn't dampened the commissioner's enthusiasm for the project, Xzardak decided it was time to take him back to the command centre.

Leaving the small house, Xzardak noticed that the transport was no longer where they had left it. "Where is the transport, Bungo?" he enquired. "Where did you take it?"

Bungo looked confused. "No idea, Xzardak," he replied. "I left it right here."

He scanned around, his head whizzing this way and that as if in a cartoon. Looking concerned, Xzardak wondered if Tesk may have had something to do with the disappearance of the transport. This was a real inconvenience.

"Oh, that's a shame," he said, trying to conceal his displeasure.

"Perhaps one of the robots has taken it in for a service?" suggested Bungo, making a similar assumption to Xzardak.

"Ah, yes, I think that's what must have happened!" agreed Xzardak. "It was due a service." he fibbed. "These robots are so efficient. They must have taken it back to the depot."

"Well, I really should be getting back," Turner said stiffly.

Xzardak feared that the commissioner was becoming irritated.

After a few uncomfortable minutes, Mono showed up in a new vehicle and Bungo dutifully opened the hatch and guided the visitor to his seat. "You know, I feel great sympathy for the child," said the commissioner wistfully as he boarded. "Having found herself, through no fault of her own, in such a strange predicament, she's just trying to make sense of it! I am quite sure the mother was correct. Any small child being asked to make such a large adjustment—"

Before he could even complete his sentence, Xzardak agreed effusively, relieved that the commissioner understood the complexity of the task in hand. He huffed out a sigh of relief.

Mono hit the pedal and drove them back to the command centre at top speed, managing to avoid any pedestrians or obstacles en route.

"I've had a wonderful visit!" the commissioner said with a simpering smile.

"Well, you must come back and see us again!" insisted Xzardak, wondering for a moment if he should ask the commissioner about the Category D files, then deciding against it. There was such a thing as pushing his luck, and so far, everything had panned out nicely.

The day had been nerve wracking enough and right now, he just wanted the commissioner to leave before Tesk reemerged. The Earth people weren't going anywhere and there would be plenty of time to investigate those hidden files further down the line.

Back at the base, Xzardak helped the commissioner with his hat and coat.

"I would love to stay and have a bit more of a poke about," said Turner. "But I've got a list of chores as long as your arm." He sighed, shook Xzardak's hand and bowed his head. "Anyway, great work; keep at it, son. You've a great future ahead," he encouraged. With that, he was off.

Xzardak waved as Commissioner Turner boarded his coalition transport.

He smiled as the cruiser zoomed up into the tall trees, speeding off across the beautiful landscape that he had created.

CHAPTER 8

"**O**kay Stevie, this is our chance!" whispered Tesk. "Let's go!" The two men ran out from the undergrowth and jumped into Xzardak's transport charger sitting idling on the outskirts of the housing complex. "And you reckon you can drive this thing?" scowled Tesk.

"Sure, I can," said Stevie. "Nothing to it. I've been studying Bungo, hauling our asses back and forth. It's a piece of cake!" He smiled, slipping the transport into gear, putting his foot flat onto the electric battery pedal and hitting the motion button. "Yeee-haaww!" he cried as the transport thrusters blasted into action, propelling them forward at great speed. "Man, that feels good!"

"This thing can sure move!" cried Tesk with a maniacal cackle. "It's like a rocket!"

"It's been a long time, baby!" called Stevie. "Just like being at home!"

Stealing cars and causing trouble had been Tesk and Stevie's favourite pastime growing up. "Sure does make a change from sitting in front of the video screen!" commented Stevie.

"Yeah!" agreed Tesk. "Let's get out of this boring dump!"

Blasting through the narrow streets of the complex, Stevie slammed on the brakes, causing the transport to spin into a skid. "That's more like it!" called Tesk. "Finally, some real excitement!"

Hearing the commotion, Marvin and Ruby came hurtling out from one of the houses.

"What's going on?" called Marvin.

"We're going for a joyride!" declared Tesk. "Hop in, we're off to raise some hell!" Jumping into the back of the transport, Marvin and Ruby strapped themselves in.

"Where to?" asked Stevie.

"Anywhere," snarled Ruby. "This place gives me the creeps!"

"Yes Ma'am! Hold on tight in the back!" He smiled as he hit the turbo thrust.

"I reckon we just drive a while," said Tesk. "Let's have a good look around this place."

"Guys, wait!" called out Ruby as they sped through the street complex. "Can we pick up Cheryl on the way?"

"Sure!" said Tesk. "The more the merrier! We should have hot-wired a minibus, Stevie, picked up Douglas and the guys, made a real day of it!"

"Douglas!" cried Ruby "Is he still alive?"

"Just about," Stevie cackled. "But for how long, nobody knows!"

Hearing the thrusters of the command transport, a few of the locals had come out onto their porches. Seeing Stevie and Tesk at the controls, they cheered and whooped and Tesk waved his hand regally just like the King of England. Stevie saluted to a group of children who had also commandeered their own transport in the shape of a freshly liberated shopping cart.

"Let's get this party started!" cried Marvin as Ruby's friend squeezed into the back seat of the four-man buggy. With the extra Earth woman on board, the transport was full.

"Hit the gas!" called Tesk and the craft launched off at speed, out across the suburban estate.

"Where're we headed?" squealed Cheryl excitedly.

"Nowhere!" replied Stevie. "Not until we get out of this dumb place!"

After a half hour on the road, Little Stevie looked at the dial. "I can't tell how much power this thing's got left," he said. He thwacked the dashboard dial, hoping to beat some sense out of the gibbering whirling dials on the display.

"Hopefully, we've got enough to get back, have we?" called Cheryl nervously.

"Get back?" Tesk muttered. "We ain't going back, baby! It's time for some answers!"

"Too right. We're busting out of this place!" cried Stevie. "See ya later, Xzardak!"

The crew cheered. The forest surrounding the estate had cleared and now, the craft was hurtling out into open land.

"Man, this sure is some lonely place." Ruby sighed, staring out onto the barren formless landscape. "Beyond the trees, there's nothing out here, Tesk!"

Tesk grunted disapprovingly.

An hour had passed and the cramped conditions in the back of the transport were making Marvin feel sticky and hot, his armpits sweating. "I'm sick of this Death Valley BS, Tesk!" he cried out in a decidedly unhappy tone. "We gotta reach Vegas soon!"

"Keep driving," demanded Tesk.

"Ruby's right!" said Cheryl. "It's a wasteland, fellas. Let's just call it a day, shall we? We've had our fun!" Becoming irritated and fearing the girls may be right, Tesk stubbornly gestured to Stevie who hit the pedal, making the little craft accelerate sharply. Farther on into the nothingness, after another half hour at top speed, Little Stevie spotted something.

It was out there in the distance, a small metal cordon with some alien symbols on it, standing out in the middle of the road.

"Must be a roadblock?" said Tesk. "This is it, guys, we must be on the edge of the compound! Better get your passports ready."

"Hit the gas!" cried Marvin with a cheer. "We're busting out, baby!" He smiled, giving Ruby, who had fallen asleep, a kiss on the cheek. "We're outta here!"

With the craft travelling at full throttle, the company braced themselves to break through the rapidly approaching barrier line. "This is it!" said Stevie, laughing, the G-force of the accelerating craft pinning him to his seat. The adrenaline buzz of blasting through the city limits in a stolen 'car' was making the veins in his forehead and neck bulge out.

Punching the black button marked 'X' on the dashboard, the craft hit maximum thrust! "Yeeeeeeooooooowwwww!" he screamed when suddenly, the craft jolted and quickly lost pace.

"What's going on?" shrieked Tesk. "Don't slow down now, Stevie! We're homeward bound!"

"Ain't me," said Stevie. "It's the damn car, losing power! Aww, trust us to steal this jalopy!"

"You asshole!" exclaimed Tesk. "You've overloaded its circuits. Driving like a street punk! Ain't you got a brain?"

Stevie tried to get the craft to respond but as they approached the limit line, the transport gently ground to a halt.

"Great!" said Tesk. "Just great!"

He got out of the transport, delivering a hefty kick to its side bumper.

"So, what now, Tesk?" asked Marvin, looking around at the arid and desolate desert landscape which appeared to go on forever. This was a godforsaken place, for sure.

"We walk!" exclaimed Tesk. "We walk out of this place and find the next. Then we steal another craft—only this time, *I* drive."

Stevie said nothing, disappointed and depressed that he had blown up the transporter and ended their day's adventure.

Tesk stormed forward as the weary Earth people leant back on the craft, each one looking tired and deflated. "And no, don't you dare suggest we give this thing a push!" Cheryl spat.

"Well?" asked Tesk. "What are you waiting for? Are you coming or not?"

The sugar rush of the joyride was beginning to subside, the humans begrudgingly standing. They gathered their things, pursuing Tesk like a brood of ducklings following a mama duck.

"Ah, it ain't so bad," called Marvin, hoping to reassure Stevie. "At least you got us to the border!" Little Stevie felt a little better and the crew quickened pace to catch up to their angry leader who was hellbent on storming the barricade.

Tesk bounded ahead, kicking over the flimsy roadblock marker which toppled and clattered to the ground. "See, Xzardak didn't think that we'd hijack one of his..."

BAMMM.

With a silent thud, he hit the ground. "What the..." cried Stevie.

"Hit the deck!" called Marvin. "He's been shot!"

Sensing a sniper, the crew hit the ground.

"Is he okay?" called Ruby.

"Well, what do you think? He ain't moving," said Marvin. "Reckon he's dead!"

Hearing that, Tesk sat bolt upright. "I ain't dead, you dummy! Something hit me!" he said, rubbing his head. "Like electricity or something!" He got to his feet.

Again, he walked forward and again, was violently repelled, knocked backwards. Still on his feet, he put out his hand. With a crackle, Tesk felt his fingers tingle as he pushed through.

"It's glass!" he exclaimed.

Getting to his feet, Stevie cautiously approached Tesk; he too lifted his hand and pushing forward, felt the jolt. "Solid, like crystal!" he exclaimed. Together, the crew all joined in, pushing and prodding at the invisible force field before them.

"He's got us sealed in!" howled Tesk. "That asshole has us under glass!" Frantically, they pushed at the barrier field but to no avail.

"We're trapped!" Cheryl said, panicking.

Looking back at the craft, Stevie had an idea. "I wonder," he said as he turned to walk back towards it. He sat in the driver's seat and putting it into reverse gear, hit the gas. The craft leapt into action. "It ain't broken!" he cried. "It must be fitted with a kill switch! So, the good news is the car works!" said Stevie excitedly.

"Yeah, but the bad news is we're trapped in a fish tank!" groaned Tesk. "Those filthy scumbags. I just knew they were up to something."

With everyone back inside the transport, Little Stevie placed it into gear and got back on to the road. "Whoa!" bellowed Tesk. "Where you going, Stevie?"

"I'm taking us back."

Tesk shook his head. "No way, man; we're only heading one way and that's out of here! Let's take this thing off road; there's got to be a way out. Let's follow around the perimeter. If the craft slows down, we'll know we're too near the edge!"

Cheryl rolled her eyes and let out a sigh. "It's over, guys. Let's just go back, you idiots!" Stevie screeched the accelerator and steered the craft from the asphalt road onto the barren plant-less dirt. The area around them was coarse, open land and the transport bobbed along, cruising across the rough purple-pink terrain. Occasionally, it would start to slow.

"You're too damn near the perimeter!" Tesk shouted, and Stevie guided the craft away from the invisible immobilising boundary.

After what seemed like hours of cruising across the bumpy, uneven ground, the craft again slowed to a stop. "Too close!" screamed Tesk, who by this time was beginning to regret the day's off-road excursion. Stevie tried a couple of times to swerve into the wall at high speed, but each time the result was the same, that their craft lost power and ground to a halt.

Ruby sighed. "There must be something around here. We're gonna die of thirst at this rate!"

"There, up ahead!" exclaimed Stevie suddenly. "Looks like a structure."

To the right of them, they could see a cluster of outbuildings and a few very tall trees.

"Maybe we should signal to them?" said Marvin but Cheryl shook her head.

"How do we know they're even friendly?" she said cautiously.

Stevie put his foot to the accelerator. Unable to approach the units, they cruised along the perimeter line until they were adjacent to the settlement.

"Hit the brakes!" called Tesk and as the cruiser slowed, he jumped out. The Earth people disembarked from the craft and together, they cautiously put their hands out in front of them. They could feel a soft tingle of electricity and then the solid glass of the force field encasing them. The Earth people looked out at the units across the vista.

"Hey, is anyone in there?" called Tesk. "Can you dummies hear me?" Tesk's words were repelled by the force field and came back at him in the form of an echo; the closer he got to it, the louder the echo became.

"It's soundproof," called Stevie. *It's soundproof,* came the echo.

"Watertight and bulletproof too I bet," said Tesk with disdain. "Doesn't look like there's much chance of us getting in... or out for that matter!"

Less than five hundred metres away from the buildings, which sat shimmering in the distance, the group stood, silently staring. "So near and yet so far," muttered Marvin.

"Who's to say they would have helped us anyway?" spat Tesk. "They're probably part of the circus show too," he said, shielding his eyes from the burning orange sun.

"You could be right, Tesk," agreed Marvin. "Hey, aren't they—" The whole group looked on in amazement as right out in front of them walked some strangely familiar creatures.

"Well, ain't that something?" said Tesk, rhetorically. "Looks like Xzardak's gone and got himself a petting zoo!" To the crew's astonishment, a number of giraffes were slowly being led out from the main unit, swishing their tails as they walked towards the cluster of tall trees. "I knew it…" said Tesk. "Didn't I tell you this place was a theme park? That just proves it."

Tesk punched the glass and cried out in frustration, but it was obvious that the docile creatures could neither see them nor hear them. "Are you sure they're giraffes?" said Marvin. "I ain't never seen one before!" he said mournfully.

"Oh, they're giraffes," said Tesk. "And this place is most definitely Florida!"

Motioning to the crew to get back into the craft, they all obediently resumed their places on board. "Keep going!" barked Tesk. Stevie once again hit the gas.

Cruising at great speed, the Earth people were soon surprised to see another cluster of outbuildings. "What they got in this one, you reckon?" cried Stevie.

"Gotta be unicorns!" howled Tesk.

Getting as close to the invisible border as the unit's kill switch would allow, they again jumped out from the transport. The glass shield was still evident and Tesk once more protected his eyes against the sun's rays, squinting to see what Xzardak had hidden away in this enclosure.

"Well, would you look at that..?" he asked. "We come all this way into outer space and look what they have here."

"Cows!" exclaimed Stevie, pointing to a herd of healthy Friesians grazing on a circular patch of lush green grass.

"I take it back," said Tesk. "Reckon we must be in Texas!"

Discouraged by the lack of an escape hatch or any discernible plan, the weary and despondent crew continued along the perimeter in the transporter craft.

Every mile or so, a new enclosure appeared in the distance. "Looks like they've got two of everything!" jeered Tesk. "Seems Xzardak's built an ark!"

"Well, one thing's for sure," said Cheryl. "With all these animals around here, we sure ain't on planet Earth!"

The origin Earth—which they had inhabited—had been completely bereft of animal life. This was the first time that the crew members had actually witnessed living creatures in the flesh. They had seen them on TV shows and movies, but almost every animal species had been extinct for at least three generations before them. No creature that was shootable and edible had survived, and even if it had, the gas cloud would eventually have choked it out.

"None of this adds up," said Tesk as they cruised past another enclosure. "Most of these critters are extinct! I only know their names because of Bible class."

"What! You attended Bible class?" Cheryl sniggered. "Are you sure about that?"

"Sure!" cried Tesk. "What, you think I was brought up by wolves?" he frowned defensively.

"Looks like monkeys to me!" Marvin smiled, referring to the next enclosure on the safari ride. A group of primates swung across a climbing frame, chattering and screeching unaware that their genetic relations were sitting gawping at them from beyond the alien force field.

"Man, this place sure is weird," said Ruby. "Xzardak must be growing them!"

"What have I been telling you?" cried Tesk. "The guy's an absolute freak!"

Ahead of them on the edge of the perimeter, Stevie noticed a vehicle. "Looks like they've sent out a search party, Tesk!"

In the distance, Tesk could just about make out a transport and two figures standing silhouetted in the late afternoon sun.

"Do you want me to double back, boss?" enquired Stevie.

"Nah, what's the point?" asked Tesk, hungry, thirsty, and resigned to his fate. "They've won this one."

As the craft approached the roadblock, Stevie was feeling quite anxious. An uncontrollable urge to escape overcame him and against his leader's instruction, he put his foot down flat onto the accelerator in the hope of blasting past the shadowy figures.

However, as they approached the mysterious humanoids, the car shuddered and slowed. One of the figures was holding what appeared to be a ray gun, pointing it toward the craft. Glancing down at the display console, it was clear to Stevie that the device was draining the vehicle of power.

Gently, the transport came to a halt right in front of the second figure.

Stevie got a sinking feeling and clutched his head in his hands; the feeling of being trapped by law enforcement was offering a familiar flashback to his formative years.

"Bungo!" growled Tesk through gritted teeth. "I might have known." Tesk leaped from the transport as Stevie angrily and desperately tried to restart it.

"Damn thing's really dead this time!" he cursed, hammering the console dash.

"So Xzardak sent you out to fetch us back, did he?" Tesk said, sarcasm brimming over.

"That's right," Bungo said with a wide smile. "How many times do we have to tell you? There is no way out."

Tesk had a sudden urge to strike Bungo. His frustration had now turned to anger, but the figure with the ray gun was watching him and Tesk feared the robot may turn the weapon on him.

"You might as well get into the transport," Bungo said, gesturing to the craft. "There's nothing out here for you."

"If it's all the same to you, Bungo, I'd rather stay out here with the other wild beasts," Marvin said, "than be back on that sterile prison reservation you call our home."

"Come on, you guys," insisted Cheryl. "It'll soon be dark."

Slowly, one by one, the Earth people got out of the broken-down cruiser and trundled over to Bungo and his transport 'home.' They were beaten and as the sun began to set, they momentarily lost their will to fight. Once on board, Bungo instructed them to fasten themselves in. "Okay, Zork, do it!" he instructed and the ray-gun-carrying robot slipped the transport into gear and forcefully blasted them into orbit, back towards the housing compound.

Ruby yawned and gazed out into the empty darkness. She laid her head gently onto Marvin's shoulder and closed her eyes.

"No way out, huh?" muttered Tesk under his breath. "We'll see about that!"

CHAPTER 9

There was a loud hammering at the door of dwelling thirty-seven. Tesk jumped up out of bed and stumbled to the window to see who it was. Cautiously peering out through the shade, he could see Mono, Xzardak's robot sidekick, looking in through the ground floor portal. Just as Tesk was just about to make a run for it, the robot looked up and immediately spotted him. "Earth man!" cried Mono. "Please do not be afraid!" But Tesk's escape plan was already in motion; he had quickly put his boots on, grabbed his hat and was halfway through the rear landing skylight when he noticed Bungo and three ugly looking service robots on the gantry beneath, looking up at him.

"Come on, Tesk. Xzardak wants to speak with you, we don't want any trouble."

"Trouble, huh?" Tesk shouted down. "Oh, I'll show you trouble." He clenched his fists but without a clear escape route and sensing that Bungo and the androids meant business, he decided it might be prudent to go along with them. Mono appeared from around the corner with two other worker drones and together, they ushered the Earthling towards a waiting transport unit.

The large grey vessel's doors opened, revealing each of the previous day's joyriders, along with a few other insubordinates sitting unhappily in the back.

"Morning, boss!" Marvin said and smiled.

Unimpressed, the other prisoners obediently acknowledged Tesk but said nothing. "What's this all about, Stevie?" Tesk asked.

"Dunno?" replied his accomplice. "Xzardak sent his heavies out to take us all in. Seems like real trouble this time."

"I knew I shouldn't have gotten into that car with you!" whined Cheryl as Mono closed the hatch and hit the motion switch.

"Hey, I didn't twist your arm, sweetheart!" Tesk replied.

Xzardak had requested that Tesk, the attempted escapees and any other malcontents be taken to his pod in the command centre. Bungo, Mono and Zork had been up since dawn, rounding up the disorderly looking crew. Each member of the band had come along peacefully; it had been much too early to run and besides, now they knew the horrible truth, there was nowhere *to* run.

The transport soon entered the massive hangar bay at the compound's edge, and a large hydraulic metal shutter opened wide to let them in, then abruptly clanged shut. The loud sound echoed throughout the vast silo. Before them now sat an impressive array of spacecraft. Two medium-sized cruisers were there, both used for local transportation, together with a larger craft for intergalactic travel. Alongside some single-unit chargers, an android transporting pod, a maintenance probe and a battered-looking garbage disposal dispatch, Xzardak's stolen transport charger sat gleaming in the morning sun. It was sparkling, freshly buffed and polished, having just undergone a full disinfection and decontamination process. Bathed in pinkish-blue sunlight, the vehicles and hangar bay were an incredible sight to behold. Tesk stood with his arms folded, as if waiting in line to be processed. "You see that ship?" he whispered. "Amazing, isn't she?"

"Yeah, beautiful," said Stevie, gazing up at the huge chrome vessel. "I wouldn't mind taking that out for a spin!"

"Looks fake," Tesk scoffed. "Probably made up of old war movie props, all cardboard and Plexiglass. I told you they were radicals." Stevie had had enough of Tesk's kooky theories but sensing they were already in hot water, he shrugged and nodded to avoid any further aggravation.

The other humans looked around in silent awe at the hi-tech array of flying machines. The collection was like nothing they had ever witnessed before.

The main hatch on the largest cruiser hissed and clicked open and Xzardak disembarked, walking casually down the duty ramp and towards the gang. His usual black suit and green robe had been replaced by an outfit best described as a flying suit or overalls, like those commonly worn by pilots and race drivers. As he approached, Tesk turned towards him and grinned. "This is quite an amusement park you have, Xzardak. Something for all the family!" he declared.

"Amusement park?" enquired Xzardak, unfamiliar with the Earth man's terminology. Their speech was often perplexing, and this was one such example. What was there to be amused about?

"Yeah, I mean this collection of yours," he said, convinced that Xzardak must be playing dumb. "Almost as impressive as that menagerie out there. Quite the showman, ain't ya!"

Xzardak looked confused and scratched his head, then suddenly realising that Tesk was referring to the attractions of the previous day, he smiled.

"I was planning on introducing you to your fellow Earth inhabitants very soon," he insisted. "But now you've gone and ruined the surprise." He looked dejected.

"All I wanna know," said Tesk, "is where do you keep the dinosaurs!"

The crew let out a bilious laugh.

"Dinosaurs?" answered Xzardak without missing a beat. "They are out on the other side of the ridge," he said calmly. "Be patient; you will be reunited with your ancestors in good time!"

"Whoa, no thanks!" Tesk laughed, holding up his hands. "We all saw that movie!"

"Gentlemen, ladies, please come." Xzardak beckoned, ushering them into a dome-framed structure sitting beneath the largest silver craft. "Take a seat inside," he insisted, and the group cautiously filed in, each finding a place to sit. Once settled, the seats rotated in the direction of Xzardak, who now stood at what appeared to be a control console.

"This feels a lot like driving detention school to me," said Stevie.

"Well listen up," suggested Tesk. "You might just learn something!"

Xzardak took a breath. "Now, speaking to Bungo yesterday," he began. "It seems to me that you people still do not understand the severity of your situation. You are unwilling to accept what I have told you and seem to want to believe that there is some form of subterfuge at play.

"Well, rather than labour the point and explain again, I thought it more prudent that I take you outside for a demonstration so that you can see the truth and we can finally put to rest your paranoid fantasies and demented delusions!"

The Earth people quietly murmured among themselves, and an evil smile appeared on Tesk's face, intrigued to see what the ring master had in store for them next.

"Fasten them in," instructed Xzardak, signalling to Mono.

The band of humans looked perplexed as the plush seats again adjusted direction. They gasped as safety belts attached themselves and the chairs began to recline. With a hydraulic whir, the platform began to rise, the domed ceiling above them splitting into sections and opening like the petals of a rose. Elevating through an ever-widening aperture, the Earth people quickly realised they were sitting inside the cockpit of the beautiful silver spacecraft.

Tesk's eyes lit up with excitement. Suddenly, he looked very impressed.

"Plexiglass, huh?" grunted Stevie dismissively. "Looks pretty real to me."

With everyone settled on board, the ship began to tremble.

Charged with electro-magnetism, it taxied forward and with a tremendous thrust, roared out of the hangar bay doors and up, off into orbit.

Once airborne, Xzardak glanced across the cockpit at the Earthlings, intrigued to see their reactions and curious to find out what effect the extreme speed of the take-off might be having on his passengers. Maybe this would be the thing that finally shut the annoying Tesk up.

Fearing that the Earth peoples' puny skulls may implode, their faces contorted by the violent thrust of the cargo craft's boosters, Xzardak signalled to Mono to slow the ship down.

"Is everyone all right?" Xzardak enquired as the vessel gently decelerated.

He gave the passengers a moment to adjust to the zero gravity, then once he was confident that they were all comfortable, he instructed Mono to cruise a while.

"Now, I don't suppose you remember the last time you were all on board a ship of this nature?" said Xzardak calmly, appearing relatively unaffected by the extreme G-Force of the take off. "Your planet had just been declared a dead star and we loaded you onto a similar class 4 craft."

"Yeah, yeah, yeah!" called Tesk, desperate to uphold his bad boy demeanour whilst struggling not to vomit. He cast his gaze around in search of a receptacle just in case but there wasn't one. He steeled himself and managed to grunt out, "Listen, man, we've had enough of your stories. We have all the answers we need! Saw them with our own eyes yesterday!"

"Really?" said Xzardak. "What is it that you think you saw?"

"It's a zoo, man. It's all fake! Virtual reality or somethin'!" he insisted, wiping his sweaty brow. "And all this…"—he gestured dismissively to the ship's cockpit—"You think we've never been on a rollercoaster before? I'm sick and tired of this Coney Island BS!"

Xzardak let out a sound which could have been a groan or a sigh as he returned to his seat. Clearly, nothing he could say would make a difference.

Instead, he motioned to Mono who hit the thruster and again, the Earth people encountered a jolt of G-Force, pinning them to their seats.

As the craft finally slowed and tilted, Xzardak stood, gesturing towards the huge port window. "Friends, this is probably the best view I can show you of your current home."

The craft banked, revealing a small, grey, purple-blue orb in the distance. The crew remained mute. "What do you think, Tesk?" Outwardly unfazed, Tesk shrugged his response.

"Nice light show, Xzardak." It seemed this man had nothing intelligent to contribute, so Xzardak did not respond, exasperated by the stubborn Earth man's foolishness. For a moment, there was stillness and silence in the cockpit. They sat quietly observing the apparent planet hanging there in the starless deep black void of space before them.

But this still wasn't enough to convince anyone.

"Spacecraft," Tesk said. "You're crazy."

Xzardak was about to instruct Mono to take them back to base when Stevie let out a sigh. "Well, for what it's worth, I think *I* believe you, Xzardak," he said quietly.

"What the!" hissed Tesk.

"Yeah, me too," said Cheryl. "I believe you too."

Marvin followed, a hint of nerves in his voice as he said, "I hate to say it, guys. But it seems on the level to me."

It soon transpired that everyone in the craft appeared to be in agreement, except Tesk. Stubborn, cynical, troublemaking Tesk.

"You're telling me you believe this bullshit. That's unbeliev—"

"It's over!" cried Stevie. "Accept it, Tesk!"

Tesk grappled with the safety belt. "Get me out of this thing! I want out!" he seethed.

A siren sounded and a light flashed. His sudden harsh tugging at the safety apparatus had triggered an alarm on the craft's console.

"Will you just cool it, Tesk!" screamed Cheryl. "You always have to make a scene. Everywhere we go and whatever anyone says, you always know better! You just had to say this is a put on, say it's all fake. But look at it, then answer me one question. Why? Why would they go to all this trouble to try and trick us? For what!"

Tesk kicked and screamed, angrily wrestling with the safety harness.

"Yeah! Nobody on Earth cared about us, Tesk!" Ruby shrieked. "Why would they put on a party like this? *That's* what's unbelievable! No one gives a shit about us."

"Grrrrrrnnnnnnngggggghhhhh!" Tesk growled, clawing at the belt. "Let-me-ouuuuuut!"

"Please, Tesk, cool it!" cried Ruby.

"It's done, Tesk. Accept it," sobbed Cheryl. "It's over."

Suddenly and unexpectedly, Tesk stopped struggling and gave up the fight. He sat back and said nothing more, appearing oddly beaten and exhausted. Unable to escape from his seat, he stared out into the blackness of space and across at the beautiful planet before him.

"Accept it." Ruby smiled reassuringly. "It's done."

Tesk sniffed. "Yeah, I know!" he said through gritted teeth, finally admitting to himself and the gang that the battle was lost. "I just wanted..."

He paused for a moment, his eyes filling with tears.

Cheryl held out her hand in an unusual show of empathy for the person no one even liked.

Unable to think of anything appropriate to say, Xzardak awkwardly motioned for Mono to proceed. "Mono, please can we approach the planet slowly so I can show our guests the conurbation? I'd like to explain a little more about my project."

As the craft hummed and shifted gears, the Earth people could feel they were drifting slowly back down towards the small pink-grey planet.

Xzardak attempted to reassure his guests.

"A vote was cast, and a panel assembled to decide what to do with your species. Initially, the government was very much in favour of letting your kind perish. Several coalition members had grave misgivings about saving you. Intel reports of countless violent episodes in your shared history did little to convince the somewhat conservative orthodoxy.

"Yet despite their uncertainties, they decided that we should intervene. Unfortunately for you, your reputation preceded you, so it was voted through unanimously that you would be relocated away from all other life settlements. Partly due to your troubling nature, but also to shield the galaxy from any germ contamination or infestation that you may have been carrying."

Xzardak looked to Tesk, and he paused, waiting for him to interject as he always did. But Tesk was crushed, looking tired and dismayed. He had nothing left to say.

"Once it was decided that you would be preserved in isolation, a home had to be found. Fortunately for all of us, a small planet was located. That planet is what you see before you. It is roughly within the same temperature range as your Earth planet; the atmosphere, although somewhat denser, is breathable and most importantly, there is fresh blue water which it seems you Earth people require to live." The craft bobbed and hovered for a while and the crew sat silently, staring out at the wispy Earth-like clouds covering half of the planet below.

Xzardak felt sure that he was finally getting through to them. This moment seemed to bring about a peculiar and unforeseen change in the Earth people. They had become acquiescent.

"It's quite a sight," said Tesk, gathering his composure. "Isn't that something?" He chuckled; the air of vulnerability having disappeared already, his familiar bad attitude had made a comeback. Regardless, Xzardak nodded his head, happy that Tesk was finally on board with the program.

There was no way that they could possibly disbelieve him now that the evidence was out in front of them. As they slowly drifted toward the planet's surface, Xzardak calculated that this was a significant and horrifying turn of events for the rescued bunch, the moment when the Earth creatures realised that all hope was lost for their home planet. He shuddered empathetically as he thought of his own family back on their own home world.

"We are all a long way from home," he said softly. "I realise it must be difficult for you to accept but your planet is dead. There is no justifiable reason to look back, no cause to be wishful or wistful." His tone was one of pragmatism. "We must look to tomorrow, not yesterday."

The crew was dumbstruck as Xzardak pointed out across the vastness of space. "This is the best world that our probes could find, and I hope under the circumstances, it will suffice."

After a moment of solace, Marvin took a deep breath. "If the government didn't want to help us, how come you came down and got us?" he asked, looking quite pleased with his question.

Xzardak beamed. "The people voted!" he said proudly. "We have many compassionate beings within our kingdoms. They lobbied the coalition, and the coalition voted to give you another chance. Surely every being deserves that."

Marvin smiled and nodded his head, delighted to have been part of the discourse.

Xzardak motioned to Mono to take the craft back into the planet's orbit and as it descended, he explained, "The large translucent dome structures that you see are where we are currently housed. Should the program work, the plan is to expand, to maybe give you the whole world. And beyond that, far into the future, who knows?"

Mono manoeuvred the ship slowly and carefully so that the visitors could get a good clear view of the entire Earth 2 unit. The humans marvelled at the shimmering glass dome configuration before them. As they descended, Tesk let out a sigh and looked to Xzardak. "Guess I owe you an apology, Xzardak," he said quietly. "Looks like you were on the level all along."

Xzardak smiled but did not respond.

"That force field looks kinda pretty from out here!" joked Tesk.

Xzardak dropped his head. "I'm sorry about your home world, Tesk. I hope that we can learn from our mistakes and together, start again?"

Tesk gave Xzardak an amenable smile. "If you're willing to give us a second chance" he said with a crooked grin. "Then sure, why not?"

The craft descended into the planet's airspace, penetrating the protective force dome. The Earth people sat in stunned silence; faced with the evidence, they were forced to accept the terrible truth. Tesk's paranoid fantasy had been just that, a fantasy. There was no way back.

The Earth was a burnt-out husk, dead and gone, along with everyone and everything on it. Contrary to what they believed, they were not the only life forms in the universe, and they certainly were not the most intelligent—far from it. It appeared that it had been their own ignorance and arrogance that had destroyed them. Everything they had ever believed had turned out to be untrue. Now, they were alone and shockingly found themselves the last of the human species, a million miles out in space at the mercy of a strange space alien and his robot cohorts.

Shivering, Little Stevie looked at Cheryl who gazed silently out of the craft window. "Are you all right?" he enquired. "You look a million miles away."

"Sure, honey," she replied. "I'm all right. Just wondering if I'm ever gonna wake up."

There had been a noticeable sense of calm during the trip back to the planet. The ship docked and once on solid ground, Mono released the hatch enabling the passengers to disembark. "I feel we have made a giant step forward, my friends!" announced Xzardak.

"Shouldn't that be a giant leap?" corrected Little Stevie. As they left the craft, Tesk insisted that the Earth people each shake Xzardak's hand. One by one, they thanked him and politely smiled as they filed out from the cargo hold, back into the compound hangar bay.

As the shuttle door hissed closed, Xzardak and Bungo respectfully wished their passengers a good day and turned to head back to the control module. Zork had been instructed to escort the Earth people back to their quarters and once on board the transit, the humans looked at each other without uttering a word. Tesk's eyes darted from side to side as he surveyed the gloomy faces surrounding him. Reality had bitten and a sense of shame had descended upon the group. They had destroyed their home world and now filled with regret, they faced the formidable task of building a new life on a new planet.

Once back at the housing complex, they disembarked from the transport.

"It's going to be okay," said Cheryl to Tesk. "You'll see."

"Yeah, I feel it, sugar," he replied with a wink.

As Zork and his vehicle blasted out of sight, the dishevelled Earth people stood in silence, each wondering what would happen next; the fatigue of the space journey and the gravity of the situation had taken its toll on the fragile Earth visitors.

Tesk took a breath and turned to the group. "What's the matter with you lot?" he croaked. "Why the miserable faces?" Tesk's mood had once again changed, and the crew looked apprehensive. "C'mon! You should be happy!" He grinned and added, "Xzardak just showed us a way off of this dump of a rock!"

CHAPTER 10

Xzardak was awoken by the sound of an interior breach alarm. Unbeknownst to him, coalition forces had already docked within the hangar bay complex.

"Mono, what's going on!" demanded Xzardak over the console monitor.

"You better get down here, Xzardak! There are coalition commissioners disembarking from a long-range craft. Looks like official business to me."

"Oh no," groaned Xzardak, jumping up out of bed and quickly dressing. Getting himself together, he bounded over to the hangar bay.

"I'm sorry, Xzardak," said Mono. "They appeared out of nowhere and demanded entry to the compound! I didn't know what to do. They don't look very happy!"

"So I see," responded Xzardak nervously.

Xzardak was fully aware that the planet was being monitored by the coalition and it was obvious to everyone that they would have noticed the boundary breach the previous day. With all of their probes and surveillance devices, it was impossible to keep anything from them and Xzardak suspected there might be trouble.

"Gentlemen," he greeted them. "I had a feeling you might pay us a visit, but no communiqué? Is everything all right?" The party consisted of three commissioners dressed in standard coalition flight suits, an envoy, the craft pilot and three members of the technical team.

Two of the commissioners held back but the smallest of the three, a squat purply blue-looking creature, approached Xzardak.

Xzardak held out his hand. "Commissioner Edward, please come over to my office and—" The commissioner barged past, refusing to shake his hand. "I'm here on government business, Xzardak!" announced the commissioner, his silver-grey eyes bulging out of their sockets. "I need to see the duty log for the past three rotations. This is not a social call. Do you follow me?"

Xzardak looked concerned. "Yes, Commissioner."

"There are reports that you escorted some of the Earth people out of the compound and took them into coalition airspace? Is this true, Xzardak? Explain yourself! It's preposterous!"

Xzardak steeled himself, the commissioner's brusque demeanour putting him on edge.

"Yes, indeed. I did take a handful of the Earth people out into orbit. But with good reason, I can assure you!"

The other two commissioners, Sirdar and Vilmos, listening in from afar, looked horrified. They stood gibbering and shaking their heads.

"Really, Xzardak!" exclaimed Commissioner Edward with a concerned tone. "Whyever would you do that? You know the protocol; you're not completely new to the game!"

Xzardak looked embarrassed and mortified at the loud admonishment.

"I only took them out a short distance, Commissioner," he said sheepishly. "I wanted to show them the compound because it would serve a vital purpose! Since the relocation, they have been in a state of shocked denial, Commissioner. They have been acting paranoid and refusing to believe that we have rescued them! It was the only way I could get through to them!"

Edward stroked his moustache. "Didn't believe you, huh?" he said. "Whyever not? What's so difficult to understand?"

"You must see, commissioner," said Xzardak. "By their very nature, they are suspicious and negativistic, almost paranoid in fact!"

"Well, where did they believe they were then, Xzardak? Tell me that. I thought they'd be pleased to be out of that festering cesspool!"

"I trust that you are familiar with the background of this case," said Xzardak assertively. "Up until very recently, the Earth people were unaware of our existence. The notion of extra-terrestrial life was beyond them. Some of the less intelligent humans expressed to me that they believed—and to some degree perhaps still believe—the idea of space aliens on far off planets to be, as they put it, 'far-fetched'!"

"Far-fetched?" repeated Edward. "Then how do they explain this?" He was pointing to the hangar bay filled with alien spacecraft and aliens.

Xzardak scratched his head. "Some seem to believe that they are still on their home world and that this is all artifice. They believe that they are party to some sort of elaborate hoax, a deception played upon them by an enemy nation. Some kind of a simulation perhaps?"

The commissioner was unable to see Xzardak's point. "Elaborate hoax?" he spluttered. "Simulation? Are they aware of how much this 'elaborate hoax' has cost?"

Xzardak was finding it difficult to explain the Earth man's unique logic. "If you like, I could bring them out and you could try explaining for yourself?" he suggested enthusiastically. "Maybe it might help if they hear it from someone in authority?" Xzardak hoped that the commissioner would decline his offer, afraid of what the Earth people might actually say.

"Well, Xzardak," the commissioner started as the two other officials joined him. "Whatever your reasoning, news of your little excursion has got back to the powers that be. The media have heard all about it and it looks like we're headed for a bit of controversy. You had no right taking them off world, no business at all! No matter how good your intentions were!"

The second of the commissioners sidled up to Edward and spoke softly. "I am Commissioner Sirdar. We have been instructed to take the Earth people back to headquarters. It is thought if we relocate them temporarily, some of this trouble might be avoided."

Edward and Vilmos nodded in agreement. The technical crew appeared on the duty ramp and opened the side hatches of the coalition craft. "We will vouch for you," continued Sirdar. "We shall explain that the reason you allowed the controlled substance to leave the compound was as a test, to see how the Earth people might handle their journey back to the Crystal Planet."

Xzardak couldn't believe his ears. "Take the Earth people to the Crystal Planet?" he exclaimed. "But they'll die. They won't withstand the journey. Besides, there are a lot of them, and they'll never all fit into your craft!" Xzardak was convinced that this was a very bad idea indeed. "What if they don't make it?" he demanded.

"Then their blood will be on your hands," Edward explained. "You had no right taking them off the blasted planet in the first place, Xzardak! And this is the best we can come up with."

The craft pilot suddenly appeared and removed his helmet.

"The gateway won't be accessible for very much longer, commissioners. If we are going to make the rendezvous, we should leave quite soon," he suggested.

"The Earth people will be quite all right as long as we get them onto the craft and through the wormhole soon!" announced Commissioner Sirdar. Xzardak was relieved to hear that an accessible wormhole had appeared as it would reduce the time of the journey quite considerably, yet he still felt reluctant to allow the Earth people out of his sight. They were still in his care.

"I'm concerned about the journey!" he insisted. "I'm not convinced they'll survive outside of the compound." Xzardak was ready to use any excuse necessary, but Edward was a step ahead.

"Well, Xzardak," returned the commissioner. "That's an easy one! We'll take the Earth people who've already breached protocol. I'm sure if they survived yesterday's little jaunt, they'll survive a trip in my shiny new coalition cruiser."

Xzardak was out of answers.

"Shall I go and get them then?" grumbled Bungo, looking to Xzardak for guidance.

"Yes, please do, my friend," said Edward, interrupting. "For all of our sakes, the sooner we get on board the better."

Xzardak tried one final time. "I really must protest!" he cried out. "I am very concerned about you taking program assets from my supervision. I respect your authority, but I'm still in charge of this project, you know! I do have some rights!"

"I'm afraid you lost your rights when you defied coalition conventions," explained Sirdar. "Besides, don't worry about the Earth people leaving your supervision. You're coming with them!"

As the craft was being prepared, Xzardak had a sickly feeling in his lower stomach. "What does the coalition want with the Earth people anyway?" he asked impertinently.

The third of the commissioners, Vilmos, turned to answer. "It's not the coalition who wants to see them," he said with a monotone cackle. "It's the government."

"The government?" spluttered Xzardak, taking a step backwards.

The commissioners instructed the flight crew, the craft's thrusters now warming in preparation for the flight. Collecting his things, Xzardak muttered to Mono, "Could this day get any worse?" Suddenly, it dawned on him that yesterday's passengers, the Earth people Bungo had been sent to collect, were again going to be Tesk and the worst of the worst.

As he made his way onto the coalition cruiser, he noticed Bungo appear in a craft transporter containing the Detroit crew. Xzardak doubled back and ushered the dishevelled looking Earth people onto the craft. "There's a problem," whispered Bungo.

Xzardak felt queasy. "What now?" he whimpered.

"No Tesk!" said Bungo, sounding anxious.

"Where is he?" Xzardak whispered as Little Stevie filed past. "As if it wasn't bad enough!"

Stevie shrugged and shook his head. "He's disappeared! That's where he is!"

Xzardak thought for a moment. "Hmm, maybe it's a blessing? He would only cause trouble."

Bungo looked concerned. "Let's just hope they don't count them going on!"

With his fingers crossed, Xzardak bade farewell to Bungo and Mono. The craft doors closed, and the passengers prepared themselves for ignition.

"You must go easy on the blast off for the sake of the humans!" Xzardak called out to the technician who was checking that the Earth people were securely strapped in.

"Don't worry sir," replied the technician. "They'll be quite comfortable. This craft is state of the art, not like that old thing!"

He pointed to the 409, Xzardak's craft, the lead ship in his fleet, sitting idling in the hangar bay.

Xzardak sat back and considered his predicament.

As a youngster, Xzardak had been taught about the benign hierarchy which oversaw the 'Everything,' the term used by the 'Civilised Universe' to describe all of creation. Right at the top sat the governors, who did not rule, but rather presided over the whole of society. Beneath them sat the coalition, made up of commissioners and envoys. It was the coalition's role to enact and enforce the suggestions of the wise old governors. Such was the shroud of secrecy surrounding the governors, however, that some believed they did not exist.

Rumours had been circulating for a million years that the shadowy elite were a coalition creation invented to keep the masses in line. However, the many had little reason to question the way of things, as the administration—for the most part—provided quite adequately for everyone.

The Crystal Planet lay right in the centre of all creation. Countless worlds and moons, galaxies, and stars spun upon its axis, many unaware that it even existed.

The recognised 'Everything' was a peaceful place in which each society looked out for the others. The government demanded this. Any kingdoms out of step with the governors' will would be excluded, banished and left to survive alone, out in the cruel black darkness of space.

Such had been the fate of the planet Earth, the earliest complex inhabitants of which had railed against any alien intervention into their practices. Yet here they were, in the final moments of their existence, on course to meet the alien creatures they'd shunned across the ages.

Xzardak trembled, considering the appointment, more than a little nervous at the thought of being hauled up in front of the coalition top brass, let alone the idea of meeting the Great Ones.

As Xzardak expected, the Earth people were taking all of this in their stride.

They were seemingly unfazed by the alien cruiser into which they'd been strapped, and by the alien commission crew transporting them to a far-off planet for interrogation and who knew what else. Xzardak marvelled at how calm they appeared, wondering how long they'd keep it up.

In Tesk's absence, Little Stevie had ascended to the role of group spokesperson. "So, tell me again, Xzardak, what is it they say we've done wrong?" he called across the transport cabin.

"Nothing, Stevie, it's me who's in trouble!" reassured Xzardak. Despite his convivial relationship with them, he was still quite wary of the Earth people and wondered when he might get a glimpse of their aggressive side. It would surely come soon; their reputation said so.

Without Mono to analyse brain, heart, or hormone levels, he thought it best to humour Little Stevie—it had been evident from the start that he was the most amiable of the bad bunch. "So why are they hauling our asses to jail?" he called over the hum of the engine.

"No one is going to jail!" interjected Edward, appearing through the cabin safety curtain. "You are not on Earth now, human! You are being taken to the Crystal Planet. The government has asked to observe you, that is all. Not for any negative or punitive reason. They just want to… consider you, as is the case with every new life form inducted into the unified society!"

Xzardak felt comforted; he too feared that they were in trouble.

Sirdar appeared and waved a bony finger at the passengers. "The Earth 2 Project has been quite a high-profile story in the intergalactic press," he mused. "Some of the coalition commissioners also want to take a look at you."

Little Stevie shuffled in his seat. "Well, it sure feels like a bust to me!"

"Maybe get some rest," suggested Xzardak. "We still have a long way to go!"

Stevie shrugged; matters were out of his control now. He laid his head against the craft window. The view outside was a hypnotising blur of coloured lights, making him feel quite sleepy. As the craft entered the gateway and hurtled through the wormhole at an unfathomable speed, Xzardak too began to nod off. He had never been comfortable with the woozy sensation experienced during high-speed aviation and was not completely immune to the exhausting effects of wormhole transit.

Many hours had passed and eventually, the ship reached its destination. The passengers began to stir as the coalition craft slowed and began its descent. Little Stevie marvelled at the glass planet below as they slowly drifted into restricted airspace. The Earth people had never encountered anything as beautiful as the small prism-like moon, glinting in the early morning sun. "I sure wish Tesk had been here to see this," he said to Marvin.

Marvin was awestruck by the celestial vision. "D'ya reckon this is where Santa Claus and the elves live?" He chuckled, the cascading light reviving a sense of childhood wonder which had lain dormant for twenty-something Earth years.

As the craft banked, the remainder of the sleeping passengers were awoken.

Bleary eyed, each one stared out in silence, overwhelmed by the most extraordinary view in all of the 'Everything.'

Xzardak awoke and for a second, wondered if he was dreaming. For a moment, he and the Earth people had become unified in a sense of enchanted bewilderment. The technical crew skilfully guided the vessel in and prepared the craft to dock. As soon as the ship had landed, the three commissioners emerged from their quarters, dressed in full coalition ceremonial attire.

"You will all be issued with breathing apparatus and contamination apparel," boomed Commissioner Edward. "The Crystal Planet is the purest in the known 'Everything.' Should it sense contamination, it may take it upon itself to neutralise and obliterate you. Please do not remove the apparel. Please do not touch anything. Please do not speak to anyone, and please stay close to us. For your own safety, I must insist on this! If any of you have questions or feel you cannot follow these instructions, it is imperative you speak up now."

No one did say a word.

Commissioner Sirdar ushered Xzardak out and an envoy enthusiastically instructed the Earth people on protocol. "Don't look so worried, Xzardak," said Sirdar. "This is just procedure. The coalition wants to see what they've let themselves in for," he added, then laughed. "Some of us still think this Earth Project is a dreadful mistake, a momentary lapse of good judgement on the part of the government. But they know best! Hopefully, your Earth friends can put us all straight!"

Xzardak gave a crooked smile. He had an uneasy feeling regarding the 'meeting of minds' that Sirdar, Vilmos and Edward had arranged for them.

"Let's just hope the Great Ones like them," Vilmos joked with an ominous laugh.

"Please, all form an orderly queue!" barked an overzealous envoy.

Xzardak rubbed his eyes, the crystal glare interfering with his vision. "All this for a day out in space," he moaned as the official positioned the group to be fumigated. "They've got me lined up like an outlaw!" he whispered.

Little Stevie chuckled. "Must be the company you're keeping!"

CHAPTER 11

Inside a crystal elevator, Xzardak and the Earth people were silent, unable to fathom how quickly the car was moving or in which direction they were travelling. Xzardak felt hot and giddy while the Earth people pushed and twisted, eager to escape. "Hey, move up a bit!" said Ruby, digging her elbow into Marvin's ribcage.

"These government types must be pretty weeny to fit in this lift" he grumbled.

"Surely, we're exceeding the weight limit with you in here," joked Cheryl, poking him in his fat belly, making all the Earth people chuckle.

Suddenly, blinded by a silver sunburst, the humans ceased to struggle.

As the lift continued to rise, Xzardak said nothing, partly because of his motion sickness but mainly due to the notion of his current surroundings.

I can't believe it, he thought. *The Crystal Planet... it exists!* To the average citizen, the Crystal Realm was a thing of fairy stories, depicted in kitsch localised folk art and sung about at school assemblies. It was an ancient sacred place, some believed, too fantastical to exist.

Yet here it was, and even more breathtaking than he could ever have imagined.

Higher and higher they climbed, the view becoming more and more magnificent. Xzardak tried to put the reason for their visit to the back of his mind. They were potentially in a lot of trouble, but for now, he would just enjoy the ride, go along with it and see how everything turned out. It was all he could do. The soft whirr of the elevator motor and the flickering rainbow colours had subdued the Earth people who now stared out, transfixed.

As they neared the top of the mountain, Xzardak's head began to spin, and he hoped they might have something to settle his stomach. Whether it was the travel or the height, he wasn't sure, but his insides were churning, and a vile cold sweat was gathering on the back of his neck.

"How long are we going to be in this thing?" whined Ruby, rousing the gang from their reverie.

"Relax. They're preparing the penthouse for us!" said Cheryl, laughing nervously.

The elevator slowed, the upper floors bathed in a beautiful cascading sunlight. "Looks like we're here." Little Stevie beamed, looking to Xzardak. "At last."

As the lift ground to a halt, Xzardak saw Commissioner Edward approaching the elevator door. "Please, all come out," he instructed, his tone much friendlier now that they were back at coalition HQ. "You must all be thirsty after your trip. Do let me know if anyone suffers from altitude sickness!" he said to Xzardak's relief.

"C'mon, crowd in, we've laid on some refreshments for you," Commissioner Turner said, joining the group. Xzardak was relieved to see a familiar friendly face; he smiled to his old associate and the commissioner even gave a sly wink. Xzardak hadn't once thought about eating but now that the commissioner had mentioned food, he suddenly became quite famished.

"Something smells good!" remarked Marvin.

"Yes," said Edward accommodatingly. "We've laid on a little banquet for you Earth visitors."

Indeed, a banquet *had* been laid on. Edward had not been exaggerating when he described it as such. In the opulent surroundings of the coalition dining room, the Earth guests and their chaperone were seated, and each issued with a silk napkin and shiny silver cutlery.

"We've tried our best with the menu," Commissioner Turner called out, bringing forth a tray of crystal glasses filled to the brim with a fine Earth wine. "We managed to salvage some of the best Earth produce in the rescue mission and recreated some dishes that I hope you will recognise. Old recipes from your homeland—your *original* homeland, that is. And this wine is as good as any I've tasted, and for this at least, your Earth species should be very proud."

"I'm not much of a wine drinker," called Marvin before Ruby elbowed him in the ribs again.

"That's all very kind of you," said Little Stevie, standing up to help the commissioner with his tray. "Tesk really would've liked to see this!" he whispered, handing Xzardak a glass of red liquid.

"I don't think I've ever tasted Earth wine," Xzardak said.

"Exquisite!" cried Turner. "Once tried, never to be forgotten. It's just such a shame that this particular vineyard withered away beneath the ash cloud. We managed to save a few crates though, for the archive records, of course!" He blushed. "Not that we are big drinkers."

Sipping the beautiful red liquid with its alluring scent and transparency, Xzardak immediately felt a little hot. "I feel... odd," he mumbled as his head throbbed.

"Give it a moment," instructed Turner. "Just let it settle." Xzardak waited a second and once the light headedness had passed, a fantastic sensation engulfed his being.

"Yes, I do like that!" he said to the amusement of the Earth people.

"Well, best get stuck in, before these guys change their minds!" suggested Little Stevie, taking a huge gulp of the red wine just as the first courses arrived.

"Chicken casserole, not bad…" said Ruby, tucking in. "I ain't had meat since I was a kid but boy, this chicken is chewy!"

"Stop complaining" said Cheryl, pulling a face. "I got birthday cake with gravy!"

"We are working on the menu, Earth friends!" reassured Turner. "However, it still needs a little… fine tuning."

After a few more sips, and by now feeling slightly sozzled, Xzardak stared out into the sunshine and surveyed the beautiful crystalscape. The accumulation of his surroundings, the Earth drink and the altitude medicine were making his head spin.

"I think I must go to bed!" he mumbled. "Suddenly, night has become day, and down is up. Everything seems to be turning on its head. Most peculiar."

"Nonsense!" exclaimed Turner. "You must eat. We're fattening you up!" He thrust a platter into Xzardak's hand.

Xzardak reached out. "I feel funny though," he muttered, sinking his teeth into the Earth bread. "I can't see straight."

"You just need to eat, spaceman," insisted Stevie. "Another few drinks and you'll be fine."

"Well, enjoy your meals, gentlefolk!" instructed Edward. "Tomorrow will be a big day! I'll let Commissioner Turner take care of you!" he boomed, heading for the door. The Earth people got to their feet to bid him a good night, but Xzardak had lost the use of his legs.

The following day had arrived and Xzardak awoke with a start. His sickly paranoid feeling had manifested into nausea. "Must be the altitude?" he croaked, his head spinning, and his vision blurred. It had been a strange night indeed, plagued with dreams and when he opened his eyes and reached for a drink since his mouth was ever so parched, the room was undulating. Even on the worst space trips, he had never felt so—whatever it was. Sick. Dizzy. Disoriented.

Washing and dressing in the freshly laid out robes, he tried to ignore the ominous feeling in his bones. "Well, here we are," he announced to the pallid looking face reflected in the bathroom mirror. "I'm not sure what today will bring, but I tried." He smiled to reassure himself before gathering his things and leaving his opulent quarters that still were moving up and down.

In the gilded glass corridor, he could hear voices. Little Stevie and Cheryl were laughing and pointing, and Ruby was cradling Marvin's head. He was lying curled up in a ball on an antique-looking chaise longue. "Seems Marvin had just a little too much of that fine living last night," said Cheryl as Xzardak approached.

"He's not the only one!" jibed Ruby, noting Xzardak's washed-out appearance. Xzardak rubbed his head and before Ruby had a chance to comment any further, Commissioner Turner appeared with a large decanter of sparkling turquoise liquid. A few faces paled, perhaps wondering if this was yet more booze. For some reason, no one had much stomach for it today.

"May I suggest we all take a sip of my national beverage?" the commissioner suggested.

Ah. It *was* alcohol—or was likely to be. Most 'national beverages' were, especially the ones showing up in decanters. Xzardak's stomach was doing somersaults.

The commissioner raised the glass canister into the air.

"An elixir of life which will soothe your sore head and cleanse your spirit!" He chuckled and smiled at Marvin, who had turned as green as Commissioner Vilmos.

Often going against their better judgement, each took a sip from the crystal vessel and immediately felt better. They developed smiles and began perking up.

Marvin rose to his feet. "I'll tell you what, Turner," he said, rubbing his head. "You guys sure know how to throw a party! Is this a new one or a continuation of yesterday's?"

Xzardak heard footsteps behind him, Commissioner Edward, William, and four envoys approaching. "Xzardak, if you're up to it, please call and assemble the Earth people. The coalition are waiting." His voice had regained its officious tone.

Xzardak stood to attention and set about rounding up the hungover Earth people.

He had little memory of the night before and decided it was probably best not to think about it. Once gathered, the Earth people, flanked by Turner and his envoy, filed into the exquisitely ornate coalition chamber. Inside, the space appeared to change, the wall decoration beginning to fade, replaced by a black, formless nothingness. Unable to discern the size or shape of the room, Ruby took hold of Marvin's arm. "Man, do they like AC in this place!" she whispered.

The chilled air was causing Xzardak to shiver, and he feared another wave of nausea. Through the dim light, he could just about make out the lectern.

Behind it, to the rear of the raised platform, were twelve gilded seats.

The envoy guided them through the blackness and once seated, an ominous musical chord could be heard. "Ah… the beloved coalition anthem!" remarked Xzardak, getting back up. He gestured to Little Stevie to do the same and all of the Earth people grudgingly got to their feet.

The droning chord grew louder, reverberating around the blackened chamber. The pitch began to lift and travelled through the entire musical spectrum until it reached its bellowing peak, then doomily subsided once more. The room in total darkness, Xzardak could feel his heart racing. Fearful of what might happen next, he took some deep breaths.

"Relax," said Little Stevie, sensing Xzardak's nervousness. "What's wrong? Have you never been in court before?" he said nonchalantly.

A single spotlight shone out from the darkness above, the light moving quickly, illuminating the faces of the Earth people in turn before finally resting on Xzardak's contorted fizzog.

Out of the gloom bellowed a booming voice. "WHO IS THIS WHO STANDS BEFORE THE COALITION?" it called. Suddenly, Xzardak realised that all eyes were on him.

"Xzardak… and the visitors from planet Earth," he replied sheepishly.

"LET THE SESSION BEGIN," the voice returned as one by one, the robed commissioners made their way up onto the stage. Varying in shape and stature, each cloaked in dark robes and with their faces obscured by heavy hoods, they slowly took their places.

"These guys look fun," whispered Marvin.

Each shrouded commissioner was suddenly bathed in multicoloured pulsating light. A soft vapour appeared to emanate from the stage below, swirling around and engulfing them.

The droning, single note accompaniment seemed to dip as the commissioners conferred with each other.

"Well, the light show ain't bad, but it sure ain't 'Sunday Night with the Stars!'" Cheryl joked, and the Earth people laughed nervously.

After a moment, the music rose again, then crashed dramatically as the room plunged into darkness. Xzardak had never been so afraid. "THE CHAMBER IS LED BY COMMISSIONER EDWARD," boomed the voice as the light source settled on Edward's unsmiling face.

"Before we begin, I would like to thank you all for coming," Edward said. "Please, be seated. I'm aware that you have travelled many light years in these few short months. We appreciate that this must be very confusing for you all." The Earth people murmured. "But we have brought you to this place as a protocol has been traversed and all such contravention must be investigated."

Xzardak shuffled in his seat. "Besides, we all just wanted to take a look at you."

Edward softly guffawed, hoping to alleviate the oppressive atmosphere created by the theatre staging, dry ice, and ominous mood music.

"Xzardak, we will each ask a question. You must then, between yourselves, answer. At the end, when we have considered the evidence, you will be taken to the high tower and into the eternal chamber. There, the exalted governors reside. Upon their judgement, a decision will be made, is that clear?" he whispered.

Xzardak couldn't find his voice. He tried to speak but nothing came out.

"Yes, that's clear, Padre," called Little Stevie.

"Please refer to me as commissioner in this most sacred of coalition chambers!" Edward castigated the Earth man.

"Yes, that's clear, Commissioner," interrupted Xzardak, suddenly engaging his larynx in response to the commissioner's earlier question.

"The questions will begin with Commissioner William." Edward smiled, launching the proceedings. William stood forward, the light source gliding toward him.

The smallest of the commissioners, and with his face illuminated, he appeared to be the most humanlike of the ensemble. "Thank you, Edward. The coalition would like to ask of you, Xzardak." Xzardak sat up. "Given that you are fully aware of the conditions applicable to the Earth 2 compound, why was it that you took it upon yourself to take these Earth people into orbit? Out of the atmosphere of the project space?"

Xzardak again felt his throat dry up. "Well," he croaked. There was an uncomfortable moment of silence.

"Would you let me speak for Xzardak, Commissioner?" interrupted Stevie again.

"If Xzardak needs a moment to compose himself, I see no problem with that, Earth creature," answered William.

"You see, what you have here," started Stevie, "is a simple misunderstanding. We all knew the Earth planet was toast. Many of us were ready to die; indeed, we were born to die! Imagine our surprise when we woke up on the other side of the galaxy. Hell, we didn't even know you guys were out here in the great blue yonder. So, waking up on a strange planet with a group of space aliens talking at us, it took us a while to get used to the idea! Let's just say a couple of people didn't buy it at first!"

William looked puzzled. "Buy it?" he enquired. "Was it… for sale?"

His face screwed up in confusion.

"No, no. It's just an Earth saying, it means we didn't believe it," corrected Stevie. "Some of us got a little upset and it was down to Xzardak to tell us what time and day of the week it was!"

"What does time have to do with this?" the commissioner scalded, once again looking puzzled. "Days of the week? I-I fear we may not understand one another. Xzardak?"

He was again casting his gaze to Xzardak to take control and shed some illumination.

Regaining his voice under the pressure, Xzardak thought it best he took over. Motioning to Stevie to sit down, he took to the floor. The spotlight finding him, the droning musical accompaniment raised up a half tone. "Yes, well, you see… The Earth people were scared. They couldn't comprehend their new surroundings, so I decided to take them out of the compound, to show them it for themselves. It was as simple as that," he explained.

"Simple?" enquired William.

"Yes, simple!" Xzardak smiled, hoping to charm the commissioner. "No malice was intended, no violation of protocol. Just a simple error on my part, a mistake for which I am willing to take the consequences." Xzardak stood back.

His spotlight moment had made him sweat terribly and it dripped from his head.

"No further questioning!" shouted William, quickly scurrying back to his seat.

Commissioner Vilmos stood up next, stooping over the lectern, his long grey face obscured by an elaborate head decoration. "What good are you?" he asked, looking at the humans.

A silence fell across the chamber. Xzardak, unsure of how to answer, looked to Little Stevie who replied with a shrug. Vilmos continued with a low-pitched growl, "I mean, simply put. What can you bring to the civilised realm? My research on the Earth's people has provided me with hopes of obtaining very little from your kind in terms of actual worth." With a grunt, he repeated his opening question, "I mean, what good are you?"

The Earth people sat bewildered, unsure of how to answer such an open-ended and abstract question. The commissioner waited a moment, but with no answer coming from the gallery, he held up his hand, smiling smugly, having perplexed the simple Earth creatures.

"No further questions!" he said. As he sat, he called out to the nearest commissioner, "Greed and hate is all they will bring. Mark my words!"

Xzardak rubbed his head, fearing that the hardest questions were yet to be asked.

"THE CHAMBER CALLS COMMISSIONER HEROD," boomed the disembodied voice. The Earth people all gasped as the next commissioner appeared to leave his seat and levitate in the air, seamlessly gliding forward and hovering before them, scrutinising each one of them suspiciously. Commissioner Edward leaned forward and gave a cough into his microphone.

Sensing that he was holding up the proceedings, Herod soared high into the air then back behind the podium. "QUESTION 3 IS FROM COMMISSIONER HEROD," announced the voice impatiently. "I would like the Earth people to take a moment to study the chamber where they stand." He held out his hand, gesturing towards the assembled party. "Do you see before you the twelve commissioners?"

The pulsating light source split into twelve separate beams, each one illuminating the faces of the coalition board as if to provide an answer to the question. He proceeded, "I would like you to study the faces of each of the assembled members and tell me, are the faces not different?"

The Earth people looked along the line of the assembled committee and quietly all murmured in the affirmative. The faces *were* different, though no one understood the question's purpose.

"They sure are an nasty looking bunch!" whispered Marvin under his breath.

Herod again waved his hand, causing the twelve light beams to form one, illuminating only his own face. "I'm sure you agree," he said rolling the 'r.' "Indeed, they are different, yet we all sit together as a whole. So, with that in mind, my question is this." He paused for dramatic effect. "Why could the Earth people not stand as we do? Why could the peoples never live in peace?"

Stevie looked to the others, and each one shrugged. He got to his feet.

"Well, sir," he said. "That is a very good question, one we've pondered many times. But unfortunately, it's not a question I can answer. It's just the way we are? Crazy, I guess."

Herod scribbled something. "No more questions," he said, motioning dismissively to Commissioner Edward.

The next question came from the largest of the commissioners, so large, in fact, that his ceremonial robes clung to his oversized frame as if he might burst their seams any minute now, his flesh coming spilling free. He lumbered towards the podium, adjusting his spectacles. "QUESTION 4 IS FROM COMMISSIONER DAVID," the chamber voice announced, and the musical accompaniment dropped four full tones.

Mopping his brow, David took a breath. "My, it's hot in here," he wheezed. "You do like it warm in the chamber!" He wiped at his moustache that was glistening with droplets of sweat. "Fellow commissioners, I won't take up too much of your time," he said, huffing and puffing, and now adjusting his steamed-up spectacles. "There has been enough bluster in the chamber for one day. I'll come straight to it if I may!" The other commissioners shuffled in agreement.

"My question for the Earth people is this. Is it true that you had weapons on your home planet, so powerful that they could destroy a million souls?"

Little Stevie stepped forward. "Yes, sir, I'm afraid to tell you that is correct," he said, bowing his head in shame.

"And these weapons I've heard about, they were pointed at us? Into deep space?"

David winced, in an obvious state of shock. He was wheezing again, struggling for every breath like an asthmatic amphibian.

Xzardak stepped forward.

"No, Commissioner David, that is incorrect," he stated. "The weapons that the Earth people had were in fact pointed at each other; that is how they find themselves here in the coalition chamber, so to speak."

"Well, I never," gasped the befuddled commissioner. "I had heard that but didn't believe it was possible. Whyever would you do that?" he barked. "That's surely insane!"

Stevie stepped forward. "To be honest, buddy, I never did understand it myself. It was meant to be some sort of goofy deterrent or something, but like everything else, it turned out to be garbage."

The commissioner gathered his papers but did not retake his seat. "Gentlemen!" he proclaimed, "I cannot stay in the same chamber as these creatures. It is too dangerous!"

The ground shook as he thundered by, making his way toward the exit.

"COMMISSIONER DAVID IS GIVEN DISPENSATION TO LEAVE," the voice boomed.

After some animated jabbering in the chamber, Edward called the members to order.

"QUESTION 5 IS FROM COMMISSIONER HENRY," boomed the hidden voice.

Of slight build and facially insectoid, Henry buzzed and spluttered into the microphone, "I would like to attthk the

Earth man next to Ttthardak, a question. Why ittth it that your planet died?" he asked. "In your opinion? What do you ttthay?"

"How come you had all the easy questions?" Stevie whispered to Xzardak as he reluctantly stood. Stepping onto the floor and into the light, he answered, "Well, commissioner, I don't rightly know," he started. "It was just the way it was, I guess. We got distracted and it just kinda happened; before we knew what hit us, it was over!"

Henry considered his answer. For a moment, he seemed to study the Earth man before shooting out his long pinkish-red proboscis-like tongue and licking his lips. After another moment, he shook his head, then buzzed and spluttered, making his way back from the altar. "No further questionttth!" he shrilly exclaimed, much to Little Stevie's bewilderment and relief.

"What the f…" whispered Ruby "Tell me that was a puppet, right?"

The creeped-out company shuddered and recoiled; commissioner Henry had taken the proceedings to the next level of weird.

"QUESTION 6 WILL COME FROM COMMISSIONER ANDREW." Suddenly, Edward stood up. "I-I suggest we take a break before Andrew takes the stage!" he stammered, mopping his brow, the whole chamber murmuring in enthusiastic agreement.

"SESSION WILL RESUME SOON," boomed the voice, the music suddenly rising up through the spectrum. The blackness in the chamber seemed to recede and the ornate mouldings on the walls reappeared. However, still a little too dark to fully navigate their way, the single spotlight shone a guiding beam for the Earth people to follow.

The musical note returned down through the range and once out of the gloom and into the brightness of the recess hall, Xzardak waited a moment for his eyes to adjust.

As his visibility returned, he looked around to see if there was a friendly face amongst the company. All the Earth people had headed over to a translucent service tube which was dispensing a plated foodstuff, but Xzardak was still in no fit state to eat.

In the far corner, he spotted a group of envoys with Commissioner Edward, all talking to the wasplike Commissioner Henry. He walked toward the commissioners and, apparently sensing his approach, Henry made an excuse and departed, heading back into the chamber.

"How are we doing?" Xzardak enquired, hoping to find that Edward was in a friendly mood.

"Splendidly!" Edward enthused. "You have answered all of the questions very well up to now. I must say the Earth people are far more eloquent than I had been expecting."

Xzardak took a deep breath. "Oh, that's good," he said.

"You mustn't worry, Xzardak; these questions are just a matter of correct protocol. You know how the coalition works."

Xzardak nodded. "Yes, I suppose I do," he replied.

"It's all theatre; you know how they like the pomp and ceremony! The real test will be speaking with the governors." Edward smirked. "They make all of the decisions around here!"

Xzardak again looked worried. "Will they close us down?" he asked nervously.

"Hard to say," pondered Edward quizzically. "Could do... or even worse!" He raised a brow.

Xzardak's head started throbbing again.

"Planet of Night?" he wondered aloud, but the commissioner would not be pressed. Instead, he feigned an excuse and turned to escape. Xzardak felt relieved; the possibilities were proving too much for him and Edward's caginess served only to confuse matters.

Over at the buffet table, Xzardak joined the Earth people noisily chowing down on the coalition regulation fodder. "It's not as good as last night's food, Xzardak, but you should try it!" called Marvin, beckoning him over.

Fearing it could be his very last meal, Xzardak took a plate. "Ozbitarian mole gruel," he said forlornly. "Take me to the Planet of Night!"

CHAPTER 12

Xzardak's unauthorised excursion from the planet had given Tesk an idea. He and a few dishevelled looking Earth people marched toward the command centre, unaware they had already triggered an array of sensors on the edge of the compound.

In Bungo's office, an alarm was sounding; someone had breached the perimeter. Bungo leapt up out of his seat. "What now? Mono, what's going on?" he called into the desk microphone. The security alarm had been installed by coalition forces as part of the compound infrastructure, and this meant pretty soon, the coalition would be notified of the intrusion.

Repeatedly, he punched the reset button, desperate to cancel the alert signal and avoid any further coalition interference.

Bungo scanned the video surveillance cameras to see if he could get a view of the trespassers. He called again, "Mono, can you hear me?" The breach flashed up onto the surveillance portal, and Bungo winced as there in front of him were Tesk and a few scruffy Earth people approaching the hangar bay, ambling as if they'd been for a Sunday stroll.

Mono was attending to his duties inside the command centre when suddenly, he heard the call. "Mono, are you there? Can you hear me?"

"Yes, I hear you," spluttered Mono.

"Tesk and the Earth people are trying to gain access to the command centre!" cried Bungo, sounding unusually alarmed. "What's going on today?" he snarled.

"They appear to be heading towards the hangar," called Mono as he scrolled through the surveillance feed. Bungo reached for his data slate and to his astonishment, found that Tesk and his invaders had broken their way into the compound block. Fearing the worst, he radioed again.

"Mono, I don't know what they want but it is imperative that they do not leave the compound; we are in enough trouble as it is!"

"I expect they are hoping to commandeer another transport?" surmised Mono. "Or worse, a spacecraft."

"Not on my watch!" Bungo cried. "Do whatever it takes!"

"Telos, Kaydar, Brogues, Legman! Secure the transport!" Mono instructed his small team of obedient worker robots to get to work. Each of the ground chargers and transport vehicles were hurriedly covered and immobilised. Mono insisted that they clear out just as the Earth people clattered through the hangar bay hatch.

Mono was startled; the hangar bay walls and ceiling above him quaked, and giant chunks of debris were falling all around him as three loud blasts rang out. Unsure of what was going on, he frantically consulted his data cell, hoping to make sense of his current predicament.

Another three blasts rang out, this time accompanied by three bright flashes of light. After a moment, an answer was supplied to him. To Mono's surprise, it appeared the Earth people were using weapons. Mono knew very little about weapons; they had only recently come to his attention whilst helping Xzardak sort through the research data for the Earth 2 Project.

"Where did the Earth man get the weapon?" he asked, consulting his data cell. Pondering the information supplied to him, he was troubled by another question. "What is he planning to do with it?" Mono's circuit board brain made a very unsettling calculation. "Earth people having weapons is a very bad thing indeed."

Whatever they planned to do, he suspected, it would not be good for anyone's wellbeing.

Mono thought it best he take cover for now; he would ponder how the Earth man obtained the weapon at a later date. Quickly scooting across the hangar floor as fast as his wheels would take him, he disappeared behind one of the disabled chargers, hoping the humans hadn't seen him.

"Hey, Bobo!" called Tesk suddenly.

"Bobo?" Mono murmured. "Does he mean me?" Mono ignored the call, hurriedly careering into the shadows and hunkering down as best he could into a small shape.

Tesk called again, "Hey you, Bobo!" This time, he let out another round of weapon fire.

Frustrated that his plan to ignore Tesk had not worked, with debris crashing down around him, Mono figured it was best to stop and pay attention. Fearing for his precious life and concerned that Tesk would destroy the entire hangar and its contents—Xzardak would be furious—Mono hoped he might be able to reason with Tesk.

"Hello, Tesk," said Mono sheepishly. "How nice to see you! And what's that you have there?" He appeared apprehensively from beneath Xzardak's spacecraft.

Tesk's eyes seemed to glow with excitement as he fired the weapon once again. "This, Bobo, is a semi-automatic rifle." He smiled, dust particles raining down from the ceiling above him. "Beautiful piece of kit, isn't she? Have you ever seen a semi-automatic before?"

Mono gulped, unsure of how to react. He decided he should go with his training. Following procedure, he answered clearly and concisely, "According to my A6 data cell, 'A semi-automatic rifle is a weapon, a gun found only on your home planet of Earth and outlawed everywhere else. Its possession and use are strongly prohibited in the enlightened universe. It would appear that your weapon violates Protocol Codes C167C and Code 18569T. Were you aware of that, sir?"

Tesk laughed loudly and let out another round of armour-piercing bullets. "No, my friend, I wasn't aware that we were contravening any codes but thank you for informing us!"

It clearly didn't make any difference. Tesk still amused himself with the firearm.

Mono felt conflicted. After an uncomfortable moment, he surveyed the room and noticed Bungo appear in the hangar bay doorway. "What's going on, Tesk?" called Bungo.

"Oh, it's you again," Tesk sneered, clearly still mad at Bungo for bringing him in after the first escape attempt. He raised the gun and pointed it at him. "We're getting out of here, and this time, you ain't stopping us." Tesk smiled a crooked smile and Bungo raised his hands, slowly backing up towards the bay entrance.

Having never experienced combat or any other form of violent disagreement, Mono realised that his memory data concerning dangerous, weapon-wielding, primitive life forms was limited and at that point in time, the little knowledge he did possess appeared to have deserted him.

While assessing the structural damage to the hangar bay and the vulnerability of the people inside, he also tried to determine what might happen next. Bungo lowered his hands.

"Okay, Tesk," he said nervously. "You win, so tell us what you want. Just no more gunfire!"

Tesk snickered. "That's more like it, *Bingo*, there's no need for anyone to get hurt. We just want a ship, a good one. Nothing personal, but we want out of this hellhole, you get me?"

"You know I can't give you a craft, Tesk," called Bungo apprehensively. "Xzardak has already been hauled in for taking you out yesterday. The coalition will shut us down for sure if—" He stopped talking.

Tesk had just raised the gun to his eye again.

"Oh, the coalition's the least of your problems, man, believe me. If you want to see tomorrow, you better give me a ship right now! Like, pronto!"

Realising he was out of options, Bungo relented.

"Okay, Tesk, but you're asking for trouble," he insisted.

"Asking for trouble?" Tesk laughed. "We *are* trouble!" he said, throwing his head back with a cackle, letting off another round of fire.

"Take the large craft," Bungo said, nervously motioning to Mono. "Fill her up!" Mono sent out the instruction, his worker drones dutifully setting about refuelling the vessel.

"The craft is new and once fully fuelled, will take you wherever you want!" croaked Bungo. "Now please put the weapon down."

"Thank you kindly, sir!" Tesk grinned, holding up the rifle and firing one last round into the air. As the ceiling buckled, Bungo made a run for it out of the hangar bay and back into the command centre via the service entrance.

Mono would do whatever it took to keep Tesk and the Earth people calm. No matter what they requested, he wouldn't stand in their way. Xzardak's shiny new ship was valuable, but it certainly wasn't worth Bungo's life, nor a trip to the repair bay.

Tesk walked towards the craft and pointed his weapon at the small blue-grey robot. Mono's circuits were vibrating—he was trembling—an action he had never experienced before. "Here's the plan," began Tesk. "Much as we've enjoyed our time with you good folks, we feel it's time for somethin' new. A change of scenery if you like! Now, Xzardak didn't seem too keen on the idea, so I'm taking matters into my own hands."

"The ship is almost ready," stuttered Mono. Tesk smiled, Mono suddenly understood the definition of the word 'intimidation.'

The Earth man turned and stepped up onto the entrance ramp. "409? Well, isn't this the big man's craft!" he exclaimed, gesturing to the shiny silver shuttle.

Mono nodded. "Yes, the finest in the fleet."

Tesk sniggered. "We'll take it! That is if it's available? I wouldn't want to inconvenience Xzardak at all."

"Xzardak has had to go away on business…" explained Mono coyly. "But I'm sure he wouldn't mind you borrowing it for a while." Quivering, he began to engage the internal communication system and check the drone squad's progress report.

Looking back down at him, Tesk's smile remained in place as he pointed the weapon back into Mono's direction. "You reckon this thing will get us anywhere we want to go?" he asked.

"Oh yes, I'm certain of it," Mono returned enthusiastically. "I'm checking the fuel status on the craft now!" The Earth people began to whoop and holler as the drone squad's progress report signalled a green light. "May I enquire… who will be driving?" asked Mono quietly, dreading Tesk's response.

Tesk's smile dropped. "Just get on the damn ship, Bobo!"

"Xzardak took us up on this thing and I want you to do the same." On board the craft, Tesk was very much in control. "Dodo, do as I say, and we'll all get along just fine!"

Mono could tolerate being referred to as 'Bobo' but 'Dodo' was going too far. Clearly disgruntled, Mono rolled his eyes, but the machine gun pointing in his general direction deterred him from voicing his concerns.

Mono kicked the ship into gear and punched some digits into the control panel engaging the ignition sequence. The hangar hatch doors cleared, the craft beginning to ascend. Tesk looked out of the viewport to see Bungo and the assistant robot, Zork, standing in the command centre window. "Too late, you dummies!" he shrieked and through the billowing magnetic thrust cloud, he blew Bungo a kiss. "Don't wait up, guys! We *won't* be seeing you later!"

The Earth people fell about laughing.

Under Tesk's command, it hadn't taken much persuasion or encouragement to get his gang of reprobates along for an adventure. "Pity Little Stevie couldn't make it," Douglas said.

"Don't worry, honey," Alice jibed. "We'll send him a postcard!"

Back on solid ground, Bungo motioned to Kaydar and the other worker drones to make their way into the control pod and secure the doors. "You gave them Xzardak's craft?" chided Zork. "But it's the best one we have!" he huffed, looking puzzled.

"Yeah," said Bungo, silently wondering if he'd done the right thing. "But it has the best tracker on board too, so at least we'll be able to keep tabs on them once the coalition gets wind of what's happened."

Where do you think they are headed?" Zork asked.

"You really need to ask?" scoffed Bungo, shaking his head.

"Planet Earth! That's right! Stick 'em up, buddy. This is a hijack situation and you, my friend, are our hostage!" Mono was taken aback. Searching his data cell, the word appeared. 'Hostage. Another Earth term and another contravention of the enlightened universe protocol codes, this time code CT510-1.' Mono was terrified, his self-preservation chip confirming he should follow Tesk's orders if he wanted to survive, at least until Xzardak or someone from the coalition instructed him differently.

The planet Earth was not a destination that Mono had ever visited. He, like everyone, knew of its reputation and he had, of course, been privy to the political discourse concerning it.

However, not having the faintest clue as to where it lay in the universe, he informed Tesk that he would have to search the charts for its location on the craft's sky map.

"Fine, do what you've got to do!" Tesk spat. "Just hurry up about it!"

He took a seat and instructed the gang members to unpack the cargo supplies they'd misappropriated from the compound kitchens. "Easy-peasy." Tesk was in his element right now; his plan appeared to be coming together without a hitch.

Studying the sky map, Mono noted a potential problem.

"It can't be done!" he blurted. "The Earth... it can't be done!"

Tesk's mood changed. "What do you mean, it can't be done?"

Mono paused, horribly aware that what he was about to say might not go down well with the psychopath—another Earth word—holding the semi-automatic gun to his head.

"It's listed as a dead star which means it's been eliminated, removed from the sky map. It's a safety precaution to prevent anyone visiting it by accident."

"Dead star?" Tesk asked. "Please don't give me that again!"

He got to his feet and paced the floor. Mono had an idea, feeling sure that if he made a suggestion, Tesk would agree and call off the entire escapade.

"Should I turn around?" enquired Mono sheepishly. "I'll inform Bungo that it was just one of your Earth jokes, or we had a miscommunication. I'm sure we could think of something between us all!" Tesk's response was not one of agreement and Mono's suggestion had only served to make the atmosphere on board even more fraught.

"Look again," he insisted with a growl.

After some deliberation, Mono was able to locate an older version of the sky map and deciphered the sector within the Milky Way where planet Earth had resided.

"Well?" asked Tesk, all agitated. "Can you get us there? Please don't make me shoot you," he added, forcing the rifle against Mono's head.

Mono was making the calculations. "Hmm… potentially," he replied. "At least I think I can."

His data cell delivered the coordinates: the craft could make it, and there was more than enough magnetic fuel on board providing they could find a gateway. "Yes," he answered. "But it's still in a restricted zone, off limits. Earth was always listed as unstable. It's not somewhere you just visit!"

He had a petulant tone for a moment but soon reverted to punching in the code, hoping that the location would tally with the newer charts on the ship's system.

"Bearing in mind the restrictions, the on-board computer says that it can certainly deliver us within 200,000 Earth kilometres of the destination."

"Fine!" cried Tesk. "Close enough! We'll get a taxicab the rest of the way!"

The cabin erupted into hysterics and although Earth still seemed like a long way off, Mono felt that the mood in the pod had lightened. Tesk had even lowered the weapon.

It seemed that Tesk and the gang were finally going home.

Removing his boots, Tesk placed his stockinged feet onto the side of the console, making Mono wince at the sight of a toenail protruding through a hole in one of Tesk's woollen socks. "Peace at last," cooed Tesk, relaxing into the co-pilot's chair.

"Can you hear me, Tesk? Mono, come in! Can you hear me, Tesk?" The video monitor in the cockpit pod crackled and fizzed into life. "Do you read me, Mono?"

Mono diligently flicked the switch. "I read you, Bungo, but I'm having a very bad day," he whispered into the microphone. The signal was faint, but Mono could just about make out the face of Bungo, who appeared relieved to have made contact with the craft.

"Mono, I must speak with Tesk!" cried Bungo desperately.

Tesk stood up and calmly walked toward the monitor screen. "Cool it, spaceman, we're just going on a little joyride, that's all. I'll make sure Bobo gets back in one piece." He laughed, glancing at the very concerned little robot. "And we'll return the ship, of course, just as soon as we manage to carjack another poor wretch!"

Bungo approached the video screen.

"Listen, Tesk, we've tried with you and failed with you, I accept that," he said. "I've an idea where you are headed, but I'm begging you not to go through with it."

"We're going, spaceman, so you're wasting your breath. And hey, guess what! There's not a damn thing you can do about it."

Bungo capitulated.

"We have no weapons to threaten you with," he said. "I have nothing left to give you or anything for you to take. It is clear that you have made your decision and there is little I can do about it. Therefore, I am sending Mono instructions on how to get you back to Earth safely."

A wide smile played across Tesk's face, revealing his broken teeth. "I ask that you do not deviate from the route or interfere with any life form you may encounter on your way. The fate of your fellow humans on Earth 2 will be greatly affected should you contaminate any planet or satellite station en route." Bungo let out a sigh before continuing, "I have one final question. Tesk, I need you to be honest with me."

"Fire away," Tesk sneered. "I'm listening."

Bungo took a deep breath. "I had the weapons on board the ship analysed; they are Earth weapons. No such weapons exist anywhere else in the enlightened universe. I need to know how you obtained them?"

Tesk looked confused and considered his answer carefully. "Well, that's a really interesting question? Are you familiar with Santa Claus?"

Mono pulled up the necessary data and sent it to Bungo. "Santa Claus, sometimes referred to as Santa, Saint Nicholas, or Father Christmas, was a well-known figure in traditional Earth planet mythology and folklore. Originating in European Christian culture, he was said to deliver toys and gifts to the homes of well-behaved children on the night of Christmas

Eve, December 24th." He included an image of a portly look-ing, bearded Earth man dressed in a red suit and white fur-trimmed hat.

Bungo looked perplexed, studying the image and report. "Yes, I have studied many of your Earth customs and tradi-tions, but what does this have to do with weapons?"

Tesk chuckled mischievously. "Seems he visited us in the night! After all, we've all been good boys and girls!" The Earth passengers let out a cheer and Bungo looked even more con-fused. "The guns were waiting for us, just sitting there when I woke up this morning!"

Tesk raised an eyebrow. "Maybe one of your guys left them there, by accident. I didn't really stop to question it, gift horse an' all." He smiled. "I've always been like that. Impulsive, I guess! They just fell into our hands. Like Christmas morning."

"According to the data archive, the weapons are semi-auto-matic rifles, most definitely produced and distributed on plan-et Earth," announced Mono diligently.

"No such weapons were ever salvaged by us!" interjected Zork.

Tesk turned to go. "Well, ain't that strange?" He laughed again. "Either way, we ain't coming back; we're going home. I miss my bed; it's where I belong! We ain't out to rob ya. I'll send the little guy back with the ship once we get there! Was nice knowing you, Bungo!"

"Please, Tesk, is there anything else you can tell me about the weapons?" Bungo pleaded "The people you've left be-hind, we want to protect them as best we can, and I need to know."

Tesk harboured no ill feeling toward Bungo, understanding that he and Xzardak were only doing their jobs. "All I know is, we got up and just outside the complex centre were some large black cargo boxes filled with semi-automatics." He was becoming irritated. "The boxes are still there if you want to go and rummage them out."

Bungo looked to Zork.

Tesk was losing patience. "Goodbye, Bungo!" he announced, pointing the gun at Mono and motioning for Mono to shut down the video link.

Submitting to Tesk's instruction, Mono switched the video monitor to black. He engaged the thrusters, slipping the craft into high gear. It was going to be a long and exhausting journey.

Tesk took a moment and retired to his seat at the back of the cockpit, beginning to feel the effects of intergalactic space travel.

Analysing the A6 data bank, Mono discovered that Christmas was a yearly Earth celebration in which the humans exchanged gifts and handwritten cards of goodwill, oddly even with people they disliked and usually wouldn't speak to. As for the semi-automatic rifles, they used these all across the origin planet, the weapons having been responsible for many billions of deaths in the time they'd been fashionable on Earth. Then he found out that hijackers were thieves, often influenced by political ideology, and almost always ending up dead.

It was all too much to take in and by now, his circuits were fizzing. He'd had orders to deliver the cargo to the dead star and that was exactly what he would do. For now, though, he needed rest and would worry about everything else tomorrow.

Back on Earth 2, Bungo and Zork were driving full speed across the dusty complex floor. Neither had uttered a word since talking to Tesk. As they approached the housing complex mess hall, Bungo motioned to Zork who pulled the vehicle over to the side of the road.

Unsure of what they were about to stumble into, he feared for his life. Nothing good would come out of this latest turn of events; Xzardak's reputation would most certainly be destroyed, the Earth 2 circus show would definitely be shut down and someone was bound to lose their life.

"I expect you'll be reporting all of this back to Dr Jay?" said Bungo with an irritated tone.

"Oh yes!" said Zork. "This will certainly add some excitement to the good doctor's paper."

CHAPTER 13

The same ominous tone which had accompanied the morning's session could again be heard emanating from the coalition chamber.

"Time to get a move on, chaps," said Commissioner Turner appearing out of nowhere. Xzardak had only managed a couple of spoonfuls of his meal, but it would be enough sustenance to get him back into the ring.

"Round two! Ding, ding," said Marvin as the Earth people and Xzardak filed slowly back into the grand hall.

The dreadful tuneless music slowly cascaded through a discordant spectrum of notes. Xzardak wondered if the piped melody was intended to unnerve the attendees.

If so, it was certainly achieving its goal.

The Earth people were seated as one by one, the commissioners filed back in. Someone had forgotten to dim the lights, enabling the humans to get a good look at their alien counterparts.

"This sure ain't no beauty contest." Ruby chuckled sarcastically. "Freaky lookin' bunch!"

"I don't know." Cheryl giggled. "Contestant eight ain't bad."

Ruby gagged and pulled a face.

Once assembled, Xzardak noticed an envoy quickly scurry to dim the house lights and again, the theatre show commenced.

The mournful soundtrack, the smoke, the luminous glow, and the lone spotlight all helped to set the stage for round two.

The beam searched out Xzardak from amongst the perturbed looking Earth faces.

Again, the loudspeaker boomed, 'COALITION CHAMBER IS IN CONGRESS. CALL COMMISSIONER ANDREW.'

Obscured by the light, Xzardak could just about see the commissioner as he hobbled to the lectern. "I must say," began Andrew in a quiet croaking voice. "I never thought I'd see the day where I'd be expected to converse with an Earth creature! Especially inside the coalition chamber. Things must be bad." A ripple of soft laughter echoed across the floor. "I'm pleased you think this is funny, my friends," he continued. "Because let me assure you, I do not!"

Shuffling in his seat, Xzardak sensed the line of questioning may be about to turn nasty.

"For a lifetime, it has been a responsibility of mine to monitor and report on the progress of the Earth people and their planet. Do not for a moment believe you were out there on your own! We have always watched over you since before your inception, since before you were you! Ever since you crawled from the swamps, sprouted arms and legs, and slowly began to converse with one another, the government and its coalition have been monitoring you. You and many similar wayward species, I might add."

The ghoulish commissioner cleared his throat and some of the other delegates fidgeted in their seats.

"Earth, such a luscious planet, so abundant with life!" he cried as if speaking to a congregation. "The proximity of the Earth to your sun, just perfect! Not too hot, not too cold. Not too dark, not too light! Located in the perfect position, enabling you to thrive and grow! *The paradise planet,* we called you!" He held his arms aloft as if a pastor preaching to his flock.

"We studied you very carefully, watching you develop and grow. We had such wonderful hopes for you. With your

intellect and ingenuity, we felt sure you would become a con-
tributing kingdom within the vastness of the 'Everything!' We
looked forward to welcoming you. But it wasn't to be, I'm
afraid. Over many millennia, we witnessed you squabble and
fight, then ultimately destroy yourselves. You seemed intent
on self-destruction, taking everything along with you."

Xzardak mopped his brow as Andrew continued.

"We discussed what should be done. Interventions were
made, but every time we revealed ourselves to you, you reciprocated with violence, hostility and contempt. Your leaders
were too stupid to realise that we were coming to help you,
and the general population at large was so desperately unenlightened, too ignorant to see that which was before them!
So, eventually, we gave up, the Earth relegated into obscurity.
Your violence and unpredictability have no place within the
sanctity of the civilised realm! Yet here you are, sitting before
us. You have spoken eloquently, and I have even heard you
joke and make light of your desperate situation.

"It gladdens my heart to be in your presence, but I still don't
think that you understand. We kept you out in the cold for a
reason."

"Not a fan I guess," whispered Marvin, hoping to lighten
the air. But the Earth people's attention was focussed on the
aged commissioner.

"Something happened to your species as you developed and
evolved," he continued. "A mean-spiritedness was consuming
you, allowing your darker, crueller urges to possess you, never
truly evolving beyond the primal urges residing deep inside
your prehistoric souls.

"The battles, the wars and conflicts on your planet, the pain,
the suffering, the greed, every single dark deed was a warning
to us, the civilised enlightened universe, that your time had not
yet come! It just wasn't worth the risk. So we watched you lan-
guish, watched you burn, and the beautiful Earth planet went
up in smoke. Personally, I was content to witness your demise.

"Once your kind were dead, I hoped that the cruelty inside
your hearts might be extinguished too. However, it appears

that wasn't to be! It is a testament to our loving and compassionate coalition members that you stand before us in the chamber.

"Unwilling to simply stand by and watch your species perish, the kinder hearted citizens of the coalition decided it was best that we intervene and save you from yourselves. Your gods disowned you. However, we did not!" Commissioner Andrew let out a deep sigh and a heavy silence hung over the chamber. "Pure folly, in my opinion! I wouldn't be surprised if you didn't take us all down with you!" he proclaimed. "But perhaps I'm just old and out of step."

Taking his time, Andrew hobbled over to his seat and took a drink. Xzardak placed his head in his hands. "It's over," he whispered, nervously anticipating Andrew's question.

Eventually, Commissioner Andrew lurched back to the lectern and stood in silhouette.

"And so to my question..." He smiled, pointing a bony finger at the subdued faces in the gallery. "Tell me, Earth people"—his eyes widened—"Why do you think we should allow you to enter our civilised society? Why would we make space to accommodate such a destructive people?"

The room was quiet for a moment.

"Gee, he's got a point," whispered Ruby. "I guess we did tear it up a little," she said softly.

None of the Earth people had an answer, the silence only broken when Xzardak got to his feet. "Commissioner Andrew, I would like to address your question if I may?" he said timidly.

Andrew lowered his spectacles and eyed Xzardak suspiciously.

"The question is to the Earth people," he said. "This is quite unorthodox!" He scratched his head and considered the situation for a moment.

"Please, if I may…" Xzardak ventured.

"When dealing with Earth people, I suppose I should expect unorthodox practice..." he rasped. "Proceed if you must!" The commissioner glared as Xzardak cleared his throat.

"I will speak for the Earth people as I do not think it fair that they should be put under such unreasonable scrutiny."

Andrew furrowed his brow, obviously wondering what was coming.

"After all," continued Xzardak, "they did not seek this audience with the coalition and its commissioners, just as I did not seek to be involved with the Earth 2 Program. It was the coalition who approached me to oversee the relocation. It was the coalition who requested we design and build a compound to house and incarcerate the Earth people. It was the coalition who administered the rescue mission. The Earth people did not cry out for assistance, they did not send out a mayday, nor in any way set about to contact the civilised realm.

"They were quite happy to live their way and ultimately, we must take it they were just as happy to die their way. To call them here and ask them to apologise for a billion years of evolutionary misconduct is not only unreasonable, but also preposterous!"

A gasp could be heard across the chamber. Xzardak stood back, wondering if he'd gone a little too far, but Little Stevie stood up and patted him on the back. "Thank you, Xzardak," he said softly. "Commissioner, may I speak now?"

Commissioner Andrew gently nodded, and Stevie began, "I ain't no good at public speaking. In fact, the last time I did was at my little sister's wedding and hell, that marriage ended badly! But I know right from wrong, and I know a stitch-up when I see one.

"Seems to me you guys have already made up your minds about us! We can't do right for doing wrong!"

The commissioners and Xzardak looked confused.

Stevie went on, "What we have here is a show trail! See, I realise we ain't perfect and I know we screwed up on planet Earth! Given the chance again, maybe we could do things a little differently, but what's done is done. Now, Xzardak has defended us and I'm grateful for that but, what I'd like to say is this. Why not just do what you guys want to do? Don't all sit there looking righteous. If you've decided we're not suitable for your fancy universe, then get rid of us and have done with it but please don't dress this up as some kind of respectable court hearing!"

The Earth people murmured in agreement.

"Sure, it was Xzardak who took us up in the craft, but we made him do it. Some of our folks just wouldn't settle down! So, he took us up, off the compound! Now let me ask you a question; did we take over the craft? Did we wreck it? Did we steal anything? Did we hurt anyone? Did we even talk bad about anyone?" He turned to his fellow Earth people.

"No way!" hollered Ruby.

"Damn no!" called Marvin, the whole company getting to their feet, calling out in agreement.

Xzardak stepped forward. "I just wanted to show them what I had done for them!" he cried. "I just wanted to show them some kindness and grant them some reassurance!"

With that, the Earth people took to their seats, showing that they could be well behaved when they had to be. Commissioner Andrew stood silent for a moment, then shuffling his notes, he turned to the commissioners. "No more questions," he said, retiring to his seat.

The proceeding questioning seemed tame by comparison and the session continued in a much more orthodox manner. The commissioners politely asked their questions and the Earth people, sensing a 'stitch up,' answered honestly but unapologetically.

"Were you aware that every other living creature on the Earth planet disliked you?" asked the small frog-like Commissioner Ludwig. "I conversed with many of your fellow Earth inhabitants and almost all held the human race in very low regard!" he said with a self-satisfied burp.

"No, I wasn't aware of that," responded Little Stevie. "I sure am disappointed to hear that, though not entirely surprised!"

Next up was Commissioner Marshall.

"Considering the size of the universe, did the Earth people not think it odd that they were the only intelligent life form in all of creation?" he said smugly.

Again, Stevie stood forward.

"Are you kidding? We knew that little green men lived on Mars, only we didn't think they'd be as ugly as you guys!" he boomed. The Earth people and commissioners all laughed as Marshall turned forlornly and sat down, wiping a tear from his eye.

"All of the madness and mayhem, the trials and tribulations," said the demure Commissioner Vega. "I'd like to ask the Earth female standing behind Xzardak…" Ruby bristled, anticipating trouble. "Did you never think to curtail your destructive activities for the sake of the children?"

"The children stopped coming!" Ruby said. "Must've been something they put in the water!"

Vega shook her head, respectfully bowed, and returned to her seat.

"Do the Earth people think they have the ability to evolve past their savage state and if so, could they give us an estimated time frame for such a prerequisite progression?" chirped the bookish looking Commissioner Arnold.

"Hey, cool it!" called Marvin angrily. "We ain't savages, okay? I'm getting sick of you fancy folk putting us down!"

Noticeably intimidated, Arnold recoiled. "No further questioning required!"

Once again, the disembodied voice boomed, "AND SO TO THE FINAL QUESTION OF THE DAY. COMMISSIONER TURNER, PLEASE STAND!"

Relieved that the questioning was coming to an end, Xzardak sat back, hoping that the congenial Turner might go easy on them. Turner stood forward, gathering himself.

He spoke softly into the microphone.

"Commissioners, I have been fortunate enough to spend some hours with the Earth people. I have spoken with them, and I have studied them, but I still am unsure *about* them. I would like to direct this final question toward Xzardak, if I may?" Xzardak let out a groan.

"Xzardak, do you feel there is any hope for the Earth people? The relocation? The rehabilitation program? Or are we, as Commissioner Andrew has intimated, playing with fire?" His tone devoid of implication, he stood back from the podium.

Xzardak was exhausted. He had given everything left to give. Unable to summon a theatrical response, he simply stood forward and gave his version of the truth.

"I don't know," he said and sighed. "If I'm completely honest, I don't know if there is any hope for the Earth people. But if you'll allow me, I would like to try and find out. I have gotten to know some of them personally. Yes, they are troublesome; the entire Earth 2 episode has been exhausting, frustrating and at times, exasperating. But hopefully, it is not worthless and without merit. If we are to consider ourselves civilised, I'd like to ask what other choice we have?"

With that, Xzardak stood back, slumping into his seat, drained of energy, on the verge of mental collapse.

"No more questions," said Turner softly.

Again, the discordant musical drone sounded and the commissioners gathered their notations. Chattering amongst themselves, the booming voice called out, "SESSION IS COMPLETE. THANK YOU, FRIENDS. COALITION CONGRESS IS OVER!"

Xzardak gave a sigh. "I tried," he said. "I tried."

"What will be will be!" said Stevie, helping the broken alien to his feet. "Goddamned kangaroo court!" Xzardak hadn't the energy to ask.

CHAPTER 14

Tesk had never left the country of his birth; in fact, he had never even boarded an aeroplane. Much of his life had been spent in the same precinct into which he had been born, so the tedious long-haul journey back to earth was an experience far beyond his comprehension. Boredom had set in, and the crew had become listless. "Can't this thing go any faster?" barked Tesk. "I knew Bungo sold us a dud! How long 'till we get back? This thing's taking forever!" he ranted. "I don't think I can take it; maybe just let me out."

Mono couldn't tell if he was joking or just saying these things to create an uproar. The worst part about it was that however Mono answered, Tesk was never going to be happy with his reply—and well Mono knew it. Faced with this conundrum, he decided the correct thing to do was to be logical and honest and give Tesk the cold hard facts.

"There is no definable notion of time in space, I'm afraid," he offered. "As we are not orbiting any planet, I cannot put it into a precise time frame."

"Well, you'd better try, Mono," Tesk demanded, still clutching the rifle.

"If you are asking me to put a number on it, I must inform you that I cannot guarantee the answer will be accurate." Tesk frowned as Mono deliberated. "At a guess, I would say four orbits of my home planet."

Tesk raised an eyebrow. "And how many orbits of *my* home planet would that be? I'm not interested in yours."

Mono took a moment to calculate before calmly answering, "Seventeen."

"Seventeen!!" squealed Tesk. "You need to put your foot down, dammit!"

"We are going as fast as the ship can physically go," asserted Mono frustratedly. The Earth people were becoming agitated, animated, up on their feet grumbling and arguing.

"What are we going to do for seventeen days, Tesk?" cried Douglas. "I didn't sign up for seventeen days!"

"This is worse than being in the can!" called Joey. "At least we got to play cards in the can."

"A bigger problem has come to my attention," interrupted Mono. "It appears to me from monitoring your supplies, that you only have enough provisions for two more orbits."

"Two more orbits?" Tesk mused. "Your planet or ours?"

"Yours, I'm afraid," answered Mono sheepishly.

The Earthlings were in uproar, angrily shouting and yelling at each other. "So, you've brought us up here, out into space with only a couple of days' worth of supplies, Tesk?"

"We must be crazy," called Chrissy. "We're going to die out here! Well done, Tesk!"

Tesk raised the gun and aimed it at the group. "You're gonna die a lot sooner if you don't all pipe down. Give me a minute, I need to think about this."

Tesk turned and paced the plane floor. "What do you think, Bobo? What would you do?"

Mono considered his answer for a moment. His data cell was telling him to say one thing, but the life preservation chip was saying something else. It would take him a few seconds to process a response. In the end the data cell won out and overruling the behest of the preservation chip, Mono blurted his reply. "I would not have started out on such a long journey without making better provision." The self-preservation chip was still stubbornly trying to override the data cell.

Sensing that Tesk's heart rate was beginning to increase again. He offered some alternative advice. "It seems to me you have a simple equation. Not enough water, or to put it another way, too many mouths."

Tesk nodded his head. "Ah ha, I'm listening."

"We have three options. First, we alter our destination or turn back, perhaps. However, as it is, we are too far from our origin point to make it back before you'd all perish."

Tesk interrupted, "That's not an option. We ain't going back!"

"Option 2. We remove half to sixty-eight percent of the mouths on board, thus eliminating demand. Freeing up supplies for the remaining thirty-two percent."

"That's definitely an option," whispered Tesk coolly.

Mono continued, "That would mean that we would need to begin purifying and recycling urine immediately."

Tesk shot Mono a crazed look. "Whoa, let me stop you there!" he cried. "There's no urine recycling option! Forget that. I'd rather shoot myself!"

Mono's eyes rolled. "Well, shooting oneself and three of the other men is an option since that would free up the sixty-eight percent of supplies for the remaining life forms."

"Well, I ain't shooting anyone...yet!" spat Tesk. "What about option three?"

"Option 3, probably the most logical option. We contact Bungo and we request that he find us supplies."

"Hmmm." Tesk smiled. "That one!" He laughed, pointing a finger. "And if that one doesn't work, we'll throw a couple of the guys out into deep space!"

He chuckled, waving his gun mischievously.

Mono had warned the Earth people that Option 3 would only be viable if he was able to contact Bungo and presuming he could, that Bungo was willing to help arrange supplementary provisions. The first obstacle would be making contact. The craft was now out in deep space and travelling at a fantastic speed. Mono would have to slow the ship and hope that he could piggyback a signal from a nearby satellite system.

He wasn't offering any guarantees, but it was the best solution he could come up with.

Once in range of a satellite platform, the craft slowed, and Mono transfigured his broadcasting equipment. He had managed to sweet talk a local station rig generator into forwarding a distress call, his logic chip twitching twice as he readied the transformer to broadcast a signal. The Earth people nervously gathered around the video view port, each one eager to see the face from which they had so gleefully fled.

Mono's anxiety levels were increasing, and his self-preservation chip and data cell were desperately trying to devise an Option 4 should Bungo not readily agree to Option 3.

After a few worrying minutes, the video view port crackled and three wavy lines appeared, pulsating and cascading across the image screen. The Earthlings stood silently as through the static, a faint ghost of a picture appeared on screen.

Bungo was standing in the command centre with Zork. Tesk let out a breath, very much relieved that Mono had been able to patch them through.

"Tesk, Mono, I thought you'd all be dead by now?" called Bungo, looking relieved and surprised. "The craft was not designed for such long-haul journeys."

"Okay, Bungo, we realise that. We need to talk turkey," hollered Tesk impatiently.

"Bungo, we need you to send us supplies!" interrupted Mono, very much aware that they were on a limited window and that the signal could drop out at any moment. He needed to get his own message across, instead of allowing Tesk to tie up the resource. "Bungo, the provisions we have on board will not be sufficient for the journey time!"

Zork interjected impertinently, "Any distribution of provisions would have to be administered by Xzardak or Doctor Jay!"

"Zork's right!" chirped Bungo. "And Xzardak is still absent. They still haven't returned and I've been unable to establish a connection with him."

"Can't you contact him and inform him that we are in trouble?" pleaded Mono.

"I'm afraid not!" explained Bungo. "The craft they are on entered a gateway, making it impossible for me to contact them. Besides, what am I going to tell him? That half of the compound has escaped? I'd rather keep this between us for now. So far, I've managed to conceal this episode from the coalition. Should they get wind of it, it will only complicate the situation further and worsen Xzardak's predicament."

Tesk wasn't convinced. "Hey, Bungo, are you on the level?" he said accusingly.

"Of course, I'm on the level," said Bungo angrily. "Xzardak will most likely be up in front of the high commission, defending you Earth people, but what do you care?"

"Hey, I never asked to be taken off the compound," said Tesk. "That's on Xzardak!"

"Listen Tesk, ever since you humans arrived, we've had nothing but trouble. Xzardak has put a lot on the line. I just hope you know that and appreciate everything he's done!"

Tesk shrugged. "Okay, cool it!" he said. "I get it, we're bad people!"

"That's the way I see it, Tesk," reproached Bungo, becoming increasingly irritated. "Xzardak is my friend, how about showing him a little respect!"

"We're the black sheep of the family. A whole damn flock of 'em, it seems. All we want to do is get back home to Earth. Once we're there, we'll never trouble you again!"

"May I be permitted to speak?" Mono meekly intervened, bringing up a technical reading on the view port's side panel. "As I explained, provisions are low. The Earth people managed to bring on board a quantity of water and supplies, but not nearly enough for the duration of the journey. I am unable to locate a suitable gateway so unfortunately, we are going to have to go the long way around. I estimate we have just enough water left for 1.46 analogue orbits.

"Beyond that, the passengers are in trouble." Douglas shot Tesk a look as Mono continued, "We are beyond the point of safe return and my instruments tell me that without a suitable gateway, we haven't enough fuel in the cell to power us back."

"Well, we ain't going back!" growled Tesk. "Not a chance in hell."

"Having explored all options, we are asking that the coalition issue us with supplies. The men are armed and dangerous and my preservation cell is all but worn down."

"We're gonna starve, Bungo!" said Tesk coolly. "If we die, Mono dies too, and you can say goodbye to the ship!"

Bungo shook his head. "You damned Earth people are a menace!" he spluttered. Chrissy looked to Tesk who was now wearing a devilish grin.

"What's it gonna be then, Bungo? Are you gonna help us or not? We could always touch down on the nearest planet. Cause some commotion, raise a little hell, all guns blazing. What have we got to lose?"

Bungo was silent for a moment, entering some information into his data slate. "I think I can arrange something, Mono," he said with an air of exasperation.

The Earth people let out an audible sigh of relief.

"Thanks, Bungo," Tesk commented. "I knew you'd see it my way."

"There's a catch, Tesk," warned Bungo, uninterested in his half-hearted gratitude. "If I do this, I'm actively helping you to break protocol. Xzardak might be happy to lose everything for you, but I am not!"

"Okay," said Tesk with a sly smile. "I don't blame you either."

"I'm making provisions to get you the requested supplies. Once you receive them, Mono will escort you to the Earth planet and return home alone. Once safely delivered, I will be forced to contact Xzardak and the coalition. It will be their decision what happens next."

Even though Tesk didn't like the Earth 2 setup, he had a feeling in his gut that he could probably trust Bungo. "Message understood!" Tesk saluted and winked. "Loud and clear, sir."

Bungo looked unsympathetic. "You're on your own, Tesk; you're essentially signing your own death warrant! I just hope you know what you're doing," he whispered in earnest.

Tesk grinned. "Don't you worry about us, big man! We'll be juuuuuust fine!" And with that, the gang of reprobates let out an enthusiastic cheer.

Technical readings appeared on the viewport panel. "You'll be intercepted in 0.134 analogue orbits," explained Bungo. "A cargo cruiser will supply you with fuel and provisions for the men and women. The food and water will need to be synthesised as no earth-like provisions are available inside your current sector."

"Synthesised?" questioned Tesk. "What's that? Poisoned?" He raised the rifle to the viewport screen. Why can't you just talk in plain English?

Mono calmly explained, "Synthesised. It's been created in a laboratory; it means it will nourish you, but might not taste as good as the food on Earth 2!"

Tesk shrugged. "Gas station food always tastes like shit!"

"Junk food," offered Mono, courtesy of his data cell.

"Mmm… Junk food!" cried Tesk. "Yee-haw! Now you're talking!"

The sombre mood had lifted, the excitement on board the craft was palpable and Mono suspected that Tesk badly wanted to shoot his rifle.

"I've one thing to add," issued Bungo solemnly. "There's another condition to which you must adhere. You Earth people are still classified as a dangerous toxin inside these sectors. My friend at the refuelling platform will insist that we vigorously safeguard against any form of contamination. A squad of specialised chemical technicians will board the craft. You are not permitted to be anywhere near the docking bay, nor must you in any way interact with any of the visiting crew. I must insist that you are put into quarantine as the delivery is made."

The mood inside the room suddenly changed, Mono could sense Tesk's apprehension.

"Hmm." Tesk smiled. "I get it. You had me there." He turned to Douglas. "Thought we were home and dry for a moment. Sounds to me like a double cross."

"That's all I've got," said Bungo wearily. "Take it or leave it; from where I'm standing, it's the only option you have left. Take the deal and don't interfere with the crew."

Tesk scratched his head.

"Bungo has nothing to gain from double-crossing you," said Mono. "He's trying to help."

Without another plan and with a sense that time and options were running out, Tesk shrugged and lowered his head. "Looks like you've got me."

The video screen fizzed and crackled and once again, Tesk and the Earth people slunk off to their seats.

"Putting you in touch with Zetland 71." Bungo smiled. "Good luck with the plan, Mono," he said, signing off just as Mono's life preservation chip finally shorted.

CHAPTER 15

"Denied!" declared Commissioner Edward. "Application denied, Xzardak! They wouldn't go for it!" Edward was red in the face. He had been upstairs to speak to the 'Controllers.' The 'Controllers' spoke on behalf of the government envoys, who in turn spoke on behalf of the 'Great Governors.' Xzardak had requested that the next meeting on the schedule be postponed.

"I haven't the energy!" he pleaded. "My nerves are shot to pieces!"

Edward had listened sympathetically. "I'll see what I can do!" he had promised, but returning from his enquiries, he shook his head forlornly. "It was a succinct 'No!' I'm afraid."

Xzardak felt he had clearly stated his position to the coalition and suggested that they might put forward a case for him.

"Not a chance; Xzardak, they want to see you, eyeball to eyeball!" voiced Edward.

Xzardak started to tremble, not at all ready to stand before the 'Government of the Infinite Everything.'

"Come now!" reassured Edward, helping Xzardak to his feet. "They don't bite, you know. Best to get it over with, don't you think? If you don't do it now, it will be looming over you."

"I'm a wreck, Commissioner Edward," pleaded Xzardak, but Edward was having none of it.

"Nothing I can do about it, Xzardak. You better gather up your things. We've just received news there's a rather heavy lightning storm heading in. Blasted things!"

Xzardak rubbed his head and Commissioner Edward patted him on the shoulder.

"Besides, it's not you they want to see, it's the Earth people. You'll just be there for moral support should things turn nasty!" he cackled loudly.

"Nasty?" Xzardak said, beginning to feel weak at the knees again.

"I'm just kidding, Xzardak," insisted Edward. "They won't say anything nasty! In fact, you'll be surprised at how little they do say. Now clean yourselves up; the cruiser will be here in a moment."

Little Stevie sat in quiet contemplation; a familiar feeling had descended upon him. It wasn't the first time he'd been in trouble with the authorities and sensing a stitch-up, he weighed up his options.

"Boy, if this were back on Earth," raged Marvin. "We'd sure sort those guys out!"

"Sit down and shut up!" scalded Ruby. "If this happened on Earth, you'd do no such thing, probably just disappear into a bottle of booze!" Marvin screwed up his face and clenched his fists. The crew sat in silence. It had been a long day and it was evident that the unusual proceedings were taking their toll.

A wailing siren called out. Suddenly, the commissioners and envoys scurried across the chamber floor. A translucent glass panel on the main hallway wall had been revealed and Little Stevie got to his feet, curious to see what the commotion was all about.

"Come now, Earthlings!" boomed Commissioner Edward as he shuffled past the crew toward the assembled throng. "Your transportation has arrived!"

"Consider yourselves very fortunate!" announced Turner, once again appearing from nowhere. "Not many life forms receive an audience with the government. You are very privileged indeed!" He smiled, awkwardly shaking Little Stevie's hand.

"Enjoy yourselves!" reassured Edward cheerily as the crystal craft docked and the envoys herded the Earth people and their reluctant supervisor aboard.

"Enjoyment," groaned Xzardak, "will only come when this terrible episode has ended!" He dropped his head and dutifully boarded the ship's ramp.

"See you around," said Cheryl.

"I do hope so," replied Turner, leading the last of the Earth people out onto the carrier.

All on board, the craft doors hissed and bolted closed with a mechanical thump as the ship quickly ascended. The Earth people stumbled up the galley, hurriedly scrambling to take their seats. "Sheesh." Ruby scowled. "At least let us get on! This ain't exactly business class!"

With everyone seated, an envoy hostess appeared. "Good day, friends," she said and smiled. "I'm your envoy today. I will be taking you to see the 'Great Governors of the Infinite Everything,' and may I say they are very keen to meet you all."

Xzardak tried to settle into his seat, but he felt hot, and his head was reeling. Little Stevie took off his shoes as Marvin twisted uncomfortably, complaining and pulling at his robe.

The mild-mannered envoy continued, "It has been brought to my attention that you have travelled some distance to meet the Great Ones. Very soon, we will supply you with refreshments—food, drink and maybe something to help alleviate any nerves. The Great Governors are well aware that it can be an intimidating experience. So please, at their request, sit back and relax."

The envoy turned and ventured behind a shimmering curtain, and within a second, her legion of helpers appeared with an assortment of multi-coloured produce and drinks.

Another moment passed, and the hostess envoy reappeared, carrying a decanter and glasses filled with a familiar blue sparkling liquid. "Might I suggest you all have a drink? It will steady your nerves, relax you and enhance your experience with the Great Ones."

As the Earth people tucked in, Xzardak put his hand up, motioning to the hostess to bring him a glass of the crystal blue elixir. "I'm coming to you now, sir!" she said, shuffling past Ruby and Marvin. "Please take two glasses," she said to Xzardak. "You look like you could use it."

Xzardak blushed, then looked relieved as he took a sip of the blue juice.

"Here, take mine too," offered Little Stevie. "I like a clear head when I go into battle." Xzardak accepted his glass, took another swig of the liquid and feeling suddenly refreshed, he began to settle a little.

"I must apologise for the bumpy ride," said the envoy. "We are travelling slightly faster than usual in the hope that we will get to the enclave before the lightning storm hits. The Crystal Planet is prone to very beautiful but violent lightning storms, the price of living in paradise."

"There's always a price to pay," acknowledged Stevie wistfully.

The Earth people enjoyed their dinner and feeling slightly more at ease, Xzardak ate something too. "We should arrive quite soon," announced the hostess. "But for now, relax and enjoy the wonderful views."

With the excitement of the day, the hurried boarding, lavish food and drinks and the crystal elixir, it occurred to Xzardak that he had not once looked out of the cabin window.

Pulling open the craft's shutters, the cabin flooded with a beautiful blue-green light. A glowing crystal cascade glinted across the mountain tops, illuminating the valley below. Light flares shining through the silver-blue gossamer clouds on the horizon caused spots to appear before Xzardak's eyes. "How wonderful," he said.

The crystal blue liquid was calming his spirit and the picturesque vista nourishing his soul.

"Wow, it sure is pretty," whispered Ruby to Marvin. Uncharacteristically, Marvin was too wrapped up in his own enchantment to say anything cynical or crude.

The craft gently banked, revealing the enclave, the home of the 'Great Governors of the Infinite Everything' and the most astounding piece of architecture that Xzardak had ever encountered. For a moment, the nervous feeling returned, flashing across his body. He took a breath. "Relax," he softly reassured himself. The silver light shimmered across the cabin roof as the craft delicately tilted. Xzardak could feel the crystal elixir coursing through his being.

He closed his eyes. Allowing himself a moment of rest, he took a breath, then from above, a loud crack and a blinding flash of lightning suddenly delivered him back into reality.

"Please do not panic!" insisted the hostess envoy, the silver-blue ship shuddering as another metallic crash sounded around them. "I can assure you the lightning will not affect the craft!"

Marvin quickly fastened his safety belt as Little Stevie grappled to put his shoes back on. Panicking, Xzardak got to his feet. "Please, sit down, sir!" she shouted. "We are absolutely safe and not in any danger whatsoever!" Xzardak appeared unconvinced but sat down obediently when the hostess shot him another look, demanding compliance.

The transport violently banked to the left, appearing to lose altitude at quite an unsettling rate. The crew members hurriedly took to their seats as the vessel vibrated and jolted. Xzardak could hear a warning beacon sounding in the craft's cockpit and looked to the hostess envoy for reassurance. The cabin crew and Earthlings all braced themselves, preparing for an impact, when suddenly, another flash of lightning hit, then another. Xzardak feared his heart might explode.

Abruptly, the ship shuddered and appeared to slow. The view through the window had changed, everything now bathed in a warm violet light.

The turbulence subsided and the ship appeared to smoothly plateau.

"I am delighted to announce that we are now inside the enclave biosphere," declared the hostess envoy over the aircraft's speaker system. "Quite safe, I assure you!" she added, looking more than a little flustered. Marvin nonchalantly undid his safety belt, forcefully yawned and stretched out his arms, in a vain attempt to mask the look of terror he'd sported moments earlier.

Xzardak's hands were trembling. Desperately wiping his sweaty brow and fidgeting in his seat, he was on the lookout for another glass of crystal elixir to drain.

The craft swiftly descended, landing as bumpily as it had taken off. "I thought we were done for there!" cried Cheryl, her face flushed, both hands clamped to the armrests.

"Me too!" admitted Ruby with a sigh of relief.

Marvin remained silent. He raised an eyebrow and shot Little Stevie a look. "No big deal," said Stevie coolly, shrugging his shoulders.

Once safely back on dry land, the brakes hissed and the transport's main doors slowly opened. A soothing purple glow filled the cabin as the craft's shutters lifted, revealing the wondrous grounds and gardens of the Crystal Enclave. The hostess envoy pointed to the High Tower. "My friends," she said, gesturing to the fantastical building before them. "The Great Palace of the Crystal Enclave." She gesticulated with a theatrical bow. "The home of the Great Governors of the Infinite Everything!" The building rose high above them, stretching up majestically into the sky and glistening in the evening sunshine. "Come, my friends," she said invitingly, "I believe the Great Ones are ready for you."

Gathering their few possessions, the Earth people disembarked from the silver coalition craft. Marvin sidled up to Little Stevie, saying, "I don't like this one bit."

Stevie turned.

"Me neither, this morning we were scum; now, they're treating us like long-lost relations!"

With a sharp intake of breath, Marvin ground his teeth. "Hey, Xzardak, what do you make of this?" he called out.

Xzardak was leading the crowd, eager to get the ordeal underway, and over and done with. He turned to answer, "I don't know." He shrugged. "They seem to be giving us the welcome treatment, but who knows what they have planned for us, I…" He hesitated.

Xzardak was aware that when it came to government and coalition business, there was always an element of artifice. "They have elaborate protocols and traditions that they like to adhere to. It's all part of their fun. The problems only really arise once you go against their protocols," he explained.

"I guess that's why we're here," interrupted Cheryl.

Xzardak nodded his head. "Commissioner Edward suggested we enjoy our visit, yet I'm finding the whole experience rather unsettling." Marvin cracked his knuckles.

Ruby interrupted, "Will you guys relax? If they were going to kill us, surely they would have done it by now." She was as bemused as everyone else but Xzardak's nervous energy and Marvin's growing paranoia were beginning to irritate her. "Besides," she purred, looking to Xzardak, "I thought you said that space people were peace loving? So why would you be worried all of a sudden?"

Xzardak frowned. "Yes, we are peace loving, for the most part, but the government has a multitude of ways to torture us should we step out of line. It's that kind of peace."

Ruby looked unimpressed. "Well, boys, let's just wait and see! Maybe I'll have something to say if they get uppity!"

Wandering the finely manicured grounds and gardens, they eventually arrived at the palace steps. The hostess envoy led them in through a magnificent crystal gateway and Xzardak peered up, his breath taken by the beautifully ornate crystalline glass carvings adorning it.

Once inside the palace, she led them down a dimly lit corridor and directed them to a chamber. "You must dress to meet the Great Ones," she whispered solemnly. "For your benefit as much as theirs. They inhabit a very sterile environment and therefore, are incredibly open to infection."

"That's us," Marvin said. "The walking germs!"

As they were ushered into the chamber, the Earth people were each given a purple-grey outfit to put on. "Please dress quickly," the envoy requested, hurrying them through the induction process. "The Great Ones are very eager to meet you and we must try to beat the lightning storm. By the looks of it, it's going to get a lot worse!"

"What happens if we don't beat it?" enquired Little Stevie, agitated by the flustered envoy's manner. "I mean, what if the Great Ones want to hang out with us?" he joshed sarcastically.

She folded her arms. "Then we will be travelling back through the height of the storm! And please be aware that red lightning is predicted," she warned.

"Sounds pretty." Ruby smiled.

"From the safety of the palace, I can't deny it is very beautiful. But from the viewport of a vessel, believe me, it is not." She huffed. "Nobody is permitted to stay inside the palace; tradition forbids it. Therefore, the Great Ones won't allow it! Once your audience with the Great Ones has finished, it will be my duty to get you back onto the transport."

Stevie held his temper. "Well, we better get this over with then."

He smiled graciously.

"That's if we get out of here in one piece," said Marvin.

Ruby elbowed him in his bruised ribs.

"The suits will emit a clear barrier which will completely encapsulate you. You must not worry; it is not harmful, you will be sealed in, and the Great Ones sealed out. It is for everyone's protection. Should the palace chamber detect contamination, I must warn you, you will be vapourised."

Xzardak began to sweat once more.

They dressed quickly and once inside the hooded suits, a clear liquid seeped through the fabric. Within less than a minute, the Earth people were completely coated by a skin of clear tasteless barrier gel. "Well, that's me sealed in!" called Ruby.

"Yes, and the creepy ones sealed out, I hope." Cheryl chuckled.

Xzardak had also been made to wear a jumpsuit, his proximity to the toxic substance categorising him as a possible pollutant. He looked quite different out of his commission standard robe and tunic. Now suited up and completely sealed in, he stood with the other lowly subjects ready to be received by the Great Ones. Leading them through the enormous, frosted crystal doors, the envoy ushered them into a chamber of pure white blinding light.

"I must leave you now," she whispered. "You will be quite safe!"

Xzardak stepped forward first, followed by Stevie and Marvin and the rest of the Earth people. Once over the threshold, they stood together and gazed out into the bright white nothingness. The colourless light pulsated and fizzed, reminding Xzardak of the mysterious gateway portals often found in deep space.

"A gateway to another realm?" he wondered, feeling strange and lightheaded.

This was the moment he had been dreading, his day of reckoning. The coalition review had been a horrible ordeal. It had clearly been a test, yet today they were being treated like guests. Another challenge, perhaps? He stood up straight, summonsing whatever inner strength he had left, staring out into the bright white miasma. He nervously took another step forward anticipating a wave of anxiety, but to his surprise, a peculiar feeling of serenity came upon him.

The light source pulsated and hummed.

He glanced over to where Little Stevie and Marvin were standing, and just behind were Ruby and Cheryl and the others. He looked along the line of faces, each one smiling and calm, at peace as the light source flickered and modulated. A light breeze brushed his face, and the Earth people all blinked in unison, contented smiles playing across their faces.

Xzardak suspected they were all sharing the same experience, the same emotion, the same serenity. A feeling like time was slowing, grinding to a halt, and a feeling like nothing mattered anymore. A feeling as though they belonged. Xzardak exhaled, and he let out a long, deep breath which seemed to last forever, his mind clear, his senses awoken, his being at peace.

Behind him, Marvin was having his own epiphany. "Are we dead?" he said, then finding himself unable to formulate thoughts into words, he realised he was unable to answer himself. He stood there, defenceless and disarmed, gently basking in the soothing luminance.

The light source suddenly intensified.

Softly and slowly, a face appeared, emerging through the searing white light. A neck, shoulders, a torso and limbs, until there, in front of them, stood a Great Governor of the Infinite Everything; he was much smaller than Xzardak had been imagining, slight in build and covered in silver-grey blemish-free skin. Little Stevie inwardly chuckled. "Now, these are space aliens!" he said to himself, hypnotised by the serene face and its halo of burning light.

The governor stood in partial silhouette, the beautiful glow pulsating, shielding, concealing, then revealing the mysterious being, its large black eyes studying its subjects.

Xzardak gazed up in awe, watching as it hovered and seemed to grow bigger. "Greetings, Earth people," the governor proclaimed. Xzardak was not able to ascertain if the words he was hearing were coming from inside his own head or via his large ears. Transfixed by the wonderful being, he awaited its next syllable. "You must not be afraid," it reassured. "We have heard much about your Earth species, and we were keen to view you for ourselves."

Behind him, the governor made a gesture, beckoning with his spindly silver arm. Through the beautiful white anti-void, another being emerged. Almost identical to the first, its large head shifted, and its big black eyes blinked as it looked curiously upon the Earth creatures before it.

"Please be at peace, Earth people," it seemed to say.

Another identical being arrived, then another and then another until finally in front of them stood twelve identical governors, indistinguishable in height, stature and shape. They gazed over, moving as if one, studying and examining the Earth people.

Seeking clarity, Xzardak glanced down and around, to his left and his right. It appeared that his kinsfolk were floating in air, the entire group glowing, suspended in the bright blue firmament. The purple-grey suits they were wearing now appeared translucent and silver rays shone right through their bodies, revealing bones, cartilage, and inner organs.

The company was at ease, transfixed, in a dream yet cognisant that they were being studied.

"We are the great governors, and we can see inside, into your souls!" they said in unison. "Much has been written about your species and many have proclaimed that you are beyond salvation!" They chuckled. "We are here to find out for ourselves. We see beyond the periphery, deeper than surface level, deep inside of you!" The telepathic voices momentarily ceased and Xzardak feared he was beginning to lose touch with his senses.

As the light source flickered and convulsed, he felt himself drift in and drift out of consciousness, his motor skills no longer functioning. He was now unable to look across at his Earth friends. He held on for dear life, resisting the abyss, a nagging doubt in his mind defying the urge to sleep and capitulate to the shimmering inertia.

As Xzardak had suspected, it was true that the company was encountering a shared experience. Yet each individual's experience of the encounter was vastly different due to the physical makeup of the species. Marvin had momentarily panicked, fearing he was leaving his physical body. He too tried to resist for fear of dying.

He gritted his teeth and attempted to clench his fists.

Ruby also felt that she had left her body behind, yet no such feeling of fear had entered into her reality. She closed her eyes, subsumed by the tide, and by the blinding soothing light and the sensation of floating in an infinite pool of pure clean energy. She smiled as images from her past appeared before her like a playbook of her life's experiences, surrounding her and engulfing her consciousness.

Little Stevie also had surrendered to the warming glow, never one to give up without a fight; he knew in his soul that resistance to such a powerful energy source would prove futile.

He, along with the rest of the crew, closed their eyes in an act of blissful rendition.

Xzardak's own life played out. Backwards and forwards, visions and memories, past, present and future. A catalogue of reminiscences projected real time all around him. He reached out to touch his father, his mother, his sister, his ancestors surrounding him. He saw his younger self and searched to see his older self, his entire tale written out in longhand for the universe to read.

The beginning, the middle but not the end.

The beings were silent, yet the conversation raged, burning brightly. They asked a million questions a minute and the Earth people reciprocated with a billion answers a second, the entire history of the species re-enacted, relived, and retold in the blink of an eye.

Fast and slow, upwards, and downwards, in two dimensions, three dimensions and four dimensions, the conversation reverberated without restriction throughout unlimited time and space. Xzardak could feel his teeth chattering; he felt cold then hot then cold again. It seemed that the memory transference was becoming too much for him, and that he was losing his mind.

Unable to establish which life was his, he felt nauseous. The ride was coming off the rails. He reached out again, desperate to anchor himself to something real. The dizzying intensity of too much information made him jolt, his body convulsing as tremors ran up and down his spine.

Then suddenly, the crescendo came, the echoing voices silenced, the images evaporated, and the searing light slowly diminished. The beings shimmered and faded, rescinding into the expiring light. Still unable to formulate thought, he opened his eyes, aware that the experience was over yet yearning that it might last for eternity.

CHAPTER 16

The purring of an engine and the wafting aroma of food had awoken Xzardak's senses. Gradually, he was rediscovering the ability to formulate thoughts. His first notion would be, "Where am I?" He started to piece together the clues, the motion, the engine, the smell.

"On board a craft!" he subconsciously deduced.

Muffled voices, flickering light, laughter, movement. The craft shuddered, gently awakening him from his slumber and all at once, a multitude of perceptions flooded Xzardak's cognition.

Desperately, he was trying to sort through the kaleidoscope of sounds and images when suddenly, a voice in his head announced, "The Everything!"

He wondered if it might be prudent to open his eyes.

"In a moment," the voice instructed tenderly, and Xzardak capitulated. He could feel his heart beating, and took a breath. He had a feeling in his aching bones that the trip was over, and the wonderful governors were gone.

"Ah-ha!"

Xzardak knew the voice, but it took him a beat to remember to whom it belonged. "So nice of you to join us."

"The envoy!" declared the voice in his head.

Xzardak slowly opened then quickly shielded his eyes, discovering that the crystal blue glow had intensified. "You've been out for quite some time!" she cooed, putting her hand on Xzardak's arm. "Come, you must eat. We are almost back at coalition headquarters."

Xzardak stirred, stretching out his arms and straightening his back. He looked across the cabin to see the Earth people. Was it a dream, he wondered? *Perhaps the effects of the elixir? It's strong stuff.* He rubbed his head. Out of the corner of his eye, he spotted Stevie, who smiled reassuringly. If it had been a dream, they had all been in it together.

"You people are very fortunate. We completely missed the lightning storm!" announced the hostess. "Sailed right through it without a scratch!"

"That's us," said Cheryl. "Born lucky!"

Now that his faculties were beginning to return, Xzardak started to piece together the events of the previous day. Marvin had gotten to his feet. "What happens next, boss?" he called, but Xzardak did not reply. He indolently closed his eyes, feigning sleep, yearning for the warm and fuzzy safety of the alternate realm. His being was too depleted to navigate his own life, let alone efficiently account for the destinies of the Earthlings.

"Good morning," said a droning mechanical voice, "I have brought nourishment." Xzardak sat up and acknowledged the service robot decanting some clear liquid into a colourful beaker.

Leaving the food on the nightstand, the robot departed. "Please let me know if there is anything else," he called as he whizzed toward the apartment door.

"Thank you," Xzardak said and yawned. "Ah… may I ask where I am?" he enquired hoarsely. But the robot was gone.

Getting out of bed, Xzardak wandered over to the tray of hot food. He was incredibly hungry and quickly tucked into the morning breakfast. "Ebonez tree stew," he said after tasting a spoonful. "Not bad." Once sufficiently nourished, he glanced over to the viewport monitor which had started to buzz and flash a light. Rubbing his eyes and still somewhat dazed, he stumbled across to the console and pressed the flashing receiver button, initiating the intel.

The irritating siren ceased, and the screen blinked on, revealing another familiar face, Commissioner Edward. "Xzardak, what on Zhim is going on?" Edward asked. "You were meant to be down here an age ago!" The fog suddenly cleared; Edward's annoyance had given Xzardak a jolt, delivering him back into the dreadful realm of reality. "Disgraceful behaviour!" Edward scolded. "Get yourself ready and join us in the chamber!"

Xzardak had started to panic again. A new day had dawned, and with it another round of wretched challenges had materialised. The lingering effects of the crystal elixir and the dreamy residual buzz from the meeting with the governors had long since subsided, replaced by the familiar feelings of paranoia and sickly dread.

"We're not out of the woods yet!" he reminded himself, splashing water onto his creased silver-purple face, and wetting his hair before hastily dressing. Gathering his things, he quickly headed down the spiral stairs into the busy recess chamber.

"Commissioner Edward, forgive me!" cried Xzardak subserviently. "I hadn't any memory of a scheduled meeting," he protested, the previous day's proceedings still swimming around inside his scrambled brain.

"Not to worry, dear boy!" declared Edward, his mood characteristically the opposite to that of Edward on the video monitor. "My fault… I don't think I even told you about the meeting, to be honest. Getting forgetful in my old age!" confessed schizophrenic Edward's more genial side.

Xzardak obediently followed him into the darkened chamber, fully expecting to see the Earth people present and seated in the trial hall. Xzardak's heart sank as he realised they were gone.

Searching for them, he frantically looked around, before figuring out that only he and the three prosecuting officials were present in the dimly lit gloom. "Xzardak, I'm sure you remember Commissioners Sirdar and Vilmos," said Edward, reacquainting him with the original arrest party. "Just us today," he said. "No need for the whole hullabaloo!"

"What of the Earth people?" inquired Xzardak.

"We'll come to their fate very soon," Vilmos said.

They've been sent away, thought Xzardak, his mind racing. *Banished to an outlying planet, dark and alone without an adequate light source or appropriate atmosphere.*

His legs gave way and tiny stars danced before his eyes. He desperately tried to quell the doubt growing inside of him.

Xzardak braced himself. Squirming in his seat, he prepared for the worst. "So, you met with the whole assembly, I'm led to believe!" said Vilmos with a sinister smile. "Not many get to meet the whole pantheon. Indeed, you are blessed." Xzardak's palms were sweating. He wished they would just reveal his punishment.

"Y-yes, all t-t-twelve," he stuttered. "What's to become of us?" he asked.

"Well," pronounced Edward as the other two commissioners made themselves comfortable. "Well," he repeated. Xzardak sensed a pause and wondered just how bad the penalty might be. "Well," enunciated Edward for a third time.

"Please!" exclaimed Sirdar, sensing that Xzardak was being trifled with. "Put the poor wretch out of his misery!"

Edward sat back. "Not a lot," he finally answered. "I'm led to believe that it went very well yesterday. Seems as though they like you! Can't for the life of me understand why."

Xzardak swallowed hard, sensing a 'however.'

Sure enough, it followed.

"However," Edward continued. "You're on probation. You have breached a very serious protocol and you know how the civilised government feels about protocol!" Xzardak lowered his head like a naughty schoolboy. "You're to go back and continue with the program, but be warned, one bad step and the whole show is finished!" Edward banged his fist on the Plexiglass desk with theatrical effect. "The Great Ones enjoyed meeting you!" he bellowed, then lowering his voice, he whispered, "But there's *our* reputation at stake here!"

Vilmos politely interrupted, "We've put a lot on the line for you, Xzardak! There's to be no more bad behaviour! You must remind the Earth people that they are our guests here on Planet A. If they mess up this opportunity, there will be no Planet B."

"No," concurred Edward. "There's little appetite for an Earth 3, even amongst their most ardent supporters."

Xzardak let out a sigh of relief. It seemed for now, he was off the hook. "Thank you, gentlemen. I really do appreciate your understanding," he said passively. With a furtive smile, he reached out to shake the commissioners' hands.

"You're to go back immediately!" Edward said sternly. "Immediately!"

Xzardak got to his feet and buttoned up his tunic. "Your Earth people are on board a cruiser," Commissioner Sirdar said. "Best go and break the good news to them. They must be wondering what's going on!"

Xzardak's ears were ringing. His stay on the crystal moon had upset his nervous system and left him overwrought. Again, he thanked the commissioners as Edward ushered him out of the chamber. "You've had a lucky break here, my boy!" he said wistfully. "I wouldn't have let you off so lightly." His demeanour was changing back to that of a tyrant. "Now get out of here, Xzardak!" he bellowed. "I don't want to see your face ever again!"

It appeared that the ordeal was at last over. Xzardak rushed excitedly to the transport and hurried up the ramp onto the awaiting craft. Looking perturbed, the Earth people sat quietly, anxiously awaiting the verdict, considering the consequences of their actions and the terms put upon their ultimate destiny. Xzardak lowered his head and said nothing, just walked solemnly up the galley and slumped dejectedly into a vacant seat. He too could play human games.

The Earth people jabbered and twitched, all eyes trained on their crumpled leader.

Betrayed by his smiling face, Xzardak could no longer continue his subterfuge. He got to his feet. "We got away with it!" he blurted cheerfully. "Don't ask me how, but we got away with it! I've just spoken with the commissioners and apparently, we are free to return to Earth 2!"

The cabin came alive.

"I knew it!" said Marvin with an air of relief. "How could they resist our charm?"

"Way to go…" said Little Stevie, slowly shaking his head. "Pretty weird trip! I had a feeling we were done for! I mean, look at us… we're the dregs of society!" he said and laughed.

"You'd better believe it. The scum of the Earth!" added Cheryl gleefully.

The coalition transporter provided to take them back was noticeably nicer than the craft in which they had been picked up. As the craft's thrusters blasted them into orbit, the Earth people excitedly chattered amongst themselves, relieved to be finally going back to the compound from which they had tried so desperately to escape.

As the ship hurtled through outer space, Xzardak closed his eyes, feeling vindicated. The governors had seen behind the mask, deep into the very souls of the Earth people. "Maybe they are worth saving after all?" he whispered. Ruby caught his eye, sleeping serenely, curled up next to her friend Cheryl. Perhaps Dr Jay and the commissioners had been wrong, and maybe there was a glimmer of light burning deep inside their tenebrous hearts.

He took a sip of crystal elixir, probably the last taste he'd ever get, relieved to be returning to the compound and beyond happy to be going home.

The wormhole which had delivered them to the Crystal Planet had unexpectedly closed. The pilot announced that they would be taking an alternate route. "We could be on board for some time!" she announced, and the Earth people let out a groan.

The journey had been a long one with still a way to go, but for now, at last, Xzardak could finally sleep.

CHAPTER 17

The journey home was taking much longer than anyone had expected, and the Earth people were becoming restless, noisily demanding refreshments from a shiny executive service robot. The android was run off its feet, diligently bringing them comestibles.

The vessel's cabin and sleeping quarters were also in a mess with food and drink trampled into its plush blue carpet. Meanwhile, the Earth people were up on their feet, singing and dancing and making a terrible din. Watching them as they pranced and cavorted in the aisle, Xzardak felt a sudden pang of despair. *What if I'm wrong?*

Shouting to a service droid and demanding yet more drink, Marvin poured the sticky liquid over the anthropoid's head, callously laughing when the poor robot began to malfunction, sparks and smoke coming from the unit's processor hatch.

Staring out of the window, trying to ignore the terrible Earth people and their appalling treatment of the crew and service robots, Xzardak had been pondering a notion. It was probably an ineffective coalition bureaucrat who had granted them a pardon. The government was keen to avoid criticism and closing down the program might have drawn scorn from the very vocal pressure groups who had lobbied for the Earth people to be saved in the first place.

For now, they were safe, but for how long, he dared not wonder.

Nestled under a travel blanket, he closed his eyes again, hoping to get some rest amid the chaos and disarray. "Hey, Xzardak!" called Little Stevie. Xzardak sighed heavily and pulled the covers up over his head. "We're all wondering, what's the catch?"

"Catch?" replied Xzardak, unsure of the Earthman's terminology.

"Yeah, catch. What's the deal? What's the trade off? They've given us our freedom. Let us off without any punishment… but there's got to be a catch?" he said.

Xzardak thought for a moment. "No catch," he said unconvincingly.

"Oh, Xzardak! You're so sweet," called Ruby. "There's always a catch, baby!"

Xzardak wouldn't believe it. Despite his own misgivings, he decided he would not feed this suspicious and devious notion flouted by the cynical Earth people.

"The coalition is giving us a second chance, that's all," he replied with an indignant tone. "And as long as we don't cause any more trouble, we should be okay!" Xzardak closed his eyes and tried to rest, refusing to give headspace to his lingering doubts.

"May we have your attention!" announced the convulsing service droid.

"Ladies and gentlemen," the hostess envoy announced. "Please gather your things as we are now arriving at your desired destination." Getting to their feet, the Earth people jostled in the aisle, impatiently pushing one another, keen to disembark after a very long and equally boring space flight. Xzardak folded down his blanket.

"Please remain seated!" instructed the hostess. "We are not yet on the ground!" But the Earth people refused to listen, shambling instead toward the craft's exit. Xzardak gazed out of the window. He would leave it to the hostess envoy and service drones to constrain the hooligans, having accepted that trying to manage them was only leading to feelings of anguish and despair.

He felt he was beginning to understand them. *They aren't bad*, he thought. *Just wild and uncontrollable.*

Xzardak was pleased to be home. Despite all the problems and a turbulent couple of weeks, he smiled as the coalition craft gently graced the giant hangar bay. He felt as though the journey into space had given him a renewed perspective on the program. He had shared some very intense experiences with the Earth people, and felt it had brought them closer together.

Xzardak decided that whatever it took, Earth 2—his very first assignment—would work! He would make sure of it. It was going to be hailed a resounding success.

The air brakes brought them to a halt and the ship landed with a hiss.

Xzardak was thrilled to see the welcoming party made up of his long-term assistant, Bungo, and the service robot, Zork. As the craft doors opened, the Earth people came spewing out.

"I bet you thought you'd seen the back of us!" hollered Marvin. "Sorry to disappoint!"

Bungo smiled through gritted teeth.

"Thank you." Xzardak smiled as he bade farewell to the hostess envoy. "It was a pleasure to travel with you." The envoy blushed and held up her hand.

"Wait a moment!" she whispered, scurrying behind the curtain and reappearing with a bottle. "Just in case things get tough, just in case we never meet again!" she said. Xzardak took the bottle from her, examining the label that stated, 'Crystal Elixir.'

He looked to the envoy. "Very kind," he whispered.

She smiled and motioned to him to not say another word.

Once the passengers were clear of the craft, it fired up its engines, ready to depart. "Great to see you!" called Bungo, patting Xzardak on the back.

"Yes!" answered Xzardak. "For a moment, I thought we were done for!" The Earth people quickly took cover as the ship noisily ascended, its thrusters propelling it up and out of the silo.

"What happened?" enquired Bungo. "We were very worried!"

"It's a long story!" replied Xzardak. "Mind if I change first?"

Bungo smiled. He would give Xzardak a moment to clean himself up before troubling him with the latest dramatic instalment. "Of course, but I must speak with you as soon as possible."

Making his way over to the command centre, Bungo had collated all the information he'd received from Mono and Tesk. He waited nervously, wondering if he had done the right thing by not informing Xzardak immediately upon his return. Zork had checked the current coordinates of the craft. At least he knew where they were, still on the Earth's flightpath and all still alive.

"Don't look so worried!" chirped Zork.

Bungo didn't reply.

"There was nothing you could do!" he reassured his colleague. "Besides, they're only humans!"

Bungo heard footsteps, turning to see Xzardak spryly jogging across the deck.

"It's good to be back!" announced Xzardak cheerfully, skipping through the command centre doorway.

"It's good to have you back, sir!" enthused Zork.

"Thank you, Zork!" he replied. "Is Mono out on manoeuvres?" he asked, looking puzzled, wondering why his obedient companion robot was absent.

Zork looked sideways. "Yes, s-something like that," he stuttered in a monotone voice.

Bungo changed the subject. "How did it go? I had feared you'd all been banished to the Planet of Night!"

"No, not this time. Somehow, we managed to get away with it!" Xzardak said and beamed. "They've given us a second chance… but issued us with a warning."

Bungo nodded. "Well, that's something," he said thoughtfully.

Xzardak looked out across the compound. "From now on, Bungo, we have to play things by the book… any more problems and they'll shut us down for good!"

Bungo waited for a moment, trying to gauge how Xzardak was going to handle the news. Zork had calculated that the odds were not looking good.

"How's Tesk?" enquired Xzardak cheerily. Bungo didn't reply, his eyes darting side to side in a shifty manner. He looked a little uneasy.

"Why do I get the feeling that I've missed something?" Xzardak said, suspecting a problem. "You did find him, didn't you?" he said, suspicious.

"Uh… oh yes, we found him."

"Well, where is he?" Sensing deception, Xzardak felt anxiety brewing in his stomach.

"He's on his way to Earth!" blurted Zork. "Tesk, Douglas, Joey, Alice, Chrissy, Nelson. All on their way to Earth!" he chirped efficiently and enthusiastically.

Xzardak turned, smiling at first, confused and with his brow furrowed.

Bungo got to his feet. "We couldn't stop them!" he bumbled. "They've taken your ship; there was nothing we could do!"

"Taken my ship?" said Xzardak incredulously. "But how would they fly it?"

Bungo looked to Zork, and Zork to Xzardak.

"Mono!" said Xzardak, putting the pieces together.

"Please believe me, Xzardak," said Bungo. "We tried to stop them, but they were armed, they're dangerous! They demanded a ship, so I gave them yours! At least we can track it!"

Xzardak looked perplexed, walking over to the console. "I met with the commissioners, the great governors. They said they liked us, and gave us a pardon, a second chance. I thought we were going to be okay," he said, crestfallen.

Bungo couldn't think of anything to say.

"You say they were armed?" Xzardak asked. "Armed with what?"

Bungo leaned in, placing his hands on the desk. "Something strange is going on, Xzardak! The Earth people have acquired some guns; they appear to be Earth weapons. They claim that they found them by the mess hall. In cases marked…" Bungo paused. "Category D."

"Category D? But that would suggest…" Xzardak looked confused.

"I didn't make contact while you were away because I feared it might adversely affect your hearing. I haven't reported the matter to the coalition and to the best of my knowledge, they don't know anything about the escape."

"But they must have registered a craft leaving the compound!" cried Xzardak, looking bewildered.

"They blasted out not long after the coalition took you away," he explained. "I suspect they thought the extra craft was part of the convoy. I thought it best to await your return," he said guiltily. "We did our best, Xzardak, we really did."

Xzardak thought for a moment. His renewed faith in the program had taken a hit, but as with previous events, he thought it best to tackle the conundrum calmly, logically and philosophically. Xzardak meditated for a moment, desperately trying to dispel the negative emotions building up inside of him.

"You did the right thing, Bungo!" he declared confidently.

Zork chirped, surprised and excited, his eyes flashing and rotating. "You must give me a full breakdown of everything that has happened," he calmly insisted.

Bungo looked relieved and rolled up his sleeves. It appeared that Xzardak was taking the news very well. The terrible feeling had returned and Xzardak's anxiety levels had begun to soar once more. He instructed Bungo to contact the ship. However, travelling at such high velocity was making it impossible to get through to the errant craft. Xzardak stood before the intel screen, staring into the fuzzy abyss. Bungo tried again and again, but to no avail.

"Looks like we'll have to wait it out," said Xzardak patiently, trying to quell any feelings of anger or frustration. 'Maybe they are beyond help?' He feared they were back at square one.

CHAPTER 18

Xzardak awoke feeling slightly worse for wear. Fully clothed from the night before, he sat forward and surveyed the room. His head was swimming. Trying to figure out where he was, he noticed his own reflection staring back at him. He was at home. With the previous day's adventures behind him, he somehow remembered he had work to do. He yawned and scratched his head, then took a swig from the bottle of crystal elixir sitting half empty on the nightstand.

With the prospect of personal, professional and financial ruin looking likely, he rolled out of bed and got to his feet. Determined not to be beaten by a bunch of under-evolved cave dwellers, he quickly gathered his things and summoned Bungo, who was already waiting outside in a cruiser.

Xzardak smiled. "Good morning, my friend."

"It's a beautiful day," said Bungo. "All things considered."

Xzardak agreed, "Yes, it's a new day and time to clear up this terrible mess. Let's pay a visit to the Earthlings… or what remains of them!"

Blasting towards the Earth 2 housing compound, Xzardak enthusiastically laid out the day's order of play. They would forensically examine the area where the weapons had been discovered, inspect all of the security footage and converse with as many Earth people as were willing to help. Xzardak wondered how their mood might be, questioning if they would even talk to him without the prompting and guidance of their leader.

Tesk and his troublemakers were gone and on entering the compound, Xzardak remarked at how peaceful the place seemed to be. It appeared that the Earth people were cheerfully going about their business, and as they disembarked from the cruiser, it felt as though the general mood amongst the inhabitants had greatly improved.

Xzardak and Bungo spotted Clive down on his knees repairing an outdated-looking mechanical device. The Earth man, in charge in Tesk's absence, stood, turning to greet them.

"Surprised to see you still here, Clive?" Xzardak mused. "I thought you'd have gone with the others?"

"No chance, Xzardak. I want out of here, but this plan to go back to Earth sounds like madness. I know there's no going back to our planet, and that you're on the level." He wiped his dirty hands on his grey overall and picked up his tools.

"I need to speak with you, Clive," said Xzardak nervously.

Clive suggested that they convene in his house. They followed him along a narrow pathway and crowded into Clive's compact but adequate dwelling.

Clive smiled as he politely ushered them inside. "How far did they get? Are they dead yet?" He snickered.

"No, they're still alive, I think?" replied Xzardak, scratching his head. "They've commandeered my best ship and assistant robot! They're quite safe, but what happens next is up to them. To be candid, I don't fancy their chances much!"

"Yeah, I hear you." Clive nodded. "To be honest, it's been nice not having Tesk around, raising hell." He smirked. "Nice and peaceful." He wiped his sweating brow with his dirty sleeve. "What do you need from us, Xzardak?" he asked. "Reckon we can work together now that the criminal element has gone?"

Xzardak liked Clive, finding him straightforward and easy to read, not wild and unpredictable like many of the other humans. "I need to know how many people are left?" answered Xzardak, relieved that Clive was being so cooperative.

"Sixty something, I reckon" said Clive. "And a few kids. The main troublemakers are gone and the rest of us just want to get on. Until something better comes along, the arrangement here suits us just fine."

Xzardak sighed. "The way things are going, the arrangement here may have to come to an end. Some individuals within the coalition are eager to shut us down. They are just waiting for us to make a bad step, and Tesk's latest escapade really hasn't helped matters."

"I can imagine," grunted Clive. "It's a real shame. As you can probably see, now that the lunatics have shipped out—Tesk, Joey, Douglas, Nelson, all of that crowd—those left are pretty cool by comparison."

"The coalition will be paying us a visit at some point soon, and once they discover what has happened, our days will be numbered. If we are to have any chance of survival, I will need to be able to give them a full explanation. I need to know exactly what happened, where the weapons came from and who discovered them." Standing, Clive walked towards the back door.

He called to his young son, who obediently ran inside.

Closing the door, Clive took the boy by the arm. "John, tell Xzardak about the cases." John nervously eyed Xzardak. He looked to his father who nodded his head encouragingly.

"S-s-some men brought them... big men. In big cases, and they left them outside of the store. Six cases, four men. I-I found them! I told Tesk and he was mighty happy once he opened them up! There were guns and ammo... And that's when all the trouble broke out. They shot a robot and broke out some windows. I-I ran and hid."

John looked frightened. He reached out and Clive put a reassuring arm around him.

Xzardak pressed on. "Tell me about the men, John... the delivery men?" John looked to his father who nodded again.

"Big men in black clothes, gloves, hoods, in a black car; they opened the cargo hold and threw out the cases! That's all I saw, sir!"

"Were you able to see their faces?" questioned Bungo.

"No, Sir!" The boy shook his head resolutely.

"And the vehicle? Black, you say?"

"Yes, sir, black. It was hovering!" the boy said excitedly. "Like a hovercraft!"

"Did it have any markings?" inquired Clive.

"Not at all," answered the boy. "Just shiny and black, like an oblong. Like a brick!"

Clive looked to Xzardak. "Okay, thank you, John." Xzardak stood, and thanking Clive, he patted John on the head. "I'll take you over if you like?" offered Clive. "I'll show you what's left." Xzardak agreed and together, they headed over to the main store.

The streets in the housing compound were all laid out in lines. Well-spaced apart, the dwellings together resembled an average neighbourhood like one on the origin Earth. Xzardak had been keen to make the compound as familiar and homely as possible for its new inhabitants. Maybe that was why half of them believed they were back on Earth, Dr Jay had pondered. "The place resembles something out of one of their terrible soap operas!"

The general store sat by the community hall on the north side of the town centre.

Worker androids had been assigned to run and restock the store; they were responsible for supplying the Earth people with all the food and essentials they required. Clive led them behind the store and Xzardak was surprised to find that the Category D crates were still there, stacked up against the wall. The brickwork was charred and peppered with bullet holes.

That was where Tesk had tested the weapon's authenticity.

"Six cases like the lad said," confirmed Clive.

Xzardak scratched his nose. "All empty?" he said and thought for a moment. "Have you any idea how many weapons each crate contained?"

Clive shook his head. "Not a clue, Xzardak... Tesk was the first man on the scene after John found them, unfortunately. He and the guys were out of here by the time we knew anything about it."

Looking puzzled, Xzardak stared up at the store building. "The cameras," he said to Bungo, pointing to the security system. "They must have a recording?"

"I'm afraid not," said Bungo. "I checked with them right after it happened. Seems someone put all the cameras out of action. This whole side of the compound was taken out by magnetic interference."

"They obviously knew what they were doing," surmised Xzardak.

"And had a diagnostic of our security surveillance system?" added Bungo.

Inside the store, Xzardak approached the main service robot. "Good morning, sir," said the anthropoid bot.

"Good morning, my friend," replied Xzardak. "I need to talk to you about an incident."

"Certainly, sir," interrupted the robot. "But if it is about the container drop, I am afraid there is nothing to tell, other than one of my service team was destroyed."

Bungo stepped forward as the android continued, "As I told your friend, on the morning of the drop, I and the other workers were taken with a terrible sickness. A case of magnetic poisoning, I fear. We were unable to function, let alone perform our duties."

"And this sickness..." asked Xzardak. "When did it come on, exactly?"

"It came on quite suddenly, sir, early rotation and lasted the majority of the day. It took us a while to get the store back and up and running. I do apologise that we were unable to fulfil our duties, sir! We will get everything back in order as soon as we can."

"Don't worry about it," said Xzardak quietly, interrupting before more apologies could come. "I quite understand."

The android bowed respectfully.

"And the damaged worker robot?" enquired Xzardak.

"Completely destroyed," said the robot, sighing. "He was a good friend, and fortunately, we had backed up his personality profile to the mainframe. I'm hoping to resurrect him once a replacement is supplied."

"I will make sure another worker is provided," promised Xzardak. "Should you receive any more information, please would you contact me?"

The robot nodded its head. "Of course, sir!" it diligently chirped and with that, Xzardak, Bungo and Clive departed.

"You analysed the area for tracks and footprints?" asked Xzardak.

"We analysed the entire place," asserted Bungo. "But like the boy said, the craft hovered, and the delivery men did everything they could to disguise their appearances. No traces of skin debris or transit matter from the cargo drop, no evidence of digital depredation or mechanical subversion. Nothing. The entire operation was carried out with scientific precision."

"And the vehicle?"

"Sounds like no transport I have ever encountered," answered Bungo efficiently. "And zero trace of it entering or leaving the compound. Clearly built for stealth."

Xzardak studied the bullet holes in the store wall. "Whoever supplied these weapons meant business."

"They are coalition crates," whispered Bungo. "Wouldn't that suggest they came from…" He paused, unsure if he should even speculate on the obvious explanation.

"I'm sure that there are those within the coalition who would seek to destabilise the program," admitted Xzardak. "But I cannot stand here and allow you to insinuate…" Xzardak also took a pause. "I refuse to believe or imagine that anyone in the coalition would seek to kill or maim the life forms. It contravenes every protocol in the book!" he declared indignantly.

"Well, someone is out to get them, Xzardak, and if they are willing to kill the humans, I'd imagine they would be willing to kill you."

Xzardak was desperate to avoid the notion that it could easily have been himself, Bungo, Mono, or one of the children cut down by the Earth weapons, but there was no way of escaping it. The compound and its inhabitants were in danger, and it was Xzardak's responsibility to protect them. Suddenly, events on Earth 2 had taken a particularly dark turn.

Xzardak nervously looked over his shoulder. "Well, we aren't going to find anything else out here!" he announced and suggested that they hastily collate their findings and take cover back at base. "Short of contacting the coalition, I fear the only person who can help us with this conundrum is Tesk!"

"Good luck with that one!" Clive said. "You're not exactly high on his list of friends."

Bungo diligently took down the details of everyone who remained in the compound and left instruction with the anthropoids to contact him should anything else turn up.

After loading the cases onto the transport and conducting a final sweep of the container drop zone, they made their way back to the command centre.

Bungo sighed. "What now, Xzardak?"

Xzardak shrugged. "Hard to say; the Earth people were in stasis when we brought them in, so they would have had no way of smuggling in contraband. These Category-D crates are coalition storage crates, meaning the coalition must have a part to play."

"Or someone would like us to believe that," suggested Bungo.

"Either way, the Earth people are in the clear as far as I see it!"

"Perhaps this Santa Claus fellow?" offered Bungo.

"If only." Xzardak sighed.

"Do you think Tesk and his crew will survive?" enquired Bungo.

"Of course, they won't!" cried Xzardak. "Which leaves us in a very difficult position. We cannot allow the six escapees to put an end to all of our hard work! The program and the deserving Earth people face a very uncertain future indeed. We need them back, dead or alive."

CHAPTER 19

As Mono had precisely calculated, after a period of six more Earth rotations, the 409 entered the toxic gloom of the planet's airspace. The craft began its descent towards the cold, dark, dead world that once had been called Earth. "Whyever would they want to come back here?" Mono said. "This place lacks atmosphere."

Tesk had just woken and wasn't in any mood for jokes. "Yeah, real funny, Mono," he said.

"Funny?" enquired Mono, bewildered by Tesk's comment. "I'm stating the fact, that I don't know how you'll breathe."

The comment's truth had flown right over Tesk's head.

"We'll be okay," Tesk said. "I lived here for twenty-nine years, never did me any harm. Look at me now. I'm perfectly fine."

Well... Mono's expression was a picture, but he said nothing.

What Mono was asserting was correct. The reality was that the atmosphere could support Tesk and the Earth people but only for a matter of days.

"You do know this is a suicide mission, don't you, Tesk?" said Mono, replaying his technical diagnostic on the video screen. The planet was badly polluted, the murk outside a putrid stew of chemical toxins and radioactive poison. "Yeah, yeah. You've told me that already," observed Tesk, half wishing Mono would put him back to sleep. "Told me a dozen times, in fact."

The crew had been in a state of sleep stasis for the majority of the journey. The consignment of fuel and supplies had been received without incident and with the Earthlings asleep, any chances of cross-contamination had been eliminated.

"Not cool!" screamed Alice on waking.

"You gave me no other option!" asserted Mono. "You would have interfered with the ground crew!"

"You roofied us, man!" wheezed Douglas. "Not cool at all!"

"It was for the good of the mission," stated Mono calmly. "A condition set by the ground operator, and the only way anyone would come near to the craft."

"The guys are damned right!" hollered Tesk, slamming his fist on the console. "That's not cool, buddy!"

Mono rolled his eyes.

"How did you do it anyway?" enquired Tesk with a devilish curiosity.

"A mild sedative added to the water supply," purred Mono cheerfully. "Not at all dangerous, and you were sleeping like babies! Xzardak ordered the solution, to help him overcome anxiety."

"Anxiety!" barked Tesk. "What's he got to be anxious about?"

"He's been having trouble sleeping. Xzardak instructed me to procure the mixture after your episode the other day. I was on my way to deliver the medicine when you hi-jacked… I mean, *borrowed* the craft."

"Why, you sneaky…!" Tesk was mad but this far out into space, it seemed crazy to start messing with the pilot. "Well… I can't say I blame you." He shrugged, quietly impressed by the inventive little fellow's show of initiative. He closed his eyes and reclined into his chair. The journey had Tesk beat and with his weapons confiscated, he wasn't in the mood to argue.

"It would appear we are here!' announced Mono gleefully.

As they slowed and descended into the miasma of fumes and smoke, the view port crackled and Xzardak appeared on screen.

"Xzardak!" cried Mono. "Thank goodness you are safe!"

"Yes, my friend!" answered Xzardak. "But for how long I cannot say."

"Where've you been, Xzardak?" Tesk asked. "You missed the party!"

"I've been having a party of my very own!" replied Xzardak without missing a beat. "I hear you've found yourself alternative accommodation."

"Yeah," Tesk said. "Nothing personal, just missed the comfort of home."

Despite the potential consequences of the Earth people's escape, Xzardak didn't blame them for wanting to return home. He too missed his family and home planet but took solace that one day, they'd be there for him when he returned, a privilege not afforded to the Earth visitors.

"I get it, Tesk, but you must understand me… we took you from the Earth for a reason."

"Yeah, I understand," said Tesk. "But don't worry about us… we'll be just fine!"

"Armed and dangerous they told me!" remarked Xzardak, shaking his head.

"C'mon, Xzardak." Tesk smiled. "You know us… we may be armed, but we ain't dangerous, are we fellas?" He motioned to the crew who let out a rousing and disparaging protestation.

"The weapons, Tesk, where did you get them? You know that weapons are prohibited within the civilised realm?"

"We ain't in the civilised realm anymore, buddy! Haven't you heard it's always open season on Earth 1?"

"For the good of your fellow humans and the program," pleaded Xzardak, "you must try and help us. Have you any idea how they arrived at the compound?"

"We've been through this with Bungo!" huffed Tesk. "I was just passing by and saw the kids playing with them. I thought they were toys at first. Hell, they could have killed someone. I took that robot right off his feet!" He chuckled. "Primed and loaded. That's all I know, big guy!"

"The cases you told Bungo about… Have you any idea what Category D might be?"

"Like I said, spaceman, we didn't steal them, someone gifted them to us. Check the cameras, man. I know you guys are filming us all the time. Maybe there's something on there?"

Xzardak was drawing a blank, but Tesk appeared to be telling the truth, his story matching that of Clive and the anthropoids in the general store.

"C'mon, man!" interjected Douglas who was eager to hit the road. "Are we going or not? We're dying of boredom over here."

Clearly, the Earth people had had enough of Xzardak's company.

Unable to make any headway, Xzardak's tone changed. He was weary and feared that if he aggravated the Earth people any further, they may cause damage to Mono or the ship. "You are free to go, Tesk. Somehow, I will sort this with the coalition but you must return my Mono to me. The craft and pilot are not part of the deal!"

"I read you, good buddy!" called Tesk. "We just needed someone to drive the getaway car. The ship will be headed right back at ya. We ain't planning on any more space adventures!"

"And you promise me you don't know anything else about the weapons?" Xzardak was exasperated but pressed one last time.

"Not a thing, Boss Hogg! Honest!" Tesk grinned, putting his hands up as if in submission.

Excited to be home, the whole crew assembled in the cockpit. An adrenaline rush had them up on their feet, groggy from the journey, but ready to face whatever the world had in store.

"What happens now, Xzardak?" asked Mono.

"There's nothing more we can do... let them go, Mono." Xzardak sighed. "Please take care out there," he said to Tesk. "I'm afraid to say it but you know you'll be dead in a matter of days?"

"Thing is, Xzardak, I've never felt so alive!" Tesk cackled.

As the intel signal began to break up, Mono gently guided the craft down into a clearing. Once on the ground, he initiated the ramp, and the doors slowly opened.

"One last thing, Tesk!" crackled Xzardak. "Mono has a call sensor. I'm going to get him to do two orbits. If you change your mind, activate it and he will bring you back."

Mono silently groaned; he'd had a feeling that something like this might happen.

"Won't need it, Xzardak, it'll be fine!" And with that, the video feed signal ominously cut.

"Aw, he's gone!" whined Tesk. "And I never got a chance to thank him!" He laughed.

The Earth people gathered their meagre possessions and following protocol, Mono reluctantly released the lock on the silo containing the weapons. "For self-defence only!" he huffed. Once fully armed, they slowly filed out. Staring into the darkness, Nelson, the last of the crew to disembark, looked over to Mono. Checking that Tesk wasn't watching, he reached out his hand, taking the call sensor from the robot and slipping it unseen into his pocket.

"Honey, we're home!" hollered Tesk with a snicker as he walked down the ramp, the chuckle becoming a cough as his feet hit solid ground. "Phew, what a stink!" He wheezed, taking in a lung full of the putrid sulphurised air. "This place has gone to hell!"

"The old town isn't looking too pretty," Tesk said, sniffing the air as he made his way along the boulevard, the other humans skulking behind him.

"What is that smell?" Chrissy gasped, shielding her mouth and nose with the sleeve of her jacket. "On second thoughts, maybe don't answer that!" She wheezed, closing her eyes as Alice took her by the arm.

Per Tesk's instruction, Mono had dropped them right back at the place he knew best—his hometown. Douglas sidled up to him. "Are you sure this was such a good idea, Tesk? I mean this district is pretty beat up! Are we sure we want to live here?"

Tesk stopped and turned. "Well, it sure beats that carnival we were holed up in. I told you… I'm not going to be a guinea pig in someone's science experiment. We're home now, we just need to fix the place up a little, that's all! We've got the whole zone to ourselves."

It was obvious to everyone that the neighbourhood was uninhabitable. Tesk wasn't sure how long he'd been away but the place had deteriorated dramatically and much worse than he had remembered it. "Listen up, you guys," he blustered. "This place is kinda messed up but it's no big deal. We just need to find a clean patch, up a mountain or something!"

"Hey, Tesk, how're we gonna find a mountain in this smog?" cried Joey. "You should have gotten the little guy to drop us somewhere nice! Why did you get him to drop us off in this dump? Look at it! It's disgusting, Tesk."

Tesk squared up. "Hey, buddy, this is my hometown. Just be careful what you say about the old place!" he growled. "If you don't like it, I'll get the little guy to drop you back with the other zoo animals!"

Douglas looked to Joey and motioned that he should simmer down. "The situation is bad enough," he said diplomatically. "We don't need any more aggravation!"

Joey stood his ground.

CHAPTER 19

"Let's find somewhere to crash," said Tesk nonchalantly. "Get some rest and in the morning, we'll go about putting it all back together!" Douglas motioned to a flickering light on the dashboard of a broken-down truck. 9:13 a.m. read the digital display on the dash. "According to this, looks like it's morning already, Tesk?"

Tesk shrugged. "The clock's wrong, so what?"

A cold breeze whistled through the burned-out buildings and Alice's eyes started to itch. As the wind gained in strength, the crew found themselves engulfed in a swirling tornado of litter and debris. Eventually finding a neglected house which looked just about habitable, Tesk kicked the door off its hinges and once inside, they began to build a shelter.

"Bunker World," Douglas said. "That's the only way we're gonna make it."

Tesk nodded and waved his hand. "Sure, Bunker World. Leave it with me. I've got it all worked out."

The next morning, to Tesk's surprise, the sun didn't come up.

The sky was still as black as night, only without any sign of the moon, stars or satellites which had filled the firmament for millions of years previously. After a listless, haunted, sleepless night, the Earth people felt nauseous, coughing and choking for air.

"We're in trouble!" gasped Alice. "C'mon, Tesk, admit it!" But Tesk would not be told.

Douglas stood. "I knew this was a bad idea! What were you thinking bringing us back here?"

"Just give me some time," insisted Tesk, raising his rifle.

The humans gathered their things and made their way out into the formless, lifeless landscape. The weather had changed. Initially, there had been an eerie stillness in the airless atmosphere, but now the wind was blowing again, hard and fast, and the reality of the situation was beginning to dawn on them. Tesk had developed a bad cough and in front of the group, he was bent over, trying desperately to catch his breath. "Damned cigarettes," he barked, attempting to look cool whilst trying not to choke.

"What happened here?" sobbed Chrissy. "It was never this bad."

Chemical agents in the atmosphere and a number of meteorological factors had been responsible for the state of the environment. It would be difficult to pinpoint one exact event which began the chain reaction, but once in motion, the conditions on Earth had deteriorated rather quickly. The nuclear wind had been responsible for the majority of the damage, cars tipped over, trees uprooted, the entire landscape turned inside out.

A few remaining buildings were left standing amongst charred ruins. Fortunately, the Earth people could only see twenty feet in front of them, the methane smog shielding them from witnessing the true devastation.

Tesk's coughing fit had subsided. "Damned neutron bombs," he cussed.

"Where do we start?" asked Joey.

Tesk pointed down to the ground. "Follow me," he said with a smile. "I have an idea."

The group found it easy to commandeer a vehicle as most traditional forms of transportation had been abandoned. Once the energy had run out, vehicles had become worthless and routinely been ditched. Douglas turned the key in the ignition. Nothing happened.

"It's dead, Tesk," he grumbled.

"Try it again."

"It's kaput!" insisted Douglas. "Must have seized."

"Damned truck!" Tesk huffed. "We'll find another."

"What's the point?" cried Alice. "You know they're all out of gas!"

Tesk scratched his head. Finding a truck had been the cornerstone to his great plan but without fuel, it was obvious they were going nowhere.

"Looks like we're running out of options," offered Douglas.

"We're almost out of water too," Alice added.

Tesk was beginning to lose his temper again, and his cough had returned. "We need to get underground!" he said before retching.

"No!" countered Alice, rubbing her red eyes. "It's over, Tesk!"

His body contorting, his eyes bulging, the burning sensation in his throat had brought Tesk to his knees. He appeared to reluctantly nod his head. The rancorous piercing wind was building again and as they headed back to the shelter, it was evident that they had made a terrible mistake. All hope was lost on planet Earth.

Once back at their makeshift headquarters, only Douglas and Alice were able to function coherently. The other humans in the group had succumbed to the fallout. Their eyes and noses were streaming, great welts appearing underneath their skin, beginning to bubble and peel.

Lying shivering in the festering gloom, Douglas thought about sending out a prayer. He pondered for a moment before deciding against it. It was clear no deity was listening that day. He glanced over to see Alice tending to Nelson, whose eyes were closing.

The air was heavy and foul and without oxygen in his system, he too slipped under, resentfully surrendering to the overwhelming feeling of helplessness.

Suddenly bathed in light, Douglas was roused from the darkness. The searing glow burned his eyeballs, but he hadn't the energy to sit forward.

"You see," Tesk croaked. "The sun is coming out." Delirious from the poison, his mind and body were shutting down for good.

~✧~

Mono had been quite happy on board the craft, joyfully watching as the time ticked away. Now as his final orbit was coming to an end, he felt confident that he had seen the last of those particular Earth people.

Reclining into Xzardak's easy chair, it occurred to him that he should ask for more leisure time. He liked being busy, but for some reason, he had recently acquired a taste for lounging about. In the pit, he was listening to some sounds emanating from the viewport monitor. To the unenlightened Earth people, these disjointed reverberations had made no sense, but to Mono it was the most soothing and captivating soundscape he had ever heard. As the 'music' lifted in tone and rhythm, Mono reclined further, at peace with the universe.

It wasn't all bad. Soon, he would be going home to Xzardak and his friends.

It was just as the music teased its crescendo that the safety beacon sounded a shrill echoing note, completely destroying the tranquillity of Mono's meditation.

Suddenly brought back to reality, his worst fears had been realised.

The Earth people were signalling for help. With a sigh, Mono dutifully put the craft into motion, obediently ignoring his life-preservation cell, which was beseeching him to turn off the beacon and head home.

Unhappy with the outcome of the evening, Mono lowered the ship not far from the spot where he had dropped the Earth people. "I thought we had said goodbye?" joked Mono, but as the destitute and broken Earth people reappeared, it was clear that nobody was laughing.

Once they were on board, Mono thought it prudent to furnish the humans with oxygen, nutrients and sickness medicine. As they settled, he got back into the pit. "Okay, homeward bound!" he announced gleefully in an attempt to rouse the spirits of the poor lost souls. The outcome of the Earth mission had been inevitable, but he had resisted the urge to sound condescending, superior or smug. He kicked the ship into gear. "Not so fast, Bobo," Tesk croaked, the sickness medicine beginning to satiate his system. "One last thing..."

CHAPTER 20

Xzardak was automatically alerted once the retrieval beacon had been activated. He had fully expected to hear the distress signal earlier and was quietly impressed that the Earth people had lasted for so long in the decaying gloom. The craft had signalled its descent and now, Xzardak awaited a progress report from Mono.

Time was passing slowly and Xzardak was beginning to wonder what was going on. He had tried to signal to Mono, but the craft was not responding. Dense chemical smoke had engulfed the Earth's atmosphere and sealed the ether like a crust, making contact with the 409 almost impossible. Xzardak would have to wait it out. Unhappy and frustrated without any form of intel, he radioed to speak to Bungo, who was attending to his duties inside the hangar bay.

Onboard the 409, the Earth people were beginning to feel a lot better. Still armed, Tesk had gotten to his feet. It occurred to Mono that he should have confiscated the Earth peoples' weapons when rescuing them. Technically, the guns were not banned on planet Earth and being such a stickler for protocol, Mono had seen no reason to withhold the death machines, especially as they were certain to meet their demise quite soon. This had been a foolish judgemental error on Mono's part, one which he was coming to regret.

He winced as Tesk lifted his rifle and pointed it at the small robot's head. Mono could sense that Tesk's adrenaline levels were running at an all-time high. Although Tesk was on the verge of collapse, something was powering him beyond his physical weakness. "You knew that was going to happen, didn't you, Bobo? You knew we could never survive?"

"Knew that you couldn't survive?" gulped Mono, the self-preservation cell whirring into life once more. "Yes, of course, I knew. You were warned. I gave you the full technical analysis on several occasions."

Mono was secure in the knowledge that he had followed protocol to the letter.

"Well, you were right," Tesk said, "and that has made me angry. So, you better make sure you help us, otherwise I'm going to put you outside. See how *you* like it out in the cold."

Mono thought better of informing Tesk that he could probably survive outside in the cold for quite a while. He also considered reminding Tesk who was flying the spacecraft but decided it was probably best not to annoy him any further.

"I'm here to help you, Tesk, don't you understand?" asserted Mono. "Xzardak has instructed me to assist you as best as I can! Just tell me what you want."

Tesk snarled. "There's an underground base 'round here, and I need you to locate it. Then I need you to take us there." Mono found himself going along with the plan just for the sake of self-preservation but thought it bizarre that the Earth people still would not see sense and abandon their mission.

He immediately ran a search for sub-level activity. It wasn't something that had been considered when the initial salvage operation had taken place. The human beings were considered surface dwellers as the vast majority of their conurbations reached up into the sky. He scanned for activity with a twenty-kilometre radius. "There has been zero activity in this region for a very long time," Mono said. "The last planet scan undertaken was on the final day of the savage mission. Nothing new shows up beyond that. Currently, I cannot find any activity, or sign of sentient life."

Tesk decided it was best if he sat down. He was uneasy on his feet and his lungs still burned. "Well, you better find something, tin man." He pointed the gun at Mono. "Or else, you're going outside." It was going to be an exceptionally long night.

"Tesk, it would help if I knew what I was looking for!" huffed Mono with an irritated tone. Tesk carefully eyed the video feed from the craft's external surveillance camera.

"Just keep cruising," he replied, concentrating all of his efforts on finding the base.

"We've been cruising for quite some time; please could you remind me of what it is you are hoping to find?" Mono was losing the will to live. Tesk said nothing.

Douglas stood and walked over to the console. "It's a rabbit hole," he said. "When we were kids and things began to go bad, it's where we used to come."

Mono consulted the data cell for the phrase 'rabbit hole.' However, the answer it returned was as unenlightening as Tesk's silence.

"People started dying. There was a reactor leak after the war and the place was a mess. Tesk's father was a military man and he told Tesk that this was where the city bigwigs and generals would come once it got real bad."

"Bigwigs?" enquired Mono.

"Powerful people!" Tesk snapped, becoming agitated at Mono's incessant yearning for clarity and logic. "Just drive the damn craft, Mono!" he shouted. "My daddy told me where it was located. We used to come down here all the time; we just need to find the entrance, that's all!"

"Thing is," said Alice from the back of the cockpit, "not everyone believes that story…"

"Are you calling my daddy a liar?" growled Tesk, turning slowly to see Alice lazily reclining across two cabin seats.

"Hey, take it down you guys," whispered Chrissy. "All she's saying is…" She paused, selecting her words carefully so as not to inflame the situation further. "A lot of folks reckoned those stories were conspiracy theories."

Tesk turned back to the monitor.

Chrissy had always had a gift for calming Tesk down. "There ain't no such thing as conspiracy theories when rich people are involved," he said and took a breath, his body still broken from his time outside of the vessel. "Just keep cruising. Mono, my daddy used to bring me here for shooting practice. We used to watch the military convoys bringing supplies to the base. It's been a while, but I know it's around here some-damn-where!"

The craft was on autopilot, cruising at around ninety feet above ground level for some time. Mono was considering a power down when an idea pulsated through his thought processor. Instigating the intel procedure, he began to compose a message to the only person he could think of who would be able—and willing—to help them.

When setting up the program, Xzardak's close friend, Dr Jay, had been an invaluable ally. Jay's input and guidance had helped them overcome many of the obstacles that had arisen during the creation of the compound. Fearing that Jay may be too close to the coalition and not wanting to create suspicion or compromise the good doctor's reputation, Mono thought better of communicating with him directly. However, his student and protege Rhodar had helped Xzardak gain access to the higher information levels at the grand directory. Mono wondered if she might be able to help out again. Knowing that it would be classed as collusion if it was discovered that she had been involved in a plan to help the Earth people escape, Mono drafted an intel, wording it carefully so as not to incriminate himself or the young librarian.

Mono silently read back his intel while the earth people bickered and argued about a mysterious secret underground base that might or might not exist. The Earth people could always be relied on to find a topic for an argument.

"Best to keep it light," Mono said to himself, devising the intel.

Good day, Rhodar,

Your help and guidance have been invaluable throughout the implementation of the Earth 2 Project. May I begin by thanking you again for your patience, diligence, and hard work.

I come to you to ask for advice. I have been handed an enquiry pertaining to the history of the original Earth planet. Unfortunately, I am coming up blank when searching through the research information at my disposal.

The subject in discussion is the existence of an underground military shelter located around the coordinates I have included. It is understood that the base was created to house humans should conditions became unliveable above ground for any reason.

It has been suggested that this base, and many structures like it, were built to house the powerful and the good once civilization began to crumble in the closing years of the origin Earth's lifespan. I have no further information and fear that the reports may be rumour and/or speculation. I realise that your talents are in high demand but would be grateful for any information should you get a moment to respond.

Mono scanned it a second time. "That should do it," he said enthusiastically, transmitting the question to the receiver at the library. "Hopefully, the dispatch will get through the smog!"

The craft continued to cruise for another hour as the Earth crew silently slept. All except Tesk whose eagle eyes still surveyed the camera feed. "Surely you must be able to do something?" he said, then cussed. "Ain't you robots supposed to be able to scan and analyse stuff? There must be something in that digital brain of yours that can help us?"

Mono powered up out of his semi-standby state.

"I can analyse data should it be at my disposal. I can monitor information, predict verdicts, outcomes, results and consequences. I can repair almost anything given a manual, I can even figure out the best course of action given the working conditions and parameters in which one finds oneself. But I'm afraid mysteries are beyond me."

Tesk said, "Well, maybe we need a better robot. What robot can we get to figure out a mystery?"

Mono paused a second. "Perhaps a mystery solving robot?" he replied, hoping to close down the conversation.

"Is there such a thing?" Tesk's eyes widened.

"Of course, there isn't such a thing!" Mono sighed, his frustration beginning to show.

Tesk laughed. "Ha-ha, good one little guy! You had me there."

"If there were such a thing, perhaps we could ask it to figure out why you're so hellbent on destroying yourselves?"

Tesk shrugged. "You don't get it do you, scrap-pile? See, everyone has a home, and this is *my* home, even if it is a burned-up rock. Everyone belongs somewhere and I belong here."

Mono consulted his data cell. "Where do I belong?" The cell was unable to provide an answer. Mono rolled his eyes. "I have dispatched an intel," he offered. "I am hoping to have some information for you very soon."

"Well, best keep cruising 'til your source comes through." Tesk rattled out a cough.

Within moments, Mono was alerted to an incoming intel. "It seems we have had a reply," he happily notified Tesk.

"Great news, trash can. Whaddit say?"

The intel flashed up on the videoscope.

Greetings Mono!

Unable to find any information on hidden military bases in that vicinity, have had my data-drones scan the entire archive. The information I have on classified military compounds and pre-existing era world war bunkers will follow. Nothing, however, about subterranean activity at the time of the intervention.

A lot of the archive appears to have been reclassified at Category D, but we will keep digging. I regret to inform you that Rhodar is no longer with us as she has been missing for some time. We are hopeful that her whereabouts will be discovered, and she will make contact soon. Sorry, that I am unable to help you.

LCLP assistant librarian.

Mono thought for a second, his concern for Rhodar greater than for the Earth man's fantastical base. "Disappeared... Category D? Very strange," he said quietly, wishing that he had access to one of these mythical, mystery solving robot units. "I'm afraid my contact was unable to provide any information. Tesk, it seems that this base you are looking for simply does not exist." Tesk said nothing deep inside his dolour, his eyes fixed on the screen.

Ahead of the craft, Mono spotted something. "Perhaps you should look at this, Tesk," he said, hoping for a breakthrough.

"What is it?" said Tesk, craning his neck to see.

"A turbine, by the look of it. Two in fact!" Tesk squinted, trying to make sense of the fuzzy images before him.

"Twin turbines!" he shouted. "That's it! I knew we'd find it!" Tesk's mood suddenly lifted.

Mono felt the craft gently ascend as it rose to avoid the tops of some burned-up trees, the husks still standing tall against the broken landscape.

Suddenly, Tesk leaned forward. "There!" he said. "That car pile-up, take us there, Mono. Twin turbines!" he declared as if remembering a secret. "I knew it was around here!"

Lowering the craft, Mono wondered what he was looking at since all he could see was bent and distorted metal. As the craft descended, the search light beam illuminated the wreckage and Mono could see clearly. Signs of violence, broken glass, contorted bodies, burned, and melted vehicles. The craft's atmospheric analysis sensor detected traces of military grade plutonium.

It was apparent that something awful had taken place here.

"Take her down," ordered Tesk.

"But it's not safe, Tesk," insisted Mono. "It's unsafe for you and the craft. My sensors detect high temperatures and radiation fallout. I will not damage the ship or its external instruments. The craft is our only way out of this hellhole!"

But Tesk would not be convinced as in his heart, he didn't want out of the hellhole; he wanted to stay. He wanted life to go back to normal, back to how they had promised. Back to how it had been before the wars, the pollution, and the final meltdown. This was Tesk's last shot, if only he could make it underground, he could maybe set up a life.

"I'm not too interested in the craft," he screamed. "Just put her down!" He reached for the assault rifle. Against Mono's better judgement, he did as Tesk requested, finding a clearing amongst the dead bodies, twisted metal and punctured uranium shells.

Nothing would stop him; Tesk wanted out. The ship hovered a few feet from the ground, but Mono was unable to touch down. "The craft won't land, Tesk. It has a preservation device. If you want out, I'm afraid you will have to jump!" called Mono.

But Tesk was already gone, followed immediately by his obedient death cult disciples. The hatch had automatically opened to allow the Earth people to disembark, then quickly closed to reseal the craft from the toxic air outside.

Once the Earth people were out, Mono surveyed the craft's instruments and decided it was time to go. He instigated an evacuation procedure and the craft zoomed up into the murky ether.

Climbing high above the torched trees, the craft sped away from the madness and the crazed Earth people.

"How could this have happened?" Mono said, surveying the debris beneath him. "What kind of creatures are they?" Mono had set the ship's surveillance system to capture the scenes that he was witnessing, planning to save the information for the good of the civilised realm.

He would be sure to give the footage to Rhodar for the Earth archive once she had reappeared. This time, he was leaving. The Earth people had made their decision, and nothing would make him return. He would face the consequences of his actions back at base, once he was home. "A billion Earth miles from here!" he said with a despairing and deliberate tone.

CHAPTER 21

On the ground, the Earth people were once again struggling with the poisonous air. This time, however, they had been prudent enough to bring along the breathing apparatus supplied in the provision drop. For a second time, the radioactive wind burned their skin and eyes, yet they stumbled forward, dutifully following Tesk on another ill-conceived mission.

"I told you there was a base!" he called excitedly, undeterred by the wretched conditions.

"You're crazy!" replied Douglas. "Even if there is a base, they won't let the likes of us near it!" Tesk shrugged. "Gotta be worth a try. We're running out of options, man! Besides, what's the worst that can happen?" Douglas surveyed the carnage surrounding them.

It seemed the news of a secret underground military bunker must have gotten out.

"I don't wanna end up fried like these dumb fools!" he said and wheezed, the stench of the rotten bodies masking the vile stink of the putrid sulphur air.

Through the smoke and gloom, in the distance, the crew could just about make out the shape of a building. Surrounded by a tall perimeter wall, it was flanked by two defunct and broken-down wind turbines. "Ha-ha!" Tesk shouted. "There she is!"

"And you think they're gonna let us just waltz straight in there?" Alice said. "Look at that wall. This ain't gonna work!"

"Everyone, just keep walking!" hollered Tesk, issuing the instruction in military fashion, sounding a lot like his father.

"Stay alert!" called Joey. "If this is the base, there'll be snipers up in those towers! Probably got thermal night sights too!" he exclaimed.

"Marine grade snipers, I'd say… that would explain why there's so many dead," stuttered Nelson nervously.

"Mown down by the rich and the powerful," Alice said. "Uncaring freaks!"

Tesk frowned, looking up and around them, surveying the high turbine gantries for munitions and military personnel. His paranoia levels were running almost as high as his hopes. "I ain't gonna lie, this is gonna be tough," he said. "Like Alice said, they ain't gonna let us just waltz straight in there! And right now, I ain't got a contingency plan."

"Whatever's in there must be worth protecting," Joey remarked. "Looks like a war zone out here!"

"I ain't interested in what's out here!" Tesk said. "I wanna see what's going on over that wall!"

Trying to make their presence a little less evident, they bobbed down, eager to conceal themselves from the eye of any sharpshooting, trigger-happy sentry guard.

"We gotta take them by surprise, Tesk! What's left of them," whispered Nelson. "Hit them hard and fast before they even know what's going on!" But Tesk did not respond. His mind was racing. Their walk to the military base thus far had been unhindered, and something just didn't sit right. He stood for a moment, surveying the battlefield.

"Can you feel that?' whispered Alice to Chrissy.

"Feel what, honey?" she replied.

"There's a feeling in the air…" She shivered. "Like there's nothing here, just empty space, silence… It's all gone."

"Don't overthink it, ladies. Just keep walking," bleated Douglas, repeating Tesk's instruction, this time not as an order but as a piece of friendly advice.

Alice rolled her eyes. "If he calls us ladies one more time..." She gritted her teeth. "I'll be doing some military grade sniping!"

"We don't have a choice." Tesk wheezed. "It's the only way we're gonna make it." He wiped his stinging eyes and undeterred by the consequences, pressed on ahead.

Sidestepping the unfortunates, they ducked and weaved through the wreckage until eventually finding themselves at what appeared to be the main gate.

"What now, Tesk?" Tesk sarcastically pre-empted Douglas's catchphrase.

Douglas did not twig and nor did he disappoint, delivering his familiar line. "Yeah, what now, Tesk?" With a crooked grin, Tesk opened his jacket to reveal a string of six grenades.

"Marine issue." He chuckled. "You're gonna detonate a couple as a diversion, attract their attention, and draw their fire! Then me and the crew will bust in!"

Douglas couldn't help but feel that he'd drawn the short straw. Just like Xzardak's spacecraft, he too had a pretty sensitive sense of self-preservation and the "Draw their fire!" part of the deal just didn't sit right with him. He screwed up his face and scratched his head but fearing a bullet in the brain from his illustrious leader, he decided it best to adhere to Tesk's instruction.

"Uh, better the devil than the deep blue sea," he wistfully grumbled under his breath as Tesk handed him two of the grenades and wished him good luck.

Douglas wiped his brow and set off, dutifully ducking and diving, dodging through the vehicle graveyard. Once out of sight of the crew, he pulled out the pin on each grenade and pitched them as hard and fast as he could.

He watched as they sailed high into the air. "Three hundred feet easily!" he cried excitedly, beating his old high school baseball record. "What a play!" he goofed. "He got him!"

On making contact with the ground at the far side of the compound, the grenades exploded within a few seconds of each other, their detonation providing blasts loud enough to make the entire derelict junkyard shudder and vibrate. The enormous sound echoed across the battlefield, gleefully puncturing the terrible silence which had befallen the dead planet.

"Yee-haw!" screamed Douglas as he raced from the explosion, his heart pounding, his ears ringing from the blasts. He crossed his fingers as he sprinted back toward Tesk and the crew, desperately hoping that they had managed to take out the snipers and breach the base perimeter.

On hearing the blast, Tesk's own survival instincts had kicked in, and he cowered in the darkness, his eyes closed tightly shut. Anticipating return fire, he hunkered down, motioning to the crew to fall back and await the first rounds of discharge. If they could establish where the snipers were set, they would have a chance to take each one out.

The blasts reverberated across the military base, but no gun fire sounded. No bird made a cry, and no voices could be heard, just the loud rumble of grenade explosions, echoing into eternity.

Tesk's heart was pounding. Unable to breathe, he desperately scanned the battlefield for clues. The derelict towers with their walkways and gantries, the soaring turbines with their busted-up rotor blades, the blackened walls and broken out windows. His eyes went darting from side to side, scrutinising every possible vantage point. But no round of fire came about.

"Stay down!" he instructed his soldiers. "They ain't going for it!"

Then, sensing movement from behind him, instinctually he spun around, quickly aiming the gun in the direction of footsteps.

It was Alice. She had stood from behind her barricade, walking casually towards the compound gate. Tesk began to panic, sensing Alice must have gone crazy! He had heard how many formerly stable men had lost their minds on the battlefield.

Was she really going to give herself up?

"Are you nuts, Alice!" he cried. "They'll tear you apart! You'll give away our location!"

But Alice did not respond, seemingly catatonic. She walked out into the clearing, stopped and shot her assault rifle into the air. Letting off an entire clip, she turned back to face Tesk.

Taking off her breathing mask, she shook her head. "Don't you understand, honey?" she said and started to wheeze, "Tesk, they're all gone!"

But Tesk didn't buy it. He backed up and ducked behind a charred paddy wagon, diverting his eyes as Alice let off another round of fire. He couldn't bear to see her mown down in front of him. There had been a moment in his life when he'd thought he and she might connect but there hadn't been time for complicated human relationships in their modern world.

Survival was all that mattered, and relationships would have to wait until the good times came around again. If they ever did.

She let out a scream, then a whistle. However, there was no hail of bullets, no reprisal of gunfire, no searchlight or siren. Nothing, just silence and as the reverberation of the grenade blast finally subsided, she dropped to her knees and began to gently sob.

Chrissy was the next to stand up, and she too let off a round of fire, the bullets ricocheting off the compound sign. "Have you read this?" she shouted over. "Twin turbines military facility. Private property. Visitors not permitted. *Danger of death!*"

Chrissy read from the sign, emphasising the bottom line.

She let off another round of fire, peppering even the sign with bullet holes.

"They ain't coming, Tesk!" howled Alice. "It's over!"

Standing, Tesk pushed past Nelson, Joey and the two women, standing out in the open. His heart was racing, expecting at any moment to experience the ringing of gunshots and the sensation of bullets tearing the flesh from his bones. But nothing came.

Angry and afraid, he walked up to the main entrance. "We're gonna need something to get these gates open!" he shouted back to Joey. However, Alice again was one step ahead. She gently pushed at the broken barrier and the gate swung open with an ominous creak.

"Lighter than air!" she said with a smile, inviting them in.

Suddenly, from out of the darkness, Douglas appeared. "Did you get 'em, guys? Are they dead? I heard the gunfight!"

"There's nobody here, you dummy!" snarled Tesk, more than a little embarrassed that Alice and Chrissy had gotten the better of him.

They wandered into the compound, the carnage on the inside way worse than that on the outside. Bent-up cadavers littered the pathway, burnt out jeeps and commandeered tanks driven into walls and across fences. Ripped up trees, the ground and walls were all scorched with a crust of thick black soot. Reapplying the breathing mask, Tesk led the way, his eyes itching, the chemical air burning his skin.

"They're just kids…" whispered Chrissy. "Just babies." She pointed to the contorted bodies of burnt-up service men strewn before them.

"An army of kids against the rest of us," Tesk said. "Don't pay it any mind. We were at war."

As they silently proceeded into the military base, Tesk almost jumped out of his skin as the main doors automatically sprang open in front of them. "Looks like they have power at least?" Nelson shrugged as the doors violently whooshed closed behind them.

"Just watch out for booby traps!" warned Joey with a nervous grin. "Booby traps and land mines!"

"Shut up, Joey," Alice called out.

In front of them stood a row of security checkpoint booths and at the far end, Nelson noticed a single guard, still sitting, hunched over at his station. They walked along the line of the broken checkpoints to see the young man, slumped uncomfortably, still gripping his pistol.

The shattered glass booth looked as though it had been punctured by a bullet hole and flickering on and off behind the boy, an illuminated sign sparked and fizzed.

'Personnel Identity Cards Must Be Presented.'

"Aw shucks, I forgot my ID!" joked Tesk flatly as he elbowed out the remaining shards of broken glass and pilfered the security guard's anti-blast sunglasses and handgun. Waltzing across the reception area, the trespassers wandered in unmolested. Then down a narrow corridor, they began to piece together what must have happened. "Man, what a party. They stormed the place!" Douglas said, taking in the destruction before him. "Everyone's dead."

The base was littered with casualties, both military and civilian, the walls splattered with blood and gore, pock marked and scorched, daubed with graffiti beseeching them to turn back.

GO AWAY! had been written in large red letters, and AMBUSHED AND AVENGED! apparently scrawled in blood. The words UNHUMAN and TRAITORS! lay scribbled on a broken door hanging off its hinges. Stepping over more lifeless bodies, shattered glass crunched beneath their feet, the corridor flooded with putrid ankle-high water.

The farther they entered into the building, the darker and colder it became. The sun outside, long since obliterated, was giving the entire planet a cold damp chill. The only light to guide them now was that of a low-powered, fluorescent, emergency lighting rig, which had triggered when they'd entered the front entrance.

"They're all dead," repeated Chrissy, surveying the evidence of the massacre. "The graffiti... I don't like this, it's time to go!" she insisted.

"No!" Tesk shouted, his word echoing around and around inside the airless corridor. "Hold the line!" he said, unwilling to accept that the mission may prove worthless. "I want to see more," he added, insisting that they push forward.

A strange determination and energy were brewing in him.

But Alice had seen enough. "We're heading back!" she cried angrily, turning to leave, resigned to the fact that nothing good lay in the shadows at the end of the dimly lit corridor.

"She's right, Tesk," Joey agreed. "This place is giving me the creeps! The heebie-jeebies!"

Tesk had become agitated too—by their reluctance and negativity. "Then go!" he screamed, angered by his mutinous crew and their lack of faith and good judgement. As they turned, neither he nor Douglas tried to prevent them from leaving, and when all was said and done, it would be their loss. The two women, along with Joey and Nelson, fell back, but undeterred Tesk and Douglas plodded on, heading farther out into the stagnant murky black water.

"I just want to see it with my own eyes," said Tesk. "I just need to see the bunker."

After a while, Douglas pointed at something. The corridor light flickered and dimmed but at the far end of the passageway, there appeared to be a service lift. The two men picked up pace, carefully and respectfully side-stepping the dead bodies bobbing in the shallow water.

As they reached the rusted-up doors, it was clear that the elevator had not been operational for some time. Tesk nervously pressed the call button and after an expectant minute, he was amazed to hear a whirring as the lift car slowly ascended towards them.

"Well, they have power down there!" he said optimistically, quietly hoping that something salvageable might still exist. Douglas gave Tesk a long look as the elevator car arrived, reluctant to enter the corroded cage, unconvinced that it would support his weight.

Uncertain whether Tesk was serious about boarding it or not, he motioned for him to go inside ahead. "No, after you…" insisted Tesk, his errant good manners finally making an appearance. Douglas carefully stepped into the lift, testing the corrugated base first with a cautious foot. Once inside, he lightly jumped up and down.

"Seems safe, boss," he reported obediently.

Tesk stepped in after him, and studying the console panel, he took a breath. "Going down!" he hollered. Tesk pushed the button, and the lift slowly descended. It seemed there were only two stops available, either the floor at which they had boarded or the floor to which they were destined. The elevator moved slowly. "We're going deep!" Tesk said.

"Might as well" joked Douglas. "We're already in over our heads."

"Aren't we always?"

Tesk needed to see but had no idea what to expect. In his mind, he had been imagining a deluxe modern utopia. The Promised Land, a hidden fortress with the very best of everything—like a high-class hotel or executive office suite, with stylishly decorated interiors, beautifully crafted furniture and sumptuous soft furnishings. It would be a wonder of contemporary engineering with every new-fangled technological device and state-of-the-art modern convenience at their disposal. Well, it would, wouldn't it?

He began to get excited; if there was a chance for another life, he was going to take it.

As the creaking elevator started to slow, Tesk closed his eyes and braced himself. He took another deep breath. "They may be waiting for us, Douglas… probably spied us on that surveillance camera. Let me do the talking, huh? But be prepared to come out shooting!"

The elevator cage jerked as they ground to a halt. They had reached the bottom of the shaft and their final destination. Tesk raised his rifle as the lift doors clanked open, and he silently motioned for Douglas to take the lead. "No, after you," insisted Douglas.

The new world was in darkness, but just ahead of them they could see a light. As they cautiously wandered toward it, Tesk quickly discovered that instead of the wonderful utopia he had envisaged, all he saw were more dingy corridors, sombrely illuminated by the back-up security lighting system. The passageways resembled those of a prison not a palace, and everywhere they looked were further signs of violent discourse.

More dead, artillery rounds and a sea of broken shards were what welcomed them forward.

"Seems we weren't the first civilians to have breached the sanctuary."

They quietly snaked through the basement compound, not making a sound for fear of waking the dead. They searched each chamber for a sign of life, finding only death. Each room had its purpose—the infirmary, administration office, storeroom, generator system bay, war room, mess hall… But all lay in darkness.

In a dormitory, they found bodies still in beds, murdered in their sleep.

In a large refectory area, they found people slumped at tables. There were broken bottles, crockery, meat bones and dead rats on the floor, dead fighters everywhere. The invaders had stormed and struck while they ate breakfast, their compound decimated.

The attack had been planned and was effective, the entire place ransacked and destroyed. "Whoever did this," whispered Douglas, "showed little mercy."

"Save your tears, big guy," Tesk said. "This lot were traitors to humankind."

Beyond the refectory door was the kitchen, and it was evident that the attack had taken place while it was busy. The cooks and servers were all lying dead, the place turned upside down. Despite the foul stench, the surreal thought occurred to Tesk that he hadn't eaten for an age; he suddenly went weak at the knees. Douglas took him by the arm. All of this carnage and mayhem was too much to take but Tesk needed to be sure that all hope was lost before they turned back.

At the rear of the kitchen was a door.

A pantry... maybe food? Tesk pondered, but the larder was bolted shut with a deadlock. "Stand back!" he ordered. The door was securely fastened, but such was the blast of high-powered rifle fire that it flew off its hinges. "Let's see what goodies they've got locked in here," he said, hoping there might at least be some salvageable morsels inside the storeroom.

Douglas pushed in first, a blast of cold, fetid air wafting out from the frozen pantry. "Why not take the food?" queried Tesk. "If they were plundering the place, why not bust out the pantry?" Suddenly, a flurry of shiny black insects scattered across the floor.

No doubt they'd been nestling inside the cold store. Douglas jumped, the lumbering giant very much afraid of the tiny creatures scurrying in the night.

The shelves were empty, the storeroom barren and above them hung rows and rows of empty metal meat hooks. At the far end of the unit, Tesk spotted one solitary carcass, bound in polythene. "That sure is some skinny assed pig hanging up there!" said Douglas.

He looked to Tesk, who stared back at him with an expression of sheer disbelief. "No..." said Douglas. "Tesk, you know what we're looking at?"

Tesk stepped forward and examined the wrapped carcass.

The frozen body was that of a man, maybe the same height and weight as himself. Douglas shivered, unable to believe what he saw before him.

"Well, ain't that a turn-up for the books, Dougie. Seems the civilised folk have gone and started eating each other! And they called us uncouth!" Douglas gagged. "Looks like the only ones left alive are me, you and the roaches!" Tesk joked, but noticeably spooked, the two men decided to make a run for the door. The bunker had been decimated.

It was beyond repair, and even with an army of a hundred men, it would take them forever to fix it up. And then what?

Tesk didn't much fancy living in a prison let alone dying in one.

The smell of decay was overpowering. The men sprinted along the concourse and out into the eerie dim light, both praying that the lift would have enough power to get them back up to the surface. At the entrance, the cage was open as if waiting for them. They both crashed in and Tesk punched the button. The lift sprang into action and quickly elevated the men towards ground level. Despite the enhanced speed, the journey back up seemed to take twice as long as the descent, both men standing in silence, desperately trying to catch their breath in the airless elevator shaft. Tesk looked to Douglas. He shook his head shamefully, silently implying that what they had just witnessed should remain underground and not get relayed to the remaining Earth people. Douglas nodded in mute agreement. They held a secret between them now.

The elevator violently jolted as they arrived at ground level and Tesk and Douglas burst out of the cage, sprinting through the disgusting corridor. Tesk let out a cry, the build-up of adrenaline in his system having overloaded his mind and spirit. Bolting through the wreckage, lumps of plaster fell from the ceiling and glass skylights exploded above them as he fired off a few rounds of ammunition. So insanely sick of the silent planet, Douglas also let out a scream, peppering the lifeless dead bodies with another round of fire. "Dance, you crazy bastards!" he cried as the repulsive bodies wriggled and writhed in the rancid water.

Scuttling along the corridor and past the poor wretch still slumped in the security box, the men burst out into the open grounds. Such was the feeling of desolation, Tesk wished that a sniper would take him down! His dreams were dead, his final hopes crushed. He let off another round but there was nobody left alive to retaliate.

Douglas froze, suddenly blinded by the beam of a searchlight. Tesk's heart stopped for a moment, then soared as he recognised the craft. Mono had waited for them and was hovering low enough that the two men could scramble on board.

Once inside, Alice ran to them, sensing their pain. "I told you it was over!" she said tenderly. But Tesk couldn't speak, his spirit broken, his hopes and dreams as dead as the lost soul in the pantry. Not only was the underground sanctuary destroyed but also, the spirit of man had died too. Putting together the pieces, Tesk knew he was never going home.

"Please, get us out of here, Mono!" he pleaded.

"At last!" replied Mono, hitting the booster pedal, and blasting them out into the safety of the void.

CHAPTER 22

"I have good news and I have bad news," said the little robot with an apprehensive tone. "Okay, the bad news first." Alice sighed. "What's the bad news?"

"The bad news is we are unable to locate an unobstructed wormhole between our current location and the Earth 2 coordinate."

The earth people groaned.

"These wormholes? I don't get it," said Nelson. "One minute, there's a wormhole, and the next minute, there's not."

"I wish I could explain." Mono huffed sympathetically. "But unfortunately, no one really understands them. It is said that the great governors know the secret, but they are reluctant to reveal it." Nelson looked confused. "They come and go as they have done for a million years," continued Mono. "Portals that cut through physical space! Much quicker than conventional transportation routes. If you are fortunate enough to find one!"

"And it's all random?" said Alice, sounding puzzled.

"Not at all!" Mono said. "They run to a system; the forefathers drew up the charts! Matching the celestial cycle, they appear and disappear at the same time and place each super-rotation. They run like clockwork!"

"Sounds like BS to me," groaned Tesk. "Snakes and ladders!"

"Snakes and ladders?" asked Mono.

"Don't worry about it." Alice smiled. "So, we're stuck in here for another month then?"

"I'm afraid so…" said Mono flatly.

"And the good news?" groaned Tesk. "What's the good news?"

"Well, fortunately, it's not all bad. Bungo and I have been able to coordinate another provision drop, ensuring we will all make it back in one piece!" The little robot looked very proud of his logistical achievement.

"Whatever?" answered Tesk, too despondent to cause a fuss.

Mono was relieved; the news had gone down better than expected. Turning to the console, he continued with his duties, checking and double-checking their route, ensuring they had everything they required for the long voyage home.

"Damned wormholes," Alice said. "What kind of crazy assed galaxy is this?"

"Relax," said Chrissy. "You know we ain't got another option."

"Hey, Mono!" asked Tesk, attempting to get to his feet. "How about another blast of that sedative?" He sat back, his lungs still not recovered from his adventures on the origin Earth.

"Yeah!" called Douglas. "Can't you put us under for another few weeks? I'm gonna go crazy, cooped up in here!"

"I share your frustration," replied Mono curtly. "The idea of spending so many rotations in the company of you lot doesn't exactly fill me with glee! Unfortunately, the mixture has been used!"

"Hey, cool it, tin man!" cried Tesk. "What did we ever do to you?" Mono bristled as Tesk sat forward. "I thought you'd be happy, out here having space adventures with us instead of being locked up on the compound with Xzardak and that other freak!"

"I was quite happy with Xzardak and that other freak!" stated Mono dejectedly.

"Happy?" Tesk laughed. "Happy being Xzardak's errand boy? Happy taking orders from Bongo? What's wrong with you, man? Don't you want to be free?"

"I am free!" insisted Mono, running Tesk's enquiry through his logic processor.

"Oh yeah! You're free all right," Tesk said, throwing an item of Earth litter at the poor robot's head. "Free to drive the craft, free to sort out provisions, free to suck up to Xzardak and the coalition!"

Mono considered the response from his logic processor.

"And what would you have me do?" he asked, turning around to face Tesk. "Give it all up so I could be as lost and confused as you are? At least I know my purpose!"

"Lost and confused? We ain't lost and confused, Mono," said Tesk calmly. "We're just trying to find our way, that's all."

Perplexed, Mono was unable to offer a retort. The Earth man's logic had conflicted with his data processor, the programmer of which had not prepared a module detailing or explaining human ideology. Plus, he had already contravened protocol by arguing with a sentient life form.

He turned back to the console. "Lost in darkness," he chirped.

"Will you guys stop arguing!" cried Chrissy.

"We weren't arguing, Chrissy, just putting Mono straight on a few home truths, telling him how it is!"

Mono ran a search. "Home truths…" His eyes widened.

"Besides, I reckon you owe Mono a thank you." She smiled. "We wanted to leave you down there, and it was his idea to wait!"

Tesk grudgingly mumbled an apology.

"Yeah, thanks, tin can; reckon I do owe you a debt of gratitude in that case."

"Man… we were lucky to get out of that freaky place alive," started Douglas. "The stuff we saw down there!" Tesk shot Douglas an evil stare.

"Oh yeah?" said Chrissy curiously. "What did you see?"

"We didn't see anything," interjected Tesk. "Just more bodies. Seems the good townsfolk got wind of the luxury hideout and decided to do a little provision run of their own."

Chrissy looked intrigued. "And…?" she said, eager to hear the gory details.

"Well," said Tesk. "All I can say is, we didn't fancy hanging around."

Douglas dropped his head.

"So, what's the next move?" enquired Alice wearily. "Xzardak isn't going to be happy once we get back. Seems the coalition is going to shut us down for good, once word of this disastrous plan gets back to them."

"Oh yeah!" said Tesk. "Well, I'll be ready for them. What exactly are they going to do?"

"I imagine they will start by shutting off the oxygen," Mono suggested. "You must remember everything on Earth 2 is synthesised. I imagine they'll shut off the oxygen and then the light!"

"Then I reckon we're doomed no matter what we do!" Douglas placed his head on his hands. "Talk about a rock and a hard place!"

"Hey, Mono!" called Tesk.

Chrissy shook her head, anticipating round two of the argument. "If you're so free, perhaps you could drop us off at the next hospitable planet?"

"There are no hospitable planets when it comes to Earth men, I'm afraid, Tesk."

"Okay, how about habitable? There has to be somewhere we could drop anchor. Someplace to hang out, just 'til I get my head straight, and come up with a plan?"

Mono pondered the idea; it was against protocol, but he ran a search regardless.

"Hmm…" He mused on it, then remembering his place in the chain of command, he sat up straight and delivered a deliberate and resounding, "No."

"Shame." Tesk smiled. "Nowhere to run, nowhere to hide."

"And we're out of sedation," groaned Douglas.

"Well, Mono, looks like you're stuck with us!" Tesk chuckled. "You poor bastard!"

Mono shuddered. Putting up with this level of antagonism for such a long journey was too much to comprehend. He began to ponder Tesk's idea. Maybe there was something to it? According to Xzardak, Earth 2 had been running quite smoothly without Tesk and his cronies. They had caused nothing but trouble since the day they had awoken, so surely it would be in everyone's better interests to get rid of the crew of troublesome life forms?

Perhaps then, Xzardak and the project might actually have a chance of succeeding?

Scanning the readout, Mono discovered that there were a dozen planets where the Earth people could potentially be dropped, many with unbreathable, unliveable atmospheres.

Even better, planets with predatory creatures which would love to feed on the freshly regenerated skin and flesh of the plump and healthy Earth folk. Picturing Tesk being ripped limb from limb by a pack of hungry space wolves, Mono scrutinised the Geo-data.

"I'd love to help you all, but the destination of the craft is already pre-set. Xzardak took control of the ship when you re-entered, for fear that you may try to commandeer it. We are destined for Earth 2, Tesk, and there's nothing whatsoever that I can do about it!"

Images of Tesk being trampled to death by a pack of wild solar ponies flooded Mono's circuitry. He chuckled, trying desperately to dispel the vision.

"Okay, trash can, if that's the way it is, that's the way it is. No use arguing." Tesk cracked his knuckles, resigned to his fate.

Mono hoped that would be the end of it. Shutting down the data map, he put in a request for carbonated sedation gas on the next fuel stop. If he could put them all back under for a nice long sleep, the journey home might just be tolerable.

"It's gonna be a long few weeks, man," declared Douglas, closing his eyes tightly, wishing the time away.

Nelson got to his feet. "Listen up, guys, I have something to show you." He walked across the cockpit and rummaged through a cargo sack. "I was going to save these for when we got back, but reckon we deserve a treat!"

He held two glass bottles of a cloudy looking liquid up into the air.

"Is that what I think it is?" cried Alice.

"Oh my! Sure, looks like it," Chrissy said.

Mono turned, looking perplexed. Nelson elaborated. "I ran a little reconnaissance mission of my own while you guys were playing house in the bunker. Found these inside one of the busted-up tanks. Reckon I stumbled upon someone's stash! What do you think?"

"May I ask what it is?" enquired Mono.

"Sure, little fella!" said Nelson gleefully. "Maybe you should have the first swig, make sure it isn't poisoned or something?" Nelson pulled out the cork and Mono placed the middle digit of his left hand inside of the bottle. Nelson rubbed his hands together excitedly.

"Hmm…" said Mono, analysing the contents of the dirty looking bottle. "Appears to be water-based but contains a peculiar compound, perhaps ethanol from some sort of fermented root vegetable. Looks quite toxic to me. What do you intend to do with it?" Mono asked.

He removed his middle digit from the bottle's neck.

Nelson gave the bottle a wipe and enthusiastically took a great big swig. Mono winced and the crew watched on in bemusement. At first, Nelson said nothing, but then after a moment his nostrils flared. Eyes wide open, he started coughing. He fell to the floor retching and gagging, clasping his throat as if it were on fire. Mono initiated a preliminary medical diagnostic on the man wriggling on the floor. "I fear he has been poisoned, so stand back!" he exclaimed.

Suddenly, Nelson let out a terrific sound, and like a wounded animal, he began to snort and hoot. "He's in pain!" called Mono. "Please stand well back!"

"He's not in pain," said Alice cooly. "He's wasted!"

Getting to his feet, Nelson took another swig then passed the bottle to Joey. Joey nervously eyed the bottle and looked to Tesk. "Go ahead." Tesk shrugged. "It's your funeral."

Joey took a gulp, reacting as badly to the liquid as Nelson. He passed the bottle to Douglas.

"Will someone tell me what's going on?" insisted Mono.

"It's booze, Mono. Do a search in your mechanical brainbox: booze, alcohol, moonshine!"

"Moonshine!" Joey spluttered. "Tastes more like antifreeze!"

"Embalming fluid!" Douglas coughed, his face turning purple. "Or rocket fuel!"

"Boy, does that kick!" exclaimed Nelson. "Take a drink, Tesk, don't be shy. I got eight bottles! Liberated from the hands of the enemy!"

By the time Mono's data chip had returned its analysis, the crew had headed out on their own journey into space. Once they'd drained one bottle, Nelson popped the cork on another.

Then came the next and then the next.

The Earthlings were quickly inebriated, and Mono was amazed at how much more annoying they had become. As they shouted and laughed, getting louder and clumsier by the minute, his head was beginning to spin.

The booze had clearly gone to Tesk's head. Enthusiastically, he wrapped his arm around Douglas' neck. Mono looked perplexed; this was the first time Tesk had shown any display of affection and Mono began to wonder what magic ingredient was contained in that drink. "You know what?" he hiccupped, "We wouldn't be out here if it wasn't for the good grace of that little fella over there!". He motioned to Mono, who lowered his head with a groan. "I mean he's ferried us backwards and forwards, halfway across the universe and he hasn't complained once!"

"Are you kidding?" slurred Chrissy. "He's done nothing but complain!" She adjusted her eyes, her vision beginning to blur. "Don't you remember, he drugged us! He can't stand the sight of us!"

"No, no, no, I won't hear it!" insisted a very merry Tesk. "Come on guys, let's give the little guy a round of applause!" The company began to whoop and clap their hands, and what happened next made Mono's eyes bulge out. The Earth folks suddenly broke out into a husky, discordant chorus of 'For He's a Jolly Good Fellow!' and Mono began to shudder and twitch. He could take no more.

"Okay!" he shrieked, taxiing across the cockpit. "That is it! Enough!" he insisted. The ensemble stopped singing momentarily and Tesk rolled over laughing so hard, tears ran from his eyes.

Mono had finally had enough.

Commandeering the craft's audio speaker, he could take no more. "Enough! Please, enough! Okay! That's it! You win, I'll help you out, Tesk! But can you all just shut up!"

Tesk's eyes were wild, and he giggled as the group collapsed into a dizzy mess.

Mono suspected that he was being played, but at that point in time, unsedated deactivation would be better than having to spend another Earth minute in the company of this lot.

Tesk smiled. "I knew you'd see it my way! What's the plan, Jojo?"

"It's Mono!" scalded Mono.

"Jeez, cool it, Mono…" Tesk said. "What's the plan then, *Mono?*"

Mono regathered his thoughts. His system was rebooting, and his stress levels were stabilising. "If Xzardak discovers that I have helped you to escape, I will be declassified *and* deactivated!" he raged. "If I help you, I would appreciate it if we could keep it amongst ourselves!"

Tesk nodded obediently. "Of course, man!" He hiccupped. "Your secret's safe with me!" Then with an evil smile, he drained the last of the moonshine as if it were tap water.

Mono set out his plan. "There is a way," he began. "The craft is set for home with a stop off at Sapphire 17 to refuel. However, if we push on a little farther, there is a planet in that sector more suited to your physical anatomy. I could tell Xzardak that I was unable to communicate with Sapphire 17 and will stop at the next available service opportunity.

"I will schedule a fuel stop on the planet Z4A, landing the craft there and I shall request that a transit tanker fills us up. There, you will need to perform your escape."

Trying not to giggle, the crew held it together as Mono continued with his detailed subterfuge. "The atmosphere on the planet is... hospitable," he continued. "But I want you to know, the locals aren't very friendly. Once out of sight, I will activate the ship, then my path is set. I can no longer help you. You will be on your own, I repeat, you will—"

"Be on our own, yes, we heard you the first time! Look man, relax," interrupted Tesk. "It'll be fine!" He turned to the crew. "Seems the little guy has got it all worked out!" he slurred as he toppled from his chair.

Three rotations had passed and Tesk's hangover was beginning to lift. "Damned turnip vodka!" He coughed. "Never again!"

The alcohol had taken the Earth people out of action for a couple of days. After the initial few hours of exuberant intoxication, they soon became weary and the following day, they appeared pallid and withdrawn. "Whatever it was you drank did not agree with you!" scolded Mono.

"Just a little out of practice, that's all!" Douglas yawned, scratching his head.

"Your purified systems are not used to such toxins. This far out in space, intoxicating substances can have a strange effect on the brain."

"You're telling me!" Alice said.

Momentarily, a feeling of serenity had ascended on Mono. Soon, they would reach their destination and he would be free of Tesk, the Earth people and perhaps even Xzardak. Mono hoped he might be demoted, given a more functional role. He had never craved adventure and after this episode, he was longing for a position more suited to his personality. Perhaps something clerical, certainly something indoors, and preferably on solid ground.

"Not long now," he said, slipping the craft on autopilot and drifting off into stand-by mode.

The silence wasn't to last. "Hey, dumb-dumb! How much longer?" shouted Tesk, sounding refreshed and reinvigorated after a lengthy catnap.

"We are in deep space, Tesk, travelling at an astonishing speed. We'll be at our destination soon enough," insisted Mono curtly.

Applying more pressure to the thrusters, the lights in the cockpit dipped. Mono winced. Accelerating at such speed was not wise, but he could sense the Earth people were beginning to stir and he feared they may start singing again.

"We are at full thrust, Tesk. We shouldn't be much longer."

When Z4A eventually appeared on the craft's navigation screen, Mono took great pleasure in announcing the news to the crew. "At last!" cried Alice.

Mono knew that what he was about to do contravened every protocol in the book, his intentions likely to be deemed irresponsible, reckless, and immoral. Yet against his better judgement, he issued the Earth people with their instructions.

Once the battery transporter arrived, Mono would exit the craft and transact with the technician, leaving the cargo hatch open and unmanned.

Mono explained that the service port on Z4A was located in the grasslands. The crew were to vacate the craft and make their escape into the long purple pampas. Beyond that, they were—just as Mono had taken great pains to elucidate to them—out on their own.

"Not much of a plan, I know," Mono confessed, "but the best we have."

Tesk thanked Mono, and as the craft approached its destination, the Earth people gathered their belongings and stood by the service hatch. "You really should sit down for the landing," Mono explained, but the inpatient passengers would not be told.

"You're coming with us, Alice?" asked Tesk with a surprised smile.

"On another one of your half-baked, escape missions?" she said, getting to her feet. "Well, it's gotta beat sitting in the dark with Xzardak and Clive." She chuckled sarcastically.

The ship shuddered and rocked as it entered Z4A's atmosphere and as the craft began its descent, Mono began wondering if he was doing the right thing. It was not the best time to be wondering it, admittedly. There wasn't a predatory creature on the planet, no space wolves or solar ponies to contend with, so he was quite sure that the Earth people would be safe. The same couldn't be said for the indigenous species inhabiting the small world, however.

Suddenly concerned for their safety, Mono began to have second thoughts about his grand scheme. Those poor innocents hadn't a clue what was about to hit them.

Tesk looked over as the craft touched terra firma. "Hey, stop stalling. Junkyard, what's the hold up?" Mono rolled his eyes, sat up straight and put the plan into action. Overriding his logic chip, he opened the hatch, engaged the evacuation sequence and hastily made his way to interface with the technician. There was no going back.

"What happens now?" asked Douglas as he sidled up to Tesk.

"Stay close to me, and I'll let you know once we're outside."

Mono had walked Tesk through the planet's diagnostics and Tesk had nodded along convincingly, so as not to appear dumb. The atmospheric and geographical data seemed to be okay, but there was much that Tesk had not understood.

Once Mono was out of view, deciding to take a punt, Tesk prepared himself for freedom.

As the robot disappeared with the technician, Tesk counted to ten, then signalled that the crew should disembark. Creeping out of the door cavity, he caught a glimpse of the purple earth beneath them. Suddenly, they were entering an alien environment and it dawned on him that Mono's plan only covered them from the ship's ramp to the long purple grass blowing in the near distance. Tesk shrugged. Beyond that was anybody's guess. He closed his eyes for a second before scurrying down the ramp, out into the sweet-smelling air.

Tesk couldn't imagine how life would be on this new world, but it had to be safer and kinder than his home planet. The gravity level, a little more extreme, made Tesk's limbs and joints feel heavy. The oxygen composition, a lower density than Earth's, made the air taste metallic. He took a deep breath then exhaled slowly. It was breathable and for now, would have to do. They didn't exactly have a choice in the matter.

As the sun was settling on the horizon, Tesk and the Earth people bravely set forward, out into the unearthly purple-red eeriness.

"Everyone, follow me!" he hollered.

"What, into the weeds?" Chrissy asked. "Then what?"

"I'll figure it out as we go along," insisted Tesk.

"This is the plan?" Alice looked bemused. "We must be crazy!"

Tesk had a feeling that if they could just get clear of the ship and away from Mono, everything would be okay. "It'll be fine!" he cried. "Just trust me!"

"We've come this far." Douglas sighed. "Doesn't look like we have an option."

Staring out across the strange new environment, Tesk took another deep breath.

"Okay," he cried out. "We're gonna make a run for it. After three. One… Two…" Chrissy crossed herself and closed her eyes. "Three!" he bellowed.

Clear of the craft and almost at the weeds, the crew bounded forward, running as fast as their impeded physiology would permit. However, just as they made it to the cover of the long grass, Tesk discovered he wouldn't actually require a plan.

Emerging from the foliage appeared Commissioner Turner.

"You filthy scumbag, Mono," whispered Tesk as he skidded to a halt, motioning to the guys to fall back.

"Great to see you, Tesk!" called the excited commissioner. "I bet you're surprised to see me here?" he asked, smiling.

Tesk's heart was racing.

"I am a little surprised," he growled as he backed away. "In actual fact, I was expecting to see Xzardak! I thought if the dustbin were going to sell us out to anyone, it would be him!"

The commissioner gently laughed. "It has nothing to do with the robot, nor Xzardak for that matter," he said, slowly and carefully approaching the crew. "We have been monitoring the craft for your entire journey. You must remember that *you people* are still classed as a biohazard in the eyes of the Civilised Realm. Once you went off course, it was obvious you would make a play for the most suitable planet within an easy distance." Tesk grappled with his rifle, every instinct instructing him to blast the commissioner. He stepped back a little further; in the distance, he could see coalition vehicles. Turner had brought reinforcements.

"So, what's the plan, Tesk?" asked Turner.

"The plan is simple, sir. You let us by, and no one gets hurt."

Turner smiled. It was obvious that he had no intention of letting the crew pass. "You know I can't do that," he said. "You're coming with me."

Tesk gritted his teeth.

"What are we gonna do?" said Alice. "We should have stuck with Xzardak!"

Tesk shook his head. "They're one and the same, Alice, don't you see that? It's the same deal as Earth. You can't trust anyone."

Picking up pace, the crew headed back in the direction of the craft. "Better hurry up, guys! He's going without us!" called Douglas. The 409's hydraulics whirred and clanged as the ramp slowly raised, before closing tightly shut.

"Too late!" Tesk cried out as the engines on the vessel fired up. "That thing is about to take off!" he called. "Better take cover!"

Forcefully approaching the commissioner, Tesk raised his rifle. "Okay, Turner," he said. "Have it your way." Turner stood his ground, and seemingly unalarmed, he was joined by his trusty mechanical assistant, Raymonde.

Behind them, the craft pulsed and vibrated.

"Let us through, man," urged Tesk. "We have nothing left to lose!"

Raymonde's visor turned from blue to red and slowly, his torso began to rotate.

"I am unarmed, Tesk!" announced the commissioner. "But I cannot allow you to pass. It would contravene subsection of clause 1060. Hazardous specimens must be quarantined!" he stated calmly and officiously.

"We're coming through, Turner, this is it!" Tesk motioned to the gang to raise their weapons.

"We are unarmed," Raymonde said, the red light in his visor suddenly pulsating as his torso rotated faster and faster.

Agitated and afraid, Tesk began to panic. As Raymonde juddered and convulsed, Tesk raised up his hand. "Okay, asshole!" he cried, instructing the troops. "It's party time! Let him have it!" A deafening blast rang out as a rain of bullets was unleashed. Tesk shrieked with joy as he fired round after round in the direction of the commissioner.

It felt good to be back in control.

As the gunfire subsided and the cloud of smoke cleared, Tesk was amazed to see the commissioner still standing, unmarked by the weapon fire.

The blast ringing in his ears, he rubbed his eyes. Horrified, he glanced to see Raymonde covered in bullets. Fully magnetised, he had attracted every shell, and with a rattle and whirr, he powered down the electromagnet, causing all the spent ammunition to tinkle to the floor.

Tesk was speechless. Raising his rifle again, he stared through the gunsight, the crosshair resting right between Turner's eyes. Raymonde swiftly powered up, changing gears, and once again he began to spin. Creaking loudly, his visor light dimmed as he stood tall and emitted a powerful electromagnetic pulse. Suddenly, the guys felt a violent jolt as their weapons dislodged from their hands, along with Joey's spectacles, Douglas's Elvis Presley belt buckle and a variety of other metal objects and random pieces of jewellery.

Raymonde's body panel again whirled to a standstill. He stood like a Christmas tree, decorated and adorned with lots of shiny objects and ornaments. With a clang, he powered down and the full arsenal of weapons and trinkets fell to the floor, as did Douglas's trousers.

Unarmed, the fugitives did as Turner had predicted—acting the only way they could in a situation like this. They panicked and fled. Each one exposed and afraid, they scattered like Earth rats into the cover and safety of the long purple grass surrounding them.

The commissioner signalled to his sentinels to gather the discarded weapons and motioning to Raymonde, the robot's visor again began to glow a burning red.

CHAPTER 23

Tesk felt his heart might explode. The conditions on this new world were not as he had hoped. The air was thin and with each stride, he was becoming weaker and weaker. His entire life, he had felt as if he was gasping for air; the atmosphere on the original Earth planet had been poisoned beyond human sustainability. But this was worse. He began to question Mono's assurances that the atmosphere on Z4A was suitable for humans. "That double-crossing little asshole knew we would choke!" he said. "What chance do we have in these conditions?"

Unarmed and afraid, he ran as fast as his legs and lungs would permit but the inevitable outcome of the situation was beginning to become apparent.

The only real question was: what would bring him to his knees first, the heavy gravitational pull or the encroaching co-alition forces?

Douglas could see Alice in the distance; always a good runner, she had left him for dust. For a moment, Douglas thought of happier times with Tesk and the crew, running from trouble, usually the police or local law enforcement. That had felt like fun, but this current predicament was something else. "This sure is some crazy shit we got ourselves into," he said.

Douglas was wheezing, aware that he had fallen behind, unable to keep pace with the younger, fitter members of the gang. Raymonde's visor glowed red then blue, then red again as the coalition cruiser cut through the long purple grass. Picking up speed, the heavy metal robot hit the thruster, propelling the craft thirty feet into the air. Climbing to the desired height, it whirred ominously, then with a shrill blast, its emanator detonated a sonic charge. The sound, like a thunderclap, could be heard from miles around. The ultraviolet flash would take down every living creature in the vicinity of Raymonde and the coalition charger.

From his high vantage point, Raymonde surveyed the field, gazing intently as each trail in the long grass ceased to advance. His targets neutralised, the craft fired into action.

With a low hum, the cargo shaft opened, and a crew of alien sentinels emerged, primed and ready to collect and safely stow the escaped bio virus.

Turner observed, smiling as the crew lifted, sorted and assembled the human prisoners onto racks in the cargo loft. Once all were accounted for, the alien army boarded, and Raymonde put the craft back into gear. With a kick, they blasted off into orbit and within a second, any trace or evidence of the incident had disappeared.

Mono watched on in astonishment, amazed at what he had just witnessed. His self-preservation chip running at burnout, he quickly prepared the craft for lift off. Fully refuelled, he fired the thrusters, and frantically adjusting the trajectory, he blasted out of the planet's airspace. For the first time in his mechanical existence, genuinely concerned for his own safety.

Once airborne, Mono steadied the ship and a thought flashed across his mind.

It was the thought that being blasted apart by the coalition might be less of an ordeal than having to face up to dear old Xzardak. Mono knew that letting the Earth people escape had been a terrible thing to do. He had acted on a whim, out of frustration and self-preservation.

The worst thing that he thought might happen was that the Earth people would be rounded up by the locals and Mono would be demoted to the station of a clerk.

The fact that this was now a coalition matter made Mono feel severely unwell. He had two options. He could blast himself into the nearest sun—he had calculated that he had just about enough fuel and forward motion to make it to Sun 15bZt—not an option he favoured, but surely better than having to report to Xzardak and explain himself to his old friend's disappointed face.

Or he could come clean and take his comeuppance. "What a mess!" he howled, painfully aware that he only had himself to blame for this current dilemma. Suddenly, Mono's self-preservation chip regained control; the only plausible option would be to tell the truth!

The signal was weak as the craft came within range of the transmitter. Once attuned to the correct frequency, Mono sent out a distress call, quietly hoping that Xzardak would be too far away from the receiver station. Much to his dismay, Xzardak answered within seconds.

Mono could just make out Xzardak's form through the digital distortion but was unable to decipher the expression on his face. Considering what he was about to tell him, Mono assured himself that this was a good thing!

"Mono, is that you? Come in old friend, are you okay?" The fact that Xzardak checked on Mono's wellbeing before the status of the mission made Mono feel all the more rotten.

"Yes, Xzardak, I'm okay."

"Excellent!" Xzardak spoke excitedly. "Once I saw you had gone off the chart, I began to worry that you may have encountered some difficulty. I know that sun 15bZt is on your trajectory. Pretty risky flying that close to a super sun! Those things fire off solar flares, you know!" Mono shrugged, desperately trying to devise some sort of fantastical excuse to mask his own stupidity, but no such fiction would occur to him.

The game was up. "Listen, Xzardak, I've done a really bad thing."

"You've not put them all back to sleep, have you?" Xzardak sounded perturbed. "I don't want them becoming addicted to sedatives! It'll take months to revive them fully and they're already a docile bunch!"

"No, worse than that, Xzardak." Mono sheepishly stumbled his words. "The humans, they've escaped!"

Xzardak didn't speak, and Mono could sense that he was trying to contain his concern. Standing silently, the lack of a response from Xzardak was making Mono feel extremely uncomfortable indeed. "They overpowered me!" he blurted. "They regained their weapons from the cargo store and over-powered me!" Mono listened with disbelief as he heard the words cascade from his own mouth. "They made me divert the craft... take them off course!"

"Are you okay, my friend?" enquired Xzardak, sounding concerned. "For a moment, I thought you were going to say you'd dumped them!" he said with a raised eyebrow. "Pesky articles. Did they injure you at all?"

Mono was amazed at how easily the lie had improved his predicament. *Lie some more,* he told himself. "I must say, they are a savage bunch," he continued so Xzardak could hear. "I'm okay, just a little shaken! I stood my ground but there were too many of them!"

"I knew I should have had Bungo come to join you," Xzardak replied thoughtfully. "Terrible Earth creatures. Do you have any idea where the humans may have disappeared to?"

Mono pondered the question for a moment; this was where the lying business got tricky. Whatever he said next would probably have dire consequences for everyone involved and could dramatically influence the next stages in the operation.

"Erm," said Mono, his gaskets working at full throttle. "Erm, none whatsoever, Xzardak!" The lie felt good. "They instructed me to drop them on the planet Z4A, then once I had fuelled, they said I had to leave or they'd destroy the ship... with me in it!"

Mono mopped his brow. Hopefully, he was now in the clear.

"Such bravery, Mono. I'll make sure you receive a special commendation for your work on this mission. It'll mean a promotion for sure!"

Mono feigned a smile.

"Now what to do with this dreaded pestilence we've unleashed upon the universe?" Xzardak sighed. "The coalition will close us down for sure!"

Mono couldn't help but think he deserved promotion. That would be punishment enough for the dreadful mistruths he had fed to Xzardak. He had a feeling that his words might come back to haunt him but for now he was safe and in Xzardak's good books. On his master's instruction, he set the destination for home. Then plugging into the mains, he switched off the lights and with his favourite soundscape playing softly in his head socket, blissfully nodded off into standby mode.

CHAPTER 24

Tesk opened his eyes, sensing he was floating. Barely conscious, still unable to recall the course of events leading him to this current predicament, he lay perfectly still as he set about trying to put the pieces back together. A dimmed light illuminated his surroundings, and catching glimpses in his peripheral vision, he suspected he must be inside a medical facility.

"Another science lab?" he whispered.

He attempted to sit up. Something was wrong. He was paralysed, that's what. He struggled, trying to escape but his limbs were frozen and heavy. Anxiety started to build, a bolt of fear shooting through his body, his frustration turning to anger.

"When I get out of here…" he raged. "They're all dead!" Trying to recollect who 'they' were, he took a deep breath and tried to steady himself.

Images flashed back and forth inside his head, dreadful twisted visions, swirling around and around. Desperate to dispel them, too much to endure, he closed his eyes tight.

His memory was returning; he was coming back to life.

Tesk clenched his teeth, sweat pouring from his forehead. What he had encountered on Earth had shattered his spirit. The situation, it appeared, was going from bad to worse, his hopes now dead, his past ruined, his future too weird to comprehend.

"Where am I?"

He struggled some more but his body felt broken.

Tesk's heart was pounding, beating faster and faster, out of control, like a train without a brake hurtling down a track. He tried to speak, to call out but no sound came, the scream only just audible inside his busted mind. "Maybe this is it?" he quietly whimpered. "People just ain't no good!" he cried again, encountering only silence.

His mind overloading, the rage came again. He would break free.

Then out of the corner of his eye, he registered movement. Someone was in the room; he could sense it. The ominous feeling of being watched grew greater and greater and Tesk's eyes darted in every direction, desperately trying to put together a mental map of his surroundings.

There were two of them, standing quietly, observing.

For a short while, nothing happened and Tesk lay in silent dread, the sound of his own heartbeat and the flickering shadow of the invaders pushing him closer and closer to the edge.

On the verge of a mental breakdown, Tesk was sinking, with a bizarre simultaneous sensation of floating, but also of falling. Movement, some clues, a hospital, a laboratory, a console and two figures. One a shadow behind glass, one standing at his feet.

"Good morning," said the indistinguishable figure, softly. "Please, do not be alarmed."

Tesk had encountered the figure before, humanoid but not human. Looming in silhouette, his voice sounded familiar. "Apologies for the sleep paralysis. You were trying to escape, so we had to give you a little shock!" His words only served to intensify Tesk's fury.

"Just you wait!" he raged.

"I want you to relax and reassure you that you are quite safe."

Figure one motioned to figure two, skulking silently behind the safety glass. Tesk was rotating, his body spinning on an axis, and he found himself upright, still floating in air but now face to face with Commissioner Turner.

Dazzled, Tesk blinked, the spotlight blazing into his eyes. "Lower the light!" barked Turner "Are you trying to blind him?"

Tesk stared into Turner's face. "You ugly freak!" He seethed. "You're dead meat!"

"That's better," said Turner softly. "I can see you now." Tesk felt a warm sensation rise through his right arm. It coursed through his body until it reached his head, not hot enough to burn but warm enough to make Tesk feel uncomfortable. "My associate has administered a medicine. It should help with the paralysis. Give it a moment and you will begin to feel better."

"You filthy scumbag!" blurted Tesk. The medicine was working; he could feel his face and heard the words tumble out of his mouth.

Turner raised his hand. "Enough medicine!" He laughed. "I need to keep you slightly subdued," he said wryly. "I imagine you're quite angry with me." Tesk grimaced. "Please don't be." Turner smiled coyly. "Believe me, you've struck lucky!"

Tesk felt dizzy, his head spinning, and with spots before his eyes, he tried to move. He had regained feeling in his body, his arms and his legs, but no control. Unable to free himself, he cried out a furious threat. "You better let me loose, man!"

"Don't worry. I will," reassured Turner coolly. "But first I want to speak to you."

Tesk lowered his head.

"We recently had a bit of a get together at the coalition headquarters. Xzardak and a few of your fellow Earth people paid us a visit. I had a very interesting evening with some friends of yours. Marvin, Ruby, Cheryl…"

"She's no friend of mine!"

"And a very nice man… Little Stevie I believe he was called." Tesk felt his head raise, curious to ascertain why Little Stevie would be conversing with Commissioner Turner. "Great company." Turner smiled serenely. "We had quite a night!" He paused and turned to examine Tesk's response.

"I'm listening," Tesk said, eager to find out where all of this was heading.

"Stevie told me you were the person I should speak to. Seems you're the one in charge, the man that everyone listens to."

Tesk slowly shook his head. "Me, no, you've got the wrong guy… Not me."

Turner smiled. "Oh, really! That's not what the others said." He paused. "Must be a case of mistaken identity, or perhaps you're just being modest?" Turner stood for a moment, studying Tesk, trying to figure him out.

Breathing heavily, staring Turner straight in the eye, Tesk said nothing, his face exposing the quiet fury raging inside of him.

After a moment, Turner motioned to his associate behind the glass.

"Sorry to have woken you," he said coldly. "Maybe you should get some more rest and we can speak in the morning." As he turned abruptly and walked out, Tesk felt a new sensation, cold, racing up his arm and through his nervous system.

His body tilted backwards and suddenly began to rise, his anger now seeming to subside. The feeling in his hands and face faded and his heart stopped pounding as slowly, his eyelids closed and slipping into darkness, everything turned black.

Floating on air within clean laundered sheets, Tesk awoke, his head resting comfortably upon a finely stuffed pillow. He stretched out his arms and legs and gently yawned. He was in a bed. He opened his eyes, the sun glinting in through a window, casting warmth across him. He was in a room; there were walls, a ceiling, and an ornately sculpted hanging light. "What's going on?" he whispered, sitting bolt upright.

He swung around, his clean feet pressed into the plush carpet beneath them. "Pyjamas?" he said, looking down at the freshly pressed night attire in which he was dressed. He rubbed his eyes in disbelief. Unable to make sense of his surroundings, he tried to stand. His body swayed, his head still reeling, his legs giving out as he collapsed back onto the bed. Disorientated, he surveyed the room. Wherever this was, it was the nicest place he'd even been.

But then came the feeling.

Memories. Xzardak, the compound, the journey, the Earth planet, the death, the mayhem... *Turner!* Tesk jumped up, but again his body gave way, and felled, he lay on the floor.

Was it all a nightmare? he wondered. *Much too vivid for a dream!*

He managed to drag himself across the carpet, crawling one step at a time, then up onto the antique dresser and to the window. He took hold of the luxurious curtain. Grappling, he rose onto the chair and then with everything he had, he yanked the curtain across. Every particle of his being wished to see the Earth, the sun shining, the blue sky, the green trees. The Earth of his childhood. The Earth they had promised him. The Earth of his wildest dreams.

Gracefully, the curtain flew open and Tesk peered out through the glass, frantically searching for something familiar, something recognisable. His heart sank. No blue sky, no trees, no birds, nothing native to Earth. Instead, an alien cityscape, its colours and shapes all unfamiliar to Tesk, and he began to tremble. "Make it end," he whispered. He glanced down at the street beneath him. Strange vehicles, driving much too fast. Realising he was up on an extremely high floor, he pushed against the window frame. If he could only break out the glass, he could jump, then it would all be over. He reached to pull the curtain back but once again, he tumbled. His body drained of energy, he lay on the floor, broken into bits.

He felt arms lift him up. "Come, my friend," said the voice. "Let's get you back into bed." It was no good; Tesk tried to rail but he hadn't the energy. Once delivered back under the covers, a flurry of service robots darted into the room. One plumped the pillow, one saw to the curtain, and another sat Tesk up straight. "You must eat," instructed a robotic voice, the service drone producing a tray of delicious smelling coffee and breakfast. Tesk took the spoon and with everything he had, he lifted the yellow gloop up to his mouth. He needed to eat.

A robot switched on the video monitor, and Tesk looked up. An old black and white western, like those they had on Earth. "A few more days in bed and you'll be fighting fit!" It was that despised voice again.

With Turner standing over him, Tesk raised his eyes. "Why are you torturing me?" he said.

"Torturing you?" Turner laughed. "This is some torture chamber!" he exclaimed. "You have everything you need. Relax! You must realise, I want to help you!"

"I don't need anybody's help!" Tesk answered, unwilling to capitulate, suspecting that the lavish surroundings might just be another mental trick.

Turner sat on a chair near the foot of the bed. "As I've told you, I have spoken with your friends, I want to work with you."

"Where are they?" Tesk panicked, suddenly remembering and reliving their neutralisation and capture.

"Douglas, Chrissy, Alice, Joey, Nelson, all of them. They are in their quarters, relaxing. They were quite open to my hospitality." Turner stood and proceeded to leave, joined at the doorway and flanked by his mechanical cohort. "This evening, I have something very special planned for you all!" He smiled. "But for now, rest."

Ravenously, Tesk devoured the food and drank the coffee, warm frothy liquid like something on Earth. Feeling slightly better, he lay back on the pillow and considered his limited options. Powerless, he would bide his time. He would play along with Turner for as long as it took, but as soon as the opportunity arose, Turner would die.

~✧~

"Please, sir, you must wake up; you've been asleep for many hours!" Tesk stirred and opened his eyes to find a service robot leaning across the bed. It was late, the room was dark, and he could see that the sky outside had turned grey and purple-blue. The robot switched on the lights and pulled across the curtain. "You must get ready, sir!" he announced enthusiastically. "Commissioner Turner has laid on quite an evening for you!"

Tesk could hear a long forgotten yet familiar sound; the hot water shower was running, and clouds of steam billowed in from the ensuite. His feet planted firmly on the floor, once again he tried to stand. Upright, he tried a stretch. "I feel marvellous!" he admitted.

"We have administered a booster!" declared the robot cheerily. "We analysed your vitals and have given your body a hit of vitamins and nutrients. You should be functioning at optimum health if our calculations are correct?" Tesk glanced over at the full-length mirror—he looked good. Wonderful aromas were drifting in from the bathroom. A companion robot held a towel and gestured for him to enter.

"I'll take it from here," he said, thanking the robot, snatching the towel and entering the bathroom. Closing the door behind him, he stepped into the shower, the horror and fear of the previous few days absentmindedly forgotten for a moment.

Bathed and anointed in redolent lotions, Tesk dressed in fresh clothes laid out for him.

"501s," he said, admiring the pair of jeans on the bed. "Brand new!" The jeans and shirt fitted perfectly. He put on the new boots and looking into the mirror at his freshly shaved and moisturised face, he smiled. "That scumbag is dead!" He chuckled, out of earshot of the companion humanoid.

A small buggy arrived and sat idling at the doorway of the bedroom. "Let me escort you down to the commissioner's quarters," said the mechanical driver.

"Thanks, but I'll walk," said Tesk cautiously, obediently following the cart along the lavishly decorated corridor. "This is some place," he remarked to the companion robot who'd insisted on tagging along. "Like one of those luxury hotels in Vegas, that they don't let the likes of me into!"

The robot chirped, "This isn't a hotel. This is the commissioner's home. Each item that you see, he's gathered from his reconnaissance missions across the vastness of the Everything!"

"Is that so?" answered Tesk, gazing up at the unfathomable array of objects and artefacts displayed in cases on the walls. He raised an eyebrow, wondering if an Earth man might one day find himself exhibited behind glass.

Tesk could smell food. Entering the great chamber, he discovered that a banquet had been laid on, their host standing expectantly at the head of the table. Tesk was placed opposite at the other end and in between them, the crew were making themselves comfortable.

Dressed up to the nines and happily chattering, each one smiled and got to their feet as Tesk reluctantly entered. "Here he is!" cried Joey with an almighty laugh.

"Great to see you, boss!" called Douglas.

"You feeling any better, sugar?" enquired Alice sympathetically.

"Yeah, I feel great," announced Tesk, looking good but more than a little uneasy.

Once seated, a service robot brought a trolley and Turner rubbed his hands together excitedly. "Now, my friends, what would you all like to drink?" he asked effervescently. "Wine, beer, whiskey, Champagne? We have everything, I believe!" Turner was giddy, happily spoiling the Earth visitors, just as he had at the coalition chambers.

"Erm, whiskey?" requested Tesk cautiously.

"I've laid on quite a meal for us tonight!" Turner smiled pouring the drink.

"Oh, yeah?" asked Tesk. "What's the occasion?"

"You are the occasion!" said Turner gleefully. "I'm absolutely thrilled to meet more of our Earth friends! That's the occasion!" He held his drink aloft. "To the Earth children!" he declared.

They all raised their glasses in a toast. The service robots scurried in, bringing serving platters of earthly and unearthly looking dishes. "Enjoy yourselves, friends! Please make yourselves at home!"

The Earth crew needed little encouragement, enthusiastically tucking into the buffet of mixed delicacies. "And here's me thinking the entire universe hated us!" joked Tesk.

"Maybe we were just hanging out with the wrong crowd?" Alice giggled.

"Exactly!" replied Turner. "And you're welcome to stay for as long as you want! Look around, Tesk, the gardens, the quarters, my home. You will see the most fantastic collection in the entire universe! Things I have acquired from a lifetime of space travel. A museum of life! Special artefacts, all of which I have picked up during my extensive service missions with the coalition." Tesk smiled, helping himself to another hotdog. "You will find many Earth artefacts!" boasted Turner. "Do you know I even have an Earth room! The finest art and sculpture, wonderful pieces, salvaged from my many, many visits there!"

Tesk nodded. "Salvaged, huh? So, you're an explorer?"

"Yes, you could say that," concurred the commissioner. "But simply put… I consider myself a connoisseur of nice things!"

"And where do we fit into all of this?" asked Tesk with his mouth full of bread. "I hope my head ain't gonna end up framed, hanging on a wall!"

Turner let out a shrill laugh. "Hahaha, of course not!" he cried. "Tesk, you must understand, I just like people. In this room, I have entertained every species of creature you could possibly imagine. I find it fascinating meeting new beings!" he enthused, putting his hand on Chrissy's, who was sitting close by. Chrissy smiled politely for a moment, but then respectfully pulled it away and took another drink. "I had such a good time with Little Stevie and the gang, I just wanted to meet you all in person." Tesk nervously eyed Turner. The rest of the crew seemed to be falling under the commissioner's spell, but Tesk wasn't buying it. "There's plenty more food, my dear!" He smiled at Alice. "Please, tuck in!"

The companion robot suddenly appeared with a tray of multicoloured drinks. Everyone took a glass, but Tesk declined. "Cocktails ain't my thing," he said politely.

"What a spectacular feast!" called out an appreciative Douglas. "I Thought we'd be in big trouble with the coalition once we escaped the compound! How come we're being treated so nice?" he hollered.

Tesk observed Turner, awaiting his response.

"I haven't informed the coalition," he declared. "It's none of their business!" He let out another piercing laugh. "They don't need to know anything about it!" He smiled, looking to Tesk. "The coalition is such a vast organisation, I don't know why we need to bother them? I'm more than happy to turn a blind eye to your mischievousness!"

"But I thought we were public enemy number one?" Chrissy huffed. "Xzardak reckoned we were dangerous and weren't permitted off of that creepy planet?"

Turner smiled again, putting his hand on hers. "Just procedure, my girl." He beamed, tilting his head. "It's nothing personal; it happens to every new species that we introduce into the kingdom. There is always a danger that they will poison us with invisible germs! The coalition are terribly cautious; they think that everything is going to kill them!" Turner chuckled. "Well, you know what?" His eyes widened. "I think tonight proves, once and for all, that our species are quite compatible!" This time, Chrissy did not remove her hand.

"Well," said Douglas, rubbing his stuffed belly, "I'm feeling pretty good! So, you space folk are all right by me!"

Turner simpered, sensing he was winning over this new batch of Earth creatures.

"Won't the coalition wonder where we've gone?" enquired Alice.

"Alice, dear, you are sitting in the company of the coalition. I am a very high-ranking commissioner. Please just leave it to me! Now, enough business. Just relax and enjoy yourselves!"

Down in the Earth room, Turner was showing off the artefacts in his collection. "Picasso, Rembrandt, Rodin," he boasted, trying to capture the attention of his guests. Douglas feigned interest while the other guys played at poker, laughing loudly, and spilling drinks on the antique floor coverings. Chrissy had passed out; the fatigue and alcohol had been too much for her.

Alice sat by her side and smiled as Tesk approached.

"Better make sure she makes it off to bed," he said.

"Yeah, preferably alone." She yawned, her eyes trained on their host. "What do you think, Tesk?" she asked suspiciously. Tesk signalled to keep her voice down, the alcohol playing havoc with the Earth people's volume control.

"What do I think?" he replied. "I think he's up to something. Give it time."

Turner popped the cork on a large bottle of vintage Champagne. "Come, friends! More drinks," he called, eager to keep the party swinging. The men, now involved in an arm-wrestling competition with the service androids, let out an almighty cheer. As Turner poured the fizzing liquid into large goblets, Tesk helped Alice pick up Chrissy and escorted them off to the bedroom. "Bolt the door and don't come out whatever happens," he said firmly. "I've a feeling it's about to get interesting." Chrissy began to stir and fearing she would demand to return to the party, Tesk made his way out of the room.

"Be careful," called Alice tenderly as Tesk, satisfied that they were locked in and safe and sound, headed back to check up on the guys.

"I thought you'd left us for the evening?" said Turner reproachfully as Tesk made his way back into the chaos of the Earth room.

"Who, me? No..!" reassured Tesk. "Just making sure the ladies are okay." He smiled, pushing past the commissioner and his henchman.

"Oh, they're quite safe," reassured Turner. "The entire apartment is hermetically sealed. Outside, you'd all fry, but inside, you're all quite safe…" He paused. "For now."

CHAPTER 25

Tesk was tired of Turner's phoney cocktail party. "Listen, man, what are you up to?" he asked, cornering, then slamming the commissioner up against the corridor wall.

"Ah, Tesk, you Earth people are so suspicious," he protested. "I'm not up to anything!"

"You've sure put a lot of effort into this shindig! If you wanted to spend some quality time with us, why didn't you just swing by Xzardak's place? What are you after?"

Indignantly, the commissioner struggled to get free. "Please, Tesk, listen to me; all you need to know is I like to take care of my friends!"

"Sure, you take care of them," Tesk replied, "by shooting, drugging and keeping them locked up!"

Turner looked embarrassed. "That was for your own good!" He squirmed. "You were very angry!"

"You ain't seen me angry!" Tesk seethed, shoving him again. "Tomorrow, we're leaving and you better not stand in our way!"

Turner's eyes lit up. "What will you do?"

"You'll see!" Tesk heard footsteps coming along the dimly lit hallway.

"There are a handful of you." The commissioner chuckled. "All unarmed, and *you're* threatening *me*?"

Tesk intensified his grip. "Don't push it, Turner."

Sensing that someone was approaching, he reluctantly released the dishevelled-looking commissioner. Turner smiled as he straightened his collar and tried to regain his composure.

Tesk shook his head, aware that the commissioner was clearly unintimidated and was still in the mood for games. "Let me show you something," said Turner quietly. "A part of the collection that few have witnessed!"

Keeping an eye on the corridor, Tesk grudgingly followed the commissioner's lead. Around a bend, Tesk noticed a doorway. Turner walked towards it and entering a twelve-character numerical code into a digital entry panel, a heavy steel door slid open to reveal a dimly lit recess.

"Quickly, come inside." The commissioner beckoned. Tesk pulled back for a moment, but then his curiosity getting the better of him, reluctantly made his way inside. Wandering into the darkness, the thick metal door clunked closed behind them. After a few seconds, they came to another entrance way, another twelve-digit code and suddenly, the pair were inside of a cavernous chamber.

"Please," motioned Turner. "Do come in."

Tesk stepped forward nervously. Before him sprawled a huge space filled with a thousand glass cases, all illuminated, their wares meticulously displayed.

"The jewel of my collection." The commissioner smiled.

Tesk inspected the immaculately kept cabinets. It was an exhibition of every kind of military artefact imaginable: handguns, knives, swords, rifles, bayonets, uniforms, flags, missiles, tanks and an array of combat vehicles and auxiliary apparatus.

"This is what I call my war room."

Tesk was awestruck.

"You see, the Earth people aren't the only aggressive species I have encountered. There have been many before you and I imagine there will be many after! I like to keep a few simple souvenirs from every society I chance upon. This is my black museum if you like, objects that appeal to the more macabre side of my nature." Astounded, Tesk stood in silence, staring wide-eyed at the abominable display. "Top secret, of course," Turner whispered in a conspiratorial tone. "I'm sure you understand?"

"Wow!" said Tesk softly, unnerved, while quietly impressed at the deadly repository before him. "You're crazier than I thought!"

Turner smiled and led him further in. "I have been across the universe countless times and have overseen so many rescue missions. We have stepped up to save a good many species from destruction, but there were those that we allowed to perish. Claiming it to be for the benefit of the many, the government has called time on a good number of rogue nations.

"The uglier the species, those less likely to adhere to the strict protocols of the law, are usually left to fester in their own misery. And those who dare to question the order of things, who will not conform to the rigidity of the structure, often simply disappear. Countless undesirables, rebels, mavericks, insubordinates, needlessly wiped out, so many in fact, that very little individuality exists anymore." Turner sniffed and wiped away a tear.

"I'm afraid to tell you this, Tesk, but the civilised universe as you see it is anything but civilised. The coalition and governors, they too have a callous and merciless side. The Earth people were next on the extinction list. Their progress had been monitored over the ages, and we had hoped that they might outgrow their primal, violent stage. But no, they just fought and fought and fought until there was nobody left." Turner looked to Tesk.

"It was decided that we would not intervene, and you would be permitted to destroy yourselves. Too violent for the civilised realm."

Tesk really needed a drink.

"If the coalition were to find out about my little collection, I don't think they'd approve! In fact, I'm sure I'd be severely punished, sent off to suffer in darkness in one of their penal colonies. Just as you Earth people will be in the coming weeks!"

Wandering through the museum, Tesk marvelled at the array of war and torture equipment the commissioner had amassed. "This is quite some toy box!" he said.

The commissioner chuckled. "Raymonde!" he called, gesturing to his companion robot. "Open it up!" With a hydraulic thrum, the wall lifted, revealing three aircraft hanging in mid-air. Two of non-Earth origin, one circular, constructed with jelly-like undulating glass, the other angular, made of a leathery, viscous, dark metal material, both clearly designed and constructed by alien hands and minds. The third resembled the fabled, mythical 'Death Bomber IV' the deadliest of the Earth air fleet. Hanging frozen in time, its cannons were pointing, following Tesk around the room.

"The coalition are hypocrites," the commissioner announced gruffly. "They operate with impunity. They claim to speak for the people, but the people are taciturn, they have no voice."

Tesk laughed. "Let me guess, you're gonna help them find that voice?"

The commissioner turned and smiled, revealing his short, sharp, piranha-like teeth. "Now you're beginning to get it."

At the back of the room, concealed from view, was another passageway. As they approached it, the commissioner's mood lightened. "I do hope you've enjoyed my little tour of the archive, but please don't think I'm showing off!" Tesk slowly shook his head. "Remember what I said," reminded Turner as if talking to an old pal. "I hope you can keep it to yourself as I am breaching many protocols here. I wouldn't want to upset anyone of a delicate nature."

"Of course," reassured Tesk slyly.

"Now we must be getting back to the party," announced the convivial commissioner, reapplying his bright and breezy demeanour.

As they exited the war room, Tesk turned to look behind him. Skulking in the shadows were two large figures, guards of some kind, seemingly armed. Tesk stepped up the pace.

Back in the Earth room, the party was in full swing. A service robot's hand had busted off whilst arm wrestling with Douglas. The broken servant picked up its fingers as another robot swept the plush carpet. "Gentlemen!" called Turner, beating a small gong. "As per your Earth tradition, the service team will bring around an array of desserts and coffee liqueurs. This is my way of wishing you a good night. Please feel free to stay up a while longer and avail yourselves of the refreshments. I, however, must retire; I have a very busy day tomorrow."

The small company let out a hardy cheer, rewarding their host with a rousing round of applause. The commissioner bowed gracefully. "Should you require anything else, Raymonde is at your disposal!" The mechanical henchmen's visor glowed a yellow colour as the commissioner departed, retiring to his quarters.

Tesk took a drink from the server as Alice reappeared and sat down next to him. "You're awake?" Tesk smiled.

"Yeah," she replied, "Chrissy's been sick, and the room's a mess! All over that beautiful carpet too!" She winced. "Where did you disappear to?"

"Oh, the commissioner just wanted to talk sports."

Alice shuddered. "He's creepy."

"Yeah," replied Tesk with a grin. "I just can't figure out if he's creepy good, or creepy bad?" He shook his head. Alice took another drink. "I'm thinking we should get out of here?" Tesk whispered. "There's something I want to see."

Taking her by the hand, Tesk led Alice out of the Earth room.

"Leaving so soon?" quipped Raymonde politely.

"Yeah, I-I don't really like parties," stuttered Alice.

Making their way along the darkened concourse, double-checking that Raymonde was out of sight, they waited for a moment, then doubled back. "This place is like a maze," he whispered, hastily leading the way back down the corridor to where he had exited the war room. Hearing mechanical footsteps from behind, the hired goon security guards appeared from nowhere.

Drawing their weapons, they approached and circled Alice and Tesk. "Going somewhere?" murmured the shorter of the guards.

"Oh, we're lost!" Alice slurred, pretending to be drunk.

"Your quarters are up there and to the left," droned the larger soldier, stepping forward and pointing with his rifle.

"Thank you, friend!" Alice smiled nervously, taking hold of Tesk's hand.

"Let's get out of here," he said without looking back.

"They looked like our weapons!" remarked Alice.

"Yeah, that's what I thought." Tesk shrugged. "That's what I wanted to see. Those weapons are higher powered than the Category D consignment, but they are definitely Earth weapons, that's for sure."

"What does that mean?" she asked with a concerned tone.

"It means the guy is crazy, he's got a whole dungeon full of the stuff. Interesting that their weapons of choice were manufactured on Earth. We really need to get out of here!"

Aware they were being followed, Tesk and Alice hurriedly ran along the corridor, making their way back to Alice's dorm. "Looks like we're out of options," she said. "Do you think those guys are going to kill us?" She trembled.

"Maybe not us…" reassured Tesk. "But give a guy like that a gun like that, and he's gonna use it on someone!"

"What are we gonna do, Tesk? Trouble just seems to follow us around." She began to sob.

"We're going to get out, tomorrow, I promise you."

"Wanna come inside and try wriggling out the window?' she smiled, wiping a tear away.

"Like I did when we were kids?" He grinned. "This time, we're on the 49th floor. Maybe another night." He smiled, letting go of her hand. "Besides… it stinks in there!"

With Alice safely locked inside the dorm, Tesk made his way back to the party.

"You again?" joked Raymonde sarcastically, his visor flashing in time with the music.

"Yeah," said Tesk, "I believe I left my machine gun in here."

Tesk had hoped to talk to Douglas, but he was too far gone. The whole crew was wasted. The free booze and convivial atmosphere in the Earth room had gotten to all of them and they'd let their guard down. Noticing that another couple of large sentry robots had appeared at the doorway, Tesk decided it was time to call it a night.

"We're out of here first thing," he whispered into Douglas's ear.

Douglas turned and stood. "No way, man," he said, swaying. "The commissioner has said I can stay! I'm going to be head of security!" he boasted. When Douglas was loaded, Tesk knew that it was pointless to argue. Shooting him a disgruntled look, Douglas toppled backwards into his chair, laughing heartily at Tesk's serious face. Tesk got to his feet and headed to the door for the final time.

"Goodnight, friend!" whirred Raymonde.

"Sweet dreams," Tesk replied.

Back in his room, Tesk tried the window again, but it was securely sealed. The companion robot awoke and got up from her chair. "I'm afraid the windows are bolted shut. I can speak to maintenance if you would like or adjust the air conditioning?"

"No need," Tesk replied, "I'm out of here in the morning."

"Yes!" exclaimed the robot. "I have just scheduled you a mid-morning convoy, back to Earth 2. I do hope you've enjoyed your visit!" she said sincerely.

Tesk frowned. "It's been terrific!"

The next morning, the service robot awoke Tesk just as he had the previous day. "The shower is running, sir," he announced cheerfully. "Commissioner Turner has requested that you join him for breakfast." Relieved that the morning had finally arrived, he got up out of the bed and made his way into the bathroom. The steam made Tesk lightheaded; he had barely slept, a million and one thoughts coursing through his brain.

Down in the breakfast chamber, the commissioner sat alone.

Tesk was led in, flanked by the companion robot and Raymonde. "Good morning!" cried Turner, getting to his feet, looking genuinely pleased to receive his cohort. "Please, sit down," he said and gestured warmly. "I trust you slept well?" he enquired. "Raymonde assured me that your friends had an entertaining evening!"

"Yeah, it was quite some night!" admitted Tesk. "A very… interesting night," he added. Turner motioned to the server who brought over a platter of fine food. "I've really been enjoying this Earth menu!" said Turner, tucking into something that resembled meat. "Ever since my first visit to Earth, I've been a real fan of your culinary delicacies! You Earth people really know how to live!" He chuckled. "Well, did…" he added with faux embarrassment. "The food we have on my planet is so… bland; in fact, everything on my home planet is bland. Awful place!" Tesk sipped hot tea from a china cup. "Please, help yourself to food!" Turner insisted enthusiastically.

"Seems like the menu is not the only thing you've embraced?" suggested Tesk.

The commissioner giggled. "Of course not! That's what you Earth people failed to understand. That planet was teeming with life, with such a wealth of resources at your disposal. There really is no other, well… *was* no other planet like it!"

The commissioner was gleefully pushing Tesk's buttons and with the sun in his eyes, his guest was clearly becoming agitated.

"Pity it went up in smoke really," said the commissioner bluntly. Tesk curled his lip. "Not to worry," said Turner. "We've managed to salvage quite a lot from the planet, a great many samples of flora and fauna, animals, plants, trees, a real menagerie!" he spluttered excitedly. "A ton of your scientific analysis, some of it is actually worth reading and of course a wealth of art and culture. You know Earth art goes for good money on the black market." His eyes widened. "You really were the most creative species!" he announced enthusiastically.

"Like you said, pity it went up in smoke," said Tesk.

Turner narrowed his eyes; there was an awkward silence for a moment as the two beings quietly scrutinised each other. "I guess that brings us to the crux of the matter?" asked Tesk.

"Yes, it does. I like you, Tesk, straight to the point!"

"Perhaps you should get to the point," suggested Tesk with deadpan delivery. Turner waved his hand, gesturing that Raymonde leave the room. The mechanical ogre silently departed, his visor glowing a warm orange colour. He closed and locked the door behind him.

"Ah, yes! My proposition…" Tesk sat back, his hands cradled behind his head.

"As I revealed to you last night, Tesk, I have amassed quite a collection of weaponry, more than enough to go around," he stated with a self-assured grin. "I trust that you discovered the ones I had delivered to Earth 2?" Tesk nodded slowly as Turner took a sip of coffee. "Just a little gift from me to you… to get you in the mood for the next stage."

"The next stage?" Tesk shrugged, nonplussed.

"Yes, the next stage of the program," declared Turner excitedly. "I'm thinking it's time for a bit of a change. Nothing drastic, just a little bit of a reshuffle at the top. Call it a power play if you like." Tesk's brow furrowed.

"I'd been putting together an army for some time. Local types, good people, but we just couldn't source enough fire power! Then, one day, out of nowhere, I heard that the Earth planet was in trouble. Kismet! It fell straight into my lap!" He beamed. "I did the right thing, of course, and stepped up. Such a beautiful planet, it would have been criminal not to intervene! Between us, we put together a program and devised a salvage operation. However, the humans were not the only things that we brought back. Now, having amassed myself an arsenal of your most sophisticated weapons, I have almost everything I need!"

"Sounds interesting," admitted Tesk.

"Oh, it is interesting."

Tesk sat forward. "If you've everything you need for your little mutiny, where do I fit in?" Turner's expression changed, becoming serious for a moment.

"Putting together an army in a universe of passive automatons is not an easy task! Many of the really effective species are gone," he said, shaking his head regretfully. "Snuffed out of existence, at the behest of the bloated ones."

Tesk suddenly had a horrible feeling.

"That's where you come in!" said Turner brightly as if organising another of his dinner soirees. "The soldiers just aren't up to scratch!" he confessed. "I need a general, someone who can school them, watch over them and train them!" Turner paused as Tesk recoiled. "The Earth people are the perfect killing machines!" enthused Turner. "They destroy everything they touch. They cannot be stopped! Who better to help me prepare my battalions? I want us to work together, Tesk! I have great plans!"

Tesk fell silent. Was Turner offering him a way out of their desperate situation or issuing him an inevitable death sentence? The only things that Tesk knew about Turner were, one, he was crazy and two, he didn't much like him. However, never one to pass up an opportunity, Tesk attempted to buy himself some time. "Well," he said graciously. "That's quite something. I'm gonna need time to process it."

"Process it?" snapped Turner, his sunken cheeks turning quite red. "What is there to process, I'm offering you a wonderful opportunity!"

"See, the problem is, I don't work with anyone else. I'm all about me!"

"Yes, Tesk!" exclaimed the commissioner. "That's why you'll be perfect for the job! You'll be in total control! You and your Earth friends will be leaders of men!"

"I'll be in control?" he repeated. "But with you as my boss? Not my style."

Suddenly aware that Raymonde had reappeared at the opened door, Tesk sat back and took a moment.

"Maybe you just need time?" suggested Turner, breaking the silence. "There's no need to decide right now. I want you to go back to Earth 2 and think about it."

Tesk had heard enough. Getting to his feet, he eagerly turned to walk away. Preventing him from leaving, the commissioner held out his hand and looked Tesk squarely in the eye.

"Please, Tesk, consider my proposition," he suggested solemnly.

"And if I don't?"

The commissioner laughed, amused that Tesk could not resist one final combative rally. "Oh, don't worry, Tesk, I've a feeling you'll come to your senses! Now come, your transport is waiting!"

CHAPTER 26

Upon sourcing and analysing an ancient and outdated Ordnance Survey chart, Zork had located a wormhole. This enabled Mono to return from his adventures on Earth in a fraction of the time it had taken him to get there. Mono had hoped that he could cruise back to Earth 2 at a leisurely pace, admiring the view, enjoying some well-deserved downtime. However, this hadn't happened. "That Zork is trouble!" he grumbled, disengaging the autopilot and firing up the ship, pointing it towards the gateway.

Once sucked into the wormhole, it had delivered the craft home at warp speed.

Xzardak had looked so happy to see Mono as the craft docked. "My little friend!" he called out. "So pleased you've made it home in one piece!" Xzardak's warmth and enthusiasm made Mono's logic chip flutter and twitch. Secrets and lies did not sit well within his self-preservation circuit. Having weighed up the consequences, Mono had decided not to come forward with any further information other than what he had already divulged.

If he were to avoid deactivation, he would have to bury all feelings of guilt and regret.

Zork's wormhole stunt had earned him a demotion. "Thank you, Zork!" said Mono curtly, back in his role as head service robot. "I will take it from here."

Zork had been enjoying the position of lead administrator but obediently handed back control to his superior. "See you later!" Zork chirped as he exited the command centre and reluctantly trundled back to the hangar bay.

"I don't think so!" declared Mono, reminding his subordinate who was in charge.

For now, the weapons haul, hijack and escape investigation had been put onto the back burner. Xzardak and Bungo's current priority was to locate and contain the missing Earth people before the coalition did. Bungo had been in contact with every friendly dispatch post and non-coalition-affiliated contact he could think of.

Xzardak had perused every intelligence transmission and communication bulletin within his badge grade but could not find any mention of the runaways.

With every avenue of investigation exhausted, the pair were wiped out.

The days were passing by slowly, and every time the intel receiver sounded, Xzardak's heart skipped a beat.

"No news is good news… I guess?" suggested Bungo brightly, in a vain attempt to put Xzardak's mind at ease. But it wasn't working. Xzardak seemed distracted and unable to sit still. His sickly, queasy, nervous feeling had returned and the anxiety becoming too much for his delicate constitution, he had finally snapped.

"If they aren't back by the morning, I'm going to inform the coalition!" he announced.

"But what of the consequences?" enquired Bungo sheepishly, feeling more than a little culpable in their current predicament. "They'll shut us down at the very least!"

"I'm past caring," muttered Xzardak. "It was foolish to imagine that we could help them!"

"I'm sure we'd have heard if the coalition had picked them up?" declared Bungo, attempting to calm Xzardak down. But Xzardak didn't reply. His spirits had hit rock bottom and he had made up his mind.

Witnessing Xzardak's disdain, Mono too decided that if the Earth people were not back by the following morning, he would own up to his own deceit and part in the second escape. Aware that he would be severely punished, perhaps even de-activated, he conceded that it was no more than he deserved and took solace in the fact that Zork would at least receive a solid promotion.

It appeared that all hope was lost, and a heavy fug had be-fallen the command centre. Then, suddenly puncturing the anxious silence, the intel siren sounded.

"This is it." Xzardak cringed. "The game is up!"

"It's a cruiser!" announced Mono. "Unmarked. I'm unable to ascertain its planet of origin. It's requesting permission to land?"

Xzardak scratched his head. "Grant it permission. We're done for anyway! Best say your goodbyes," he groaned, ac-cepting their imminent deportation to the Planet of Night.

Reluctantly, he got to his feet and opening the hatch, pro-ceeded along the gantry to greet the mysterious visitor ship.

"Nice transport!" exclaimed Bungo, joining Xzardak on the ramp, both shielding their eyes from the craft's blinding head beam.

"Very nice," agreed Xzardak. "Too nice for coalition…" He wheezed, the pair enveloped in smoke as the ship cooled its thrusters.

Once the cloud had cleared, the craft's hatch opened and Xzardak squinted, trying to make out the identity of the figure walking towards him.

"Good to see you, spaceman," called a voice. Xzardak im-mediately recognised it.

"Tesk!" he cried, thrilled and relieved that the prodigal son had returned, his excitement soon turning to fury like a parent receiving an errant child. "Where have you been!" he scolded, not entirely certain that he wanted to know the answer.

"It's a long story," called Tesk with a concerned tone. "I think we're going to have trouble."

"Trouble?" cried Xzardak. "So then, what's new?"

The others emerging from the hatch, Xzardak was relieved to discover that all of the missing human beings were alive, present and correct.

Following their leader, they all crowded into the command centre.

"I never thought I'd say this," confessed Tesk. "But it's really good to be back!" He had lost weight; he looked gaunt and Xzardak noticed that his demeanour had changed. Whatever had happened to the earthman over the preceding weeks, it had affected him greatly.

"Please, Tesk…" begged Xzardak. "Tell me where you have been!"

Tesk began to tell the story. Discovering the weapons, the break in, the hijack, the journey to Earth, the aborted mission, the journey back and the second escape. He looked to Mono as he skirted around the actual detail of the Z4T breakout. As Tesk relayed the modified scenario, Mono felt dizzy, the complexity of the mistruth burning through his circuit boards.

Then to the pertinent part of the story.

"Seems like we have a buddy in the coalition," began Tesk. "We just spent a couple of nights with an old friend of yours." He smiled slyly at Xzardak.

"A friend of mine?" enquired Xzardak. "I don't have any friends… anymore."

"Commissioner Turner," said Tesk flatly. "Seems he's the Earth people's biggest fan. He has some wild plans for us, he reckons!"

Xzardak looked confused. "We've been expecting an intel from the coalition any day now, informing us that you'd been captured and neutralised, but not a word? Why did Commissioner Turner not notify me of your whereabouts?" Xzardak looked suspicious. "This news just doesn't add up."

"None of it adds up," agreed Tesk. "Seems Turner sees himself as a bit of a free spirit. He wants to take over the world. The guy's crazy! Kept us prisoner for a few days, wined us and dined us, then brought us home in his fancy new ship."

Xzardak was having difficulty processing the information. "What do you think, Bungo?"

"Not sure, Xzardak, but I don't like the sound of it." Bungo shrugged.

Again, the intel buzzer sounded. Answering it, Mono spoke into the receiver. Then reaching out his arm, he switched on the viewport. "That was Dr Jay," he announced. "He told me to switch on the evening news."

CHAPTER 27

"**B**reaking news, terrible news," announced the female News 36 anchor. "Coalition headquarters destroyed as the Xzardak Project takes yet another dramatic turn! Governors and commissioners feared dead and injured!" Xzardak watched in total dismay, the news channel reporting that the Earth people, fully armed, had infiltrated the highest of coalition offices.

"Acting lead enquirer, Commissioner Turner, had this to say." She handed over live to a familiar face.

"We are shocked and deeply saddened that a terrible crime of this nature could have happened here, in the peaceful surroundings of the high commission." Ashen faced and visibly shaken, Turner stood outside the burning government building and spoke into the oversized News 36 microphone. "This seat of high office has watched over the cosmos for so many millennia," he said solemnly, "ensuring peace and prosperity across the universe…" He looked down the camera lens. "What has happened here today has left us all heartbroken. Such honourable souls, cut down in the service of their duty."

Xzardak could not believe his eyes. Scenes played out of the dead and injured being tele-lifted from the charred remains of coalition HQ. Teams of emergency workers fought to extinguish the flames while paramedics attempted to resuscitate the wounded.

"I have taken it upon myself to locate and incarcerate the perpetrators of this terrible event! A crime of this magnitude must not go unpunished!" Turner had a wild, crazed look in his eye. "If the Earth people are watching, I suggest you pack your belongings and get ready for the Planet of Night! We are coming for you!" Xzardak trembled.

Handing back to the studio, the presenter continued, "Independent sources have confirmed that the Earth people are responsible for today's attack. Commissioner Turner, who as you've just heard exclusively live on News 36 is heading up the investigation, has urged anyone with any information regarding the whereabouts of the Earth people to come forward.

"Earth 2 administrator, Robert Xzardak, could not be reached, believed to be with the Earth people. It has not yet been established if he is being held against his will or is involved with the renegades."

Xzardak's head was swimming. "What's going on?" he spluttered.

"Who would have thought it?" Tesk said. "Turner would use our weapons against the other commissioners then pin the blame on us little old Earth folk!"

"I-I don't believe it," stuttered Xzardak. "Tesk, is this true?" He turned to face the Earth man.

Tesk lifted his head and stared Xzardak squarely in the eye. Bungo slowly backed away, anticipating trouble.

Tesk grinned. "Come on, Xzardak, we're bad but you know we ain't that bad!"

"I'm sorry, Tesk, but I need to know. If you are involved in this, you must tell me. I am sure together—"

"Hell no! Of course, we aren't!" cried Tesk, getting up and walking toward Xzardak. "Listen, man! Like I told you, the guy's nuts! He's created an army, every deadbeat and fruit loop in the galaxy! He wants me and the guys, Douglas, Stevie, Alice, all of us to train them up! He's got a ton of our weapons too!" Tesk was raging. "We've got a lot of work to do. I dunno what his next move will be, but I guarantee we'll be in the picture!"

Xzardak's heart was racing. Such horrible scenes! Unsure of what to do next, he paced the floor. What if Tesk and the Earth people were guilty? A coalition convoy would be here any minute to arrest them and take them away. Were they really that evil? What if Tesk was telling the truth? Turner's attempt to overthrow the coalition had worked and now the humans were the most wanted creatures in the whole of the universe.

As administrator of the program, surely he would be a suspect too? After all, the virus had escaped and he hadn't even notified the authorities.

Either way, it seemed obvious they were done for.

"But why?" pleaded Xzardak. "Why would Turner do such a thing?"

"He's crazy!" answered Tesk. "He wants to run the show! This is his way of getting rid of the other commissioners and it seems we just walked straight into a set up!"

"Did you know he was planning this attack?" inquired Bungo. "Did he indicate such an action?"

"Hell, no! He told me he had plans, but I thought he was bluffing, mouthing off. He's a freak! He's the one who organised the Category D drop!"

Bungo gave Xzardak a sideways glance.

"He's got it all planned out. Him and his army of nasties, all lined up and ready to raise hell! Wanted us to join up, but I told him to stick it!"

"Was anyone else privy to this conversation?" enquired Xzardak.

"No, just me!" insisted Tesk. "I didn't want to get the other guys involved."

The other guys looked as perturbed as Xzardak.

Mono had taken it upon himself to run a medical diagnostic on everyone present in the room.

Tesk was losing his cool. "If we'd been responsible, why would we come back here? We're public enemy number one! We'd be long gone! If we were responsible, the first thing we'd do is shoot up the compound, shoot Bungo, shoot you!"

"You did shoot up the compound," exclaimed Bungo, "when you commandeered the 409!"

"What, that? Nah, we were just goofing around!"

Unsure whether it would help or not, Mono interjected, "Xzardak, I believe the Earth man is telling the truth. His brain patterns would suggest that he is not lying."

Tesk gave Mono a knowing look, now they were even.

Xzardak wiped his brow. "What do you think, Bungo?" he enquired.

Bungo shrugged, aware that Tesk was becoming angry. "If they were evil enough to murder the commissioners, I'm sure they would have murdered us by now? It would explain who supplied the weapons, I suppose."

Xzardak collected his thoughts and stood up straight. He asserted that the correct plan of action would be to try and deal with the situation calmly and rationally.

"There must be some sort of misunderstanding?" announced Xzardak calmly and rationally. "I suggest we follow protocol."

"Misunderstanding!" Tesk chuckled. "Oh man, this guy!" He looked to Bungo. "Okay, brainiac, let's get them on the phone, see if we can't sweet talk them into playing nice."

Xzardak nodded. The correct course of action would be to report their location to the relevant authorities. Bungo lifted the receiver from the control console and tried their direct line to coalition HQ. "It's dead, Xzardak."

"Try Turner directly," suggested Xzardak. Bungo entered the code but to no avail.

"That one is dead too."

"Try the press office of News 36," offered Alice. Bungo pulled up the code from the telex network but again, the line failed to connect.

"Seems they've cut us off," said Tesk. "You sure you paid the bill?"

"Impossible!" muttered Xzardak, punching the mayday distress button installed into the system by Dr Jay.

"It ain't working, is it?" said Tesk.

"I won't believe it!" cried Xzardak. "There must be some kind of power outage, a meteor shower or something?"

"There ain't no meteor shower!" declared Alice. "It's as clear as day, we're being set up! Tesk's right; the guys were wasted but I saw the weapons in his apartment. The guy's a creep!"

"Yeah, I'll testify to that!" Chrissy sighed, still nursing her hangover.

"Let us handle it, Xzardak!" insisted Douglas. "From what Tesk says, it seems like a total set up to me. You're way out of your depth here, soldier. This is our war!"

Bungo shrugged.

"What we have here, Xzardak, is a maniac!" asserted Tesk. "Now you space folk are always eager to tell us Earth types how primitive and violent we are, but tell me, Mr Perfect, who comes next on the list of undesirables? I know that there are other misfits out there in the universe. Turner told me so. If we are the worst of the worst, who's the second worst of the worst?"

Xzardak sat forward and placed his head in his hands. "Mono, what do you think?"

Mono's eyes flashed as he processed the data. "Most likely, erm...The Nova! They are next on the government's list of least wanted."

Xzardak looked horrified. "Oh no, the Nova! Please, not them!" Bungo furrowed his brow and cleared his throat. "It would make perfect sense. They'd be stupid enough to get involved. They live out in the farthest reaches of space, banished to the dark lands! They were part of the kingdom at one time; however, they were exiled after some... high jinks."

"High jinks, huh?" chuckled Tesk. "I like the sound of these guys! Well, that explains why Turner ain't knocking on our door just yet. My guess is he's rallying these Nova creeps and as many other rejects as he can find. Tell me, how long would it take them to get over here from—"

"The dark lands!" Mono interjected. "Their vehicles were impounded many, many cycles ago, but in a coalition craft, I would imagine with the benefit of a chartered wormhole they could be inside of our territory within a rotation or two?"

Mono looked to Bungo, Bungo looked to Xzardak, and Xzardak closed his eyes.

Tesk stood up. "Well, let's imagine, two days to arrive, a couple more to brief them, train them up."

"Oh, they won't need training up, Tesk," Mono declared. "They really are quite despicable, savage entities! They're already quite...capable."

"Bad guys, huh?" Tesk scratched his head. "Well, in that case, they are probably headed over already and we're sitting around shooting the breeze," he bellowed.

"We need to work up a plan!" demanded Nelson impatiently. "We need to rally the troops!"

"The Nova?" Xzardak shuddered. "Headed here... I don't believe it..."

"Believe what you want, Xzardak, but trouble's coming, and we need to be ready!" announced Douglas.

Xzardak got to his feet. "If what you have told me is true, there must be a peaceful way out of this mess. If only we could make contact with the authorities."

"Don't you see it, Xzardak? Turner *is* the authorities!" insisted Alice.

"You must allow me to negotiate!" said Xzardak. "I cannot sanction a campaign of violence!"

"I hear you, boss," replied Tesk cheerily. "But he's coming to kill us, Xzardak! Don't you understand? I turned the guy down. We've served our purpose. There's no campaign of violence; the way I see it, we're acting in self-defence!"

"Protocol 68331 states that one may engage forceful coercion as a form of self-preservation!" Zork announced cheerily, reappearing at the entrance hatch. "It's an outdated protocol but it still stands in the eye of the law." Mono rolled his eyes.

"Brute force is the only language these freaks understand," asserted Dougie. "If they want a war, they'll get a war!"

"Don't look so worried, Xzardak. They don't stand a chance against us!" assured Tesk.

"Only one problem," wailed Xzardak. "You haven't any weapons!"

"Are you kidding me, Xzardak? Leave that to me. I had a feeling something like this might happen!"

Mono didn't much care for Tesk's plan of going down in flames but feeling somewhat responsible for the dreadful circumstances in which they had found themselves, he did not voice his concerns. "In lieu of any other plan, it would appear that enacting protocol 68331 could be our only option!" he announced, so as not to be upstaged by his insubordinate counterpart. "We are totally within our rights to act out of self-preservation!"

"Yeah, and I bet Turner's familiar with that protocol too!" growled Alice.

Eventually, it was decided that when Turner arrived, Xzardak would explore a peaceful and mutually beneficial resolution with him. However, if a suitable compromise could not be agreed, Tesk had convinced him that they should have a plan 'B' in place.

Xzardak capitulated. However, he remained apprehensive.

"I have a feeling that Tesk might be somewhat disappointed should plan 'A' succeed…" he confided to Bungo who rolled his eyes.

The weaker, older, and more placid Earth people, those who had so far abstained from any trouble making and 'high jinks' would be categorised as 'Civilians.' "I have no need for any weak-willed, yellow bellies!" ranted Tesk. "Leave them out of it; they'll only hinder our progress. Set them to work building shields and gathering rocks!"

'The Hellraisers.' Those who had been up for a fight since the moment they had awoken in this strange new reality, would provide the real action.

Having once again commandeered Mono and a transport, Tesk, Dougie, Alice and Little Stevie re-emerged from the housing complex. The land charger was primed and loaded with enough guns and artillery to equip a small army. Xzardak marvelled at the armoury of munitions the Earth man had managed to stockpile. "I'd love to know where that lot was hidden," he admitted, looking puzzled. Land probes had scanned for any leftover weapons when Tesk and the marauders had departed on their ill-fated origin Earth mission, but the search crew had been unable to locate any firearms, let alone confiscate them.

"Yep, they certainly are resourceful," agreed Bungo.

As Tesk had explained, it made total sense that Commissioner Turner had been responsible for the weapon drop and Xzardak conceded that if his plan had been to fire up the Earth people, it had most certainly worked. All assembled, brandishing their firearms, the small band strutted around the compound, their faces flushed with excitement, armed, dangerous, and crazy enough to face down whoever or whatever came over the horizon.

The Earth people were given their duties and obediently got to work. Xzardak monitored their progress from the video screen in the charge quarters. The civilians went about their chores while Tesk rallied his hellraising legion, preparing them all for the conflict. "You know what they've said about us!" he cried into a microphone. "They called us savages, monsters, devils!" His words were echoing out across the compound speaker system. "Hell, they even categorised us as a toxic entity!" The crowd jeered. "Well maybe they're right. Maybe that is what we are? But this conflict isn't ours. Trouble has sought *us* out this time! Perhaps that's all we're good for? In which case... Let's not disappoint those news cameras. If the folks at home are expecting fireworks, let's give them fireworks! Light up the sky like the Fourth of July! You know what we have to do!" The compound crowd whooped and cheered.

"Tesk seems incredibly calm," remarked Bungo.

"Yes, it's almost as if he's enjoying himself," replied Xzardak.

As night fell, the Earth people gathered outside the charge quarters. The civilians were put into the confinement of the command centre and Tesk briefed those remaining, before finally instructing the battalion to retire. The next day would be a test of everyone's wills.

As Xzardak wished Tesk a good night, Mono appeared. "There's a convoy, Xzardak," he said solemnly. "I've just spotted it on the control scope, and it appears to be headed by a coalition ship. They are heading in our direction."

CHAPTER 28

Xzardak thought it bizarre that the lead ship in the coalition convoy would request permission to land. After all, if Tesk was to be believed, the incoming invaders were there to destroy everyone and everything on the compound. The fact that the commissioner was adhering to protocol would surely suggest that he hadn't gone completely off the rails. The Earth people anxiously chattered amongst themselves. "Just play it cool, people," reassured Tesk. "If they wanted us dead, they'd have blasted us already," he said cheerfully, polishing his shiny new rifle.

The larger of the ships cooled its boosters as it gently docked inside the hangar bay. Zork dutifully guided it clear then immediately rushed to take cover. Douglas excitedly sidled over to Tesk. "Shouldn't we have started shooting by now?" he whispered.

Tesk smiled, staring down the sight of his rifle. "Let's just get them down on dry land. Something tells me there's more to this visit than meets the eye."

Douglas nodded enthusiastically and got back into position, reassured that despite their limited options, Tesk had a plan.

All the cruisers had landed and the atmosphere in the pod suddenly changed from wild excitement to mild dread. Xzardak and the Earth people sat quietly for a moment, staring out through the contact viewport, Xzardak anticipating and Tesk considering the first move.

With a crackle and a burst of feedback, the lead ship's public address system sounded its fanfare. "This is Commissioner Turner speaking, I am armed and have brought with me reinforcements," his booming, distorted voice reverberated across the compound. "Xzardak, I wish to speak with you," he announced with an ominous tone.

Xzardak looked to Tesk. But Tesk's eye remained on the cockpit of the lead ship. He tipped his head, motioning to the microphone on the main console.

"See what he wants," he instructed.

Xzardak took a deep breath and placed his finger onto the intercom switch. "Commissioner Turner, this is Xzardak. There is no need for further bloodshed, and we will listen to what you have to say."

After a slight pause, Turner spoke again. "I think it is better that we converse eye to eye, so I am coming out of my craft. Please do not attempt anything. I know that you are suitably armed, but I must remind you that you are also vastly outnumbered."

"How could he know we're armed?" remarked Tesk sarcastically, giving Bungo a sideways glance. "Unless…"

Xzardak looked to Tesk, but the Earth man slowly shook his head. "Too risky," he insisted. "Look, stay where you are, we'll do it my way."

"I'm going outside!" declared Xzardak. "If there is a peaceful way to settle this, Tesk, I must try to find it!" Xzardak got to his feet and stood tall, reasserting his role as commander of the program. "You are still my responsibility, remember, and it is my duty to pursue a nonaggressive settlement!"

"Plan 'A'?" Tesk rolled his eyes and snickered. "We have you covered, Xzardak. We'll try it your way, and if that doesn't work, just holler!"

Xzardak straightened the collar on his robe and checked what was left of his hair in the viewport reflection.

"Plan 'A'," he announced confidently.

"It was nice knowing you." Little Stevie chuckled as the commander marched out with a swish of his cape.

Emerging through the main unit doors, Xzardak paced along the gantry ramp and approached the coalition cruiser, his footsteps echoing across the grimly silent hanger bay.

"So good to see you," called Turner cheerily as he disembarked and swaggered toward his old friend. "It's just a shame I'm here under such terrible circumstances."

Xzardak was unnerved by the commissioner's dishevelled appearance. It was evident that his mentor and ally had dramatically changed since the last time they had spoken.

"I need your help," he announced.

"My help?" Xzardak paused.

"Yes. I would like all of the Earth people loaded aboard my ship. They are to be transported to the Planet of Night to await trial for treason."

"Treason?" baulked Xzardak. "There is no evidence that they are involved in any act of treason."

Turner smiled. "Have you not seen the news reports, Xzardak? I would be happy to show you, aboard my cruiser."

Xzardak shook his head. "I'm not entirely certain that those news reports are accurate."

The commissioner smiled. He had intended to perpetuate his subterfuge, but the temptation to gloat and bask in the glory of his terrible deed was too much to resist. "I am offering you a way out, Xzardak." He beamed. "Stand aside, I'm here to take the Earth people, with or without your cooperation. Testify against them and you will be free. As their hostage, I will attest that you had no part in their diabolical scheme. I have no quarrel with you."

Xzardak took a deep breath and gestured to the armada of cruisers docked in the shuttle bay before him. "Who have you brought with you, Commissioner? The Nova?"

"Yes, that's right, Xzardak!" giggled Turner. "However did you guess? Or did the vile Earth people figure that out for you?"

Xzardak began to sweat. Despite his recent reassertion of guardianship, his newly acquired bravery and bluster had suddenly deserted him.

"The Nova are just here for moral support, Xzardak!" insisted Turner innocently. "Let's not forget you have an infestation of your own, and how better to protect oneself against a dangerous virus than with another dangerous virus? The Nova won't interfere. They are just here to see that justice is served."

"I came out here to discuss a peaceful resolution to our problems. With the Nova behind you, it is clear that was never your intention. There is no way that you and your monsters will take the Earth people; they are armed and willing to do whatever it takes to defend themselves."

The commissioner chuckled. "Bring me Tesk, and let's see if together, we can't broker you a peaceful resolution." Xzardak turned and looked to the control deck, able to see Tesk still staring down the sight of his rifle. "You can't intimidate the Earth people, Commissioner. Tesk wants nothing to do with you and your plans. None of them do."

"But Xzardak!" Turner protested. "I'm afraid they don't have a choice!"

He clicked his fingers and suddenly, two ugly looking Nova emerged from the lead ship. Xzardak stepped backwards, appalled to see the despised Nova disembark and set foot on his beloved compound. The bigger of the two grunted into a transponder and the hatches on all five coalition crafts opened with a crack and a hiss. Xzardak nervously stood his ground as the battalion of scaly green Nova troops lumbered out from the idling vessels. All dressed in ill-fitting, grubby looking military attire, they marched out of step in the direction of their commander. Turner held up his hand, instructing the lizard-like legion to halt.

Xzardak stood frozen to the spot, hearing the dreaded in vaders' primitive rifles powering up.

"You must realise that it is in everyone's better interests that you listen to what I have to say," said Turner. "After all, you have played your part and I believe you should be duly rewarded," he declared. "You've done everything by the book and kept the powers that be at bay. You've enabled me to work with impunity, to formulate and execute my plans while all eyes in the galaxy were upon you. As my project's unwitting custodian, I am eternally indebted to you."

Turner signalled to Raymonde and with a heavy clunk, the robot released a catch on the side of his cruiser's fuselage. The side panel dropped open with a thud, revealing the interior of the cavernous craft. Xzardak stared into the vast open vault, crate upon crate, piled ten high and fifty wide, each one loaded with an unimaginable cargo.

Each one was branded with the simple insignia 'D.'

The leader of the Nova cackled, revealing his shark-like yellow teeth and Xzardak slowly took three steps backwards.

"Human innovation at its finest!" bellowed Turner. "Guns, ammunition, grenades, rocket launchers, explosives! Enough technology to destroy the entire Everything!"

The wide-eyed commissioner grinned.

Inside the pod, the Earth people jostled to see what was inside the silo. "Those freaks are giving me the creeps!" cried Cheryl.

"The crates," asked Alice. "Do they contain what I think they contain?"

"Yeah… more guns!" said Little Stevie. "He's a wacko!" Beginning to lose his cool, he turned from the viewport window as the Hell Raisers cooed and craned their necks, eager to get a clearer view of the prohibited bounty.

The commissioner turned as if to leave, motioning to the largest of the Nova troops. The battalion took two steps forward, presenting their fully charged up arms. "I'm grateful for everything you have done, Xzardak," he called. "But you must understand, the program was never about the human beings, the planet Earth or any of it. It was all about the weapons."

Safely back inside his freighter, Commissioner Turner addressed the Earth people from his dispatch post, his voice echoing across the compound.

"My dear Earth friends!" he began. "It seems we find ourselves at a difficult impasse. The vicious attack on the coalition headquarters has made your tenancy within the civilised realm unworkable. Therefore, with the power invested in me, I am here to ensure that justice is carried out. You are to be escorted from the sanctity of Earth 2, off to somewhere more suited to your darkened hearts!"

It was clear that plan 'A' had been a terrible idea. Out on the gantry, Xzardak slowly backed away. However, a coarse grunt from the lead Nova warrior stopped him dead in his tracks. Now trapped directly in the line of fire, feeling vulnerable and alone, he bowed his head.

The commissioner continued from inside the lead ship, "It is with great regret that I come here today. We had such high hopes for the program, but true to form, it has failed and now you find yourselves on the brink of oblivion. In many ways, this most recent tragedy is down to your illustrious leader. Not Xzardak, the man inaugurated to see you on your way to a brighter future but Tesk, your self-elected master. I offered Tesk a way out," insisted Turner, "but he has declined my kind offer, as has Xzardak. Sensing the hostile reception we have received today, I am forced to conclude that you Earth fools would rather perish than prosper. However, I will give you one final chance to make amends, one final proposition."

Xzardak shook his head. "You've lost your mind, sir!" he cried at the top of his voice.

"Perhaps," Turner replied with a sinister whisper. "But let me assure you, there is a method in my madness."

Xzardak felt dizzy and unsteady on his feet. He took a breath but the heat and the fumes from the multiple exhaust ports had contaminated the clean, purified, unpolluted atmosphere.

Fearing he might pass out, he turned to view the command centre.

Inside the pod, the Earth people were listening intently. "Shouldn't we go out there and help him?" cried Little Stevie.

"Not yet," replied Tesk. "They'll shoot him if we make the first move."

"They're gonna shoot him anyway!" cried Stevie. "C'mon, man. We have to do something!" But Tesk did not respond.

Xzardak closed his eyes. A single tear ran down his face as the commissioner cleared his throat. "For many Earth rotations, we'd been watching your world. The coalition had turned its back upon the plight of the Earth people, claiming they were too far gone to be saved. Ignoring your pain and suffering, your species was added to the extinction list, considered too wild and uncontrollable for the civilised realm. I watched you with a curious interest; you didn't appear primitive to me. In fact, you displayed startling ingenuity."

The Earth people were silent.

"I witnessed you destroy your own world. I saw how you polluted the oceans and poisoned the air that surrounded you. I watched as the forests were felled and the fauna hunted to extinction. I watched you tear each other limb from limb, and I revelled in the scenes of savage cruelty. Much too horrifying to comprehend, it seemed so alien to a member of the civilised order. Yet I was transfixed, and couldn't look away!

"At first, I accepted the common misconception that the Earth people must be deranged, a pestilence set upon the Earth. An uncontrollable virus hellbent on destruction. But the more I studied you, the more I related to you. The acts that you perpetrated were not acts of self-sabotage or folly; on the contrary, they were acts of survival, each one part of a singular quest for permanence, for continuation. Out in the dark, you felt unsure of who you were or what you were for, each of you ceaselessly running from God and your own demise.

"What bemused me was that your quest for existence did not bring you together as a people. What would have appeared obvious to a child in my realm, did not seem to occur to the most intelligent or enlightened of your brethren. Your fears did not unite you or spur you on to a unified spiritual quest. Instead, you set out to surmount each other.

"Rather than moving forward as a kingdom, it appeared that every Earth man just wanted to be a king. This is where our stories merge."

Turner disembarked again. He spoke into his transponder, broadcasting across the speaker system. He paced back and forth, talking enthusiastically with conspiratorial glee.

"I'd been disillusioned with the coalition for so long, it was time for a change! But how could one achieve it? The system within which we exist is much too rigid, the might of the civilised realm, far too strong for one being to dismantle! You must understand that the rules are the rules and *protocol must never be breached!* That is our despised doctrine.

Sitting pondering this conundrum, I suddenly had a thought. As my beloved Earth planet began to expire, I wondered what would become of its unique inhabitants? Would they be permitted to perish? All of those fables of fire and fury deleted from our data repository? That's when the notion occurred to me, a brain wave! That's when I had my idea!"

Tesk felt a strange mix of emotions. He felt vindicated, yet the fact he had been right all along left him far from elated. The coalition had had little interest in preserving the Earth people, as he had suspected from the very start. Now that the terrible truth was out, he realised they hadn't a friend in the universe. He watched as Raymonde and the other worker drones selected individual crates, bringing them forward and placing them at Turner's feet.

The commissioner bent down and flipping open the lid, he reached inside. Selecting a fearsome looking combat rifle from the open container, he held it aloft. "Oh look!" he shouted. "Property of the U.S. Military! Nothing but the best!" He lowered it and pointed it in the direction of Xzardak who slowly held up his hands, much too terrified to flee.

"Around the time of the elections…" continued the crazed commissioner. "A pressure group emerged. They were advocating a distress convoy be sent to the Earth planet to try and assess the extent of the damage."

"Let me guess. *You* assembled the group?" Xzardak asked.

"Ha-ha, yes! That's right, Xzardak, I and a few like-minded acquaintances put together a plot. The other commissioners hadn't a clue! We had this whole thing planned out from the very beginning. All we needed to do was tug at the heart strings of the gullible populace and we knew we'd have ourselves a mercy mission. Once public opinion was on our side, we established a convoy to salvage what we could, a sample of every existing life form on the planet.

"While the land probes searched and collected what was left of the flowers and butterflies, I had a special drone task force collect as many weapons as they could. The Earth people were too distracted to notice. The project had been allocated very little resource, so we were not required to provide any form of itinerary for inspection upon our return.

"The coalition had no interest in saving the planet. To them, it was just about appeasing the people, who by this time had organised marches, petitions and fundraisers, to save the poor beleaguered inhabitants of the trash planet. The humans were too busy squabbling amongst themselves!" Turner jeered. "They didn't even notice the alien convoys harvesting as many keepsakes as they possibly could! All in the name of science, mind you!

"By the time the planet's ecosystem had collapsed, and the Earth had been declared a dead star, we had amassed enough specimens to create a whole new planet Earth!" He held up his hand and evidenced the new world around him. "We made sure we brought back some Earth people, of course, just for the sake of legitimacy." He giggled. "Then everyone rejoiced, the politicians remained in their places, the sickly Earth people were saved, and the gentle folk enjoyed a warm feeling of self-satisfaction. Most importantly, I got some shiny new artefacts for my museum—the Museum of the Apocalypse I'm going to call it! A warning to everyone about the horrors of war!" he added sarcastically. "The rest is history, Xzardak, surely you can work it out for yourself!"

"What's this I hear about a new proposition?" called Tesk, appearing in silhouette at the control centre doorway.

The commissioner squealed with delight. "Ah, Tesk, we meet again! I had a feeling you'd see sense. Xzardak is a good man but he's so prim and proper. There's only one thing more powerful than fear, I find, and that's curiosity. I knew you'd be intrigued!"

"Oh, I'm intrigued." Tesk smiled.

Turner's eyes lit up.

Walking down the ramp and across to the coalition cargo bay, Tesk eyed the Nova warily.

He showed little emotion as he approached Turner and squared up to him. A little too close for comfort, invading his personal space, the commissioner attempted to politely back away.

Turner had expected the Earth creatures to come out fighting, but his plan to provoke them had clearly not worked. He smiled awkwardly, pleased to have Tesk's attention but apprehensive in such close proximity to the unpredictable Earth man proudly brandishing a shiny new rifle.

"Please don't worry about our associates." Turner smiled, gesturing to the Nova army.

"The hired goons?" remarked Tesk with a growl. "I ain't worried."

He sniffed, tilting his head and fixing his eyes squarely on Turner.

"I'm sure you've seen the news reports?" he announced. "You understand the gravity of the situation we find ourselves in?"

Tesk shook his head nonchalantly. "Not really," he whispered.

Turner switched off the transponder and took a breath. "I've had many disagreements with my fellow commissioners, they see…" He paused to correct himself with a chuckle. "Well, they *saw* things differently to how I did. Put simply, they continually stood in the way of my plans. Good plans, fair plans, plans that could vastly improve things. D-do you understand me, Tesk?" he stuttered, beginning to become unnerved by the Earth man's cold, hard stare.

Tesk smiled. "Sure, I understand; you've got to jive to stay alive, my friend!" he concurred.

Turner backed up to a more comfortable distance. "Most sensible creatures knew to avoid your people, but the more I heard about you, the more I admired you. I became obsessed, transfixed, mesmerised. I felt sure that you could help me, so I studied you. I wanted to discover your central drives. What it was that made you so volatile, so destructive, so different from every other life form we had encountered?"

"Like you said," said Tesk. "We were part of a machine. We were fighting for survival, you called it right. Each man for himself, we did what we had to do!"

Turner shook his head and took a moment to compose himself, narrowing his eyes and cocking his head, looking to redress the balance of power. "Something happened to you along the way, your quest for survival became corrupted, debased, perverted. Even when you'd acquired everything you needed, it still wasn't enough. Survival at any price became dominion at any price. You were out of control, slaves to your own desires and impulses. That's what destroyed your world, wiped out your kind and that's what piqued my interest.

"If only every species had in them, that spark which resides inside an Earth man. Personally, I celebrate your wild spirit, your insanity, your recklessness, your lack of respect and disregard for consequence! I revel in it, and it is that which I wish to harness!"

Inside the command centre, the Earth people were becoming restless. Turner had turned off his transponder and the conversation was no longer being broadcast across the internal tannoy system. Mono was relaying as much as his receptors could detect but it seemed just as the conversation was getting interesting, the humans inside the pod could no longer hear.

"What the hell is going on out there?" demanded Chrissy. "What is there to discuss?"

Mono tried to appease the Earth woman. "Xzardak and Tesk are trying to find a peaceful compromise to the situation. I'm sure they will come to an amicable agreement quite soon!"

"Amicable agreement?" cried Ruby. "Just shoot the damn gun already. There's no use in talking to this nut job. Just blast him away and we can get back on with our lives!"

Mono could not think of a logical retort.

"I've had enough of this!" announced Little Stevie. He headed to the exit, en route to join his friend.

"No, stop, wait!" cried Mono. "Tesk demanded we all remain in the pod!"

"I wanna hear what's going on!" insisted Stevie. "No one is going to fit me inside their amicable agreement!"

Stevie marched out of the command centre and down to where the others were gathered. He baulked as he saw the number of troops assembled behind the commissioner. As Stevie approached, Turner smiled and bowed to him. "Thank you for joining us, my friend!"

"What's going on, fellas?" called Stevie.

Tesk motioned to the open cargo. Stevie marvelled at the number of unopened Category 'D' crates and the vast armoury it likely contained.

"Whoa, that's some firework display!" he joked. "What's the big occasion?"

"The commissioner's kindly laid on a little going away party for us!" Tesk chuckled.

Turner smiled. "When I brought you into my home, I showed you my war room. You saw that I had many, many weapons inside there, but I did not show you everything." Turner once again signalled to the Nova Captain, who in turn instructed his man to drop the second of the cargo bay doors. To Turner's disappointment and frustration, the frontage would not open.

Fearing that the oafish Nova soldier had botched his big reveal, he barked an order to his superior. The leader marched over to the silo door and together, the two Nova hammered and bashed at the latch. Turner dropped his head with embarrassment.

"Incompetent fools," he muttered to himself.

Suddenly, with a loud clack, the latch was released, and the heavy door clanged to the ground, revealing the bounty inside. With a sharp intake of breath, Tesk and Stevie stepped backwards, chilled by the vision before them.

"The jewel in my collection!" cried Turner. "The ultimate weapon. Nuclear warhead N19H5TU. This silo contains eighteen in total." He grinned mischievously.

"Hey, maybe go easy on that cargo door, fellas!" Tesk, shouted forgoing his cool demeanour. He looked to Stevie, then Xzardak, both standing speechless.

"It wasn't until I saw the scope and scale of your war machines that I realised how useful you could be to me. So inventive, so creative, the ability to destroy yourselves a million times over! Who else could create a weapon, the sole intention of which was the annihilation of its own species? This anomaly in rational or abstract thought couldn't be allowed to perish with the planet."

"Okay, Turner, you have the missiles. Now what?" Tesk asked.

"The human spirit must not be permitted to expire!" raved Turner. "With our physical attributes and your imagination, just think of the society we can create! The ultimate coalition! Just as the Earth people had their dominion across the Earth, I shall have my dominion across the Everything!"

"But the Earth is gone!" declared Little Stevie.

"Yes, but the Earth people are not!" cried Turner. "Somehow, they always survive."

"You're crazy," Stevie said, wishing he had never left the safety of the control pod. "You saw it for yourself, man. We blew it!" He turned to walk away. "C'mon, Tesk. It's over."

"Let's not be hasty," suggested Turner. "What I have to say won't take long."

"I've heard enough!" screamed Little Stevie. "Let's get out of here!" With the butt of his rifle, he encouraged Xzardak to walk. But Tesk did not follow.

"We're out of options, guys. Let's hear the man out." He shrugged.

"Are you kidding me?" exclaimed Stevie. "He's a nut!"

Tesk remained in place, staring into the deranged commissioner's cold, dead eyes.

"Please, Tesk!" insisted Xzardak but Tesk did not move. Xzardak turned to go, afraid that the tide could be beginning to turn.

"It can't hurt to hear what the man has to say, fellas!" suggested Tesk with an evil smile, but Little Stevie and Xzardak were gone.

CHAPTER 29

Xzardak had made it safely back inside the pod, but it was evident that the atmosphere amongst the Earth people had changed. Watching the proceedings closely, they seemed captivated by the commissioner and his box of tricks. The huge bombs had made them gasp then chatter and applaud, seemingly so impressed that Xzardak feared they may be seduced by the manic commissioner and his ridiculous scheme. The project had been a sham and Xzardak felt a fool.

Questioning the legitimacy of his position in Turner's game, he wondered if he should just call it quits, break protocol and head for home. Pondering this notion, he felt a sudden pang which prevented him from fleeing. He realised that he still felt an obligation towards the humans.

He had worked so hard, and they had come so far together, and for them to revolt and defect now would break his heart.

The commissioner had switched on his transponder and scrambled up onto a large Category D crate. His eyes bulged as his voice boomed out, "I have utilised your wonderful war machines and begun my plan! Now I intend to harness the human spirit, to enable me to implement and enforce my design." He looked to Tesk whose eyes were fixed on him.

"You must understand," he implored. "Passive subordinates and docile imbeciles surround me! We exist in a state of ambient inertia and the time has come to act! I have a team reverse engineering and reproducing your weapons. I have the firepower, and I have the numbers; all I lack is the guile and ingenuity! Greed, cunning and cruelty do not come naturally to my species, so if I am to succeed with my operation, I will need you to guide me!"

The leader of the Nova snorted, unable to decipher the commissioner's words but suspecting that something exciting was about to happen.

The commissioner turned and smiled, gesturing to his battalion. "The Nova have all of the savagery of the human race, but none of the style." He laughed. "However, they are great in number, obedient and given the signal, will destroy any opponent that stands in our way!"

Tesk considered the alien invaders for a moment. "They really are an ugly bunch," he said. Turner laughed and the leader of the Nova bristled, suspecting an insult. Gripping his ancient weapon, he growled and double-checked that it was fully charged.

"Ugly and stupid!" announced Turner. "Brainless, yes, but loyal and eager to please!" Tesk laughed along, cautiously eyeing the troopers.

"Don't worry, Tesk, they can't understand us!" reassured Turner. "They're just happy to be here, out in a civilised zone. Out on this beautiful planet! They've been banished you see, restricted from coming into contact with other complex life forms. Sent off to the Planet of Night, far away, out of harm's reach."

"Too much chatter!" called out the Nova captain in their native tongue. His legion grumbled and twitched. Tesk had an uneasy feeling, sensing that the Nova were becoming impatient, that they craved action and extreme violence.

The commissioner approached and placed his hand on the captain's shoulder. "The coalition wanted them dead!" he explained to Tesk in a parlance the Nova could understand. "They said that the Nova were too violent, that they didn't deserve to live! Fortunately for us, the do-gooders got involved and a vote was arranged. The Nova survived! But on the condition that they'd be banished. A fate worse than death in my opinion."

The Nova captain hung his head in shame.

"They are just happy to be out in the fresh air. They live in near darkness you see, out on a tiny planet, quite far away from any sun system. Without transportation, without light, without hope. So, a day out to them is a real adventure!"

The Nova began to jabber excitedly, thrilled to be part of the day's proceedings. Approaching one of the smaller soldiers, Turner cried, "They just want to be loved, don't you, fellas!"

The Nova held their weapons aloft and began to call out, gurgling and snorting, growling in a kind of celebratory war call.

Turner switched back to the language that the Nova did not understand. "Most importantly, Tesk, they're killers. Desperate killers, cold-blooded, remorseless, and easy to control."

Mono had calculated that 380 Nova soldiers were present. Commissioner Turner and his staff of envoy, flight crew and technical support made up twenty-six. So, it was true that the Earth 2 phalanx were vastly outnumbered. "It doesn't look good," he whispered.

"Keep your voice down!" hissed Bungo, eager to keep the Earth people on side, quietly suspecting that Mono had a point. The Nova race were known for their savagery and brutality, but they had never posed a serious threat as they hadn't the intellect to organise themselves. Now with Turner and company at the helm, it appeared that things had changed. Standing with their new leader, clutching their fully charged weapons, they diligently awaited instruction.

Turner approached Tesk. "You'll be my first in command," he said cheerfully. "I want you and the Earth people to lead my army, to enrol and train the troops. There are a hundred species like the Nova out there, in the darkest corners of the 'Everything.'

"In exile, each one cast out into the shadows, festering and vengeful. I have evaluation analysis data on all of them! You would have your pick of the weirdest and most wonderful misfits in the galaxy! And if you think this lot are ugly, just wait 'till you see 'the Zonk'!"

The Nova captain's ears pricked up as he picked out the mention of his sworn enemy. The only word he'd recognised from the alien psychobabble, he spat on the ground in disgust.

"That is just to begin with…" The commissioner paused. "You haven't even heard my ultimate plan!" He smiled and rubbed his hands together excitedly. "To breed and reproduce! My top scientists are already experimenting with gene supplementation. We'll splice together a super being! Our physiology and intellect combined with your cunning and deviousness! We'll be running the show together, the scum of the Earth will take over the universe!"

"What did he just say?" exclaimed Ruby inside the command centre.

"Breed and reproduce, I believe?" said Cheryl.

Ruby shook her head. "I don't think so!"

"What do you think, Tesk?" bellowed Turner, holding up his hands.

Tesk did not respond.

With all eyes upon him, he stood silently and considered the situation. The vengeful and bloodthirsty Nova, Turner and his crew of outlaws, the Earth people in the command pod, Xzardak, Mono, Bungo and Zork, each of them awaiting his answer.

So much had happened to Tesk in the previous months. Each morning, he would wake up and expect to find that the entire episode had been a bad dream. As the Earth planet had slowly died, Tesk had become quietly resigned to the fact that they were all going to perish. He had come to terms with the notion of his own death, so this second chance at life had come as a surprise and nothing could have prepared him for what it would involve. Strange worlds, alien life forms, talking robots, space travel, it was all too weird to comprehend.

He nervously eyed the missiles, stacked precariously, one on top of another. A Nova guardsman was leaning on the silo hatch, yawning and scratching his behind, oblivious to the power of their payload. The situation was way out of control.

Tesk was used to conflict. He'd had to fight to stay alive his entire life. However, this was something else and the absurdity of the scenario was not lost on him. A guy from Detroit arguing the toss with an alien in outer space! It had to be a put on, a bad trip, a nightmare? *The destiny of the universe in my hands?* he thought. *None of it adds up.*

Sure, they had plenty of weapons and ammunition. Turner had at least granted them a fair fight, but even if they defeated him and his army, they were still the most wanted outlaws in the galaxy. There was no way out, and consequence would catch up with them eventually.

Breaking it down, Turner was offering him everything he had ever wanted, everything he could possibly need! An end to the running and fighting, an end to the daily battles and the quest for survival. Now he would be calling the shots. Sure, the fighting would continue but at least he'd be a general, no longer out on the frontline. He thought about Xzardak and the dreary housing compound. It would do for now, but what about long term? Could he really imagine himself lying in bed watching reruns on TV for the rest of his existence? *No way!*

Maybe this was what the Earth people needed... a new direction, a plan and a reason to live. Wasn't this what they had always wanted? The upper hand? Would it be such a crime to take the easy option this one time? He felt sure his crew would follow him whatever he decided, and they would deal with Xzardak along the way.

As long as everyone plays along, no one will get hurt.

Tesk had nothing left to live for, his home planet destroyed, the war already lost. Almost everyone and everything he had ever loved were gone. The party was indeed over, and the old

Tesk had died with Earth 1. This, however, was Earth 2 and Tesk 2, the next chapter.

Looking around at his friends, facing imminent demise, he knew what he must do for the good of the species.

"Tesk, there's something else," said Turner slyly, switching off his transponder.

"Oh yeah?" Tesk looked intrigued.

"There's another part to my plan, something to sweeten the deal," he whispered so as to evade Mono's amplification device. "I'm going to need to return to your Earth planet. I mean, just think of all those wonderful weapons down there rusting away in the toxic gloom. I'm going to be flying convoys down there, many convoys. To strip the planet of its war machines, I'm gonna need someone at the other end, an entire crew. I could build you a compound bigger and better than this one… you'd be in charge. You'd be home. You'd be a king and the Earth would belong to you!"

Tesk thought for a moment. "All mine, huh?"

He grunted, the words of Turner's tantalising offer echoing around inside his head. A vision of the origin Earth played inside his mind, the burned-out cars and buildings, the fetid air, the dead lying out in the dark, unburied and uncared for, the cruel cold wind whistling across the barren land, the derelict army base, the soldiers, the roaches, the pantry, the meat hook.

Stepping forward, he spoke softly. "It's incredible that you'd come all this way to ask us simple Earth folk for help, and truly, we are very grateful for your offer!"

Turner smiled. "I knew you would be, Tesk." The evil grin that played on the commissioner's face sent Mono's logic receptor into a spin.

"But you see," continued Tesk. "We had people like you back on my home planet, back on Earth." He smiled, raising an eyebrow. "In fact, the reason I'm here today is because of people like you. Commissioners, leaders, despots, maniacs. You, my friend, are what I would call an 'oddball.'"

"Oddball?" repeated Turner.

"Yeah, a loose cannon if you like?" He smiled.

Analysing the phrase "oddball," Mono motioned to Xzardak, suggesting that they step back, away from the window.

"And the problem with an oddball is you never quite know what they're gonna do next!"

Turner considered Tesk's words, bewildered by his terminology.

"I mean, we had armies back on Earth, but that lifestyle never really appealed to me, all of that marching and shouting, taking orders and all of that." He turned around to see his crew all lined up together outside the command centre doorway. Ruby, Alice, Marvin, Cheryl, Dougie, Nelson, Chrissy, Little Stevie; they were all together, cool, calm and collected, their weapons raised and pointed in the direction of the commissioner, his battalion... and him.

"What do you think, guys?" he called out.

"Tell him to shove it!" cried Cheryl. "He's a lunatic!"

"You reckon?" said Tesk.

"Yeah, come inside, Tesk! Come home!" insisted Ruby. "That guy's weird!"

"You're crazy, Turner," said Tesk, "I've seen what's left of the Earth and it ain't worth having. You're welcome to it, you and your uglies! Our time on Earth is over." He hesitated for a moment and turned back to look at his crew, Xzardak, Bungo, Mono, Zork.

"Forget it," he shouted, "I have a better idea."

Turner looked hurt. "I don't understand. I'm offering you something bigger than all of us!"

But Tesk began to walk away. "You're a fruitcake, Turner!" he exclaimed.

Suspecting another insult, Turner panicked; he looked to Raymonde for a translation, but his android had already boarded the weapons silo.

"You must know, Tesk, if you are unwilling to cooperate, I will be left with little choice other than to finish this!" he called. The Nova will wipe your people out. I have several battalions on standby waiting to intervene. Please, for all of our sakes!"

Tesk approached the command centre, then he held up his hands and motioned for the Earth people to take cover.

Turner seethed. "Xzardak! Tesk! See sense, the government, the coalition, the commission, it's over!"

But walking away, Tesk would not see sense. He gave the signal. "Plan B!" said Xzardak excitedly. Tesk smiled and Mono killed the lights.

CHAPTER 30

"**K**ill them!" cried Turner and the captain of the Nova army let out a blood-curdling call to arms. The Nova excitedly opened fire as Xzardak, Tesk and the small Earth army took their places inside the hastily assembled bunker. 'Plan B' was in action. Mono extinguished the lights in the compound, plunging everyone into total darkness. The Nova started firing indiscriminately into the night, enraged at being thrust back into the loathed state of blackout. The flashing laser bolts from their rifles, the only visible light source in the pitch-dark hangar bay, illuminated their grimacing faces. After a moment, Tesk radioed to Mono. "Strobe light!" he cried. Mono dutifully hit a button, causing the pre-programmed lighting system to flicker on and off at a nauseating rate. For the Nova army, the blinding flashing light was too much to bear. Repulsed by the flickering sensation, they staggered around dumbfounded. After a few moments, many were brought to their knees, the dizzying strobing light causing them to writhe and convulse.

"What's wrong with them?" screamed Turner.

"The light! We can't take it!" squealed the captain, shielding his eyes.

Xzardak was back at the control console in the command centre. "They're so used to the darkness on the Planet of Night," explained Mono. "They are unable to take the pulsating luminescence!"

"Whose idea was that?!" Xzardak happily enquired.

"Mine!" interjected Zork, looking very pleased with himself.

The Earth army had also opened fire. "Try not to hit that silo!" screamed Tesk as he dodged another laser bolt. "If that thing goes up, it's over!" he called out, but his cry went unheard as their retaliatory gunfire echoed across the compound floor. Tesk was not the only one concerned with the volatility of the nuclear missiles. Raymonde and his worker drones leapt into action, bullets sparking and ricocheting off them as they frantically worked to seal the reinforced cargo hatch. "Maybe it's a good job he is bulletproof," said Tesk.

Turner opened fire with his Category D machine gun. A primal latent madness had awoken inside of him. "You asked for this, Earth scum! I gave you an option!" he screamed, firing off several rounds with an unrealised hatred.

Xzardak hastily made his way into his shuttle chamber as Tesk had instructed. The cell had been built to withstand any impact whilst travelling in the void of space, so Xzardak knew he was quite safe providing he stayed inside. Watching on as the battle commenced, Xzardak felt very afraid. Tesk had armed him with a rifle and given brief training on how to use it, but Xzardak had been unable to retain the information. His mind now blank, he cradled the gun in his arms. Gunshots pinged and fizzed as they grazed the shuttle screen, Xzardak closed his eyes and covered his ears, terrified, useless, and confused.

Against Tesk's strict instructions, many of the Earth people had left the control module. This was the most exciting thing that had happened to them in a long while, and they were eager to get in on the action. Mono was keeping an ongoing tally of the mounting casualties and it was obvious that the Nova army lacked the combat skills required to take over the universe.

Many were dead, some gunned down by their own soldiers whose dexterity and aim were way off. It was evident that the Nova would never be able to master the sophisticated Earth weapons and it had become clear to Mono why Turner was so keen to employ the humans.

The Earthlings seemed to be revelling in the bloodshed, skilfully picking off the Nova troops one by one, unaffected by the strobing light and unintimidated by the ugly looking army and their antique firearms.

"Their rifles are junk!" exclaimed Little Stevie gleefully. "This should be a walk in the park!" he cried as way off-target laser bolts whistled by him.

As the battle raged, Turner managed to avoid the open fire and scurried back inside his ship. He had a plan. He switched on the cruiser's guiding lights then radioed to the Nova drivers to do the same. Suddenly, the compound was flooded with a blinding white glow which served to eliminate the pulsating strobe effect. "Too bright!" called the Nova captain. "Too bright!" But Turner was one step ahead of him. He instructed his flight captain to engage the craft's thrusters and the pilot hit the switch.

"Removing motion brakes," announced the flight assistant.

"No!" said Turner. "Hold the brake in place."

"But the cruiser will overheat," replied the pilot.

"Hold the brake in place!" demanded Turner. The ship rocked and vibrated as the thrusters fired. "Full power!" he barked.

"But we'll burn up!" insisted the co-pilot.

"*Full power!*" Turner screamed.

The full thrust of the oscillator caused the ship to jolt back and forth. Unable to take off, a thick plume of black smoke bellowed out from the cruiser's exhaust system.

The dense acrid smog filled the hangar bay, diffusing the searing white light. Suddenly, the human beings began to cough and choke, unable to handle the noxious toxic fumes pumping out from the grounded machine. "Sir, I must insist!" demanded the pilot. "With the weapons on board, I fear the cruiser will explode!"

"Okay, kill it!" Turner shouted to the relief of the flight crew and tech team. Instructing the pilots of the other crafts to follow suit, a poisonous chemical discharge had filled the air. The bright light now fully diffused, the Nova could just about see again, their superior physiology impervious to the exhaust emissions. The smoky battle arena now a little more even, they took aim at the Earth people who coughed and retched, desperately trying to catch their breath.

Xzardak was reminded of his Earth planet research findings.

He shuddered as he remembered the footage he had seen of warfare on the origin Earth. Now it was playing out here in the otherwise peaceful depths of space.

High above the compound, Tesk had secured himself a perfect vantage point. Out of view of his adversaries, he precariously clung to a radio mast. He could see that the Nova death count was high, with many bodies slumped on the ground. There were Earth casualties too but not nearly as many as their boneheaded opponents. Laser bolts whizzed by him as the Nova fired haphazardly into the air. The enemy soldiers were raging, charged with adrenaline but as Turner had surmised, they were no match for the lethal Earth task force. Tesk fired down, taking out the better of the Nova snipers one by one. Unaware of his elevated position, each one of them collapsed, the piercing bullets coming out of nowhere.

The Nova had begun to panic, the cloud of smoke had begun to lift, revealing many of their dead kinfolk. Bathed in a diffused blinding white light, a few of them fled into the dark woods only to be pursued by the Earth people. Each one was deftly marked and eliminated.

Xzardak was scared out of his wits, garnering little comfort from the numbers that Mono was projecting onto the video monitor. Like one of Earth's sporting scorecards, it revealed that the Nova numbers were falling. The Earth people were taking the upper hand. He nervously radioed to Mono. "I bet Tesk is loving this…" he called. "If he's still alive?"

Mono's eyes whirled. "Oh he's still out there; sensors show he's still with us!"

Tesk was indeed enjoying himself, deliriously gunning down his adversaries. He had a perfect view of the ensuing carnage and as the light grew brighter, he reached for his black

anti-blast sunglasses and slipped them on. "Just like the good old days, huh, Stevie!" he cried out into the murky gloom. Little Stevie was out of sight, but Tesk had a feeling he was safe.

These were easy pickings for the crew. Once resources had started to run out on Earth, the humans had formed gangs and taught themselves to fight. If you were to live, you had to be armed and proficient with your firearm. The weak-willed had long since perished.

Only the strong, the mean and the lucky had survived and fortunately for Xzardak, these Earth people were all of the above.

Tesk's instructions had been to keep the command centre doors closed and locked, and Mono had obliged. However, against his orders, several more Earth folk had impatiently rushed out of the centre to watch the fireworks. To Tesk's horror, he glanced down from his vantage point to see a handful of Nova enter the control centre.

Tesk panicked.

Some troopers who had managed to escape the Earth people and avoided being shot down by their own forces, were now out deep in the woods. The Nova were better at running than fighting and when faced with oblivion, their primal instinct had been to flee. Once out of the reaches of the main compound, they arrived at the perimeter shield.

With a thud, thud, thud they crashed into the invisible force field. Angry and bewildered, they got to their feet. They rubbed their heads and tried to figure out what had hit them.

"Force field!" cried the smarter of the three fighters.

"Stand back!" instructed the larger of the trio. Raising his rifle, he blasted a hole into the invisible shield. "Again!" he cried, and the soldiers raised their weapons. Together they fired, creating an opening big enough to enable them to escape.

"There's been a perimeter breach!" called Mono, eagerly dispatching a surveillance drone and its camera zeroed in on the sector. Xzardak and Mono were able to monitor the renegade's progress as they smashed their way out of the compound.

Xzardak shuddered as he watched the grainy video feed of the bewildered Nova running to their certain deaths.

It had taken coalition forces a while to figure out that not all of Earth's inhabitants got along together. "Is every creature on Earth a barbarian?" asked Bungo as they intervened in yet another murderous episode. It was decided to put the most savage species such as big cats, crocodiles, and bears, etc into their own enclosures, as no matter how hard they had tried, Xzardak's team could not incentivise the beasts to stop fighting and eating each other.

Unfortunately for the Nova, this turned out to be one of the enclosures they had breached. It took only a few moments for the incarcerated Earth creatures to hunt out and strike down the disparate group of defectors. Thinking they had escaped the battle, the confused Nova ran obliviously into the jaws of the second wildest wild Earth creatures on the planet.

Now with the compound perimeter breached, Xzardak wondered if the wild beasts might venture into the battle zone. However, for now, it appeared that the savage critters were happily distracted by their tasty Nova platter.

Xzardak's radio flashed a light. Answering it, he heard a familiar voice, "Xzardak can you hear me? Are you there, Xzardak?"

"Yes!" came the reply. "I hear you, Tesk, where are you?"

The signal was weak due to the heavy charge of static electricity hanging in the atmosphere, but Xzardak could just about hear the Earth man. "The Nova are in the building, Xzardak!" screamed Tesk frantically. "I told you to keep the doors shut! What happened?"

"Your people busted the lock!" spluttered Mono. "I could not stop them!"

"You need to get out of there and defend yourselves!" insisted Tesk. "You'll be dead meat if they make it to the pod!"

Xzardak was unaware that the alien horde had managed to infiltrate the command centre. Mono's receptors had been concentrated on the perimeter breach and the group of striped animals now tentatively making their way out into the compound.

Xzardak got to his feet. "Tesk, where are you?" Suddenly, with a crash, the centre rocked.

"Xzardak, they've seen me," cried Tesk, his radio channel breaking up. "You're on your own!" Xzardak jumped as a blast and then another blast came from above the pod and with a screech of feedback, the radio went dead.

"The building should be quite secure," announced Zork, "Dr Jay designed it himself."

"Dr Jay didn't think we'd open the door and let them in!" answered Xzardak curtly.

The command centre had been designed to be impregnable, Dr Jay had insisted on this when taking the job. "These humans are dangerous, savage creatures!" he reminded his bright-eyed partner as they filled out the manifest document. "It's not too late to change your mind." He chuckled. Despite Jay's reservations, Xzardak blithely accepted his position, motivated by the doctor's curiosity and his own boundless and often irritating optimism.

Xzardak meditated for a moment; this happy memory seemed like a lifetime ago. "If only I'd listened," he mumbled to himself.

Mono had successfully sealed and secured the control quarters, but Xzardak remained concerned. "We can't just sit here and allow the Earth people to be butchered!" he exclaimed. "We must try to intervene!" On the internal security monitors, he could see that there were human casualties; a few of the weaker, unarmed humans had been overpowered by the lumbering Nova soldiers. However, some of the Earth creatures were putting up a fight and Mono marvelled at the ingenuity on display.

"Such resourceful minds," he remarked as they fashioned for themselves an array of primitive looking protections. A chair became a weapon, a table leg became a weapon, a curtain, a light stand, a shoe, not to mention a fist or a foot! Each became a unique implement of torture to inflict pain on the gawkish Nova invaders. An eating utensil could be used to gouge an eye, a writing implement to stab or scratch. Any heavy object could be used to crush a skull.

These were the humans that Xzardak had seen in the archives, not the meek, mealy, mannered humans he'd got to know on Earth 2. Here they were, the wild and violent, vicious creatures from the video log, living up to their reputation and even without their firearms, defending themselves against the encroaching alien enemy. Xzardak recognised that once provoked, the seemingly lazy and lethargic Earth people would reveal their true latent natures. Old or young, big or small, they had transformed into killing machines.

Together, they battled on.

Transfixed by the commotion on the internal video screens, Xzardak had been distracted from the ensuing battle outside. Another alert sounded. "Oh, what now?" he cried.

"Bad news I'm afraid," said Mono sheepishly. "Another cruiser is about to dock!"

Suddenly, and with a loud crackle, the radio set let out a burst.

"Is anybody listening? This is Stevie! Control centre, can you hear me?" Stevie's voice fizzed and broke up into abstract syllables.

"Stevie, it's Xzardak; are you okay?"

"They're overpowering us, there's too many!" he cried.

Mono shuddered. "We're being overrun."

"We need to close the hangar bay doors immediately!" demanded Xzardak. "Lock them out, if more troops enter, we're done for!"

Mono instantly sprang into action, punching in numbers and twisting dials, implementing the sequence that would bring down the gate. The star port was the only way into or out of the compound; this had been another of Dr Jay's directives, to secure the base and prevent the Earth creatures from escaping. Once the hangar doors were secured shut, no further coalition cruisers containing Nova troopers would be able to land. The area would be secure, for now.

"Stevie, can you hear me?"

"I'm here, Xzardak!" spluttered Stevie. "Do you know where Tesk is? We could really use some help out here!"

"I am unable to detect neither Tesk nor Turner at the moment," replied Mono flatly.

"We can hold their fire for now." Stevie coughed. "But I don't know how much more of this smoke we can take, and we are running out of ammunition!"

Xzardak fell silent, unsure what to do. He realised he was useless in a combat situation, Plan 'B' after all had been Tesk's idea and there had not been time to discuss strategy.

Each of the six cruisers was producing a cloud of toxic smog. Turner had instructed his flight crew to keep the thrusters burning with the motion brakes in place. With such little visibility, the Earth people and Nova now shot blindly into the miasma of foul-smelling smoke.

"The hangar door is stuck!" Mono said. "It must be damaged! It appears that the internal signalling mechanism is not responding. I will have to go over there myself and reset the console."

"No!" cried Xzardak, shaking his head. "Who will control the command computer?" Xzardak was beginning to lose his mind.

"I will leave Zork with instructions," replied Mono. "I'm handing control over to you and will access the hangar via the supply tunnel. Hopefully, I can reset the system from there." With a whirr of his circuits, Mono was off, out into the big bad world, leaving Xzardak to fend for himself. Still cradling his rifle, Xzardak sat at the control desk and scratched his head.

Leaving the safety of the control pod, Mono hurriedly sped down the supply tunnel. "Protocol must be followed, and the Earth people must be protected!" he chirped. "Protocol must be followed, and the Earth people must be protected!" he repeated, not fully convinced by the mantra put forward by his logic board.

At the exit, he sprang the hatch and once outside of the main building, he scurried across the hangar floor. The visibility in the bay was bad but he was able to navigate through the noxious gloom with his inbuilt controller compass.

All around him, everywhere he looked, Mono could see signs of brutality, the mutilated bodies of deceased Nova and Earth people all lying twisted and lifeless. He shivered, witnessing the hangar bay walls and freighter ships, all pockmarked and peppered with weapon fire.

"But why?" he questioned. None of it made any sense.

Mono had never encountered anything like this before, and unable to comprehend the senseless loss of life, he repeated his mantra. "Protocol must be followed, and the Earth people must be protected!" he sang, again secretly questioning the validity of his own statement.

Deafening gunshots echoed out across the base and laser bolts whipped by him as Mono raced at full speed toward the workstation. At last, he made it to the console and managed to access the unit's main computer. He punched in the codes and the sequence began. The mechanism creaked and very slowly, the hangar bay doors started to close.

"I'm going to demand a vacation after this…" he said to himself. "Vacation?" he repeated. "Another Earth word?"

"The doctor will be thrilled with the data!" announced Zork.

Xzardak was jogging through the security monitor databank. The events of the day had been captured by the camera system installed by Dr Jay.

"At least something good might come from this," sighed Xzardak to himself.

At the inception of the project, while the surveillance equipment was being installed, Dr Jay had predicted there would be chaos. "This analysis footage will give us a valuable insight into the workings of the human mind!" he announced grandly. "We will monitor the progress of this dangerous virus and chart their destruction in real time!"

Xzardak had naively put forward the notion that the Earth people could well be vindicated. "After all," he said, smiling nervously, "how bad could they be?"

Dr Jay had played along. "I'm sure you're right, Xzardak. Perhaps the surveillance footage will capture their altruistic side! The little devils!" he scoffed. "You'll see, Xzardak; I've encountered these types before! Watch and learn, my friend!" He chuckled. "Watch and learn!"

One thing was clear, and this was that when the findings were analysed, and all was said and done, Dr Jay would certainly be the toast of the scientific community. What had seemed like a prudent action at the beginning of the program would now provide invaluable information to the research librarians.

Xzardak scanned the compound, eager to find Tesk and desperate to hunt down Turner.

"Are you sure you can't locate the commissioner?" radioed Xzardak to Zork who had also disappeared.

"I am unable to locate individuals," replied Zork. "The observation system has gone haywire! There is too much electromagnetic interference in the atmosphere and my sensors are all but shot! I am trying to re-establish a connection!"

From the surveillance footage, Xzardak observed that amongst the vast number of dead Nova lay many of the Earth people whose safety had been entrusted to him. "How could this have happened?" he wondered aloud. "My very first case, a total disaster." He rubbed his eyes. "Who would have thought it could go so wrong?"

"You must have known there'd be trouble," Turner whispered into Xzardak's ear. Startled, Xzardak turned and sprang to his feet, dropping his rifle which clattered as it hit the floor.

As Mono had departed, Turner had entered the service corridor and now stood with a pistol at Xzardak's head. "I want you to reconsider my offer, Xzardak; it's still valid. In fact, after this display, I'd say you've all passed the test with flying colours! Quite unbelievable!" he said. "The Nova dispatched with such ease!"

Paralysed with fear, Xzardak felt his heart rate increase, his head starting to spin as Turner stepped closer. "They've excelled themselves, surpassed all of my expectations and lived up to their glorious reputation!" he bellowed excitedly. His mood suddenly changed. "I need all of the surviving Earth people loaded onto my cruisers immediately."

Turner was breathing heavily, Xzardak trying to back away. "They'll never go along with you Turner, you must realise that. They're wild! You can't control them!"

Turner pointed to the surveillance screen.

"Oh, I think they will, Xzardak, because if they don't, I'll detonate my bombs and destroy the entire compound! I'll kill everyone and everything on the planet. It's what the Earth people liked to call 'the nuclear option.'"

Xzardak was very much aware of 'the nuclear option.' It was one of the anomalous notions that he had read about in the Earth log but simply couldn't comprehend. Now it made even less sense and only made Turner appear all the more deranged.

"I must say I'm a little disappointed in Tesk's attitude," said Turner. "I really thought he would want to join me. Maybe now, he'll reconsider? Perhaps today's excitement will have re-ignited his sense of adventure."

"Turner, it's no good!" protested Xzardak. "Tesk is dead and they'd only listen to him! They've gone berserk! They won't do as I tell them! You're wasting your time!"

Turner smiled. "I'm very impressed that you've made it this far, Xzardak, I gave you a job to do and you've done it. Now, however, it's time for the final stage of the program, it's time for you to let go…" He motioned to the console. "Address the Earth people," he said in a deathly tone. "Thank them for the beautiful display, but tell them, the ship is primed and ready to blow." Turner's eyes narrowed and turned red. "Announce it!" he bellowed.

The compound dispatch speakers let out a shrill static blast. "Hello! This is Xzardak speaking. Please listen." He trembled, the pistol placed at his temple. "Commissioner Turner has breached the control module and is holding me captive. He thanks you for your enthusiasm in dispatching the Nova horde. The way in which you have eliminated so many of the invaders has made the commissioner even more excited about your up-and-coming collaboration!"

The Earth people stopped firing momentarily and listened carefully as Xzardak continued. "The commissioner ensures me that if we all play along and help him, there will be no need for him to enact his new plan. However, if we do not, we will all be destroyed. The commissioner has stated that if everyone does not file onto the cruisers, he will detonate the ship containing the nuclear devices. Taking us all into a fiery inferno… Instant annihilation."

Xzardak felt weak at the knees. He tried to steady himself but slumped into the console chair. "How long have we got, Turner?" he said quietly.

"Not long, Xzardak, not long."

Eager to stay alive and with nothing left to give, Xzardak surrendered. He held up his hands and attempted to get to his feet.

"Stay where you are, Xzardak. I want you to know I appreciate everything you've done for me. But I'm afraid this is where our partnership must end." He sympathetically smiled and raised the shiny black pistol to Xzardak's head. Xzardak closed his eyes tightly, whimpering, too afraid to cry out. It had all been a set up and now that he had played his part, the commissioner had no further use for him. This was it; the moment had come. It was all too much to take, but maybe soon, the ordeal would be over. Gripped with fear and resigned to his fate, he lowered his head and awaited the inevitable blast. Inhaling slowly, he listened carefully as Turner cocked the pistol. "You survived a good deal longer than any of us thought you would. Don't worry, Xzardak, I'll make sure you're remembered."

The commissioner laughed and Xzardak braced himself. He clenched his teeth and took a deep breath as suddenly, the piercing sound rang out.

But Xzardak did not fall. Instead of the dreaded gunshot, a blast was heard from inside the hangar bay, a boom, a rumble and then an explosion. "No! My babies!" cried Turner.

Both he and Xzardak turned to the viewport just in time to see the commissioner's ship blast out of the hangar gate. Turner raised his weapon again and pointed it at Xzardak.

"You'll pay for this, Xzardak!" he said. Xzardak sprang back as Commissioner Turner suddenly let out a bloodcurdling scream. "Aaaaaaaargh, my leg! My leg!" he shrieked. He stumbled backwards. "You devil!" he cried, swinging the pistol. He let out a shot, then another shot but his bullets did not connect. He screamed again, such was the searing pain.

Xzardak was amazed to see the small girl from the compound at Turner's feet. Her teeth firmly clenched, she had squeezed under the security shutter and had bitten onto his leg. With no sign of letting go, the commissioner let out another shot. "Let go!" he cried as she dug her fingernails into his bony limb. He fired again and the bullet grazed her face.

Fearing for her life, she released her grip, spitting out his blood as the commissioner turned.

"Why, you little..." he cried, taking aim but before he could fire, Xzardak seized his Category D rifle and swung it, smashing Turner across the back of his head. Turner stumbled as again and again, Xzardak beat him with the rifle butt. Xzardak had lost control.

The time he had spent researching the Earth people, the hours and hours of ancient newsreel he had viewed had permeated his psyche. He had witnessed so much violence, chaos and mayhem that the administered beating came quite naturally to him. Every news report, every TV melodrama, every book, every play, everything from Earth he had witnessed… had prepared him for it.

He already knew the motions; he had seen them so many times before. The commissioner tried to fight back as Xzardak repeatedly struck his face and head. Reaching out to grab the rifle, Turner tried to stand, but Xzardak was too quick and kicked the commissioner to the floor.

Releasing the safety catch, Xzardak raised the rifle, then per Tesk's instruction, he efficiently aimed and shot both barrels into the beseeching commissioner's head.

Just like in the movies.

CHAPTER 31

"That's some nice shooting!" Little Stevie stood in the doorway, looking down at a blood-splattered Xzardak. With Turner dead, the Nova captain had signalled the retreat and every one of the coalition cruisers had blasted out of the space port. "I didn't know you had it in you, Xzardak!" chuckled Stevie, Commissioner Turner's head had been taken clean off his shoulders.

"Neither did I," murmured Xzardak, noticeably shaken by the ordeal.

Little Stevie reached out a hand. "Well, you're one of us now, Xzardak."

Xzardak was trembling, horrified that he had taken the commissioner's life, while greatly relieved that for now, the ordeal was over. "Someone left the security hatch open." Stevie tutted with a furrowed brow. "You should maybe have a word with Mono!"

Xzardak looked confused for a moment. "Mono!" Xzardak jumped up and trampling the commissioner's dead body, he ran over to the control panel.

"Mono!" he cried. "Are you there, Mono. Mono!" he called.

With a crackle of static, a voice could be heard. "Xzardak, is that you? Come in, Xzardak…" Xzardak was thrilled to hear his faithful assistant's voice.

"Are you okay Mono? Where are you?"

"Hard to say. Headed toward Sector 12, I believe," Mono's distorted response echoed faintly. Xzardak was taken aback.

"Sector 12? What are you doing there?" The signal was beginning to break up.

Mono hesitated. "I... I've someone who would like to speak to you!" he stuttered.

Xzardak looked to Little Stevie, then back to the control panel as another voice called out, "Xzardak! How's it going?" Little Stevie laughed, relieved to hear that his old compadre was still alive.

"Tesk? Is that you?" asked Xzardak cautiously.

Tesk sounded excited. "That's right, Xzardak, Mono is taking me and these nukes out for a little joyride. I hope you don't mind."

A million possibilities fired off in Xzardak's brain. Suddenly, he encountered a moment of doubt. "Tesk, what are you saying?" He looked to Little Stevie, who appeared to be thinking the very same thought. Would Tesk really commandeer a ship and blast off with enough firepower to take over the galaxy? The Crystal Planet sat not far from Sector 12.

Could Tesk single-handedly enact Turner's plan?

"He wouldn't, would he?" said Xzardak, turning to Stevie.

Stevie shrugged, looking as bemused as Xzardak.

Xzardak still found it impossible to comprehend the thoughts and actions of the human being. He gazed through the viewport; the smoke had cleared, and the dust was settling.

"What a mess," he muttered. The compound he had helped to create, design and build was all but destroyed, the coalition were dead, and one of its commissioners had died at his own hand! Now the virus had escaped and armed to the teeth, was headed in the direction of the governors!

Xzardak's entire world had been turned upside down. Accepting the worst of his assumptions, he attempted to plead with Tesk. "Please come back, Tesk, whatever you are planning to do will only get us into further trouble!" The line was dead for a moment, but then with a rumble, he heard that familiar laugh.

"Trouble?" hollered Tesk. "You know me, Xzardak, I love trouble! Trouble is what keeps me alive!"

The following rotation would be an extremely stressful time for Xzardak, who by this point was almost broken. The perimeter shield had been damaged and the compound was now overrun with escaped Earth animals. "I thought the humans were bad," grumbled Bungo as he watched the wild beasts feast on the dead Nova carcasses which lay rotting in the warm afternoon sun.

The remaining Nova horde had fled, retreating into the forest once their commanding officer was no longer around to tell them what to do. Fresh meat for the recently liberated lions and tigers.

The remaining Earth people had made it back into the safety of the control centre. The hangar bay had been secured and now, everyone sat awaiting news. Sipping hot tea, Ruby chuckled.

"You look good on TV, Stevie!" Her eyes fixed on the video screen.

Xzardak had sent out a telex to every media outlet in the galaxy, copies of the surveillance tapes, complete with the exchanges between Turner, Tesk and Xzardak, included.

The footage had been played and shared across the entire universe.

Xzardak and the Earth people were in the clear since it was obvious that Commissioner Turner had been responsible for the entire episode. Xzardak was hopeful that the coalition overthrow might herald a new beginning for everyone. Bungo wasn't convinced.

As the remaining coalition resource fleet descended into the docking bay, Xzardak hoped to put the entire episode behind him. It was time for a fresh start. However, there was still one cloud on the horizon. The lost ship, the nuclear bombs, and the Earth man.

What had happened to them was anyone's guess.

"Well, Xzardak," said Bungo. "This is where we find out if it was worth saving the Earth people."

Zork let out a shrill cry. "Xzardak, he's back! I knew he'd return!" he called.

Xzardak ran to the viewport, thrilled to hear that the traveller had at last shown up. Expecting to see a coalition craft, he was surprised to see a Science Division crest on the fuselage panel. Confused, he cried to Zork, "How could Tesk have commandeered a research ship?"

Zork's gears whirred. "It's not Tesk, it's Doctor Jay!" he said. "I knew he would return! I do like the good doctor."

Crestfallen, Xzardak paced back to the command console. "Dr Jay," he said. "That's all we need! No doubt here to gloat!" He sat at the desk and put his head in his hands. "Earth people!"

A million miles away, on board the commission ship, Mono sat upright in the pilot's seat.

"Now approaching Vector 77, Tesk."

Tesk got to his feet. "Now you're sure this is far enough out? This is some pretty serious firepower. I don't want any blowback!"

Mono's gears grinded and whirred. "Yes, my calculations are double, and triple checked, that is correct. We are out of range of any civilised settlement, cargo route, transport route or satellite system, and there are no wormholes present in the jurisdiction. The detonator is set. The auxiliary craft is primed. If you'd like to board it, I will begin the ignition sequence."

Setting the timer to zero point three rotations, Mono and Tesk quickly evacuated the dead commissioner's ship. The auxiliary pod zoomed out from the coalition craft's hub and Tesk peered out through the back hatch. "You're sure this thing will get us all the way home?" he asked with an unconvinced smile.

CHAPTER 31

Mono rolled his eyes. "Yes, of course! These commission auxiliary ships will run 'til Doomsday!" he announced authoritatively. *Doomsday?* pondered Mono, *another Earth concept.* "Do you want me to notify Xzardak that we are on our way back to the compound?" he asked excitedly.

"No," Tesk said, smiling as the little craft hurtled through space. "Let's surprise him."

Made in United States
Troutdale, OR
12/07/2025

43233959R00187